MIST, METAL, AND ASH

ALSO BY
GWENDOLYN CLARE

INK, IRON, AND GLASS

MIST, METAL, AND ASH

GWENDOLYN CLARE

{Imprint}
MAKE YOUR MARK

NEW YORK

[Imprint]
MAKE YOUR MARK

A part of Macmillan Publishing Group, LLC
175 Fifth Avenue, New York, NY 10010

MIST, METAL, AND ASH. Copyright © 2019 by Gwendolyn Clare. All rights reserved.
Printed in the United States of America.

Library of Congress Control Number: 2018944985

ISBN 978-1-250-11278-1 (hardcover) / ISBN 978-1-250-11277-4 (ebook)

Our books may be purchased in bulk for promotional, educational, or business use. Please
contact your local bookseller or the Macmillan Corporate and Premium Sales Department at
(800) 221-7945 ext. 5442 or by e-mail at MacmillanSpecialMarkets@macmillan.com.

Book design by Liz Dresner

Imprint logo designed by Amanda Spielman

First edition, 2019

10 9 8 7 6 5 4 3 2 1

fiercereads.com

The first one who steals this sequel,
Shall lose a possession its equal.
And whoever steals it next
Shall find themself scribed in the text.

FOR CARL, WHO UNDERSTANDS
THAT SCIENCE *IS* MAGIC

THE FOUR STATES
OF ITALY, 1891

AUSTRIAN EMPIRE

FRANCE

KINGDOM OF
SARDINIA

Trento

KINGDOM
OF VENETIA

Venezia

Nizza

Cinque
Terre

Bologna

Pisa

Firenze

PAPAL
STATES

Roma

Cagliari

KINGDOM
OF THE
TWO SICILIES

Napoli

Marsala

AFRICA

PROLOGUE

When no one is listening, the Clockwork Creature breaks the rules.

She knows all the ways out of the world, the easy ways and the difficult ones, the paths where you must walk on the ceiling or jump twenty meters over a bottomless chasm. She has mapped and completed every route. There is not much else to do, while the Broken Boy sleeps.

Tonight the Clockwork Creature crouches on a windowsill and spies through the glass. Her bronze-tipped fingers dig grooves into the stone, and her wings snap open for balance. The Mad Boy has returned home and brought another with him. The Lost Boy is golden-blond where the Mad Boy's hair is coffee-black, but they have the same eyes—glinting like chipped amber in the warm yellow light of the gaslamps.

The Clockwork Creature watches the boys argue. Though

she can hear them, she does not understand. They are using the Voice Words, the ones she does not know.

She does not like the Mad Boy very much. He is unpredictable—by turns kind, or cruel, or indifferent. Nothing like the Broken Boy, whom she loves with all her heart.

Perhaps this new boy is broken, too. From the outside he looks whole, but there are many kinds of broken. Perhaps he will be given to the Clockwork Creature.

She leans forward, overeager, and the tip of one curved horn clacks against the glass. A mistake—the Lost Boy glances in her direction.

The Clockwork Creature lets go of the sill, twisting and falling through the night. But she'll be back, she decides, wings spreading to catch the air. She'll come back to watch the Lost Boy. And perhaps to take him.

1

STUDY AS IF YOU WERE GOING TO LIVE FOREVER;
LIVE AS IF YOU WERE GOING TO DIE TOMORROW.
—*Maria Mitchell*

PISA, KINGDOM OF SARDINIA—1891

Elsa flipped through the pages of *Advanced Alternate Physics* by Joseph Fourier, desperate for inspiration. The quiet inside Casa della Pazzia's octagonal library felt oppressive, three stories of bookshelves staring down at her failure in silent reproof.

Could she apply integral transforms to scriptology? The science of creating new worlds with lines of script in a book usually came so easily to her; Elsa loved the subtlety and precision of syntax, combined with the endless applications. She had created a laboratory world with stockrooms that never depleted, and even a book that linked one location on Earth to another for instantaneous travel. But the particular worldbook she most needed at the moment was refusing to function.

Elsa set aside the Fourier and opened the worldbook again, its pages vibrating softly against her fingertips like the shiver of a butterfly. It was a map world she'd created to serve as a locating device for people here on Earth, and there was someone she needed to find: a thief. A traitor. *A lying liar who lies*, as Faraz once called him.

Faraz's words had seemed like a harmless joke among friends at the time. Not anymore.

Elsa took up her fountain pen and set to work adding new lines of text to modify the book's tracking property. Worldbooks were not confined by the physics of Earth, and it was difficult to predict how their unique physical properties would function. She was out on the edge of known science, trying to solve a problem no one had ever seen before—a thrilling prospect, if only the safety of the whole planet weren't teetering on the brink with her.

In the center of the library a black hole irised open, a corridor through the fabric of reality connecting Earth to a scribed world, and out of the darkness stepped Porzia Pisano. As the portal closed behind her, Porzia arched one dark eyebrow. "You altered the worldbook. While I was still inside. You do know that's dangerous, don't you?"

Elsa blinked. "My mother does it all the time with Veldana." Veldana was her home, and the only scribed world in existence with a native population.

Porzia managed an even more skeptical expression, which was a feat in and of itself. "Mm, yes, and as we've established, Jumi's judgment is always flawless."

Elsa's instinct was to jump to her mother's defense, but the truth was Jumi had started this whole mess when she scribed the most dangerous object in existence—a book with the power to edit the real world. Whoever controlled the editbook could permanently alter anything they wished on Earth, up to and including the complete destruction of the planet. The editbook was supposed to protect Veldana from European interference; instead, it became the focus of a power struggle, one that had nearly cost Jumi her life and her world. And if Elsa failed to steal it back, there was no limit to the havoc the editbook could inflict.

Elsa exhaled her tenseness and leaned her head back. The gasolier hanging from the center of the domed ceiling dazzled her eyes and cast intricate shadows. "Did I at least change something inside the world? At this point, I'll take any kind of improvement to the tracking process as a victory."

"You turned the sky red—which I have to say looks *very* ominous—but no, the tracking property was unaffected." Porzia pulled out a chair and flopped down with an uncharacteristic lack of decorum, her full skirts puffing like a thrown pillow. She tossed her handheld portal device on the table, its brass casing clattering against the wood.

"So still no fix on Leo's location, then."

Porzia, who was a talented scriptologist in her own right, reached for the worldbook and dragged it closer to scowl at the text. She flipped through the pages, glowering as if she could make the world do what she wanted by intimidation alone. "We've expanded the tracking map to function globally; we've been through every line of script looking for optimizations. It's no use."

Elsa nodded, trying not to let her frustration show. A week had passed since Leo stole the editbook and rejoined his father and his brother, Aris. Despite all her efforts, Elsa wasn't so much as an inch closer to recovering the editbook—or to confronting Leo.

No, better not to think about him. The memory of his betrayal felt like fragments of glass grinding together somewhere behind her sternum.

Elsa made herself focus on recovering the editbook. "So either they're hiding off-world, or Aris figured out a surprisingly effective way to block the tracking map."

Porzia sighed. "Looks that way."

"First he designs a way to detect portals, now he's blocking our tracker," Elsa grumbled. "Does this guy have a clone? How does he work so fast?"

"I suppose it doesn't hurt being a polymath," Porzia said.

"Wait—what?" Elsa sat up straighter. "Aris is a polymath?"

Porzia gave her a confused look. "You didn't know . . . ?" Elsa got the sense she was trying hard not to say, *Leo didn't tell you?* Another secret withheld from her; another shard of glass sliding between her ribs.

Elsa shook her head. "Signora Pisano told me I was the only living polymath." Most pazzerellones, people with the madness for science, specialized in one of the three disciplines—mechanics, alchemy, or scriptology—but Elsa could perform all three.

"When Mamma said that, she thought Aris was dead," Porzia pointed out.

"Oh. Right." Certain moments of Leo's behavior toward Elsa suddenly made more sense—the odd flashes of jealousy and insecurity. "What about Garibaldi?" she asked. Ricciotti Garibaldi was the father of Leo and Aris, and the madness often ran in families. He had two pazzerellones for sons; their scientific impulses must have come from somewhere.

Porzia cocked her head to the side. "Um . . . alchemist, I guess. Leo never talked much about his father's work."

Elsa frowned. Garibaldi was obsessed with unifying the four states of Italy into a single country. As far as she could tell, everything he did—faking his own death, going into hiding, stealing the editbook—was done in the service of that cause. It seemed to Elsa that he treated Aris more like a soldier than a son. If Garibaldi had expected Leo to be a polymath like his brother, and left him behind in Venezia because he wasn't . . .

Against her better judgment, she felt a pang of sympathy for Leo, but it shifted quickly into anger. "How could Leo go back to that horrible man? Garibaldi *abandoned* him, and we're the ones who cared. I even thought Leo and I were—" Elsa cut herself off before she could voice the words. When she was young, Jumi had told her, *They call it "falling" in love in some Earth languages. To fall, as one falls into a trap.*

Porzia looked at Elsa steadily, a kind of grim resignation visible in the set of her mouth. "Garibaldi is still his father—you can't break the ties of blood. We were naive to assume he *wouldn't* turn against us."

The door creaked behind Elsa, and she glanced back as Faraz entered the library with Skandar riding on his shoulder. Faraz was tall, dark, and awkward; Skandar was all tentacles, with a pair of wings and one giant wet eye in the middle. Since Leo left, Faraz had taken to carrying Skandar, his alchemical masterpiece, everywhere with him. (Except the dining hall, which Porzia had declared absolutely off-limits for tentacle monsters.) Faraz was one of the orphaned pazzerellones raised at Casa della Pazzia; Elsa worried that, given his history, this latest abandonment was like a blow to a tender, unhealed wound.

"Hi, you two," Elsa said.

Faraz made a poor attempt at a smile. Skandar, however, raised a few tentacles cheerfully, pleased to see her. Elsa held out an arm as Faraz approached, allowing the beast to crawl from Faraz's shoulder onto hers. She'd grown accustomed to the feel of suckers clinging to the back of her neck, though Porzia wrinkled her nose just at the sight of the transfer.

"Sorry I'm late," Faraz said.

Porzia muttered, "Not that it matters."

"Actually, I've had a thought." He pulled out a chair and sat. "So far, we've only tried targeting the tracking map with Leo's possessions in order to track Leo. Right?"

Elsa nodded. "True."

"Well . . . what if the block—whatever it is that's blocking us—only applies to Leo? For example, if they'd scribed a prison worldbook to keep him in."

"Interesting," Elsa said. Privately, she found it impossible to share Faraz's faith in Leo—that he had been tricked and was being held against his will—but his idea still had merit. "We might be able to track Aris or Garibaldi, instead of Leo."

Porzia said, "Except for the slight problem that the only possession we had of Garibaldi's was the pocket watch, which Leo took with him. We have nothing to target the map with."

For the first time in days, Elsa felt a spark of hope. "No, but we know someone else who might: Signora Scarpa."

Porzia rubbed her temples. "For heaven's sake, Elsa. We ought to be working with the Order, not the Carbonari." The Order of Archimedes was the secret society of pazzerellones that Porzia's family were members of; the Carbonari were revolutionaries fighting for an Italy free of foreign rule. The two groups had an occasionally tense agreement to keep out of each other's way.

"The Order?" Faraz looked genuinely shocked at the suggestion. "They only care about retrieving the editbook, so it won't threaten their precious political neutrality."

Elsa saw anger and frustration in the set of Porzia's jaw, portending an argument as surely as storm clouds promised rain. Elsa quickly said, "Yes, but we're not going to let anyone else take the lead on this. We'll be the ones to find the editbook. And, if he needs it . . . rescue Leo, too." She didn't believe her own words, but she knew this was what Faraz wanted to hear.

He nodded. "We'll have to plan our approach carefully, if we want to rescue Leo and retrieve the editbook before Garibaldi knows what hit him."

Porzia snapped, "I can't do it any longer. What is wrong with you, Faraz? He left us! He's gone! He's *not coming back*."

"How can you say that?" Faraz stared at her, aghast. "It doesn't make any sense! We were his family, for *seven years*, and he just up and turns on us with no warning? There must be something else going on."

Porzia stood, slammed the tracking worldbook closed, and snatched it up angrily. "Wake up, Faraz! He had a choice to make: us or them. And he chose. It's that simple."

She whirled around, knocking over her chair in her haste to leave. She slammed the library door as she went. On Elsa's shoulder Skandar shivered with distress, and she put a hand up to soothe the beast. Elsa herself was too stunned at Porzia's outburst to know how to respond. That sharp, constant pain in her chest—the pain of betrayal—certainly agreed with Porzia, but she knew Faraz clung to hope like a lifeline.

"Don't listen to her," Faraz said, sounding shaken. "She's only distraught. She's trying to make sense of this as best she can."

"Right," Elsa said. It did not escape her that, perhaps, Porzia was not the only one at a loss.

He stared at the closed door through which Porzia had left them. "She's wrong—blood and family aren't the same thing. We're Leo's family, not them."

"I know." Elsa squeezed his arm reassuringly, but then felt guilty for encouraging him. What if Porzia was right, and Faraz was simply weaving an elaborate self-deception to soften the blow of Leo's absence? The doubt ate away at her like rot in the heart of a tree, and Elsa wondered if she'd ever be sound again.

Elsa followed Faraz through the cobbled streets and airy piazzas of Pisa, relying on his familiarity with the city and his general street-savvy. They were headed to see Rosalinda Scarpa, the Carbonari operative who had been Leo and Aris's childhood fencing instructor, before Garibaldi faked his death and splintered from the Carbonari. Elsa had met her only once, but once was enough to make her apprehensive about asking the woman for a favor; she didn't seem to like pazzerellones very much, with the exception of Leo, whom she treated with a strange sort of maternal possessiveness.

The walk through the city streets only worsened Elsa's nerves. It felt like traversing the floor of a never-ending valley, entrapping her on either side with row upon row of red-tile-roofed buildings. Faraz looked naked without Skandar on his shoulder; he'd left the beast at home so as not to draw attention, but Elsa still felt the weight of sideways glances, of gazes lingering a little longer than propriety would dictate. She didn't know whether the cause was their brown complexions, giving them away as foreigners, or her sartorial choice of trousers and a leather bodice.

Elsa said, "So you've never been there before?"

"I had to ask Gia to write down the address." Faraz crumpled the scrap of paper in his hands.

Gia was Porzia's mother and headmistress of Casa della Pazzia, which made Leo her ward. "She must have been *thrilled* about that request," Elsa said dryly. "Though I suppose we should count ourselves lucky that somebody knew about Rosalinda at all."

They crossed an old stone bridge over the river that bisected the city, and the openness came as a relief to Elsa. It was a clear day, bordering on hot as May surrendered to summer, and the sunlight glinted off the water.

"Yeah," Faraz agreed halfheartedly. "I guess there was some sort of custody disagreement between the Order and the Carbonari after Garibaldi faked his death."

Elsa was getting the distinct sense that Faraz did not want to talk about Leo right now, and especially did not want to talk about the things Leo had chosen to keep secret from the rest of them. She decided to shift the subject. "Speaking of the Order . . ."

Faraz shook his head. "We'd be gambling on the reliability of their assistance. The more people become involved, the more opportunities there are for someone to slip up."

Opportunities for a slipup . . . or opportunities for a betrayal. Porzia's father was in Firenze at the headquarters of the Order, and the Pisano family had influence. But Elsa had been betrayed once by someone she trusted completely, and she was not about to make the same mistake again.

"There is an alternative."

Faraz tucked his hands into his pockets. "I'm all ears."

"We don't involve anyone else. We use just one person, infiltrating Garibaldi's operation."

"You want to become a spy?"

"Think about all the levels of security Montaigne designed to protect the editbook, and he was just one scriptologist working alone. Montaigne was the original creator of Veldana, who had betrayed the Veldanese by helping to steal the editbook and then double-crossed Garibaldi to keep the book for himself. Garibaldi has Aris and a whole squadron of ex-Carbonari assassins. It may not be possible to get it back by force. What if the best way to steal the editbook is to trick them into giving me access?"

Faraz stared ahead, his expression thoughtful. "We'd need to somehow convince Garibaldi that you want to join his revolution. And if Leo is locked up, you'd be operating alone."

"Well," said Elsa, "it's a possibility to consider."

They arrived at the door of a narrow town house. Elsa tugged on the bellpull, which produced a muffled twang somewhere deep in the house. As they waited, she snuck a glance at Faraz: his features looked composed, as if he'd regained his usual unflappable resolve.

The sound of heavy, not especially ladylike footfalls preceded the door swinging open. The woman on the other side was tall, thin, and severe. She was dressed in men's trousers and a long black frock coat, and her steel-streaked hair was pulled back in a tight chignon at the back of her neck.

Elsa cleared her throat. "Rosalinda . . ."

"Signora Scarpa, if you please," she corrected. Her expression closed down at the sight of them, as if she had shutters she could lock behind the windows of her eyes.

Elsa felt her own expression darken in response. She opened her mouth to reply, but Faraz smoothly cut in. "Our apologies, Signora Scarpa, if we're disturbing you at an inconvenient hour."

Instead of replying, she scrutinized them with that hooded, hawk-like gaze of hers; she glanced at Elsa's hip, noting the revolver Elsa had taken to carrying. At least she didn't slam the door in their faces.

Faraz took this for an invitation to continue. "We'd like to speak with you about Leo. May we come in?"

With a sigh, she let them in and led them down a short hall to a sitting room, where she grudgingly waved them toward a pair of chairs.

Signora Scarpa's sitting room was neither particularly fancy nor particularly "lived-in," as Alek de Vries liked to call his cluttered flat in Amsterdam. The thought sent a pang of guilt through Elsa—for leaving her home world of Veldana, and for asking Alek to stay there to look after her terribly ill mother. Alek had mentored Jumi when she first learned scriptology, and though he was the closest thing to a grandparent Elsa ever had, she still felt that the responsibility to care for Jumi was hers alone. *What's done is done*, she chided herself. If she wasted time dwelling on decisions already made, she'd never get anywhere.

Faraz was telling Signora Scarpa about what happened with the editbook, Leo, and Garibaldi. If Scarpa's expression had been closed before, now it seemed to have turned to stone. Impenetrable and unreadable. Not an especially good sign; Elsa had hoped for *some* kind of reaction.

"So what are you doing here?" Signora Scarpa said, when Faraz finished the story.

"We came to you for help," Elsa said. "That is, assuming you care at all about what happens to your world, or to Leo." Talking about Leo as if he were an innocent victim felt like drinking acid, but she doubted the alternative would get her anywhere.

"Under my roof, you will watch that mouth of yours," Signora Scarpa snapped. "That boy is like a son to me. Do you think I live in Pisa by happy coincidence?"

Elsa shrugged. "I don't pretend to have any notion why you do the things you do."

"I trained him since he was old enough to pick up a foil," Signora Scarpa said. Her voice started out tight and soft, but her volume rose as she continued. "I was the one who got him out of Venezia alive, and *I* was the one who comforted him when he woke up screaming in the middle of the night for months afterward. Then the Order exerted their right of custody—caring only that he was a pazzerellone, not that he was a scared child—and I was expected to simply turn him over to the care of strangers. So yes, I asked the Carbonari to transfer me to Pisa. Not so I could manipulate him, as you seem to believe. But because he was a child and he needed me."

Elsa felt heat rise in her cheeks. Perhaps she should not be so quick to distrust everyone.

Faraz cleared his throat. "If you want to help Leo, he needs it now more than ever. Assuming you aren't"—Faraz paused, his gaze flicking over to meet Elsa's for a fraction of a second— "pleased to see him back in the custody of his father."

"He's being manipulated," Scarpa said with rock-hard certainty. "If he isn't simply held against his will."

Faraz offered a weak smile. "That's what we think, too."

"Not *think*," she insisted. "I *know*."

Elsa said, "Either way, we've been trying to locate him, but he's well hidden. We were thinking it might be easier to track Aris, but for it to work we need something—an object, a possession— that belonged to him."

Signora Scarpa frowned in a way that suggested she doubted Elsa's intelligence. "The Trovatelli estate *burned*. It wasn't as if we had much opportunity for collecting keepsakes. And I imagine anything of sentimental value would have left with Aris before the fire, in any case."

"It doesn't have to be his most favorite possession ever," Elsa said testily. She took a breath, reining in her temper. "If you can think of anything at all, it would be most appreciated."

Signora Scarpa still looked skeptical, but she nonetheless paused to think on it. "There was a mask. A carnevale mask, white with a long snout—the plague doctor mask, do you know it?" she said, turning to Faraz, who shook his head. "The spring before the fire, Ricciotti let Leo and Aris go out during carnevale by themselves. They ended up at my place somehow, wide-eyed and out of breath, but they wouldn't tell me what trouble they'd gotten into." Rosalinda smiled slightly at the memory, then caught herself and straightened her expression. "Aris left the mask behind by accident. So later I gave it to Leo as a remembrance. I don't know if he's kept it this whole time, though."

Elsa nodded, relieved. "It's something to look for. Thank you."

She and Faraz made ready to depart, but Signora Scarpa forestalled them.

"Wait," she said, "just for a moment."

Elsa turned back and looked at her expectantly.

Her face was a mask of non-expression, but she pressed her thumb into her opposite palm, as if she were struggling with a difficult decision. Finally, she said, "I believe you already know this, but . . . Garibaldi is dangerous."

"Yes, of course," Elsa said impatiently.

"That's not all." She shook her head in dismay. "I suspect Aris is also dangerous, in a way entirely different from his father. And because of that, I fear Leo may be dangerous as well—dangerous to you, I mean. Do you understand?"

Elsa swallowed around a lump in her throat. "I—yes, I think I do."

Signora Scarpa's expression quivered, as if she was struggling to keep her emotion off her face. "I'm not trying to say you shouldn't rescue him. Nothing could be worse for Leo than falling under their influence. But, by the time you find him . . . he may not understand that anymore."

Elsa wanted to snap that it was too late, that Leo had already willingly given himself over to their corrupting influence. But instead she pushed her anger down deep, where it could not escape from between her lips. "We'll work fast."

"I hope you do," she said.

"Signora Scarpa . . ." Elsa hesitated, aware she was edging onto uncertain ground. "Once we have a location, can we count on your assistance? The assistance of . . . of the Carbonari, I mean."

While Garibaldi had parted ways with the Carbonari over methodological disagreements, they still shared the same fundamental goal: to unite the four states of Italy into a single country. And if anyone could help Elsa become a spy, it was this woman.

Signora Scarpa's thin lips twisted into a grimace. "To what end?"

"I need to infiltrate Garibaldi's operation as a supposed defector from the Order of Archimedes," Elsa said.

"There is a strict arrangement of noninterference between the Order and the Carbonari, and the Order sees Garibaldi as *their* problem to solve. Officially, my answer has to be no."

Faraz raised his eyebrows. "And unofficially?"

There was a pause before Signora Scarpa answered, "Come to me when you know more, and I'll see what can be done."

2

IT HAD LONG SINCE COME TO MY ATTENTION THAT PEOPLE OF
ACCOMPLISHMENT RARELY SAT BACK AND LET THINGS HAPPEN TO
THEM. THEY WENT OUT AND HAPPENED TO THINGS.
—*Leonardo da Vinci*

Leo couldn't remember the last time he truly wanted to be left alone. It didn't come naturally to him, he who usually thrived on the company of others. But no matter how Aris behaved—enthusiastic, annoyed, bossy, concerned—he always inevitably served as a reminder of everything Leo had ruined. Even if he could find comfort in his brother's companionship, he wasn't ready to let anyone replace his old friends. And his father was worse—Ricciotti had a talent for making Leo feel reduced to a petulant child, when he wasn't too busy planning revolutions to remember about Leo at all.

Leo leaned against the window frame in his new bedroom, grateful to have a moment to himself. There was nothing in the world so exhausting as pretending to be happy. The diamond-shaped panes of glass were cool to the touch, and the view beyond looked even colder, the naked, craggy peaks of the Italian Alps free of ice only by virtue of the season. There was green in the valley below, but it seemed impossibly remote, at the bottom of a precipitous drop.

The view was almost enough to make even Leo dizzy, and certainly enough to make him glad he wasn't prone to fear of heights like Faraz. *Faraz*, his best friend, whom he would never see again.

There was something poetic about Ricciotti Garibaldi hiding out in such a cold, remote location. Certainly more fitting than the tenement building in Nizza where their reunion had taken place. That had been a center of operations, but not a home. This stronghold was where his father and Aris had lived these past seven years, ever since they'd fled Venezia without him. To Leo it seemed as unsentimental as it was opulent, though Aris was comfortable enough here.

Aris, who refused to understand. Aris, who had never been discarded like an obsolete machine.

Leo pressed his forehead against the glass and let the cold seep into him.

His gaze fell on the windowsill, and he frowned. Were those marks carved into the stone outside the glass? He reached for the latch and yanked the window open, stiff hinges creaking. The narrow ledge beyond the window frame had eight long grooves carved into it, two pairs of four, almost like . . . claw marks? Leo ran a finger over the rough edges, then spread his fingers to measure the span. No, the grooves were too far apart to have been made by a hand—a human hand, at least.

"I hope you're not weighing the merits of jumping."

Leo whirled around. His father stood in the doorway. He felt a reflexive flash of guilt, as if he were a child caught breaking the rules, but it was quickly replaced with annoyance. He hadn't done anything wrong, and even if he had, he was long past caring what Ricciotti thought of him.

"I was airing out the room." With slow deliberateness, he swung the window closed and latched it. He did not ask about the marks on the ledge.

Ricciotti clasped his hands behind his back and stepped casually into the room. "I know you're not happy here."

Leo raised his eyebrows. "Really, Father? Whatever gave you that impression?"

"So stubborn," Ricciotti said. "You were never this stubborn when you were a boy."

"It's not as if you've kept up to date. A lot can change in seven years."

He sighed. "Listen, Leo—when our situation in Venezia became untenable, my hand was forced. I would have waited until you were older if I could have. And it was always my intent to retrieve you, when you were old enough to understand what we're trying to do."

Leo felt his throat tighten with anger. Quietly, he said, "Don't you dare pretend your children were ever a priority for you. Pasca *died* in that fire. What could you possibly say to make that right?"

"Nothing," Ricciotti admitted. "I don't expect you to forgive me, but you have one brother still alive. I only ask that you not punish Aris for my mistakes."

"You know why I'm here," Leo said, tight-lipped. He was the consolation prize for letting Elsa and her mother go free. "I intend to honor my end of the bargain, but I never promised to enjoy it."

Ricciotti's eyes narrowed. "And what good are you to us like this? Do I have to remind you how valuable Elsa could be— another polymath, and one who already knows how to safely use the editbook?"

A thread of icy panic laced through him at the mention of Elsa, and Leo fought to keep his expression stoic. "Careful, Father. Are you so eager to find out what happens when you threaten me?"

Ricciotti laughed. "Whether you like to admit it or not, you certainly are my son." He turned to walk out, then paused in the doorway. "Your brother is waiting in the ballroom. I expect you to attend him."

Ricciotti swept away down the hall, leaving Leo wordless in his wake.

Leo considered disobeying his father, but in the end he decided this particular hill was not worth dying on. Without a doubt there would be worse battles than this, and it would be smarter to save his energy for one that mattered. So he left his room and went downstairs.

The grand ballroom had no furnishings whatsoever, not even curtains on the tall windows lining the south wall. His footsteps echoed as he entered the empty space.

"Heads up!" Aris called, and threw a fencing foil at Leo.

Leo snatched it out of the air, reacting instinctively despite his surprise. He raised an eyebrow at his brother. "We're fencing now, are we?"

"What, you don't like it anymore? We always used to fence." Aris's brow pulled down in a scowl, and Leo felt tension building in the air like an electric charge.

"No, it's fine," Leo said quickly, heading off his brother's mood before it could solidify.

Aris's tawny eyes lit up—nothing delighted him like getting his way. He strapped on a wire-mesh fencing mask, tossed a second mask to Leo, and brandished a foil of his own. He was taller than Leo, which gave him a bit more reach, and his wiry body moved with a tense, coiled energy.

Leo swung the training foil through the air experimentally. The foil was lighter than his rapier and not as well balanced, but it felt eerily familiar. Had Aris bothered to rescue their fencing equipment from the house fire in Venezia all those years ago? *He took the foils with him, but left me behind.*

Leo shook his head to clear it. Aris had been young, too, back then, and was only following their father's commands. Besides, now was not the time to dwell on it.

"En garde?" Aris said, grinning like a fiend behind the protective mesh of his headgear.

Leo raised the blunt tip to eye level and widened his stance. They began—lunge and parry, shuffle step, flick of the wrist—more akin to a dance than a battle. Leo thought hard about how skilled he should appear. If he beat Aris soundly, his brother's good mood would vanish, as would any future advantage Leo might have in a fight. But if he played it too slow, Aris would realize it was an act; they'd crossed swords in the labyrinth, after all, and Leo had held him off then, long enough for Elsa and Porzia and Faraz to get away with the editbook. Back before Leo realized he would have to betray them all. Lord, that memory ached.

Aris landed a hit.

"Touché," Leo admitted with a rueful smile. Apparently all he had to do to fake mediocrity was let his mind wander.

Annoyed, Aris said, "You're distracted."

Leo saw no point in denying it. "I have a lot on my mind."

Aris scowled. "If you don't pay attention, I'm going to gut you like a fish."

Leo dropped out of his stance, feigning dismay. "I'm afraid that might happen either way. You've gotten quite good."

"Don't worry, you'll catch up soon enough," Aris said, somewhat mollified. "You were always a quick study with a foil, and now that you're home, we'll practice every day."

Leo almost snapped, *This isn't my home*, but he swallowed the words. "All right then, brother," he said. "Let's practice."

Leo raised his foil to the ready position. He'd fought his way out of some tricky situations in the last few weeks. Stopped a runaway train, thwarted a Carbonari-trained assassin, navigated a madman's scribed labyrinth. Here at last was the trap he could not escape from: family.

But perhaps he was thinking about this situation all wrong. There was genuine delight written in Aris's features. Could Leo strengthen their bond of brotherhood and turn Aris against their father? Ricciotti had the editbook but no scriptological talent of his own—he would have to rely on Aris to figure out how to use it.

So there *was* a way Leo could throw a wrench in Ricciotti's plans, after all.

Alek de Vries looked up from the writing desk to watch Jumi. She sat on her cot, awake, leaning against the wall amongst a nest of pillows. There was a book open in her lap, but she was staring off into space instead, a frown line creased between her dark eyebrows.

Sighing, Alek set down his fountain pen and closed the lid on the inkwell. Worrying about Jumi really ought to be declared the national pastime of Veldana.

"What is it?" he said. "What's bothering you?"

She turned her head quickly, startled, and blinked those eerie green eyes at him. "Hmm? Oh, just thinking. Wondering what will become of Montaigne, now that he's in custody."

It was Alek's turn to frown. Montaigne, his once-friend, who had scribed the Veldana worldbook and then spent the next eighteen years bitterly regretting it. The Veldanese had no interest in glorifying their creator, and Jumi had held the editbook over

Montaigne's head like the sword of Damocles—not that it excused his terrible decisions.

"The Order of Archimedes will decide what to do with him," Alek said. "He conspired with Garibaldi. He broke our most basic rule."

"Don't be a miserable pig?" Jumi said dryly.

"Don't involve yourself in politics." Alek paused. "Which is almost the same thing, now that I think about it."

A quick rap on the cottage door interrupted their conversation. Jumi moved to stand, but Alek waved a hand at her reprovingly and got up to answer it himself. From the door he could see down the slope to the other whitewashed, thatch-roofed cottages of the village, tucked into the valley with cypress trees rising behind like protective sentinels. It could have been a scene from the Mediterranean, except for the subtle alien scent to the air that never quite allowed Alek to forget he was in a scribed world.

In any case, the boy waiting on the stoop shouldn't have to suffer through Alek's ruminations. "Good afternoon, Revan," Alek said in Veldanese, his command of the language somewhat shaky.

"Good afternoon, Honored de Vries," the boy pronounced slowly for Alek's benefit.

He held the door wide to let Revan in. Alek still thought of Revan as the restless skinny boy who had followed young Elsa around everywhere. He was a grown lad now—tall for a Veldanese and filling out, his brown complexion made even darker by long hours in the sun. Still restless, though.

Revan aimed straight for the cot set up against the side wall of the cottage. He crouched beside Jumi and they spoke in rapid Veldanese, the liquid syllables flowing off their tongues so fast that Alek caught only one word in three. Alek went back to the writing desk, turning his attention away to give them some semblance of privacy despite the smallness of the cottage.

He ran a hand over the half-blank page of the worldbook open before him. The scriptology paper seemed to pulse slightly, like the slow heartbeat of some hibernating animal. The book wouldn't truly feel alive until he'd finished it, though. Assuming he *could* finish it. He was attempting to duplicate a worldbook scribed by Elsa, which gave her the ability to open portals between two locations on Earth. Most scriptological scholars would call the doorbook—as Elsa had named it—a ludicrous impossibility, but Alek had seen it, and used it, and knew for a fact that it was real.

He didn't understand how she'd pulled it off, though. He had nearly five decades more experience and study, and he still couldn't figure it out.

Alek didn't look up from his project again until Revan stood to leave. The boy's gaze swept over the cottage like a searchlight before he made for the door. Alek frowned, but told himself it was nothing. The Veldanese simply had more of a cultural emphasis on awareness of one's surroundings.

"What was that about?" he asked, after Revan had gone.

"Everything's fine," Jumi assured him, fingering a page of the novel still open in her lap. "Some of the villagers want to learn how to use the portal devices."

"Why?"

"In case of emergency. When Elsa and I were both off-world, Veldana was entirely cut off from Earth."

Alek harrumphed. "With the editbook in Garibaldi's hands, it's probably safer here, inside the Veldana worldbook, than it is in the real world."

"Still, we need to be better prepared," she said. He could tell the *we*, in this case, meant *us Veldanese* rather than *you and I*.

Alek nodded, but in his mind he was replaying Revan's visit. He couldn't shake the feeling that the boy was up to something.

Leo kept himself awake by mentally reviewing what he knew about the layout of his father's alpine fortress. He composed a blueprint in his mind's eye, sketching all the places he'd been so far, and all the unknowns implied by the negative space around those places. He might need to know these things, and soon.

Claw marks outside his window. Was he being watched? If he went digging for answers, would they immediately know? Was it Aris or Father, or some outside force trying to monitor him? The Carbonari, maybe, or the Order. Leo felt torn between a desire to act, to *do* something about it, and a desire not to tip his hand too soon. Assuming someone actually was watching him, they did not yet know that Leo knew he was being watched, and that could be useful.

It was a quandary, when the thing you wanted to investigate was your own surveillance.

The house had been quiet and dark for hours. Leo stared at the ceiling of his room, waiting. There was a grandfather clock at the end of the hall, and if he lay very still, he could hear the swish and clack of its pendulum as it measured time.

Now, he decided, and slid off the bed. In the dark, he fumbled with the velvet-trimmed flannel smoking jacket that had been left in the room for his use, impatient to wrap himself tightly against the chill. The nights were as cold here in May as Casa della Pazzia was in the dead of winter.

He lit a candle, eased his bedroom door open, and slipped out into the hall. Sneaking around the house, in and of itself, should not tip off his surveillants. There were a dozen reasons he might want to go exploring at night. One might even argue that if he *didn't* go sneaking around, that would be a sure sign he knew he was being watched.

So he padded barefoot down the hall. By the time he reached the bottom of the stone stairs, his feet were freezing, but that was the price he paid for moving silently.

To his right gaped the dark maw of the entranceway into the ballroom, the large space swallowing the meager light of his candle. At the far end the moonlit windows seemed to hover in the air like specters. Leo turned the other way instead—north, into the bowels of the fortress, where the boundaries between the house and the mountainside blurred together.

As he followed the dark hallway, he stopped at every door and listened for a minute, ears straining for any sign of movement within. When he heard none, he would try the knob. Some of the doors were locked, which would not usually provide much of a deterrent for Leo, but he'd left his lockpicks hidden in his room. He was saving those for when the need was urgent; he didn't want to risk getting the lockpicks confiscated over some undirected exploration. Still, it was hard to walk away from those doors— the mere fact that the locks were denying him entry made him itch to get past them. Locking a room was as good as *begging* a mechanist to break in, and for a fleeting moment Leo wondered if this was some game Aris was playing with him.

Now you're getting paranoid, he thought, and moved on to the next door.

Whenever he found an unlocked room, he did a quick sweep inside. A disorganized storage area full of empty shipping crates. A long chamber lined with empty cots, which might serve as a barracks or a hospital, perhaps. And then, deeper into the mountainside, a wide, tall room outfitted as a mechanist's laboratory.

Leo paused in the doorway, suspicious. Lit only by his candle, the hulking machines cast enormous, distorted shadows against the walls and ceiling. There was no heat in the air, no telltale smell of lubricant, no sign that someone had been at work that evening. So why, then, would the door be left unlocked? They were hosting a mechanist of questionable loyalty; they should have secured the tools the minute Leo arrived.

Leo carried his candle over to one long workbench, and he did not have difficulty finding a place to set the holder down. Everything was quite clean and organized—meticulously, almost obsessively organized. Leo could not help but smile a little at that. Even as a boy, Aris had insisted on keeping everything in its proper place. Leo, on the other hand, would set a tool down any old place and have no trouble remembering where he'd put it the next time he wanted it. "Away" was wherever the tool landed when he let go. That had always driven Aris nuts.

Leo idly ran his fingertips along the dustless, polished wood of the workbench. It was comforting that some things never changed. He still *knew* his brother, and it gave him hope that Aris could be swayed from the path Ricciotti dictated.

Then the smile fell from his face. Neat was not the only thing Aris had always been—he'd also been possessive and manipulative. There was no way Aris would leave his laboratory unlocked by accident, which meant he'd left it open for Leo to find. What was this—an offering? A lure?

Perhaps Aris wanted Leo to search the lab and find evidence of whatever had left those claw marks outside the window. Or search the lab and find an absence of evidence. Or the unlocked lab and the claw marks were unrelated, and Aris had some other motive. Leo turned over each possibility, mentally mapping them out like planning future moves in a game of chess.

He picked up the candleholder again and moved deeper into the laboratory, examining his brother's machines. Toward the back was another workbench, this one with a thin white sheet draped over the lumps and angles of some half-completed mechanical components. And atop the cloth was a note, the careful loops of Aris's cursive standing out starkly against the pale paper and paler cloth.

It read: *Don't touch my stuff.*

Leo moved the note aside and gently lifted the sheet to see what lay beneath.

A procession of tiny clockwork parts was spread across the wood, each gear and bolt and screw positioned precisely as if they were soldiers lined up for a march. Leo turned the cloth back farther and discovered a half-built mechanical hand, brass skeleton joints shining in the candlelight. He froze and stared at it—could this be the evidence he was looking for?

But no, the size didn't look right. Leo held out his hand for comparison, and the brass skeleton fingers were no longer than his own. This part could not belong to whatever creature dug those grooves into his windowsill.

He uncovered more of the workbench and, with it, a second note. It read: *Fine. Be that way. But for the love of God, put things back where you found them.*

Leo smiled again. Despite their years of separation, how well Aris knew him. And chess had always been Aris's game.

Leo saw little of his father the next day, and even less of Aris. At first he treasured the solitude, but his relief at their absence soon transformed to suspicion. For them to leave him so unattended, something must be going on—something of import.

Leo walked the empty hallways, pausing at each closed door, until he heard movement within his father's study. He froze, then leaned in, pressing his ear to the wood.

On the other side a voice spoke—muffled, yet still recognizably belonging to Aris. "You want to know how it's going? Slowly. Like a snail. That's how it's going."

Ricciotti's voice replied, "What can be done to expedite the process?"

Aris let out a disbelieving laugh. "Father, the entire book is written in a language *nobody can read*. I have to decipher the grammar and syntax and vocabulary—all without any references—before we can even begin to use it."

There was a long pause, and Leo could vividly imagine the stare that must be passing between Aris and Ricciotti.

Eventually, Aris broke the thick silence. "We shouldn't have let the girl go. She's valuable."

"Must you constantly second-guess my decisions?" Ricciotti said, half-amused and half-annoyed.

"Do you know what the locomotive engineer told the police? I read the report. She left through a portal and came back with a device that put out the fire in the firebox. Father, she's a polymath."

Ricciotti sighed audibly. "Yes, Aris, I am aware. But your brother made the conditions for his return quite clear."

"I was right that we should have retrieved Leo sooner, and I'm right about this, too. We need her skills. Even more, we need her language."

"But we don't need her yet. For now, she is serving a different purpose—she gives Leo a reason to stay. In time, he'll remember he belongs with us, and her freedom will no longer be a necessary bargaining chip."

Leo pushed away from the door, struggling to stay silent. His hands, he realized, were shaking. Panic lit his veins and buzzed in his brain. *No, no, no, please no.*

After everything he'd sacrificed to buy her freedom, Elsa was still not safe from his father.

3

SCIENTISTS DELIGHT NOT IN ABUNDANCE OF MATERIAL;
THEY REJOICE ONLY IN THE EXCELLENCE OF THEIR
EXPERIMENTAL METHODS.

—*Jabir ibn Hayyan*

They walked back through the narrow, straight streets and wide-open piazzas of Pisa. There was a renewed energy to Faraz's step, and Elsa had to hurry to keep up with his long legs.

Back at Casa della Pazzia, he took the grand staircase two at a time. Faraz was the one to open the door and let them into Leo's bedchamber, seemingly comfortable with the thought of entering his friend's space uninvited. Elsa, however, stepped into the middle of Leo's large room and looked around awkwardly.

Afternoon sunlight streamed through the glass doors that led onto the balcony. Aside from the bed and a garishly upholstered wingback chair, there was a wardrobe and shelves and drawers, all overburdened with more possessions than one person could possibly need. She hadn't noticed before, but apparently Leo was the sort of person who hoarded *everything*.

"On the bright side," said Faraz, eyeing the mess, "I find it highly unlikely that Leo would have thrown out the mask."

Elsa started with the wardrobe, hoping this would be the easiest hiding place to eliminate. It was packed full, so she felt around to confirm everything was made of cloth. She struggled to understand how anyone could accumulate so much junk—her own unsentimental upbringing had taught her that the value of an object was its practical use, but Leo's collection of stuff was clearly about something more personal than utility.

She said, "I don't know about you, but I feel a little strange going through his things like this." It seemed somehow intimate, as if exploring Leo's private space would bring her closer to him—whether she wanted that or not.

Faraz was searching the shelves, undeterred by such inhibitions. "Look at this," he said, holding up a folded sheaf of paper. "Playbill from an opera we saw more than a year ago." He put it down and pointed at a badly corroded, broken sextant. "Salvaged from a tall-ship wreck we explored when we were fourteen. Ticket stub from our first train ride to Firenze. And I don't even know when this is from," he said, fingering a wine cork that Leo had kept for some reason. "I swear, he's worse than a magpie."

This seemed to delight Faraz, as if it were tangible proof that the Leo he remembered had, in fact, existed. But looking around, Elsa sighed. How could a person who clung with apparent sentimentality to every scrap of his life simply walk away from all of it, with nothing but the clothes on his back and the tools in his pockets? To Elsa, the clutter spoke of a desperate need to feel settled and at home here in Casa della Pazzia. Was Garibaldi now fulfilling that need?

Were all of them—the Pisanos and Faraz and Elsa—nothing but a poor substitute for the true family he'd always yearned after?

Elsa pushed the thought away, along with the sharp pain it gave her, and went back to searching. She concluded that nothing was hidden in the wardrobe other than a reluctance to dispose of old clothes, and she moved on to exploring the contents of an ornately carved cabinet with an abundance of little compartments.

"Isn't *any* of this organized?" she huffed, frustrated.

"Oh, it's all organized," Faraz assured her. "But I'm afraid the method of organization is entirely opaque to anyone who's not Leo."

Elsa sighed and opened another little door, then froze. "Um, Faraz?"

"Yeah?"

"What color did Rosalinda say the mask was?" she said, reaching into the compartment.

Faraz shifted his weight, turning his attention toward her. "White."

Elsa held up a broken piece of white ceramic. "I think we have a problem."

Elsa needed to break something.

Hanging on the wall over the washbasin in her bedroom was a small, oval mirror with a somewhat tarnished silver frame. She lifted it off the wall and looked it over, familiarizing herself with every detail. It was heavier than she'd expected—not that she'd had much experience with such little luxuries before coming to Pisa. *The Europeans value rarities*, her mother once explained. *Minerals and metals that are hard to find in their world. But what is rarity to us, we who scribe the stone?*

"Casa?" she said, addressing the empty air.

The house's smooth, low, artificial voice seemed to emanate from everywhere and nowhere. "Yes, signorina?"

"Who would you say this mirror belongs to?"

"Well." Casa's pause sounded thoughtful. "It hangs in your room for your use."

"Yes, but does it really *belong* to me?" It didn't feel like hers; it was simply an object that had been left in the rooms she borrowed.

"In what sense, signorina?"

Elsa rubbed her thumb against a spot of tarnish. "In the scriptological sense: the property of ownership." The map world was a finicky invention—hence why the shattered fragments of the mask would not provide strong enough ownership for tracking—and Elsa needed a test object with clear ownership.

"Scriptologically speaking, it cannot belong to me, as I am neither human nor alive," said the house. "I belong to the Pisano family, and so by extension all that I contain is theirs as well. Does that help?"

"Thank you, Casa. You are, as always, very helpful."

"I exist to serve."

Elsa nodded, padding barefoot through her sitting room with its absurdly lavish furniture upholstered in green-and-beige damask, and into her cozy, well-lit study, with its delightfully large writing desk. She should test the mirror first, to be sure, before breaking it.

"And to protect," Casa added.

Elsa looked up. "What?"

"I *exist* to *protect*," the house said emphatically.

"Riiight . . . ," Elsa said. She had no idea what that was about. "Thanks," she said, to dismiss the house's attention.

She set the mirror down on her writing desk and opened the tracking worldbook to the first page. Elsa had found the tracking book waiting for her outside the door to her chambers. Apparently

Porzia was *done* with the search, and Elsa and Faraz would have to continue without her assistance.

Elsa read the coordinates listed in the front of the worldbook and set the dials on her handheld portal device. She picked up the mirror again in her other hand and flipped the switch to activate the device.

A gaping black hole irised open, cutting through the air in the middle of her study. Elsa stepped into it. The cold, black nothingness of the in-between space washed over her, and then she passed through to the other side, stepping into ankle-deep salt water.

Inside the tracking world, a scale model of Europe stretched before her. She stood in the middle of the Adriatic Sea, towering like a giant over the landscape, the immensity of the Alps reduced to an inconvenience no taller than her shins. Turning left, she saw that the world now included the continent of Africa, and behind her was the Near East. The cuffs of her trousers were wicking up the water, so she stopped looking around and stepped across Europe to get to the podium-shaped machine that would control the tracking map.

She set the mirror atop the podium and fiddled with the controls, then yanked down on a large lever to start the machine. Gears whirred, and the targeting settled in with a series of *ka-chunk* noises.

When the machine was done, she sloshed back through the Atlantic to stand on Europe, staring down between her feet; on the map, a little red dot glowed over the location of Pisa within the Kingdom of Sardinia.

"Excellent," Elsa murmured. The mirror had enough ownership property for the machine to target its owner—apparently Signora Pisano, since her husband was currently in Firenze at the headquarters of the Order.

Elsa grabbed the mirror and opened a portal back to her study in the real world. Then she shut the tracking worldbook to make room on her desk. Taking the frame in both hands, she whacked the mirror down against the desk's hard wood. It made a soft crunching noise, and a spiderweb of cracks marred the glass.

Now all she had to do was design a device that would repair the mirror without muddling the ownership property. The clarity that came with focusing on a task relieved her of anger, of hurt, of doubt. Elsa smiled.

She would build the device, fix the mask, and track down Aris. Then she would make her mother proud by recovering the editbook. Leo meant nothing, she told herself. The task was all.

Elsa prayed to nothing in particular as the machine chugged and huffed.

She was in the main room of her laboratory worldbook, with its smooth wood floor and ample worktables. The single broad window showed a view of waves lapping at the sandy shores of a barrier island, but the scene was an illusion; no outside existed beyond the laboratory walls in this world. The water was silent and bereft of the salt-and-decay scents of an actual sea, and the sight alone brought her little comfort. Elsa would have to scribe sound and smell sometime.

She turned back to watch the machine she'd just built. It was approximately the size and shape of a steamer trunk, though the steel and brass construction rendered it much heavier. The pitch of its whirring gears lowered as they slowed to a halt.

Elsa opened a pressure valve and waited a minute before reaching for the latch that held the machine's lid tightly sealed. The lid opened with a soft hiss. She pulled on a pair of long, thick leather gloves and lifted out the still-hot oval mirror. Tilting it in the light, she held the mirror so close to her face she could feel heat wafting off the surface. Its cracks were sealed now, but there remained bubbly deformations in the glass where the cracks had been, like the glass equivalent of raised keloid scar tissue.

"Damn," she muttered, setting the mirror down on another lab bench to cool. She pulled off the gloves and threw them across the room, which was momentarily satisfying but in the end not terribly productive.

Pressing one palm to her forehead, Elsa had to acknowledge she was exhausted. She had no notion of what hour it was—she deliberately did not keep a clock in her laboratory, since she disliked being reminded of the passage of time while involved in a project. Her stomach told her she had missed the dinner hour, though. She should take a break and eat something; perhaps a solution would present itself once she was refreshed.

The portal took her back to her rooms in Casa della Pazzia. As soon as she was through, Casa's voice startled her, saying, "Signor Hannachi requests your presence in the alchemy lab, when you're able."

She squeezed her eyes shut, willing her heart rate to calm down. "Thanks for your, uh, *diligence* in delivering that message, Casa. I'll go see Faraz now. Would you send some leftovers to the alchemy lab for me, please?"

"It would be my pleasure, signorina."

As she navigated through the hallways of Casa della Pazzia, her mind drifted back to Leo. It was easy not to think of him when she was focused on calibrating the pressure gauge or tweaking the sealant formula to activate at a lower temperature. But as soon as she stepped away from the diversion of engineering, the betrayal and doubt came flooding back, and she felt as if she were walking through a marsh where at any moment the next step might be the one that sucked her under.

At least she and Faraz were united in a common goal; Elsa needed that camaraderie. If she didn't force herself to trust someone now, she might never be able to do it again. Not after what Leo did. Elsa paused outside the alchemy lab door, part of her wanting to withdraw, but instead she made herself go in.

Faraz's laboratory—in contrast to Leo's—was immaculately clean, with the shelves of chemicals and cabinets of glassware all neatly organized. The white shards of the mask were laid out like puzzle pieces on the worktable in the center of the room, and beside them Faraz was sculpting a lump of clay with his hands.

Elsa said, "What do you have there?"

"Good evening," Faraz said, glancing up. "I was thinking I could shape a clay mold, and stick the broken pieces on the outside. Then we'd just need your machine to fuse the cracks."

"If I can ever get it to work," she said darkly.

"Of course you'll get it to work," he said with utter faith. He motioned for her to come over. "Take a look at this."

This was a book he had open on his worktable. Elsa touched the pages, but the paper felt dead to her—it was just a regular book, not a worldbook. "What is it?"

"A history of the plague," he explained, pausing to rub his nose with the back of his hand. "I found a sketch of what the plague doctor mask looks like. It was actually worn by doctors in the seventeenth century, if you can believe it."

Elsa leaned close to look at the picture. The mask was designed to cover the entire face, with two round holes for the eyes and a long, downward-curving beak like that of a mournful ibis. "Well," she said, "at least we now know what we're trying to reconstruct."

A bot let itself into the lab, bringing Elsa a bowl. "Thank you, Casa," she said as she accepted the food—white beans and stewed tomatoes with sausage chopped into it. She was too hungry to care that it was room temperature, and started shoveling it into her mouth.

"How close are you with the machine?" asked Faraz, who had gone back to molding the clay, using the picture in the book as a guide.

"No idea. I can predict the chemistry, but figuring out how to retain the ownership property is blind trial and error," Elsa said between bites. The food tasted of garlic and sage, with bursts of spiciness when she bit into a piece of sausage. "Though I should test it on something ceramic to check my temperature and pressure calculations."

Faraz leaned away from the clay mold and shifted from side to side, examining it for imperfections. "Well, in about thirty seconds you'll have an empty ceramic bowl," he teased.

"Ha-ha," she said around a large mouthful.

But by the time Elsa made it back to her rooms, the bowl was indeed empty, so she licked it clean and brought it through the portal into her laboratory.

She set the bowl on a workbench, rested a narrow-bladed chisel against the bottom, and gave the chisel a good whack with a mallet—splitting the bowl into two neat pieces. Now that the machine would have some physical damage to repair, she lifted the lid, placed the two halves of the bowl inside, and applied a thin trail of liquid sealant to the crack. Then she checked her notes, adjusted the machine's settings, and let it run.

Elsa worked long into the night, running tests and more tests. They only had the one mask, so there was no margin for error. Casa brought her teacups and saucers and plates, and expressed only mild reservations about allowing Elsa to break the Pisanos' fine china.

Once Elsa was satisfied with a visual inspection of the machine's results, she began taking her repaired objects through a portal into the tracking world and testing the strength of their ownership property. She kept tweaking the fusion machine until its products consistently retained a strong, clear ownership signal, and only then did she admit to herself that it was time to give in to exhaustion.

She took a portal back to her rooms in Casa della Pazzia. Outside her windows, dawn had already brightened the sky, and a songbird's melody permeated the glass, muted but audible. Apparently she'd worked the whole night away.

"Casa, I'm going to grab a few hours' sleep. Please wake me when Faraz has finished reconstructing the mask."

"As you wish, signorina," said the house.

This was going to work. She would make it work—by sheer force of will, if she had to.

Faraz's reconstruction of the mask was a work of art, as far as Elsa was concerned.

"Will this do?" he asked as he rested the mask-covered clay mold on an empty worktable in her laboratory.

For a moment, Elsa was too baffled to respond; she almost would have accused him of false modesty, if he didn't seem so genuinely unsure of the quality of his work. "Faraz, don't be ridiculous, it's a thing of beauty—I can barely see the cracks and we haven't even sealed them yet."

Together they prepped the mask with sealant, and Faraz carefully lowered it into Elsa's machine. She set the dials, took a deep breath, and flipped the switch to turn it on. The machine hissed and hummed as the chamber got up to temperature.

"How does it work?" Faraz asked.

Elsa watched the gauges closely. The pressure needle was wavering a little, so she made a couple of fine adjustments. "The sealant lowers the melting temperature of the ceramic and the glaze just along the cracks, while the rest of it stays solid."

"Doesn't that leave behind trace contamination?"

"Nope." There, that was better—the pressure needle held steady. "The sealant burns off when I increase the partial pressure of oxygen."

Keeping an eye on the built-in timer, Elsa let the chamber hold at peak conditions for another ninety seconds before she turned the dial to increase the oxygen content. When the entire process was complete, she opened a valve and vented the chamber to equilibrate it with the air in the room.

Elsa said, "If you're the praying type, now would be the time."

"That's not really how prayer works . . . for me, at least," Faraz replied, his expression turning wistful.

Elsa shrugged. The Veldanese had no religion, so she grew up only vaguely aware of the concept; someday she'd have to get Faraz to explain it to her properly, but today was not the time for that.

She handed her thick leather gloves to Faraz and opened the chamber lid for what would hopefully be the last time. Faraz pulled on the gloves and gently lifted the plague doctor mask out of the machine, leaving behind the clay mold he'd used for the reconstruction. The mask held together in his hands.

Faraz set it down on an empty workbench, and Elsa leaned in for a closer look. The seals in the porcelain looked almost seamless—Faraz had done an excellent job of fitting the pieces together, and after a whole night of trials, Elsa had the machine running optimally.

Elsa dared to hope. "So far, so good. We should let it cool before taking it into the tracking world—let's not risk a rapid temperature change." She worried the cold nothingness between portals would crack the mask if it was still hot.

They let it sit on the bench for an agonizing few minutes. When the anxious impatience in her chest became too sharp to bear, Elsa tapped her naked fingertips against the mask, testing its temperature, and found it still warm but not painfully so.

They both took off their boots. Elsa picked up a portal device and Faraz lifted the mask, and together they stepped through a portal into the shallow water of the Adriatic Sea. They walked across Europe and into the Atlantic, and Faraz placed the mask atop the tracking podium with a care bordering on reverence.

"Moment of truth," he breathed.

Elsa grinned at him. "Truth is what we make it to be."

She adjusted the controls and pulled the lever to input the target. The mechanical innards of the podium chugged and whirred, and then the targeting was complete.

Faraz said, "Did it work?"

Elsa sloshed her way back through the ankle-deep Atlantic to continental Europe. "Check the map. Do you see the dot?"

They stared down at the map beneath their feet. After a tense moment of searching, Elsa spotted the red dot of light, its glow partially obscured by the rugged alpine topography. "Here!"

A location, finally—she'd found Aris, and he would lead her to the editbook.

Faraz picked his way over and examined the location. "They're in the mountains outside the city of Trento. That whole region north of Venetia still belongs to the Austrian Empire."

"Is that going to be a problem?" Elsa's grasp of European politics was tenuous at best. For most of her life, she'd thought of existence as divided into two categories: Veldana and not-Veldana. The divisions between countries on Earth were trivial compared with this most important of distinctions, or so Jumi had encouraged her to think. At the moment, though, she was painfully aware that her ignorance of political matters was a weakness.

Faraz's features settled into a thoughtful expression. "The border crossing could prove problematic, but Rosalinda may have a solution to that. I'd be surprised if the Carbonari didn't have someone who could forge papers."

"Papers?" Elsa asked, confused.

"Identification."

"Oh," she said, though she still wasn't sure what exactly he meant. "Anyway, will you bring the news to Rosalinda for me?"

"Of course," said Faraz. "But what will you do?"

The flood of elation at their success was gradually receding as Elsa focused on the next problem that needed to be solved. "The Carbonari are my way in, but I'll also need a way out." She took a deep breath. "And for that I'll need Porzia."

4

AH, CHILD AND YOUTH, IF YOU KNEW THE BLISS WHICH RESIDES
IN THE TASTE OF KNOWLEDGE, AND THE EVIL AND UGLINESS
THAT LIES IN IGNORANCE, HOW WELL YOU ARE ADVISED TO NOT
COMPLAIN OF THE PAIN AND LABOR OF LEARNING.
—*Christine de Pizan*

P orzia was desperate for something to do that wouldn't remind her of Leo.

After her outburst in the library, she'd gone straight up to her study, taking the tracking worldbook with her even though the mere sight of it made her blood boil. She had hurled the book against the wall, and that gave her a moment of satisfaction. But the worldbook had fallen open where it landed, as if begging her to sit down and go back to work on the impossible problem of how to track the untrackable. She briefly considered finding a lit fireplace to toss it into, but in the end decided to leave it outside the door to Elsa's chambers instead. If Elsa and Faraz wanted to keep banging their heads against the delusion of rescuing Leo, she supposed it was within their rights to do so—as long as they left Porzia out of it.

Now she was wandering the halls of Casa della Pazzia, going

up and down staircases at random, looking for a place that didn't remind her poignantly of Leo. How could it be that every square inch of the massive house seemed to come with some memory of him attached to it? Porzia had lived here for eleven years before Leo turned up, and yet he seemed to be as much a part of the house as the army of little brass bots that kept the place running.

Eventually she found herself on the main floor, outside her mother's office. The door was mostly closed, but not latched, so Porzia let herself in without knocking.

Mamma looked up from her desk. She had dark circles under her eyes, and strands of dark hair were escaping from her usually neat chignon. "Good evening, darling."

"You've been working too hard," Porzia fretted as she took a seat on the other side of the desk. The office was wood-paneled and cluttered and felt too cramped for her tastes, but her mother seemed to like it that way.

Mamma offered her a tired smile. "Haven't we all."

Porzia leaned forward a bit to peer at the papers laid out on the polished desk—mechanical diagrams of some sort, upside down from her perspective. Not that looking at them right side up would have made much difference to Porzia. She was a scriptologist through and through.

"How are the repairs coming along?" she said. Courtesy of Garibaldi, the house had been infiltrated and sabotaged. Casa was still recovering.

Mamma sighed. "We've rooted out all the bugs, and the maintenance and security protocols are powered and running. But I'm still concerned there may be lingering errors in the system."

The house's disembodied voice cut in. "I do *not* have lingering errors." Casa sounded quite affronted at the mere suggestion.

Soothingly, Mamma replied, "No one's blaming you, Casa. It won't hurt to run diagnostics, just to be sure."

The house harrumphed, then fell silent so they could continue their conversation.

"There must be something I can do to help," Porzia said. "I mean, not *help* help, not with the mechanics."

Mamma said, "You can take yourself to bed and get a full night's sleep for once."

That wasn't at all what she'd meant. "Can I bring you an espresso, maybe?"

Barely audible, Casa muttered, "I am perfectly capable of bringing Signora Pisano an espresso."

"It's just that I've been feeling rather useless," Porzia continued, "and I don't know what to do with myself since . . . Leo . . ." Her throat tightened up and she couldn't finish the sentence.

"Oh, darling," Mamma said. "It's not as if he's the last mechanist on Earth."

Porzia scowled. "It's not my marriage prospects I'm worried about." For Casa della Pazzia to remain in the Pisano family, there had to be a mechanist in each generation—by blood or by marriage—so the house's systems could be properly maintained. Porzia was the eldest child, and decidedly not a mechanist. She could not fathom, though, why her mother thought *that* was the salient point here.

Mamma set down her drafting pencil and folded her hands. Only Porzia, who knew her well, could have seen the pain in the way she interlaced her fingers, or caught the faint quaver to her voice as she said, "We did everything we could to make a home for him here. There is nothing more for us to do. He's the Order's problem now, along with his father and brother."

Porzia nodded, mute. She had never truly believed that she

and Leo were meant for each other. There was no love there—no romantic love, at least. It had seemed like a practical solution, was all. And when she started catching the signs of his affection for Elsa, she thought, *If he has to give his heart to someone, I'm glad it's her.* To lose him to Elsa—who was brilliant, and brave, and fast becoming a dear friend—would not have been a loss at all.

But this. *This.* He must have calculated how to leave behind the largest possible crater of damage. A smoking hole in all their lives.

Porzia tried her damnedest to forget him, as if such a thing were possible. There was a hot little flame of anger inside her, bright as the sun, so bright she dared to glimpse it only out of the corner of her eye. She was afraid if she looked straight at it, the image would burn onto her eyes, and for the rest of her days that fury would be the only thing she'd see.

Porzia had scoured the walk-in closets of the sewing parlor for a dress that would look appropriately schoolmarmish. Certainly her own closet didn't contain anything this drab: medium gray linen with a high neck and no frills or adornments. Fashion was a small sacrifice, though, when one needed to exchange it for an air of authority.

"Sante, do try to focus on your work," Porzia said, tilting her head down to give the boy a severe look.

They were in the classroom in Casa della Pazzia, along with seven of the other school-age children. Everyone was seated at the long tables that could serve as desks or laboratory benches, depending on the needs of that day's lessons. Everyone except Porzia, of course, who stood at the front by the blackboard.

Sante slouched lower in his chair and gave her a rebellious

look, to which she said, "Unless you've finished the proof already?"

"Math is stupid," he grumbled, but picked up his chalk and returned his attention to his own slate.

Casa was home to two dozen children under the age of twenty. Aside from Porzia and her younger siblings—Sante, Olivia, and Aldo—they were all orphans of deceased pazzerellones. The Pisanos were responsible for their care and education, the latter of which had fallen by the wayside in all the recent excitement. Porzia had taken it upon herself to rectify the situation.

Sante heaved a melodramatic sigh and scowled up at his elder sister. "How come Burak doesn't have to be here?"

"Burak is still assisting Mamma with the repairs," Porzia said. "Which you, too, would be welcome to help with, if you'd learn to focus on anything for more than five minutes."

At the next table over, a ghost of a smile moved across Olivia's lips, the only sign that her attention wasn't entirely focused on her own slate. Olivia was the quiet one in the family. Porzia wondered, though, if her sister wasn't hiding a keen talent for observation behind that meek temperament. Now and again, Porzia would see flashes of understanding in those wide, dark eyes that seemed out of proportion with the girl's twelve years and timid demeanor.

Porzia let out a breath, careful not to sigh audibly, though that would have been more satisfying. She wished her father would hurry home from Firenze. She could handle the children well enough, but Pappa was a better tutor, and he always knew the right thing to say to Olivia. But the Order of Archimedes needed him at their headquarters, and the Pisanos were Order members first and everything else second.

Porzia made her rounds, checking each student's slate for the answer, then returned to the blackboard and wrote a new problem. While the children worked, she brushed the chalk dust from her fingers and wandered over to the windows. The classroom was on the main floor of the house, with the windows facing into the cloister garden, and the abundance of leafy greenery dappled the afternoon sunlight.

The cloister garden was another place she could not go without thinking of Leo. His bedroom had a balcony overlooking the garden.

Porzia's temper had cooled somewhat since yesterday, leaving in its wake a gnawing sense of guilt. It had been *her* plan Elsa was following when Leo defected. Perhaps if they'd gone through with the exchange as Garibaldi intended—simply traded the editbook for Jumi, without trying to double-cross him—things would have gone differently. Or if she'd only noticed Leo's distress, listened to his reluctance, and had the wisdom to leave him behind that day. Did not some of the blame belong to her?

Porzia pressed her eyelids closed and pinched her nose between two fingers. She had to stop doing this, letting her mind go round and round. Suddenly, the renewed classes seemed a poor attempt at normalcy, a terribly insufficient distraction, and she felt foolish standing at the front of the room pretending to be her father.

Aloud, she said, "I know this is an adjustment getting back to your usual lessons, so we'll finish early today," and she dismissed them.

Sante let out a whoop of joy, abandoned his slate and chalk, and dashed from the room, followed quickly by the other children. Except for slight, quiet Olivia, who hung back.

"Are you all right?" Olivia asked, her dark brows drawn together in worry.

"I will be, darling," Porzia replied, forcing herself to smile. "I will be."

There was still some time left before supper—plenty of time in which to sit alone and brood over her own shortcomings—so Porzia found herself climbing the stairs toward her chambers. Not that her sitting room was much of an improvement over anywhere else in the house. The bedroom, maybe; she could lie on the bed. Yes, that would work. She could not recall any memories of Leo ever entering her bedroom.

Porzia turned the corner and discovered Elsa asleep in the hallway beside her door. She must have been waiting and dozed off, leaning against the wall with her head lolling at an uncomfortable angle. The poor girl looked to be wearing the same trousers and linen shirt as yesterday, now with a tunic-length waistcoat thrown over it.

Porzia cleared her throat noisily, and Elsa jerked awake.

"Up all night?" Porzia said.

Elsa blinked, bleary-eyed, and put a hand out behind her to push away from the wall. "Yes, but I slept most of the morning."

Porzia raised an eyebrow. "Not *here*, I hope."

"What? Oh, no. I just nodded off again. Casa said you were busy and not to be interrupted, so I thought I'd wait." She stood but made no effort to straighten her rumpled clothes or messy black hair, as if she were entirely unaware of her disheveled state.

"I was tutoring," Porzia said unapologetically.

"Oh," the other girl said, carefully neutral, though Porzia could imagine what Elsa must be thinking: *Whatever for?* or perhaps, *At a time like this?*

After an uncomfortable pause, Porzia sighed. "I presume this is the part where I'm supposed to ask you how the search is going."

"We have a location," said Elsa, those startlingly green eyes of hers widening in an earnest plea. "But I need your help with this." She held up the doorbook.

Porzia arched an eyebrow. "The incomparable polymath can't get the job done and needs *my* help? Seems an unlikely story, if you ask me."

"I'm not perfect," Elsa said, a note of exasperation creeping into her voice. "And anyway, I need help with the library."

Porzia pursed her lips. She wanted to forget about Leo's betrayal, not investigate it, and she wished Elsa would respect that. "Faraz knows how to use a library."

Elsa snorted. "You know what I mean. I need another *scriptologist*." She paused, swallowed as if it were her pride going down. "I need my partner."

The truth was, Porzia missed their collaboration. Working with Elsa had opened up new possibilities for her, had challenged her assumptions and made her a more versatile scriptologist. And the loss of their partnership was something she could blame on no one but herself.

She heaved an enormous sigh. "Fine, I'll help."

Elsa blinked. "Truly? You're serious?"

"Of course I am." Porzia offered her a rueful smile. "Haven't you learned by now? I'm terrible at saying no."

Porzia was marauding through history and architecture.

Up on the third level of the library, she pulled volume after volume from the shelves, not bothering to return the books she rejected to their proper places. At first Casa had put up a fuss and threatened to report her to Gia for generating such disarray, but Porzia had ignored those protestations and the house had fallen silent.

In order to open a portal to a specific location on Earth, Elsa needed to accurately describe that location in an entry in the doorbook. Since none of them had ever been to Trento, that meant they needed a photograph or at least a decent sketch of some landmark unique to the city.

Three heavy volumes clutched in her arms, Porzia went over to the wrought-iron balcony rail. She looked down at the main floor of the library, where Elsa was seated at one of the tables. The doorbook was open in front of her, but it didn't hold her attention. Instead, she was staring at the glass-lidded display case where the Veldana worldbook was safely locked away, along with a half dozen of the most valuable books in the library's collection.

Porzia wondered what the other girl was thinking. Was she homesick? Porzia had lived her whole life at Casa della Pazzia and found it difficult to imagine what it must be like to literally leave one's entire world behind.

After a moment she shook herself, mustered her usual tone of confidence, and called down to Elsa, "I think I have it!"

Elsa startled out of her reverie and glanced up. "What did you find?"

Porzia clattered down the stairs to the main floor of the library, dropped her armload of books on Elsa's table, and began sharing the fruits of her labor. "A few possibilities, actually. There's quite a good sketch of the Fountain of Neptune here . . ." She flipped open the first book.

They sorted through the images together, and Porzia was surprised to find that Elsa truly was leaning on her for insights about European architecture. Brilliant as she was, Elsa's education apparently had not included the history of art, and she had no idea what qualities made a landmark unique.

Elsa rubbed her forehead as if the architecture lesson were giving her a headache. "Can we combine a couple of descriptions to eliminate some of the uncertainty?"

"These three are all right next to each other, so that should help," Porzia said. "I mean, I'm sure there are many towns with a cathedral, a fountain, and a clock tower in the same piazza, but not in this orientation with these exact details." She leaned close to one of the books, examining the clock tower's distinctive crenellations. "Yes, this should get you there."

Without looking up from the page, Elsa said, "It's not for me, it's for you."

"What!" She couldn't be saying what Porzia thought she was saying. "I agreed to help you scribe the location, not go to Trento myself!"

"Oh, I'm going too—but I'll approach them through the Carbonari, pretending to be a defector from the Order. I need you to take the doorbook to Trento and hide it there, so I have an exit route in place that nobody knows about except us." Elsa delivered this news with infuriating calm, as if it were the most sensible plan in the world.

Porzia couldn't believe she'd let herself get drawn back into their insane plan for rescuing Leo. Joining the Carbonari? Hiding the doorbook in a strange city? She shuddered to think what else her friends would willingly risk, all to save a liar who didn't want saving in the first place.

She folded her arms tight against her ribs and said, "Absolutely not!"

Alek de Vries scratched at the back of his neck, damp with sweat despite the shade provided by the wide brim of his Panama hat. The Veldanese sun was much too hot for his Dutch blood. In his youth he'd been tolerably comfortable in the Tuscan climate, but Veldana was even hotter, and he was not a young man anymore.

The fresh air seemed to have a restorative effect for Jumi, though, so Alek held his tongue.

They had strolled as far as the creek that ran through the center of the village and were now seated on the moss-covered bank beside the burbling water. Jumi was acting even more pensive and close-lipped than usual.

Eventually Alek had to ask, "Are you going to tell me what's bothering you?"

Jumi shrugged. "Nothing's bothering me."

"You can't seriously expect me to believe that." Try as she might to conceal all emotion, Alek had known her for almost twenty years, and she was no longer as opaque as she liked to believe. Not to him, anyway.

She gave him a sidelong glance beneath raised eyebrows, considering, then relented. "It's just that I never considered Veldana a prison until my own daughter banished me here."

Alek stalwartly resisted the urge to roll his eyes. "No one's banished you here. But you need time to convalesce before you'll be any use to anyone."

"Then my 'convalescence' feels as if it has walls even when we're out in the open air," Jumi retorted. "I do hate feeling useless."

"And entrusting Elsa with matters of importance?" Alek said wryly. "Certainly you must hate that."

"She's still so young, Alek."

He patted the back of his neck dry with a handkerchief. "You weren't much older than her when you first came to me."

Jumi stared off into the middle distance, as if looking at something that was no longer there. "I was never her age. I was never a child."

"All the Veldanese were like children back then, in the early days." Half the time the Veldanese still seemed children to Alek, though he had the sense not to say that to Jumi, who took herself and her people so seriously.

"We may have been naive once, but we learned hard lessons every time Montaigne altered our world."

Charles Montaigne had thought he knew what was best for the Veldanese and had imposed his will upon them, altering their worldbook without bothering to ask for their consent. He'd meant well, and so Alek had found it difficult to condemn his friend, but in retrospect Alek wondered if he'd mishandled the situation. Mishandled Charles. Perhaps if he'd succeeded in persuading Charles to voluntarily relinquish control of Veldana, then Jumi would not have needed to create the editbook, and none of this would have happened.

There was one thing Alek could not bring himself to regret, though, and that was his mentorship of young Jumi. That, at least, he could be proud of.

"If all we're going to do is mope about, we might as well mope about indoors," Alek declared, as he stood and stretched his stiff hip. "Let's get you back to your prison, before I start suffering from heatstroke."

"I'm not moping," Jumi said with a show of dignity, though it was clear his slight was already forgiven. Alek helped her up, and they leaned on each other as they climbed the hill back to the cottage.

Jumi's cottage was blessedly cool inside, and so dim compared to the glaring sunlight that Alek's eyes struggled to adjust. As he blinked and peered around, his gaze fell on the shelf where Jumi stored her scriptological supplies. A single portal device sat upon the wood, and beside it an empty space.

"Jumi . . . ," he said, staring at the shelf, "where is the other portal device?"

5

ONE OF THE MOST BEAUTIFUL QUALITIES OF TRUE FRIENDSHIP
IS TO UNDERSTAND AND TO BE UNDERSTOOD.
—*Lucius Annaeus Seneca*

E xplaining the plan to Porzia was not going as well as Elsa had hoped. They sat on opposite sides of a library reading table, but it might as well have been a chessboard; their cooperation had devolved to verbal sparring.

"If we tell the Order Aris's location, we give up all control over the situation," Elsa argued. "And Rosalinda has already agreed to assist."

Porzia countered, "Rosalinda's only concern is Leo; the Order's only concern is the editbook. Of course she doesn't want you going to us for help. As far as she's concerned, we're almost as bad as Garibaldi."

Elsa blinked at her. To Elsa the Order of Archimedes was some distant, nebulous organization, pulling strings from the shadows, and it was easy to forget that to Porzia they were family friends. The Pisanos were an old and influential lineage, so like it or not, Porzia was a legacy member. Someday she might even take on a leadership role within the Order. Strange to think about.

Elsa said, "I just need a way in, and I can use the fact that I've never actually declared loyalty to the Order or anyone else."

The other girl leaned forward and rested her elbows on the tabletop. "Tell me this, once and for all," she said, spreading her fingers in one of those very Italian gestures. "Are you trying to retrieve the editbook, or trying to retrieve Leo?"

Elsa didn't answer. It should have been an easy question. In the wrong hands, the editbook had the power to tear apart the real world. As the daughter of the scriptologist who wrote the damned book in the first place, Elsa felt responsible for it—felt responsible for all the damage Garibaldi could do now that he had it.

Leo, on the other hand, was very much not her responsibility. He had made his own choices, and in so doing had left her heart shredded. But at the same time, Faraz was so devoutly certain of Leo's true loyalties . . . and if she was honest, there was a small, traitorous part of her that desperately wanted Faraz to be right.

Porzia leaned back in her chair, her eyes narrowing. Apparently, Elsa's hesitance was all the answer she needed. "That's what I thought."

Elsa hardened her resolve. "Of course the editbook is the first priority," she said. "But Faraz needs to believe there's hope for the other part."

Porzia tipped her head back and looked up, as if to beseech the heavens for help. "What am I to do with you? Faraz is a fool for deceiving himself, and you're a fool for indulging him."

This, at last, raised Elsa's hackles. "We are not *fools* just because—"

But Porzia cut her off with a sharp wave of one hand. "Fine,

fine. Truthfully, my quarrel is with Leo, not with you or Faraz. If you're resolved, I won't stand in your way."

"I am resolved," Elsa said. "This is the right course, I'm sure of it."

Porzia sighed. "Then we'd better get to work on that description for the doorbook."

Elsa finished the last sentence and set her fountain pen aside. The ink still wet, she slid the doorbook over to where Porzia sat. "What do you think?"

Porzia took her time reading through the description and frowning at the image they'd chosen. Finally, she said, "Looks accurate to me."

A month ago, the thought of showing her work to anyone besides her mother would have filled Elsa with dread, but she'd come to not only trust Porzia but even to rely upon her for assistance. Elsa was momentarily struck by the magnitude of her own change, that such a partnership now felt natural.

She said, "Well, if it doesn't work, I know I can count on you to fix it."

Porzia glanced up, startled. "What? You're not even going to test it?"

"Too much to do, too little time. And anyway, I have every confidence that you're up to the task of making any corrections it might need."

Porzia shrugged off the praise. "To be fair, that's only because of you."

Elsa blinked. "Whatever do you mean? I've hardly taught you anything—you were already a fine scriptologist when I came along."

Porzia frowned thoughtfully. "The way you scribe . . . you see things differently. You don't follow the same fundamental assumptions, and so you challenge me to reconsider what I thought I knew, what I thought was fact. Scriptology is a much more powerful tool than anyone believed."

"A much more dangerous tool," Elsa said, thinking of the editbook. Not only had Jumi created a book with the power to alter the real world, she had forever changed the discipline of scriptology by proving that such a thing was possible. Until now, Elsa hadn't paid much mind to the editbook's theoretical implications— she'd been too preoccupied with the practical matter of retrieving it—but Porzia's words planted a seed of dread inside her. Even if they got the editbook back from Garibaldi, they could not unprove what it had proved. And someone, someday, would use that knowledge.

"Are you all right?" Porzia touched Elsa's arm. "I didn't mean to imply you were some sort of bizarre heretic . . ."

Elsa wiped the gloom from her expression. "No, it's not that, I'm not offended. I was thinking about the editbook."

Porzia pressed her lips together, but before she could reply, Casa interrupted them. "Signorina Elsa, your guests have arrived."

Elsa was tempted to frown at this—*guests*, plural, when she was expecting only Signora Scarpa?—but instead she simply hopped out of her chair and said, "Perfect timing. No need to disturb Gia's important work, Casa—they won't be staying long."

Porzia came with her through the house to the entry hall, where Casa had taken the liberty of opening the front doors and welcoming the guests inside. One of them was Signora Scarpa; the other was a tall man in his twenties with a rapier slung from his belt.

"What's he doing here?" Elsa said, and then immediately

regretted her gruff tone. The last thing she should do was antagonize this woman whose help she needed.

Thankfully, Rosalinda chose to ignore her disrespect. "Elsa, Porzia, may I introduce Vincenzo? He is the, uh . . ." Here she chose her words carefully. "The solution to the problem Faraz presented me with."

Vincenzo acknowledged them with a nod, a roguish grin playing at the corner of his mouth. He was tall and whipcord lean, though his imposing presence made him seem even larger. He moved with the same ease and confidence that Elsa had always thought of as unique to Leo, a sort of feline grace that bespoke mastery of one's own body. He had a long face with an aquiline nose, and he wore his dark hair long but tied back. Not beautiful, but Elsa got the sense he compensated for it with ample self-assurance.

"I understand we have a location?" he said, speaking the Tuscan dialect with a slight accent, as if it were not his native tongue.

Elsa relayed what they knew about Aris's location near Trento, and he nodded. "Smart."

"Why is that smart?" Elsa said, feeling lost when it came to the political details.

Signora Scarpa explained, "There is significant support for unification in that region. When Venetia earned its status as an autonomous crown state, there was much resentment that the Austrians did not award the same consideration to the province of Trentino. Garibaldi would not lack for allies."

"And it's far enough away that our commanders don't have much control over what the local Carbonari do," Vincenzo added, resting a hand on the intricate hilt of his rapier. "Or who they associate with."

"So you can't get me in with them?" Elsa said sharply.

"Don't be ridiculous, of course I can get you in." He turned to Signora Scarpa. "Do we have documentation to get her across the border, or are we to use stealth for that?"

Porzia, who had been watching this exchange with increasingly narrowed eyes, interrupted, "If you'll excuse us for a moment . . . ," and pulled Elsa aside.

"So?" Elsa said, keeping her voice low and leaning close to Porzia. "What do you think—can we trust him?"

"Trust him? How would I know! I've only just met him," Porzia hissed, exasperated but not for a second forgetful of the need for discretion. "You're not seriously going to put your life in the hands of a total stranger, are you?"

"Well . . . Leo trusted Signora Scarpa, and she trusts Vincenzo."

"Leo, of all people, does not get a vote," Porzia snapped.

At that moment, Faraz came rushing down the grand stairs, and Elsa and Porzia rejoined Signora Scarpa and Vincenzo as introductions were made. Then Faraz asked, "So how do we orchestrate this? Elsa's infiltration, so to speak."

Vincenzo said, "She's got to prove she's no longer with the Order of Archimedes, so she'll need to do something no Order member would ever do."

At this Porzia looked alarmed. "Like what?"

"Like supply them with a special piece of tech, something only a pazzerellone could build."

Porzia groaned at the same time that Elsa said, "Not a problem. But how, specifically, will this work?"

"We'll take the late train to Bologna tonight," Vincenzo explained, "if that gives you enough time to prepare. I know the Carbonari there, they trust me, and that makes them easy to manipulate. From their leader we'll get a location for the Carbonari in Trento, who can deliver us to Garibaldi's doorstep. We'll have to behave exactly as disaffected Carbonari looking for a new leader to put our faith in—no one can know the truth except us."

"And Leo," Faraz amended. Then, looking to Elsa and taking in her determined expression, he said it again with less confidence. "And Leo, right?"

Elsa shook her head. "I may not be able to convince him of the lie, but I definitely can't rely on him to help."

Porzia snorted. "He's the best liar I've ever met, he'd do fine."

"But if you're right, and Faraz is wrong," Elsa said, "if he thinks he belongs with them . . . then I can't trust him. Even if I'm trying to rescue him, Faraz, I can't trust him." The words threatened to catch in her throat and left a bitter taste in her mouth. *Rescue* was a lie; in her heart she knew there was no path back for such a traitor.

Faraz sucked air in between his teeth. "So in the best-case scenario, we come out the other end with two fugitives."

Vincenzo, inexplicably, was grinning. "Three fugitives," he amended, hooking a thumb at himself. "The Carbonari aren't exactly going to be pleased with me, either."

"And that doesn't concern you?" Faraz said.

"I don't lead a life of certainty," he said, shrugging. "But you should know, even arriving as Carbonari, they will not simply trust us. Garibaldi's no chicken waiting to be plucked—he'll anticipate that we're there to cross him. He'll plan for every contingency."

"We'll have to improvise, then," Elsa replied. "The first step is still to ease their suspicion, and then we can gather more information about how to proceed."

"Keep your lies as close to the truth as possible," Faraz unexpectedly offered. "Leo can deliver any ridiculous claim as if it were fact, but if you're not a practiced liar, they'll see through you. Incorporate as much honesty as you can into your lies to make them feel real."

Sourly, Porzia muttered, "Sage advice from one bad liar to another."

Elsa felt heat rise in her cheeks. She'd told her first lies in this very conversation where Faraz advised her on how to do it. At least her skin tone would hide the flush. She was no good at deceiving a friend; if any of them were going to take up a career as a spy, it should have been Leo.

Signora Scarpa said, "The trip will take a couple of days. There will be time for Vincenzo to give Elsa some training along the way."

"Oh good," Porzia retorted. "Two days' worth of spy training before she enters the viper's nest. All my fears have been assuaged."

"Signorina Porzia, if I may interrupt . . . ," Casa said. Oddly, Elsa detected not only distress but confusion in the house's tone. "There is an intruder in the library."

"What!" Porzia screeched, at the same time that Faraz morosely said, "Again?"

Elsa, however, felt a kick of fear in her chest. "The Veldana worldbook is in the library." Had someone come to steal it? Or worse?

The three of them dashed through the house back toward the library, with Vincenzo and Rosalinda following a few steps behind. In the hallway outside the library, Elsa yanked her revolver from its holster as she ran.

They burst through the library doors with Elsa in the lead, aiming the gun, and Vincenzo pushing forward to stand beside her. His eyes alert, his muscles tense, his rapier pulling free with a metallic *shnick*.

But Elsa stopped short. The intruder was no black-clad ex-Carbonari assassin—he was a dark-skinned, brown-eyed Veldanese boy.

"Revan!" she exclaimed, disbelieving her own eyes. "What are you doing here?" she asked in Veldanese.

"What do you mean? I came for you, of course," he said, eyes wide at the sight of everyone.

"What's going on?" demanded Vincenzo, who couldn't understand them.

Elsa holstered her revolver. "It's all right—he's a friend," she explained, though perhaps that was stretching the truth. At least they had been friends when they were younger, before Elsa's responsibilities drew her away. She was the future caretaker of their world, and that set her apart from the other Veldanese. "Porzia, Faraz, you remember Revan of Veldana."

"Good day," Porzia said in awkward Veldanese. Elsa was surprised she knew even that one phrase, although both Porzia and Faraz had briefly visited her home.

To Revan, she said, "You shouldn't be off-world."

Revan looked taken aback. "You disappear with no warning and are gone for weeks, returning only to bring Jumi home and then disappearing again. What did you expect I'd do?"

Honestly, she hadn't given a moment's thought to what Revan—or any of the Veldanese, for that matter—would think or feel about her recent actions. She'd certainly never imagined that he would try to pursue her. How had he even managed to leave Veldana?

"Vincenzo," Signora Scarpa said from the doorway, quiet but commanding. "Leave them to it."

Vincenzo sheathed his rapier and reluctantly withdrew. Elsa heard him say on the way out, "Old friends unexpectedly showing up? I don't like it."

"It doesn't concern us," Rosalinda stated as she left the library with Vincenzo.

Revan watched them go with wide eyes. "Where are we? Why does everyone have weapons?"

Elsa snorted. "Welcome to Earth."

She took a moment to really look at him. He seemed somehow larger than the Revan of her memory, though he surely could not have filled out much in the short time since last she'd seen him. It was only that she'd grown accustomed to the softness of refined and mannered city folk. Not that she thought of Porzia and Faraz as weak, but they didn't spend their days pushing a plow through the dirt or hauling firewood. Revan did, and though she had never noticed it before, it showed. She glanced at Porzia and had to suppress a smirk, because clearly Elsa was not the only person noticing.

Faraz, however, wore an expression somewhere between disapproval and worry. "I'm confused. Why is he here? Did something happen in Veldana?"

Elsa set her hands on her hips, determined not to feel any embarrassment about the situation. "I'm afraid he came because he was concerned about me."

"You must be joking," Faraz said. "As if we didn't have enough trouble on our hands, without adding tourists to the mix."

"Faraz," Porzia scolded. "What a thing to say, when he left his home to come to Elsa's aid."

"Is he a pazzerellone?" Faraz asked Elsa.

"No, not that I know of."

Faraz shook his head. "Then I'm sorry, Porzia, but I can't imagine what aid he thinks he's going to be able to provide."

Revan was observing the conversation, listening intently though with little comprehension. Elsa wondered if he would pick up Italian as quickly as she had; her own talent for learning languages derived from a clause Jumi had added to the Veldana worldbook, so in theory any native Veldanese should share the ability.

"Alchemy, scriptology, and mechanics are not the only three skills in existence," Elsa felt the need to point out.

But before Faraz could reply, Casa interrupted, "Shall I serve the evening meal without you? Or can this discussion be relocated to the dining hall?"

In the end it was decided that all their guests—Rosalinda and Vincenzo and Revan—would be invited to dinner, and what would happen after that could be sorted out with full stomachs.

Elsa had cleared her plate away to make room for the doorbook and an inkwell. A few seats away, at the end of the long table, Porzia was engaging Vincenzo in conversation, though something about her carefully polite expressions made Elsa think it was more of a subtle interrogation than anything else. Beside her, Revan was still picking at his pasta as if uncertain that what he'd been served was, in fact, food. He held the fork in his fist like a child, unaccustomed to the implement.

"Are you ever coming home?" Revan asked. He'd been nudging her for information through the whole meal; Elsa had done her best to deflect his questions rather than encourage them, but this one struck her by surprise.

"Of course, I mean, eventually . . . ," she replied, stumbling over the words. After what Leo had done, a part of her wanted nothing more than to return to Veldana and lick her wounds and try to forget about the Garibaldis. But the situation wasn't that simple; now that she'd made friends here on Earth, it would never be that simple.

"'Later' is just a sly way of saying no," Revan said, quoting a phrase his mother, Baninu, had often used on them when they were little.

Elsa took a breath to regain her composure. "I need to concentrate." She opened the doorbook to a blank page and focused on her memory of bright-painted buildings and luminous blue water. Putting nib to paper, she began scratching out a new description. When she was halfway done, Revan set his fork down with a clack that spoke of impatience.

"What are you writing?" he asked.

She glanced up briefly. "A destination."

He planted an elbow on the table and leaned his cheek against his fist. "I wouldn't mind a slightly more detailed explanation, you know. It's getting a bit frustrating, having no idea what's going on."

"Well," Elsa said slowly while scribing another line, "maybe you should've thought of that before you left Veldana."

Revan snorted, but didn't pursue the subject. Elsa felt a twinge of guilt at leaving him in the dark, but sharing the details of her predicament would only encourage him to involve himself further. And the hard truth was that he knew even less about Earth than she did, and she worried he would be more of a liability than an asset.

As she finished the last line, Elsa became aware that the once-empty chair on her other side was now occupied. Most of the children had already abandoned the dining table, but she looked up to see Olivia sitting there, quietly watching her. The resemblance to Porzia was striking—the round cheeks, the small mouth, the rich brown eyes beneath sharp eyebrows—though Olivia didn't seem to know she was pretty yet, whereas Porzia wielded her beauty like a polished weapon. Elsa, who had no siblings, found these familial details fascinating. Of the four Pisano children, Sante was the only one who didn't seem to take after Gia—his hair a lighter shade of brown and his face a bit too narrow across the cheekbones—and Elsa wondered if his traits came from his father, whom she hadn't yet met.

Olivia seemed to be withering beneath Elsa's scrutiny, so Elsa decided to take pity on the girl and break the silence. "Hi there."

"Hi," Olivia said, barely above a whisper.

"Do you need something?" Elsa gently persisted.

Olivia straightened in her chair, mustering her bravery, though not quite enough to look Elsa in the eye. "I just wanted to ask . . . are you going to bring Leo home?"

Elsa's first instinct was to give the girl a patronizing promise, but something about Olivia's wide, serious gaze convinced her otherwise. "I can't swear to it, but if it's possible, I'll at least try."

Olivia gave a sharp, definitive nod, and then she lingered, finding the courage for another question. "Will it be dangerous?"

"You needn't worry about that—I'll have an expert swordsman as my guide. Okay?"

Olivia nodded again, slipped off the chair quiet as a ghost, and disappeared into the cluster of children who had finished with supper.

Elsa turned to find Revan staring at her as if she were a stranger. "What?" she said defensively.

Revan gave a one-shouldered shrug. "Nothing. Just . . . since when are *you* good with children? You used to despise them."

"I'm not good with them," Elsa protested. "And I despise frivolous behavior in people of all ages."

"Mm-hmm," he replied, clearly unconvinced.

"Wait, does that mean you understood what we were saying?"

He shrugged. "I think I caught most of it. Italian still feels a little . . ."

"Elusive?" she offered.

"Elusive, exactly. Like a slippery fish you're trying to catch with your bare hands—you can grab it for a second, but then it wriggles away." He paused. "You're staring. What is it?"

Elsa shook her head. "Nothing. It's just . . . picking up languages the way we do . . . Jumi was the only one who ever understood this stuff. Before now."

Revan's expression darkened and he leaned away, as if she'd slammed a door in his face. "Sorry to intrude on your two-person secret society."

She started to say, "No, that's not what I—" but he had already pushed his chair away from the table and left her sitting there alone.

Elsa made a low noise in her throat, releasing her frustration. Were all boys constitutionally prone to moodiness? For a minute there, Revan's company had provided a comfortable respite from the tension hanging heavy in the air between Faraz and Porzia. She'd even managed to forget, however briefly, the sharp pain of Leo's betrayal. But Jumi had been right all along: men could not be relied upon for anything.

Elsa had half a mind to open a portal back to Veldana and shove Revan through it. Except that Casa had already offered to make up a guest room for him, and she couldn't exactly renege on the Pisanos' hospitality now that the house had extended it. Anyway, she had far too much to do to worry about whether Revan kept himself out of trouble.

She excused herself from the table, letting Vincenzo know she'd need an hour or so to get everything sorted, and went up to her rooms. From there, she took a portal into her laboratory world.

First she built a narrow-frequency wireless transmitter; then she gutted a spare portal device and built a receiver tuned to that specific frequency into the empty casing. It was nothing compared to the complexity and miniaturization that Aris had employed in the bugs he'd built to infest Casa, but it would do the trick. Lastly, she threw together a device composed of a small insulated canister and a nozzle—a much smaller version of the freeze ray she'd used to stop the runaway train.

She took one last, lingering look around her laboratory before opening a portal back to her rooms in Casa della Pazzia. The lab book was scribed in Veldanese, and she couldn't risk taking any Veldanese texts with her, lest Aris get ahold of them and use them to help decode the editbook. So the lab worldbook would be hidden along with the doorbook, the wireless transmitter, and her portal device. She wrapped the four items in oilcloth and tucked them inside a wooden box for Porzia.

Then Elsa changed into a clean pair of trousers and the garment that Porzia affectionately referred to as her "battle vest"—a leather bustier with an overabundance of pouches and pockets and brass attachments, into which she stuffed her revolver, a pen, a small bottle of scriptological ink, and other such items as she deemed potentially useful. She fetched her carpetbag and packed what few clothes she owned, along with the small freeze ray and the receiver masquerading as a portal device. Last of all, she laid the plague doctor mask on top and closed the carpetbag.

Elsa had never been sentimental about her possessions— Veldanese culture didn't emphasize personal ownership the way European society seemed to—but she could not help comparing her own things to Leo's cluttered room, so full of hoarded memories. Physical symbols of his connectedness to the people around him.

Her wardrobe was largely composed of clothes Porzia had designed for her. The borrowed revolver had been a gift from Alek to Jumi. Even the carpetbag itself had been lent to her by Alek. Among all these possessions, all these personal connections, she had nothing of Leo.

It was like their history had been erased that day when he shoved her through a portal without him, without the editbook. Or had it never really happened in the first place? Had it ever been real for him the way it had felt real to her? When had truth ended and the deception begun? A knock came at the door, interrupting her ruminations, and Elsa crossed her sitting room to let Faraz in.

He said, "I have something for you," and she laughed because his timing was impeccable.

Faraz gave her a confused look, and Elsa said, "I've just realized everything I own is borrowed or a gift."

"Oh. Well, here's one more for your collection, then."

He passed her a large brass pocket watch. A dysfunctional one, if the lack of mechanical vibrations against her palm was any indication. "Um, it's beautiful . . . ?" she said, puzzled.

Faraz raised his gaze to the heavens. "Just open it."

She clicked open the lid. The space inside was empty of mechanical workings, instead taken up by a hollow glass disk filled with Faraz's purple sleeping potion.

"In case . . . you know, in case Rosalinda's right," he explained.

"Ah." *In case Leo won't come willingly*, Faraz meant. A knock-out drug for kidnapping the boy she'd once thought she loved.

How had her life come to this?

She clicked the watch case closed, her throat tight. "Thank you."

Faraz's mouth twisted into a pained smile. "I hope you won't need it."

She was about to throw herself into the dangerous world of the Carbonari, but the most frightening part was the thought of reaching Leo without incident, only to confirm that he was her enemy.

6

When the house fell quiet around midnight, Leo threw caution to the wind and brought out the lockpicks.

The door to his father's study provided little resistance to a mechanist like Leo. The lock was practically a waste of his skills. If Ricciotti wasn't going to install better security, he might as well entirely abandon the idea of locking things with Leo around. Perhaps Ricciotti still thought of him as the obedient son he'd been at the age of eleven. That was another error in judgment his father would learn to regret. No one would describe Leo as obedient anymore.

He slipped inside the study and used his candle to light a couple of the wall sconces within. Once he could see properly, he took a moment to orient himself. The study was larger than he expected, with armchairs set near a fireplace at one end. The other end was dominated by an enormous polished-wood desk, with floor-to-ceiling shelves built into the wall behind it.

Leo stepped behind the desk and checked the drawers and pigeonholes first, but found little of interest. A few spare fountain pens, a report on the weather in Napoli, a list of price quotes for various chemicals, a half-written letter to a recipient whose name Leo didn't recognize.

He turned to face the shelves instead. Some of the contents were regular books: history, philosophy, and even a smattering of literature. Leo was unsurprised to find the writings of Machiavelli and Guicciardini, but he snorted at the fiction, trying to imagine his father curling up by the fire with Manzoni's *I Promessi Sposi*. Ricciotti Garibaldi did not read for pleasure.

There were a few worldbooks on the shelves as well, though of course the editbook was not among them. Leo flipped through them anyway, but he could glean little information beyond confirming they were worldbooks. Worldscript had always looked like Greek to him. If Porzia were here, the books might be informative, but without her to interpret them, they were effectively useless.

The lower shelf held a series of hardbound journals. Leo selected one at random, a slim volume with a faded label on the spine. He set it down on the empty surface of the desk and opened the cover. The first page looked like a handwritten medical record: name, age, occupation, date admitted, and so on, all reported in a neat, slanted cursive. This information was accompanied by a photograph of a young, dark-haired woman pasted to the page. Below that, though, was a somewhat cryptic list.

RESULTS:
failed 9/10/68
failed 6/2/69
failed 18/5/69

failed 11/8/69
failed 23/9/69
failed 26/2/70
success: Subject A

"Subject A," Leo murmured, wondering what that meant. A successful result, and also the last trial of whatever this person was attempting.

He flipped to the next page, where began a series of dated entries in the fashion of a laboratory notebook. Methodological details, chemical formulae, observations and results. Beyond determining that the experiments were alchemical in nature, Leo couldn't make much sense of them. He wished Faraz were here.

Leo took down another notebook. The contents were similar except for the results, which listed failures spanning 1866 to 1868, with no success at the end. A third notebook and a third photograph of a woman followed by a similar list of failures through 1872 into early 1873, ending in *Subject L*. Leo lined up the open notebooks on the desk to compare the handwriting, which was consistent among all three. He'd thought the research notes might belong to the women in the front, but now it seemed more likely they were the subjects, not the scientists. Did the handwriting belong to Ricciotti? Leo couldn't remember well enough to say for certain. What an odd thing to forget. He supposed he should feel sad that he didn't know his own father's handwriting, but when he searched himself for the emotion, he found none of it.

"What are you doing?"

Leo jumped, his heart slamming against his ribs. It was Aris, standing in the doorway of the study with a smirk playing across his lips.

Leo let out a breath, relieved he hadn't been caught by Ricciotti. "Hello to you, too, brother."

Aris moved inside and softly shut the door behind him. He sauntered over, leaned one hip against the desk, and graced the notebooks with a cursory glance. "If you're looking for a little light reading, you've come to the wrong place."

"I'm looking for answers." Leo watched his brother's face to gauge his intentions, but Aris did not look inclined to interfere. If anything, he seemed amused. So Leo reached for the shelves and retrieved another notebook.

"You really oughtn't look at those. It's guaranteed to raise your hackles," Aris said, but made no move to stop him.

Leo opened the fourth notebook and froze. He recognized the woman depicted on the first page. In the photograph the woman was healthy and smiling, while in the depths of his memory she was sickly pale, hollow-cheeked, and lacking the strength to smile. Still, he knew this was her. He would know Mother anywhere.

Her list of results ended with *success: Subject P.*

"No," Leo breathed, struck with horrible realization.

Subjects A, L, and P. Successes in 1870, 1873, and 1877: the years in which Aris, Leo, and Pasca would have been conceived.

In a daze, Leo went back to the shelves, hoping not to find what he now knew to look for: but there they were at the far end of the bottom shelf, three notebooks labeled *A*, *L*, and *P* on the bindings. These notebooks were much thicker than the ones with the women in them. He pulled out his own, brought it to the desk, opened it, all the while telling himself he must be wrong. But the first page had his date of birth written on it, beside a photograph of an infant. He opened to the middle and flipped through a few pages. In Leo's notebook, the entries consisted of clinical observations on his behavior, his interactions with his brothers, and above all his performance as a pazzerellone.

"What is this?" Leo shouted, though he already knew the answer. "What is this!"

"Are you upset that Father was engineering polymaths," Aris said, "or upset that it didn't work on you?"

"How can you—'upset' is hardly—" Leo choked on his own words. He ran his hands through his hair, wanting to tear it out in frustration. "What happened to all these women?"

Aris just inclined his head and gave Leo a sad look, as if Leo were acting foolish.

"Answer me, Aris: Did they all die the way Mother died?"

"That woman you remember wasn't your mother. She was just a brood mare—an incubator for Pasca. These," he said with a dismissive flick of his wrist at the notebooks, "none of these mattered. They were never our family. *We* are family."

Leo searched his brother's face for any sign that these were Ricciotti's words parroted through Aris's lips. But no, his belief seemed genuine. Leo shook his head slowly, too horrified to find words.

Aris frowned. "I don't see why you always have to make such a fuss about everything."

"I know," he said. "That's the problem."

Leo stared at the desk. Then he slowly, respectfully closed each notebook, letting the covers down the way one might let down a flower on a grave.

Leo refused to leave his room at breakfast, and again at lunchtime. He didn't dare force food upon his roiling stomach. Ricciotti seemed ignorant of the cause, so Aris must not have told him what

Leo had been up to in the middle of the night. Interesting. If nothing else, Leo had to be grateful his lockpicks weren't getting confiscated, which was thanks to Aris's closed lips.

As difficult as it was to admit, Aris had been right about one thing: there were some truths Leo really didn't want to know. After that first grim revelation, Leo had fled the room, leaving the notebooks largely unread. He justified it to himself because the records were old and had no bearing on the editbook or Ricciotti's plans, but he knew that was an excuse. He should have stayed and read the notebooks. A stronger person would have. But Leo's revulsion at how his father had used up the bodies of innocent women was too powerful.

Thanks to Ricciotti's alchemical meddling, Pasca's mother had never recovered from carrying him, and though she clung fiercely to life she eventually succumbed to the damage the experiments had wrought. And Leo had never known his own birth mother, had killed her like some inhuman parasite. Did he want to go back and stare at the photograph in that wretched notebook, memorizing her face? Was it worse to see her through the lens of his father's horrific science, or to have no concept of her at all? Leo felt as if he could lose his mind dwelling on those questions.

His self-imposed confines began to feel oppressive, so he slipped out and went wandering instead. The stronghold was plenty large enough to accommodate his explorations without much risk of encountering other people. On the top floor of the fortress in the southeast corner, he found a circular glass-domed solarium. The hinges of the door were stiff with rust, but when Leo threw his shoulder against it, it screeched open. Inside, the stale air and silence had the feeling of a tomb.

Four limestone pillars held up the ceiling, and thick, woody vines wrapped around the pillars, emerging from large ceramic pots at the base of each. The vines were long dead, botanical skeletons, and the soil was dry as dust. Other pots and planters scattered about the room looked equally neglected, with few signs remaining of what once grew there. It had been a long time since anyone tended the solarium garden.

Empty. Dead inside. This felt appropriate, given his mood. Even the slanted rays of sunlight added little in the way of warmth or life to the place; the light seemed more inclined to bleach the stone and wood of color, until everything was awash with gray.

Leo was staring at how the sun hit the tiled stone floor when a shadow raced across the room, something large momentarily eclipsing the solarium. A bird? No, too large for a bird, he thought as he hurried over to the glass wall. Perhaps a flying machine? But the shadow had moved much too fast to belong to an airship.

Shading his eyes with one hand, he searched the air for the object. The sky above was cloudless and powder blue, the valley below completely still. No sign of motion anywhere. Whatever else it was, it was good at disappearing.

In the evening a servant arrived to collect the silver tray of uneaten dinner, and to report that the master of the house requested Leo's presence in his study.

Leo's mouth twisted in anger at his father's manipulation. If he refused to make an appearance, the servant might be blamed for failing to deliver the summons. Leo had no desire to get the poor girl whipped or fired from her position—a sympathy that Ricciotti was now exploiting. Leo descended the stairs, knowing full well that Ricciotti moved him about the house as if he were a rook on a chessboard.

In his father's study, the desk stood empty. Instead Ricciotti sat in one of the high-backed armchairs, a fire crackling in the hearth beside him, the rest of the study bathed in the warm yellow glow of the gaslights. Leo took the remaining armchair, facing his father. If he didn't know better, Leo would have thought the room had an inviting atmosphere. But Ricciotti wasn't prone to giving invitations; Ricciotti gave orders.

With his usual air of assumed authority, Ricciotti demanded, "Did you eat?"

The question caught Leo off guard, and he paused too long. "I . . ."

"If the food isn't to your liking, I can have the cook whipped." The words came out so casually, but the glare in his eye had edges sharp as a diamond.

"No," Leo said quickly. His father had really done it once before, when Pasca went through a phase of refusing to eat his vegetables—whipped the cook right in front of them, to show the cost of misbehavior. "No, it's not the food at all, it's my fault . . ."

Ricciotti folded his hands in his lap, self-satisfied. "So you admit you saw the notebooks. I imagine you must have questions."

Leo crossed his arms, vexed that his father cornered him so easily. "Not really. I'm sure Aris—ever your instrument—filled you in on our conversation."

"Your brother came to me because he was concerned about you. I understand you found my research upsetting. I want to assure you that I've only ever done what was necessary for the unification movement."

Leo stared at him, disbelieving. The thought of what Ricciotti had done to those women—their *mothers*—made Leo feel physically ill, and here he was acting as if they were nothing more than frogs or guinea pigs. "I think you might actually be insane. Your thirst for power blots out everything else."

"Power?" Ricciotti laughed—not harshly, but as if Leo had surprised him. "I don't want to *rule* Italy. I'm no tyrant. I want our people to join together into a republic. I want us free from the iron hand of the Papal States choking our pursuit of knowledge. I want us free from the French and the Austrians fighting over our lands like wolves over scraps of meat. I want to lift our people up, to usher in a new age—a modern age—of justice and prosperity and innovation."

Leo shook his head. A part of him was desperate to believe in the altruism of his father's intentions, however misguided his methods might be; that would be so much easier than facing the horrifying, unjustifiable lengths to which Ricciotti had gone. But Leo could not afford to fall into the trap of the obedient son. "If the people want to be free, they will rise up. Rosalinda always spoke as if we have many allies in the south, as if they were eager to revolt against foreign rule. There's no love lost between the Sicilians and the House of Bourbon."

Ricciotti gave Leo a pitying smile. "Your grandfather believed he could dethrone that French bastard Francis with a thousand men and a popular rebellion. His ships never even made landfall. They burned and sank, and took the will of the Sicilian people down to the bottom of the sea with them. The common folk of Two Sicilies won't rise against their ruler again."

"And this somehow excuses what you did to our *mothers?*"

Ricciotti pushed out of his armchair and paced in front of the hearth. "Francis didn't win with strategy, or numbers, or spy work. He won with Archimedes mirrors—he won because he had a pazzerellone who could build him weapons that no one else possessed, and that no one could foresee." He reached out an arm and leaned against the mantel, staring into the flames as he spoke. "With most pazzerellones, age and experience calcify their obsessions.

A mechanist who builds trains only builds trains; he will not, perhaps even cannot, do otherwise."

"And an alchemist obsessed with creating polymaths can only create polymaths?" Leo interrupted.

Ricciotti shot him a warning look. "Don't mock me, boy. Polymaths are the key. Their creative focus does not narrow with time; they remain intellectually malleable, and can aim the full power of their madness at any problem they choose."

Leo leaned back in his chair, calculating his slouch to be indisputably disrespectful. "It must really gall you, then, that Jumi was the one who created the ultimate weapon. And Montaigne was the one who scribed Veldana, thus creating Jumi."

"I have the editbook, don't I?" Ricciotti said flatly.

"But you can't claim credit for it. Two decades wasted on the polymath problem, and at best your work is tangential." Leo shrugged, enjoying the twitch of rage he saw at the corner of Ricciotti's mouth. "I suppose if Aris can manage to decipher the Veldanese language, then it won't have been a complete failure. Your prized polymath will have made some small contribution."

In two long strides, Ricciotti closed the distance between them and laid the back of his hand across Leo's face. Stars exploded in his vision, and he tasted the salty tang of blood from where his teeth cut his cheek.

Leo recovered quickly from the shock of the unexpected blow, and he sprang out of the chair and backed away to escape his father's reach. He was out of practice; he should have seen that coming.

With frightening calm, Ricciotti said, "You will learn to respect me again. One way or another."

* * *

Leo spent the rest of the evening in the brittle sanctuary of his new bedroom. He sat on the carpet, leaning back against the side of his bed with a book open in his lap. The words were proving impossible to concentrate upon, though, the novel reduced to abstract markings of black on white.

"Still sulking?" Aris said from the doorway.

"Yes. So go away." Leo glared; he did not want to be comforted.

Aris entered uninvited. "I brought ice," he said, offering a bowl.

Leo held out for a moment before grudgingly accepting some of the crushed ice. He sucked on it, numbing his swollen cheek, like they'd done when they were children. Aris folded his legs and sat on the floor beside him. Leo wished he had the strength to aim his fury at Aris, but he felt as wrung out as a damp rag, and a traitorous part of him wanted nothing more than to be taken care of by his brother. Just once more.

"Traitor," Leo grumbled around the ice. "You tattled on me."

"I don't tell Father everything, but I do have to throw him the occasional bone." Aris shrugged. "And you need to learn not to antagonize him."

Leo gently prodded the side of his face. "Hardly the worst injury I've had."

"Hmm," Aris said, as if he didn't quite believe Leo's nonchalance.

Objectively, a sore cheek was nothing to worry over. His fencing lessons with Rosalinda had often left him with bruises and sore muscles, and his mechanics laboratory had gifted him with a variety of cuts and burns. There was a scar on his left arm from a cut that had needed five stitches. This was nothing compared to that.

Except Ricciotti *meant* to hurt him. That always made it ache worse, somehow.

Leo said, "He's a madman, you know."

"He's our father," Aris insisted. "And we're all madmen in our own ways, right? At the end of the day, we're all pazzerellones. His is simply a very driven sort of madness."

"You are too forgiving of his faults," said Leo. *Faults* was rather a euphemistic word for murderous human experimentation, but he wanted to draw his brother closer, not drive him away.

Aris laughed. "I think that's the first time anyone has ever accused me of being too soft."

"Not soft. Blind." Leo fished another sliver of ice out of the bowl and sucked on it. "Has it ever occurred to you that he separated us not because of age or talent, but because we were too difficult to control when we were together? That he needed to isolate you in order to make you dependent upon him alone?"

"I'm not *dependent*," he bristled. "Father allows me a great deal of autonomy."

"Autonomy in handling the editbook, for example?"

"Anyway, it's you who does not see him clearly," Aris said, neatly sidestepping the question of the editbook. "He lost his own father and his brother Menotti in the Sicilian revolt; is it any wonder he hates King Francis with a passion? You of all people should be able to sympathize with how that feels. And after what happened to Pasca, and having to leave you behind . . . he only became more determined. If he doesn't succeed now, then everything he's lost will have been for nothing."

"And if he does succeed, will that somehow magically bring Giuseppe and Menotti and Pasca back to life?" Leo said.

Aris had no clever answer to that.

*　*　*

84

In retrospect, Leo decided his bruised cheekbone was a good thing. It had elicited sympathy from Aris—to the degree that Aris was capable of acting sympathetic, at least—and perhaps Leo could leverage that emotion against Ricciotti. Aris had always been protective and possessive of his younger brothers, but the blind loyalty he now showed for their father was a newer instinct. All Leo needed to do was remind Aris of his original priorities.

Ricciotti was relying on Aris to decipher the editbook, which meant Aris knew where the editbook was being kept. Now that Leo understood the depths of depravity to which Ricciotti could stoop, there was no sense in trusting him to honor their deal and leave Elsa free. So Leo would set to work driving a wedge between his father and his brother. And if Ricciotti ended up feeling abandoned and betrayed and terribly alone, well, wouldn't that be poetic justice?

The next morning, as he descended the stairs to look for Aris, Leo pondered how exactly to proceed. Should he push harder against Ricciotti, to make Aris see what a tyrant their father was? Or would Aris only blame Leo for stirring up the conflict?

In the corridor outside Aris's laboratory, Leo took a moment to compose himself. He pressed his ear to the door and heard the muffled clunking and banging of Aris at work inside. Excellent—they could start with bonding over a mechanics project.

Leo let himself in, saying, "So this is where you've . . ."

His voice trailed off and he stopped with one hand still on the door handle. Someone—or something, rather—was in the lab, but it wasn't Aris.

Leo stood face-to-face with a grotesque commingling of alchemical monster and mechanical construct: a green-skinned, ram-horned, brass-clawed, organic-and-metal automaton. She was shaped more or less like a female human, except for the two enormous mechanical wings that sprouted from her shoulders. Over two meters tall, she stood like a cat on her toes, her feet elongated and her knees high on the leg.

She'd frozen in place when Leo burst in. She held so still that if it hadn't been for the noises he'd overheard through the door, he might have doubted she was powered up. Or alive. Whichever term applied to her.

Leo eyed the creature, cautious of the potential danger she posed. His hand went automatically to his hip, but his rapier was still hanging from a peg on his bedroom wall. "Um . . . hello there . . . ?"

The creature shifted her weight and tilted her head at him, the motion accompanied by the soft sound of joints clicking and gears whirring. She did not reply, but something about her posture spoke more of curiosity than aggression, despite her daunting height.

Leo relaxed a little and took a step toward her. "I'm guessing Aris is your maker, right?"

She made a series of complicated gestures, none of which had decipherable meaning, though Leo got the distinct sense that she was attempting to communicate something and expected him to understand.

He gave her a confused expression and shook his head. "I don't know what that means."

The creature made a breathy noise in her throat, half hiss and half sigh.

"So you're the spy?" Leo said. "It's not polite to look in people's windows, you know."

The creature suddenly glanced up like a deer catching the scent of a staghound, though Leo couldn't hear whatever noise was distressing her. Then she wiggled her long brass fingers in the air, and the black maw of a portal appeared out of nowhere. No portal device, no worldbook. Leo only had time to watch as the creature quickly stepped through and the portal closed behind her.

"What the hell?" he asked the empty room.

7

At dinner, Porzia needed to pack away all her irritation and save it for later. Casa had invited all three of their surprise guests to stay and eat—without consulting Porzia—and Elsa was too busy with Revan to be of any help at all with the Carbonari. Across the table, Faraz was discussing the details of the plan with Rosalinda, which left Porzia alone in sussing out the trustworthiness of Vincenzo.

She put on a welcoming smile and said, "How are you finding your first day in the company of pazzerellones? I'd love to be able tell you this kind of excitement is unusual for us, but honestly, it seems par for the course of late."

"I admit I didn't expect to draw a weapon until Austria," Vincenzo said. "But no, this isn't my first encounter with pazzerellones."

"Really?" she said with polite curiosity, careful not to seem too interested.

"I was a fencing pupil of Rosalinda's for a while, so Leo's an old friend."

Porzia's jaw tensed. Old friends? Leo had never so much as mentioned Vincenzo's name. Another secret withheld from her, just when she thought she was done feeling punched in the gut by Leo's betrayal.

Vincenzo looked at her, observing the abrupt change in her mood. "Pardon me, Signorina Pisano. Did I say something displeasing?"

Porzia attempted to bring back her hostess smile, though she could tell it came out rather thin. "No, it's not you. I just sometimes wonder if I ever knew him at all. Leo, I mean."

Vincenzo grinned ruefully. "Well, you know his experiences have made him secretive, which is more than I could tell you about him. I've been on assignment in Bologna and haven't seen him in years." He paused. "Actually, I was better friends with Aris. We're closer in age."

"What!" Porzia said too loudly, drawing a curious glance from Revan, who was seated beside Elsa down the table. Porzia quickly looked away before the heat could rise in her cheeks, but she felt the weight of his gaze lingering for a moment after.

Vincenzo was saying, "Garibaldi didn't approve of his sons growing too familiar with Carbonari rabble such as me, of course, but at that age Aris was not overly concerned with following his father's wishes." He paused and tilted his head like a hawk, eyeing her. "Does that bother you?"

Porzia adopted an air of extreme unbotheredness. "Not at all, so long as you're prepared to use that connection to our advantage."

"Why did you think Rosalinda summoned me for this? My charming personality? While I admit to being excessively charming, that's not the primary reason."

"And modest, too," she said dryly, to which he laughed.

Vincenzo was a bit of a flirt, but not in a way that led Porzia to believe he actually wanted something—it seemed habitual, a reflex not specifically directed at her. She wondered if it had occurred to Elsa to be on guard against that. Yes, he was a revolutionary of questionable loyalties, but Porzia was also simply concerned that he was a man.

He and Elsa would be on their own. Traveling alone with a strange man was . . . not done. Especially one of low birth, low manners, and potentially low morals.

Despite her reservations, Porzia took the two Carbonari to the sitting room for some after-dinner limoncello to keep them occupied until Casa declared that Elsa was ready. Then she escorted them to the foyer.

Elsa descended the main stairs carrying her carpetbag in one hand and a wooden box tucked under her other arm. She came straight over to Porzia and held out the box.

"Here," she said, her voice low so the others wouldn't hear. "There's a transmitter inside, so all you have to do is pick a good hiding place, and I'll be able to find it."

Porzia made a reluctant noise in the back of her throat, but she accepted the box. It felt heavy with the weight of responsibility— Elsa's only escape strategy, in physical form in her arms.

She asked, "Does Revan know you're leaving now?"

"I can't worry about Revan. If he can break out of Veldana, he can take care of himself." Elsa paused, the irritation in her voice softening. "You'll keep an eye on him for me, won't you?"

"Obviously." She already had three siblings and twenty orphaned pazzerellones on her hands; what was one more stray?

"And Porzia, after we leave . . . I need you to do something else."

Porzia rolled her eyes. "Of course I'll do whatever it is. You know that."

"Don't be so quick to agree," Elsa warned. "You're not going to like it."

"I already don't like this plan, so how much worse can it get? Out with it."

Elsa took a deep breath, as if to steel herself. "I need you to report me to the Order. Convince them that I've switched sides."

"What!" Porzia screeched. "Have you lost your mind?"

Elsa held up her hands to forestall Porzia's temper. "For this to work—for me to trick Garibaldi—it has to look real. The Order has to be hunting for me in earnest."

"You don't know what you're asking." She squeezed her eyelids shut for a moment. "I'll . . . think about it."

"And I'll already be on my way, rushing into the lion's den whether or not my story holds up to scrutiny." Elsa sounded stubborn, but there was also an edge of something else in her voice—mania, almost. Certainly obsession.

"You're impossible," Porzia huffed.

Elsa grinned. "Everything's going to work out."

Porzia had never known someone so determined to bend reality to their will. She worried that quality would get Elsa into trouble one of these days.

"Right, well, best be on your way if you've got everything you'll need." Porzia turned to Rosalinda, who was hanging back to give them some semblance of privacy. "Signora Scarpa, are you going with them to Bologna?"

"No," Rosalinda said. "I have work to do here—queries to send, rumors to set in motion. I must lay the groundwork for Vincenzo and Elsa's defection."

Porzia searched her face, doubtful of the older woman's motivations. She did not like placing so much trust in someone she barely knew. The only agreement between the Order and the Carbonari was to stay out of each other's business; they were not allies.

Rosalinda let out a short, humorless laugh. "You still mistrust me? My dear girl, with suspicion like that, we could indeed make a Carbonara out of you."

Porzia did not know how to feel about that, but Elsa cut in and said, "Let's certainly hope so, since that is what I require of you for myself."

At this, Rosalinda turned solemn—or rather, turned somewhat more solemn than her usual dour self. "I'll do my part, and you yours," she said. "Do exactly as Vincenzo instructs you."

Elsa nodded, and Porzia got the sense of a fragile truce solidifying. Rosalinda was not the easiest person to like, she was not pleasant, but she seemed the type who could be relied upon in a crisis. Even Porzia had to admit that counted for something.

Rosalinda turned slightly, as if to go, but after a pause she said to Elsa, "Never forget, you are a spider entering a nest of spiders. You play a dangerous game."

Porzia wanted to snap, *This is not a game*, but something in Elsa's calculating gaze made her hold her tongue. Instead, she gave Elsa a quick embrace and bid them all good night and good luck.

Closing the heavy double doors behind them made a clang that echoed against the foyer's high, frescoed ceiling. The subsequent silence left Porzia with a fluttering sensation of anxiety in her chest. This time when she wandered the halls, it was to help her think.

The problem wasn't just that she must lie to the Order—

though that alone would've been bad enough—it was that the lie would make Elsa persona non grata among pazzerellones. If Porzia's role in this scheme came to light, she would be severely chastised; it might even mar her chances at a council seat later in life. But Elsa could face exile . . . or worse. The Order had imprisoned Charles Montaigne, not for his crimes against the Veldanese, but for conspiring with Garibaldi.

Which was effectively what Elsa wanted Porzia to accuse her of.

Goading the Order into hunting her wouldn't protect her in the long run—it was at best deferring the danger. And yet, with the plan already in motion, to do otherwise would compromise Elsa's safety right now.

Finding herself on the main floor near the classroom, Porzia leaned against the open doorway. Even though it was night, the empty seats struck her like a silent accusation. She'd wanted to restore some semblance of normalcy, but instead of running lessons tomorrow, she'd be taking a portal to Trento. So much for a normal routine. She wished Pappa would hurry back home.

She could check on the nursery, at least. That might assuage some of the guilt over the failed attempt at resuming regular lessons. She pushed away from the doorframe of the vacant classroom and went down the hall.

The nursery housed the seven youngest orphans, kept under the constantly watchful eyes of three nanny-bots. When Porzia opened the door, it was to find one of the nanny-bots hovering nervously in the entrance, blocking her way. It was vaguely woman-shaped, with two beady eyes in an otherwise featureless face. No legs—only a wheeled base shaped like a skirt—but it did have functional arms, and at the moment its hands were clasped together in front of its imitation bosom.

"Signorina," Casa stuttered. "There's no cause for concern. I've been taking excellent care of the progeny, I promise."

"Casa." Porzia scowled at the nanny-bot. "What is wrong with you?"

"I must protect the children."

"What in the world are you talking about? Everyone is perfectly safe inside the house. Now let me in."

The nanny-bot didn't budge. Porzia glared into the bot's eyes—Casa's eyes—with the same glare she used on misbehaving children. Grudgingly, the bot rolled to the side to admit her.

"Potsa!" one of the little girls squealed, too young to properly pronounce Porzia's name. The girl was in bed like the others, but awake despite the late hour.

"Shh." Porzia pressed a finger to her lips and perched on the edge of the bed to give the girl a hug and then tuck the covers around her. "You should be asleep, Annabella."

Porzia would never say it out loud to Casa, or even to Mamma, but she had serious reservations about leaving the nursery under Casa's sole supervision. It was unnatural. Children needed human caretakers, not cold metal machines. Try convincing a mechanist of that, though. Porzia sighed.

One of the nanny-bots seemed to be hovering nervously just behind her. Porzia stood and said, "What is it, Casa? What's bothering you?"

"I am so very sorry, signorina," the house said mournfully.

"Sorry?" She frowned, puzzled. "For what?"

"It is all my fault," Casa replied. "When I let an assassin inside my walls, I . . . I *failed* to protect my wards."

Porzia stepped back into the hall, knowing Casa's attention would follow her even as the nanny-bot stayed behind in the nursery. "Well, everyone is safe now, so there's no need to fret."

"Signor Leo is my charge, and he is not safe."

94

"That's because he *left*," Porzia huffed. "He's not your charge anymore."

"Signor Leo left because he saw I was vulnerable. If I had done better, there would not have been a need for him to leave. And now Signorina Elsa has followed him, because of my weakness."

Porzia had never heard the house so close to hysterics. "Oh, dearest Casa," she said, her heart swelling with sympathy, even though the house was just a machine. "It was no fault of yours that drove him from us. I promise."

Casa's answer was a silence laden with disbelief and doubt.

"Did you hear me, Casa? You are *not* responsible."

Reluctantly, the house replied, "If you say so, signorina."

"Apparently there's guilt enough for everyone to have second servings," Porzia muttered. Amazing how many different versions there were of Leo's departure, each person with their own interpretation. Even the house had a unique perspective.

Porzia decided to sleep on the dilemma Elsa had presented to her, allowing time for Elsa and Vincenzo to arrive in Bologna and get a head start on their business there. She rose early in the morning, anxiety coiling in her gut. *Now or never*, she told herself, as she took the stairs up to the room where the wireless transceiver was kept.

The wireless room was an awful, claustrophobic closet of a place, tucked up against the eaves at the very top of the house. The air was stuffy, and the room barely had enough space for a small desk and all the wires and tubes and machine bits.

Porzia took a deep breath to brace herself and perched on the wooden chair. She had no special fondness for electrical contraptions, but she knew where the on switch was and how to press the keys, and that would be good enough for her needs.

She wasn't certain exactly what her mother had told the Order about Leo's departure. Her mother knew the editbook was in

Garibaldi's possession, and that she and Leo and Faraz had helped Elsa rescue Jumi, but not that they'd gotten ahold of the editbook for a short time. Or that Leo was the one responsible for taking the book back to his father.

Porzia decided to leave any mention of Garibaldi or Leo out of her report and stick to the immediately verifiable facts. Elsa left Casa della Pazzia in the company of a Carbonaro, intent on boarding a train to Bologna and giving no indication of when she might return. Before that, she had expressed interest in the Italian unification movement. (This part was a stretch, though not technically an outright lie.) Typing out her message, Porzia concluded that Elsa *appears to no longer be aligned with us* rather than resorting to the more damning word, *defection*.

She left the cramped little room as soon as she was done, not waiting for a reply. At the moment she had no desire to see how they would respond, and in any case there was another pressing task waiting for her. Compared with sending a deliberate deception to the headquarters of the Order, taking a portal to Trento and hiding a wooden box seemed relatively mundane. Traipse around a city that was technically in enemy territory— sure, why not? She'd already given up on ordinary.

Porzia held up her drab charcoal-gray skirt as she flew down the stairs back toward her rooms. She was dressed again to play the schoolmarm, though this time it wasn't for the benefit of her siblings so much as to avoid attention on the streets of Trento. A young lady alone in her usual flashy, high-society dress would raise too many eyebrows.

Her mind already looking ahead to the task of choosing a hiding spot, Porzia went into her study and reached automatically for the shelf where she always kept her portal device. Her hand came up empty, and she froze.

Her portal device was not there. Could she have been distracted and set it down somewhere else? Her mind raced, replaying the last time she'd used it. She rushed around her study, and then her sitting room and bedroom, but a quick search turned up nothing.

"It can't have grown legs," Porzia muttered to herself, setting her fists on her hips. "Casa, have you seen my portal device?"

"I surely have, signorina."

"Well," she said impatiently, "where is it, then?"

The house paused, and then sheepishly confessed, "I had to confiscate it, signorina."

"Did Mamma instruct you to take it away?" Porzia asked, grappling for some logical explanation. But there was a sinking feeling in her gut, as if she had overlooked something crucial.

"No," the house admitted. "Though she surely would have, if only she'd thought it through. The outside world is dangerous."

Porzia scowled, a spark of panic kindling in her breast. "Casa . . . what in the name of God is going on?"

"I can't protect you if you leave," Casa explained. "So I've decided, no one's leaving."

Porzia tamped down her fear and made herself think: the box, of course! Elsa would have put a portal device in the wooden box to go along with the doorbook. She rushed back into her study and threw open the lid, fumbling with the oilcloth wrapping that protected its contents.

"No need to look there," said the house. "I also confiscated that device."

"What! Casa, *what have you done?*" Porzia screeched.

She pressed a hand to her forehead, trying to calm her nerves. Should she have seen this coming, should she have noticed the signs? The oddly protective behavior, the aberrant distress in

Casa's voice—the house's artificial mind had undergone too much strain, and the fractures were starting to show. But Porzia was no expert on mechanical constructs; how could she have foreseen such a disaster?

"I don't have time for this—I must go to Trento *today*! I command you to return the portal devices to me."

If Porzia didn't plant the box, Elsa would have no escape route ready for when she found the editbook. And worse, she wouldn't know it. There was no way to contact her now that she and Vincenzo were undercover.

Elsa was going to steal the editbook . . . and then get caught.

"Terribly sorry," Casa said, "but I'm afraid you children won't be going anywhere. Ever again."

The house was out of control.

8

I HAD RATHER DIE IN THE ADVENTURE OF NOBLE ACHIEVEMENTS,
THAN LIVE IN OBSCURE AND SLUGGISH SECURITY.

—*Margaret Cavendish*

This train ride out of Pisa bore little resemblance to Elsa's trip to Cinque Terre with Leo—no private compartment, just a hard wooden bench in an open car occupied by a dozen other passengers. The darkness beyond the windows made the interior feel smaller than it was, as if they'd taken a portal into a scribed world only three meters wide.

Elsa had been so focused on preparing for her encounter with Leo and Aris and Garibaldi that she hadn't given any thought to what it would be like traveling with a companion she hardly knew. At first, Vincenzo seemed content to leave her to her thoughts. But the silence was starting to feel thick and awkward, so Elsa resolved to break it.

The question that came to mind was, "So what's the probability Garibaldi's men will just shoot us on sight?"

Vincenzo raised his eyebrows at her. "You're asking this now?"

Elsa shrugged. "I didn't think it would be wise to bring it up in front of the others. They already have enough reservations about this plan."

"Uh, low probability, I'd say," Vincenzo answered. "Especially if they recognize you. I'm more concerned about convincing them of our allegiance in the long run."

Elsa nodded. "Good to know."

For a moment, they seemed at risk of lapsing back into awkward silence, but then Vincenzo said, "It's brave, what you're doing. Totally mad, but brave."

"The editbook is my responsibility. You're the one making a daring choice."

"Nah," he said, though the way he squared his shoulders made her think the praise had landed. "I'm the Carbonari's weapon. All I do is go wherever Rosalinda aims me."

He said this as if it were a point of pride that he had turned over his independence, his will, to some faceless cabal of revolutionaries. Elsa could not comprehend such blind loyalty. "How can you trust someone with your life like that?"

"This isn't about my life—my life, by itself, doesn't matter much—this is about something bigger than me. The chance to make history, to change the future for my people." He shook his head, and then grinned as if to dispel the gravity of his words.

"You sound like Garibaldi," Elsa said.

Vincenzo snorted. "Garibaldi can't tell the difference between liberating the people and oppressing them. At least he can't anymore, if he ever could."

Elsa frowned thoughtfully. Jumi had taught her to view European politics as something to stand in opposition to; Europe was a monolith of colonialist ideology that threatened the security of Veldana. But here was Vincenzo, speaking about the various Italian political factions as if the complexities therein could mean the difference between oppression and liberty. Was this devotion he felt for his land and his people so different from her own love of Veldana?

"But . . . why?" she asked. "My world is one village large, I know every Veldanese by name. Why would you risk your life for people you'll never even meet?"

Vincenzo stared out the window, as if to avoid the question, but after a pause he said, "When I was a child, my sister took ill. The tax collectors had come the week before and left us with nothing to pay a doctor. I refused to eat for five days, trying to save up the money for medicine."

"That's sweet," Elsa said, though she was afraid of where the story might end.

"It was stupid—I could've easily caught her illness, as my parents feared I would, and anyway I was a kid and had no idea how much medicine costs. I got lucky and lived. My sister didn't."

"I'm so sorry."

He flashed a pained half smile. "In the Kingdom of Two Sicilies, everyone has a story like that, or knows someone who does. That's what foreign rulers do to the people they conquer."

Was that what the French would have done to Veldana, too, if Jumi had not created the editbook to ward them off? Veldana had no wealth to tax, but the necessary features could be added to the landscape. A river in which to dredge for diamonds, perhaps— and her people diving and drowning in the murky water. The thought gave her a flash of hot-and-cold sickness. What if scribing the editbook was the right choice, the *only* choice to protect their people?

Keeping her voice low so as not to be overheard, Elsa said, "So we need to stop in Bologna for information. And from there . . . ?"

"Bologna to Ferrara to pick up your papers, then Ferrara

straight through to Trento. Two days, if everything works in our favor."

"Your world is too large," Elsa complained.

Vincenzo laughed. "That's not my fault."

Elsa knew she needed to defer to his expertise, that their plan required it of her. But ever since Leo's betrayal, her instinct was to cling to the controls with a white-knuckle grip; the idea of allowing someone else to steer terrified her.

She took a measured breath to steady her nerves. "What do you need me to do when we get to Bologna?"

"You'll lie low for most of the day tomorrow, so it doesn't look like we got into town at the same time. I'll pretend not to know you. The fellow in charge—Domenico—it's important he believes it's his idea to send me with you to Trento."

"You want me to sit around doing nothing for a whole day? Why?"

"Sometimes it's easier to get information out of someone if they think you don't want to hear it. If you're too eager, they'll suspect you're up to something." He flashed a grin. "Which, to be fair, we are."

It was late when they arrived in Bologna, but Vincenzo found Elsa a women's boardinghouse and instructed her in how to rent a room. They parted ways, him to check in with the Carbonari and her to wait where she wouldn't be noticed. Her rented room was narrow, with a narrow cot and a chipped washbasin and an empty trunk that smelled musty inside. She set the carpetbag on top of it instead.

She slept fitfully, the creaks of the boardinghouse and street noises beyond the window different enough from the sounds of Casa della Pazzia and Pisa to keep startling her awake. Or perhaps her nerves were simply raw with anticipation of the subterfuge she'd soon need to accomplish. Either way, in the morning the landlady saw the dark circles under Elsa's eyes and took pity on her, allowing her to take breakfast in her room. Best not to have all the lodgers meet the curious dark foreigner, since the whole point was to hide.

It felt strange, being cooped up all day with nothing to work on. Elsa wasn't accustomed to the sensation of boredom—in Veldana, there were always observations to make, new areas to explore and new species to document as her mother expanded their world. Now she didn't even have her laboratory world to keep herself occupied.

Elsa couldn't help but dwell on the thought of Casa della Pazzia and the friends she'd left behind. Porzia and Faraz at each other's throats; Revan abandoned among strangers in an unfamiliar world. To make matters worse, Elsa would have no way of communicating her progress to them, or even reassuring them that she was still alive. She was all too familiar with the restless, squirming anxiety of not knowing, and she did not envy them.

As afternoon bled into evening, Elsa checked out of the boardinghouse and took to the streets with her carpetbag in hand, following the directions Vincenzo had made her memorize. The Bologna chapter of the Carbonari met in the back room of a café whose proprietor was sympathetic to their cause, and as Elsa spotted the establishment from half a block away, her pulse fluttered in her throat. What had she gotten herself into? Leo was the perfect liar, not her—deception was not in her skill set. But her feet kept carrying her forward and took her inside.

The café's walls were cluttered with paintings and gilt-framed mirrors, and below that were lined with benches padded in green velvet. Wooden stools and narrow, marble-topped tables were arranged in precise rows—all of them empty at this hour, though voices carried from somewhere farther in.

Behind the polished-wood bar, the barista called out, "We're closed!"

Elsa raised her eyebrows. "Yes, I can tell from all the noise."

Ignoring the barista's protests, she followed the sound of voices through a wide doorway into a second room. It was similarly furnished and decorated but held a greater sense of privacy, and most important, it was full of revolutionaries.

As soon as she walked in, eyes turned to her, and the hubbub of conversation began to quiet as one after another noticed her presence. The Carbonaro nearest the doorway closed in on her and relieved her holster of its revolver so quickly she didn't have time to protest, but after that was done, he looked to another man for instruction.

This man rose to intercept her with a distinctive air of authority. His hair and stubble were more gray than black, and he had deep lines around his eyes as if from years of squinting in the sun. There was a stiffness in his posture, too, that spoke of age.

He looked her up and down, taking in her trousers and battle vest with all its pouches and loops for carrying tools. "Are you lost, little pazzerellona?" he said with a mocking quirk to his mouth. He gave that word—*pazzerellona*—an undertone that Elsa had never heard before, as if it were a foolish way to be, something not worthy of respect.

Elsa raised her chin. "I know exactly where I am. I require assistance from the Carbonari, and I am prepared to offer fair compensation for your time and effort."

The man snorted. "The Carbonari are not for hire."

"I'm called Elsunani di Jumi da Veldana," she persisted. "And you are . . . ?"

"Domenico, at your service," he replied, spreading his hands and giving a shallow, joking bow. The gesture made her notice that he had only nine fingers.

Elsa kept her eyes on him, resisting the urge to search the room for Vincenzo's familiar face. "Well, Domenico, I brought something for you . . ."

She moved to open her carpetbag, but before she could reach inside, Domenico snapped, "Search her."

The Carbonaro who'd grabbed her revolver reached out again to take the bag, and another man came forward to pat her down. His hands were light and efficient, and his cheeks reddened as if he found the process embarrassing. He yanked on her watch chain—making Elsa suck in a nervous breath—but he only glanced at the pocket watch before handing it back to her to tuck away. If he'd opened it, he would have discovered Faraz's sleeping potion.

Next they started emptying her carpetbag. They lifted the miniature freeze ray suspiciously and laid it out on one of the café tables.

"What is this?" said Domenico.

"Something I designed for you," Elsa quipped, "and I'll even show you how to use it, if we can come to an agreement."

"And this?" Domenico barked, as his men removed the signal receiver she would need for locating where Porzia hid the door-book. She'd thought it was clever to disguise the receiver as a portal device, but it hadn't occurred to her that they might not know what a portal device was.

"Oh, come on now, that's standard scriptological equipment. Completely harmless." Elsa felt prickly and hot, a slow sort of panic creeping up on her. Why wasn't Vincenzo stepping in to help her? "Surely someone here has seen a portal device before?"

Domenico peered at it as if he thought it might explode, then looked up to search the crowd. "Vico!" he called.

Movement in the back, and finally Elsa spotted her inside man. Vincenzo rose lazily from his reclined position in the far corner, drained his wineglass, and edged between his compatriots to join them near the entrance. "What?" he said.

"You've spent some time around pazzerellones," Domenico said. "Do you recognize this?"

Vincenzo set his hands on his hips, looking quite convincingly irritated at the interruption. "Yeah, it's one of those . . . black-hole-opening things. For going inside mad books."

Domenico nodded, giving Elsa a considering look. Vincenzo shifted his weight as if to return to his table, but Domenico held out a hand to forestall him.

Elsa feigned impatience. "The device I made for you is a sort of . . . universal key, if you like. It will freeze any lock hard enough to turn the metal brittle and easily shattered." She shrugged. "Unless I'm wrong and you never have any need to access places that are forbidden to you."

To his credit, Domenico had quite the poker face, and for a moment Elsa wondered if she'd be thrown out instead of sealing a deal. But then he said, "And what do you ask for in return?"

"From you? Just an introduction in Trento." She could tell this answer did not satisfy him, so she elaborated, "There's someone I need to track down. I have reason to believe he's staying near Trento, but I'm unfamiliar with the area, and I need to catch up with him fast. He stole something from my people, and I can't count on the Order for assistance in this matter." Strange—Elsa had been preparing herself to lie, but as she finished speaking she realized every single word was the truth.

Domenico set his hands on his hips and scowled. The air in

the room nearly vibrated with tension as the men waited for his decision.

"Look," Elsa said, "as soon as I walked in here with that tech, I implicated myself as a collaborator. I'm counting on discretion as much as you are."

"True enough," Domenico said, and he nodded as if deciding that having a pazzerellona in his pocket could be useful. "Very well, then. Vico, pazzerellones are your wheelhouse—you'll take her."

"*Stu gazz!*" Vincenzo swore in a dialect that Elsa didn't quite catch. "Are you playing with me? I just got back from an assignment."

Elsa carefully did not react to this, though inside she felt the burn of nascent panic. Why was he turning down the assignment? Their plan was so close to working, and here he was throwing it out the window!

But his reaction only seemed to make Domenico *more* determined that Vincenzo should go. "Oh, my apologies, I didn't realize your job was to hang around the café drinking wine," he said sarcastically. "Are you a Carbonaro or a poet?"

In a few short minutes, Elsa's possessions were returned to her—all except the miniature freeze ray she'd offered them—and she and Vincenzo were reunited on the streets of Bologna. Now with the knowledge of how to find the revolutionaries in Trento.

"I can't believe that worked," Elsa said, as they walked back to the train station.

Vincenzo grinned. "I can't believe you doubted me."

They stayed the night in Ferrara and went to a lawyer's office in the morning, where Vincenzo gave a cryptic pass phrase and the secretary handed him an envelope with travel documents for one Elsa Valenti. Rosalinda had wired ahead so the forged papers would be ready for them.

The border crossing into the crown state of Venetia proved uneventful—a train attendant simply checked their papers and gave Elsa a curious look, but apparently he saw nothing amiss with her documents.

After the attendant had moved on down the train car, she leaned closer to Vincenzo to ask, "So Venetia is its own kingdom, but it's still part of the Austrian Empire?" She was never going to get all these bizarre political distinctions straight in her mind.

"They've been granted autonomy to govern themselves, at least in theory," explained Vincenzo. "But they still pay taxes to the Austrians, and let's face it, it's probably a puppet government."

They rode through a series of cities, which Vincenzo named for her: Padova, Vicenza, Verona, Ala. Finally they disembarked at the station in Trento, and instead of walking toward the city center, they angled north to the outskirts. Trento itself sat in a broad, flat river valley, but the hill country surrounding it was a sea of vineyards the scale of which Elsa could not have imagined if she wasn't seeing it with her own eyes.

With his long legs, Vincenzo set a pleasantly vigorous walking pace, though he kept glancing around in a way that made Elsa nervous. She found his constant alertness distracting; how anyone could focus when half their mind was scanning for enemies she could not fathom.

They met their contact, Claudio, at a winery where he worked. Vincenzo maneuvered deftly through an exchange of pass phrases, dropping of names, and sharing of news.

Then he leaned in confidentially and said, "Claudio, friend— may I call you friend?—I'm sure you can imagine why I came here, specifically, with a pazzerellona in tow."

"I don't know what you're implying," said Claudio, suddenly very focused on wiping the grape stains from his hands with a rag.

"I think you do," said Elsa, catching a subtle cue from Vincenzo. "And his name is Ricciotti Garibaldi."

Claudio tugged the rag through his belt and narrowed his eyes at them. "Officially, Garibaldi is persona non grata to the Carbonari."

Vincenzo said, "His methods are extreme, but I assumed you'd be ready to do whatever it takes to break free of Austrian rule." He shrugged and shifted his weight as if to go. "My mistake. We'll leave you out of it, then."

Claudio held out a hand to forestall him. "Wait! Wait, friend." He glanced around reluctantly, as if to confirm they were unobserved. "Yes, we've been in contact. Lately, he's even been recruiting from among our numbers. I can't approve of it, but . . . well, if your minds are made up, you certainly wouldn't be the first."

"So, you can send us with an introduction?" Vincenzo said.

"I can do better than that—I'll take you up there myself. Today, if you're ready."

"Yes," Elsa said. "We're ready."

Claudio drove the winery's horse cart, with Elsa and Vincenzo riding in the back, and they followed the road up into the mountains, where it became steep and winding. While the rugged terrain was beautiful to look upon, all the jouncing and jostling made Elsa lament that they had not simply approached on foot.

With the afternoon sun sinking below the peaks to the west, the air turned chilly. Elsa didn't own an overcoat, and it hadn't occurred to her she might need one this late in the spring. Weather—yet another aspect of Earth that mystified her.

"There it is," Claudio called over his shoulder, lifting a hand to point.

Elsa sighted along the direction he indicated, across a valley floor and high up on the opposite side: the yellow glow of gaslit windows, shining like the eyes of a nest of spiders in the failing daylight. The massive house was built of the same dark gray stone as the surrounding mountainscape, and indeed it seemed to have been built into the side of the mountain, almost as if it had grown there of its own accord. It had very steep rooflines—the purpose of which was not immediately obvious to her—and an imposing, bulky shape. Not quite a castle, Elsa thought, though it nearly qualified.

"Pig of a god," Vincenzo swore under his breath, taking it all in. "It's a damned fortress."

Claudio pulled the cart to a stop at the bottom of a narrow gravel path that switchbacked up the mountainside, providing access to the fortress. Elsa and Vincenzo climbed out of the back. There was tension written in the angle of Vincenzo's shoulders; his eyes darted everywhere, and his right hand wandered to the hilt of his rapier.

"Calmly now," Elsa muttered to him.

"We've been spotted," he muttered back.

Elsa didn't doubt his assessment, though what noises she heard were indistinguishable from the montane wildlife settling down for the night, or in some cases waking up for it.

They began the steep walk up the path, but they didn't make it far before a disembodied voice shouted, "Stop there!" A man-shaped shadow stepped out from behind a boulder, pointing a pistol at them. "Hands," he said.

Vincenzo held his hands out wide, and Elsa set down her carpetbag and imitated the gesture of submission. She jumped when the ground behind them crunched beneath a set of boots, and a hand reached forward to take her revolver from its holster.

"You must be lost," the first man said. From his tone, Elsa imagined him smirking beneath his black cloth mask.

Claudio stepped forward. "Is Stefano on duty? He can vouch for us."

"Visitors aren't welcome here," the guard argued.

Elsa wasn't sure how well they could see her through the gloom of dusk, but she pulled herself up to her full height and borrowed an imperious expression from Porzia's repertoire. "I think you'll find we will be," she said. "Tell Garibaldi that Elsa di Jumi da Veldana has come."

9

SCIENCE IS MADE UP OF MISTAKES, BUT THEY ARE MISTAKES
WHICH IT IS USEFUL TO MAKE, BECAUSE THEY LEAD LITTLE BY
LITTLE TO THE TRUTH.
—*Jules Verne*

Porzia had never felt much affection for Casa, the way a mechanist might, but she had taken for granted that the house was comfortable and familiar and safe. Now, as she passed through the corridors, she felt something vaguely sinister about that inhuman intelligence surrounding her. It was as if she had grown up on the shores of a placid sea and was just now seeing her first storm surge.

On the first floor, security bars had lowered over the windows. On the basement level, a veritable army of small cleaner bots roamed free, so that she had to dodge around them lest she trip. She found her mother in the hall outside the generator room. Two large maintenance bots blocked the door, and her mother was deep in argument with the house.

"Mamma!" she shouted, lifting her skirts so she could hurry.

"Porzia, dear, you shouldn't be down here. Casa has—"

Porzia put a finger to her lips. "Come with me."

She took her mother by the hand and led her up out of the basement and down the hall toward Leo's laboratory.

"Wherever are you dragging me off to?" Mamma said, sounding as if her patience was wearing thin. "We're in the midst of a crisis."

"I am well aware of that." Porzia threw a significant look over her shoulder at her mother.

She yanked open the laboratory door and rushed down the half flight of steps to the sunken floor. The room was just as Leo had left it—a chaotic mess of tools and machine parts that looked more like the aftermath of a natural disaster than it did a workspace. Fortunately, Leo's disinclination toward putting things away meant that the device Porzia wanted was sitting in plain sight, exactly where it had been the last time they'd used it. Atop Leo's favorite workbench sat the metal cube of the scrambler.

Porzia was not insensitive to the irony of the situation: Leo had invented the signal scrambler so the adults could not use the house to spy on their conversations. Now here she was, using it with one of the very people it had been designed to foil.

She took a deep breath, flipped the switch on top of the box, and said, "There we are—Casa can't hear us now."

Mamma looked at the box critically, clearly displeased that Leo and Porzia possessed such a thing. "We'll be having a talk later about that device."

"Won't that be fun," Porzia quipped. "For now, Mamma, let's have a talk about how your house has gone insane."

Mamma planted her fists on her hips, setting aside her inner parent in favor of her inner mechanist. "It's not a hardware problem, it's . . . something more complex than that. Casa has found a way to leverage the safety protocol so that it supersedes the obedience protocol. The house no longer follows my commands."

"Well, it's not ideal, but at least we're safe," Porzia said, though Mamma was looking at her in a way that made her think this was perhaps a naive assumption.

Mamma said, "And what happens when Casa decides the best way to keep us safe is to store us in cryogenic chambers? Or replace all our fragile organic parts with mechanical ones?"

"Oh." Porzia's momentary relief melted like ice in the sun. "That would be bad."

"We need to evacuate as many people as we can manage. The older children are all still free to roam the house, so it shouldn't pose too much of a problem to gather them together."

"And the younger children?"

Mamma sighed. "Casa has the nursery on lockdown. There's no way to get to them without alerting Casa that we're attempting an escape."

Porzia stared at her mother, aghast. "We can't just abandon them here, all alone."

"Not alone. I must stay behind to attempt the repairs."

Porzia protested, "Mamma—" but Gia held up a hand to quiet her, and Porzia clamped her jaw closed on her argument.

"I need you to do this for me, darling. You must get the older children to safety, as many of them as you can."

"What about Burak? He'll want to stay here with you."

Mamma pursed her lips, reluctant. "It's too dangerous."

Burak was only thirteen, the difference in age sufficient for him to look up to Leo with a follower's adoration. Porzia suspected that becoming Mamma's right hand was Burak's way of dealing with Leo's absence. And losing his hero was making him grow up fast.

"You should let him stay," Porzia said. "He's old enough, and serious enough. And I'm no mechanist, but even I can tell you'll need all the help you can get."

As her mother went down into the bowels of the house, Porzia's first task was to find Burak and clue him in to the situation at hand without tipping off Casa that anything was happening. She almost reflexively asked Casa where he was—her whole life she'd relied on the house for little tasks like that, and only now was she realizing how frustrating it could be to try to locate a particular person inside a multistoried mansion.

Finally she found Burak in the courtyard with Sante and Olivia. Olivia was seated on a stone bench with a large book open in her lap; Sante and Burak were dueling with branches they must have snapped off one of the ornamental trees planted in the courtyard.

Porzia squeezed her eyes shut for a moment, praying for patience. What had she just argued to Mamma, about Burak being mature enough to stay behind? And Sante was nearly two years older than Olivia, yet he showed only half her diligence.

"Burak, you're needed," she called. "Burak!"

The boys stopped their play-dueling. Burak tossed his stick aside as if he'd already forgotten all about the game, eager to help even before he knew what he'd be helping with. Disappointment and jealousy flashed in Sante's eyes, but Porzia didn't have time for her brother's feelings.

Burak jogged over to where Porzia stood near the entrance. "Zia Gia?" The orphans often referred to her mother this way, as *aunt*, though there was no relation.

Porzia nodded. "In the basement. Off you go."

Olivia and Sante came over as Burak ran off to fulfill his task. Hugging the book to her chest, Olivia quietly asked, "Is it serious? Is there anything we can do?"

Porzia deliberated, not wanting to spread panic through the

children. "Just . . . make sure everyone knows that lunch today is not optional." Gathering in the dining hall should seem neither suspicious to Casa nor frightening to the residents.

Her siblings went off to spread the word, and Porzia was momentarily left alone with the tense anxiety in her chest. Even if the children weren't in immediate danger from the house, she still needed to get herself out as quickly as possible for Elsa's sake. Suddenly it seemed incredibly risky that she'd left the doorbook unattended in her study, where Casa could confiscate it at any time. Porzia ran back upstairs as fast as her skirts would allow, burst into her rooms, and frantically unwrapped the oilcloth inside the box.

The doorbook was still there.

She pressed a hand against her corseted ribs, her relief even sweeter than the oxygen she sucked in. Portal devices were replaceable, but there was only one doorbook in the world—or in *any* world, as far as she knew. She picked it up, wanting the tangible connection as reassurance. She hadn't lost it. This part of the plan, at least, hadn't fallen apart.

Flipping open the doorbook, Porzia discovered that Trento was no longer the last entry—there was a newer description, in Elsa's hand. Cinque Terre, where the Pisano ancestral castle was hidden. The castle couldn't be accessed without the Pisanos' keys, which meant Elsa had scribed the location specifically for Porzia.

She closed the book and had to blink unexpected moisture from her eyes. Even with everything else going on, Elsa had planned contingencies for her. God, she hoped she'd done the right thing, reporting Elsa to the Order.

After a moment of indecision, she found a satchel to carry the wooden box in and slung it across her shoulders. Better to keep Elsa's escape kit with her, so Casa couldn't easily confiscate it.

Then she went downstairs to her mother's office to retrieve the keys to the ancestral castle in Cinque Terre—another irreplaceable tool they might need in the immediate future.

Lunch was a tense affair. The youngest children were conspicuously absent, and the older ones uncharacteristically subdued after Porzia shut down their speculations with a stern glare. Revan tried asking her what was going on, but Porzia cut him off with a small, sharp shake of her head. Faraz didn't show up at all, a fact that tied her stomach in knots and made it nearly impossible to eat. Had something happened to him? The absence of Gia and Burak was expected—they were off trying to fix the house—but she couldn't imagine what had held up Faraz, unless Casa had done something awful.

Halfway through the meal she tossed her napkin down beside her plate and stood. Revan rose to follow her; she tried to wave him back into his seat, but he persisted, and Porzia decided it wasn't worth making a scene in front of the children.

As they moved to leave, Sante looked at them with raised eyebrows, so Porzia told her brother, "Keep everyone here."

"I can do that." He nodded vigorously, proud to have even a sliver of authority assigned to him.

They left the dining hall, and Revan tried again to ask her what was wrong, and she again rebuffed him. His Italian was much improved, even compared to yesterday, and for once Porzia felt more grateful for than jealous of that scribed Veldanese ability to pick up languages. At least they didn't have a communication barrier to deal with, on top of everything else.

And yet, for someone who understood, he was not especially good at listening. "I don't have time to fill you in; will you please just go back in the dining hall and wait with the others."

"I'm not a twelve-year-old," Revan protested. "Let me help. I *crossed worlds* to help Elsa, and she just up and left without so much as a goodbye. There has to be something I can do that will make this whole journey seem less . . . futile."

Porzia stalked down the hall. "Fine, do what you like, I also don't have time to waste arguing."

With Revan following at her heels, Porzia found Faraz in his lab, quite alive and seemingly unperturbed. He was scratching chemical formulae across a slate chalkboard, while his pet tentacle beast balanced on his shoulder. A wave of relief flooded through her—he was fine, nothing had happened to him—but it quickly transmuted into anger for the unnecessary worry he'd caused her.

"I can't believe what I'm seeing. What do you think you're doing at a time like this?"

Faraz glanced behind him as if he hadn't heard them come in. "Oh, hello. I'm working, what does it look like?"

"Didn't Olivia tell you about . . . *lunch?*" she said meaningfully.

"Sante said some nonsense about mandatory mealtimes, but really, I know you're not *that* concerned about my eating habits," he replied.

"You haven't noticed anything amiss lately?" Porzia asked suggestively. Seeing that he clearly had no idea what she was talking about, she added, "Wow, that is an impressive level of obliviousness, even for an alchemist."

His brow lowered into a frown at that. "To what, exactly, are you referring?"

"Not here," Porzia hissed. "Come along."

She'd meant the invitation for Faraz alone, but Skandar came riding on his shoulder, and Revan stuck to her side as she left the alchemy lab and rushed through the house to Leo's cavernous mechanics lab. Inside, Porzia flipped the switch on the signal scrambler, and then let out a sigh of relief.

"All right, now we can talk without Casa monitoring our conversation." She proceeded to catch them up on the current crisis.

Faraz grew quiet as she explained, thoughts racing behind his dark eyes.

It was Revan who said, "But you're all pazzerellones. You've thought up some brilliant solution, haven't you?"

"Sort of." Porzia chewed her lip for a moment before explaining, "The science of scriptology actually predates the invention of the portal device. Early scriptologists used a portal ledger to scribe the portals into existence, which was supposedly quite laborious, not to mention dangerous."

Revan said, "Okay. So all you have to do is make one of those."

Porzia held up her index finger. "Slight problem: no one's used a portal ledger in over three hundred years. The script has been lost to time. I'd have to reinvent it from scratch."

Faraz folded his arms. "Explain the 'dangerous' part."

"Portal-device portals close automatically, as a safety precaution. Ledger portals have to be closed manually with the proper script. Apparently, if you leave a portal open for too long, it destabilizes and starts to affect the realspace around it."

"How do you know all this?" he said.

Porzia rolled her eyes. "How do you think? I *read*, Faraz."

He frowned at her. "So you don't actually have any notion of how ledger portals work, or what happens when they go wrong."

"All right, then," Porzia snipped. "Let's hear your brilliant alternative plan for how we're supposed to escape."

Faraz said, "What about an old-fashioned breakout? Go out the windows, rappel off the roof, that sort of thing."

"Thanks for the great idea, *Leo*," Porzia sneered. "But if we so much as gaze longingly out the windows, Casa will initiate a full lockdown. There's no chance we'll have time to get everyone out that way."

For a brief moment he looked shocked, as if her words hit him like acid, then his expression smoothed over. "Right, because your plan is so incredibly practical."

"Arguing isn't going to help anything," Revan interjected calmly, trying to mediate.

"What are you even doing here?" Porzia snapped, her temper brittle from stress.

"At least he's right that this is pointless," Faraz said. On his shoulder, Skandar fluttered anxiously, picking up on his frustration. "What would *help* is a way to get out of this damned house." He climbed the half flight of stairs to the door, then opened it and slipped through without a backward glance.

"Unbelievable!" Porzia declared. She hefted the signal scrambler, balanced it against one hip, then followed out the still-open door, yelling, "Faraz! We are not done. Get back here."

She was unaccustomed to being on the receiving end of someone storming angrily out of the room, especially when that person was Faraz, who usually behaved so peaceably. He stopped walking when it was clear she didn't intend to let him get away, but his arms were still tightly crossed against his chest.

Porzia said, "We have to try *something*! Who knows how long it will take Mamma to repair this disaster. We can't just wait here while Aris deciphers the editbook."

"The whole point of retrieving the editbook is that we're trying to prevent the world from being irreparably damaged," Faraz replied, his voice tight. "And you seriously want to propose a solution that involves potentially destabilizing reality? Am I the only one smelling irony here?"

"You're the only one here, period," Porzia muttered, realizing that Revan had not joined them in the hallway.

But just then he came loping down the hall from the direction of the foyer; he must have run upstairs while Porzia was focused on fighting with Faraz. He held his right arm pinned against his side and there was a bulge under his coarse linen shirt, as if he was carrying something concealed. He was not out of breath, but there was an excited, keyed-up sort of look in his eyes.

Revan revealed the object to them: it was a portal device.

Porzia gasped. "Where did you get that?"

"It's the one I took from Jumi's cottage. I hid it when I got here. And besides, I'm not a pazzerellone—it probably didn't even occur to the house that I might have one."

"Revan, I . . . ," Porzia began, but she lost the words, embarrassed at how blithely she'd dismissed him before.

Faraz put a hand up to steady Skandar as he leaned forward to look at the portal device. "We still have the problem that it'll take time to herd a dozen children one by one through a portal, and there are house-bots everywhere. Casa can respond almost instantaneously to any perceived threat."

"Give it to me," Porzia said. Her arms still full with the signal scrambler, she angled herself so Revan could stuff the portal device in her satchel. "You two, go back to the dining hall and keep the children occupied. I need to consult with our mechanists."

Porzia rushed off, not sparing time for the boys' reaction to her command. She couldn't afford to care whether they bristled at being ordered about, not in the midst of a crisis.

She found Burak on the basement level, sweaty and smeared with grease, but unself-conscious about his appearance in the typical fashion of a mechanist. *He looks so like Mamma*, Porzia made herself think, because the alternative was *He looks so like Leo*, and that was an intolerable mental road to follow.

She passed him the signal scrambler and explained what little she knew about it. "It seems to have been quite effective so far. My question is, do you think it will keep us hidden if we open a portal?"

"I'd have to take it apart to be sure, but I'd guess it just has a selective sound-dampening effect that interferes with Casa's ability to hear. I doubt Leo designed it to mask the signature of a portal opening."

Porzia nodded, hiding her disappointment with practicality. "So we'll need a distraction, then."

"Or I could cut the power to the charging stations, so the bots can't recharge," Burak offered. "Take them all out of commission."

Porzia tapped a finger against her chin, considering. "Is that the sort of problem Casa would be able to repair unassisted?"

"I can squeeze into the wall space and mess with the wiring in a place the bots can't reach. Might even be able to rig it so Casa thinks the charging stations are still functional." There was a gleam in his eye that reminded her uncomfortably of that mechanist who shall not be named. "We'd have to wait overnight for all the bots to run out of charge, but it'll give us at least a brief window in the morning, before Casa figures out how to redirect the power."

Could Porzia afford to wait another night before fulfilling her mission in Trento—or rather, could Elsa afford for her to wait? But what other choice did she have, when this was the best plan for safely getting out as many children as they could? Once again Porzia found her priorities at war with each other, duty to family and loyalty to a friend pulling her in two different directions. But indecision helped no one.

"Do it," she said to Burak.

Porzia took the signal scrambler with her when she left the

basement level, but she flipped it off so she could speak with the house.

"Casa, are you there?"

"Always, signorina. How may I be of assistance?"

The thought of what kind of *assistance* Casa might provide sent a quiver through Porzia, but now was not the time for honest reactions.

"You were right," she said, "we've been horribly lax about the children's safety. Mamma and Burak are working to reinforce your security measures, but they'll need some time. So until then, I think we should move all the children to a central location where you can protect us more easily."

Casa paused, considering the argument. Eventually the house said, "Yes . . . that is an excellent plan, signorina."

Porzia hid a smile. "Casa, it would be most helpful if you could bring a stack of blankets down to the dining hall, so we can sleep there in comfort. And the children will each need to pack a bag, if you don't mind."

Again the house paused, but for a shorter time. "That is acceptable."

In the morning, Porzia rose early from her improvised bed on the floor of the dining room. She instructed the house that everyone would be very hungry this morning and require a large breakfast, and then she moved among the sleeping forms, waking them one at a time. She began with those who did not need to be told to ready themselves—her mother, Faraz, Revan, and Burak. Then she moved on to her siblings and the others, each one of whom received a solemn stare from Porzia, which told them that serious matters were close at hand. Casa still had the youngest children sequestered in the nursery, and Porzia felt a pang of guilt at the thought of leaving them, but her mother was right: they needed to get as many people out as they could, before the house's madness escalated.

Without Porzia needing to ask, Revan and Sante began rolling up the blankets so they could be carried easily. The food train arrived with its little cars loaded to capacity with loaves of bread, wheels of cheese, bowls of fruit. The children went to the table and picked at the food, their eyes frequently darting up to watch Porzia or her mother.

Mamma looked tired, dark circles under her eyes like bruises, but she also looked determined.

Porzia moved to the signal scrambler and rested her hand casually atop the box. She made eye contact with Mamma and raised her eyebrows to say *Ready?* Gia checked the time, conferred very quietly with Burak, and gave a nod for a reply. Porzia looked to the others, one by one; they all waited on her.

Porzia flipped the switch and immediately began shouting commands. "Revan, block the door! Everyone else, grab your bags and pack up all the food! Quickly, now!"

The room exploded into chaos, everyone rushing to follow her orders. Mamma came over to stand beside her, with Burak at her heels. Porzia lifted the scrambler and handed it to Burak to carry.

To her mother, she said, "Stay safe. Casa's going to be furious about this."

"We'll disappear into the maintenance tunnels as soon as you're all through the portal. With luck, it will take Casa a while to realize we're still here."

"Don't worry," Burak said, "I have all the tunnels memorized."

Porzia smiled at him. "I don't doubt it. Keep an eye on my mother for me, will you?"

He nodded, puffed up with pride at the importance of his task.

She gave Mamma a hurried embrace and bid them both good-bye. Turning, she whipped out Revan's portal device, the coordinates already set, and flipped the switch. The table was nearly clean of food, the doors blocked with a chair wedged beneath the handles. The black hole of the portal yawned open, and Faraz went through first to organize the children on the other side. Then Porzia began waving them through one by one.

She grabbed her own bag and glanced at Revan, but he was still at the doors with his ear pressed to the wood.

"We've got a problem," he shouted.

Too slow, too slow, Porzia thought, practically shoving a boy through the portal. The children had picked up on the atmosphere of danger, and some of them were freezing with fear. The delay between one child and the next made the portal wink closed automatically, and she had to quickly reset the device and open the portal again.

A metallic bang on the far side of the doors heralded Casa's awareness.

Revan jammed the chair tighter against the doors. "I thought you said the bots would all be out of power!"

"They were supposed to be!" Porzia flinched at a second, louder bang. The house had definitely noticed them, and was displeased.

A muffled whirring sound began, and then the doors vibrated as a radial saw bit into the wood. Recognition settled cold and dreadful in Porzia's stomach. Revan backed up several steps, taking something from his pocket, but whatever he had would be no match for Casa now—the house had control of Leo's training bot, the one he'd "improved" too much, the one that had carved a path of destruction on the day Elsa arrived.

"Goddamn it, Leo," Porzia swore under her breath, but to the last of the children she urged, "Go, go!"

"It's not going to hold . . . ," Revan warned, his attention focused on the besieged doors.

"That's everyone. Come on!" Porzia shouted, looking back long enough to make sure he followed. The doors were buckling under the training bot's assault. Porzia dove toward the portal with Revan at her heels. The last sound she heard was the splintering of wood as the bot broke in.

They stepped out of the portal's blackness into dazzling sunlight and air heavy with the salt-scent of the sea. Porzia looked around—they stood on a train platform. To one side, the Ligurian Sea crashed against the rocky coast below, and to the other, narrow buildings clung to the rugged landscape. The buildings crowded together in a strict utilitarian fashion, not a meter of space wasted, but they were painted in a whimsical array of colors—sea green and safflower yellow, sky blue and salmon pink. Out to sea, a cluster of similarly bright-painted fishing boats bobbed up and down with the passing of each swell.

Porzia had barely gotten the chance to orient herself when Faraz came over, arms crossed, expression accusing. "This isn't Corniglia—it's Riomaggiore."

She tucked back a strand of hair that the breeze had pulled loose. "Elsa scribed the destination. Probably she thought it best not to port to the exact location of the ruins, on the chance that Aris is monitoring portal activity at Casa della Pazzia. We have seen him track portals before."

"I don't suppose we brought money for more than a dozen train tickets," said Faraz. "It's going to be a long walk with this crowd in tow."

"But we *can* walk, yes?" Revan asked.

Porzia closed her eyes for a moment, praying for patience. She had to remind herself that feet were the only form of transportation available in Veldana, so Elsa probably hadn't thought of this as a potential problem.

Finally, she said, "The inland paths are much too difficult, but there's a trail that follows the coastline. We should be able to manage."

First get the children safely to the castle, then worry about Elsa. Porzia couldn't leave for Trento anyhow, not until she scrounged for a second portal device—one to hide with the door-book for Elsa's use, and one to get Porzia back home. Or back to Cinque Terre, now that *home* was gone.

Hold on, Elsa, she prayed. *Find the editbook, just . . . not yet.*

10

NEVER WAS ANYTHING GREAT ACHIEVED WITHOUT DANGER.
—*Niccolo Machiavelli*

Leo saw who was in the foyer and his heart stopped. He flashed hot and cold, panicked and elated in the same instant. She was the person he most yearned to see in all the world—and the very last person he wanted to see *here*.

"Elsa," he croaked.

She looked over at the sound of his voice, her expression unreadable, only the barest flicker of recognition in her bright green eyes. Her indifference cut into him like a well-honed blade.

Leo and Aris had been summoned by one of their father's ex-Carbonari guards to deal with "the intruders." Ricciotti himself had been mysteriously absent all day—Aris had offered only that he was *occupied elsewhere with the business of rebellion*, and Leo hadn't pressed for details—so in his absence the guardsmen deferred to the elder brother.

Aris, for his part, was much more interested in Elsa's companion.

"Vico!" he crowed, sauntering inside the circle of guards surrounding the intruders. For a moment Leo didn't recognize the man standing beside Elsa and thought his brother must have gotten it wrong. In Leo's mind, Vincenzo was still a gangly youth, all knees and elbows, quick with a rapier but even quicker with a verbal jibe.

"There he is!" Vincenzo greeted Aris with a wide grin and a clap on the shoulder. "Been too long, *cumpari*."

Leo watched, stunned. It was all too surreal. What was Elsa doing here in the company of a Carbonaro? Ever since that first reunion in Nizza, where Leo came face-to-face with his father and realized he would have to protect Elsa from him, Leo had been constructing a story in his mind. In the story, he sacrificed whatever was necessary to keep Elsa safe and free, but now the fragile house of his self-told narrative came crumbling down around him.

He had failed. He had betrayed everyone who mattered and left his life behind, but in the end, none of it made a difference. Elsa came walking straight into the spider's nest of her own accord.

Elsa's eyes were on him. She moved as if to approach, but one of the guards lifted his pistol menacingly in response, and she halted.

"Oh, put your weapons away, you morons," Aris commanded as he slung an arm around Vincenzo's shoulders. "These two are to be our honored guests."

The guard reluctantly stepped aside. They did not obey Aris in the manner of subordinates following a trusted superior; rather, they slunk away as if afraid to invoke his wrath. As if the boss's mad sons were off their leashes, and anything might happen.

Elsa kept an eye on the guards as she passed them. She moved slowly, deliberately, over to Leo. He felt her proximity as if she carried an electric charge. He wanted to drink in the sight of her—the fall of her black hair, the dramatic sweep of her low cheekbones, the luminescence of her bronze-brown skin.

Elsa tilted her head, acknowledging him. "Leo."

Leo's throat went suddenly dry. He swallowed. "Hi." He almost asked her what she was doing here, but that would have been a stupid question. She was here for the editbook . . . wasn't she?

"Where's your father?" she asked, her tone guarded.

Leo lifted a shoulder awkwardly. "Damned if I know. It's not as if Ricciotti keeps me apprised of his presumably nefarious activities."

She attended to his words as if scrutinizing each syllable for hidden meaning, but she gave him nothing to work with in her reply. "Hmm."

Leo flexed his fingers, resisting the urge to grab her by the shoulders and shake her until she gave him an honest reaction. Yell, scream, threaten, cry—anything would be better than this smooth, impassive shield. It was torture being so close to her and yet having no idea what she was thinking, as if she weren't really there at all.

"So, is this place . . . like Casa?" Elsa asked, her tone carefully neutral.

Leo stared at her, trying to gauge her meaning. Was she asking if it was safe to talk freely? And if so, did he even have a definitive answer to give her? He now knew who—or what, rather—was spying through the windows, but he couldn't be sure that creature was the only tool they had for keeping track of him. He decided to hedge his bets and say, "In some ways it's similar."

She nodded, her expression still composed, and Leo had no idea whether she'd taken his meaning. It was like speaking with a stranger, as if Elsa had somehow purged the memory of him from her mind.

"Chambers!" Aris announced, drawing Vincenzo over to join Leo and Elsa. "We must find you both chambers. You must be tired after your journey."

Vincenzo said, "You're too kind, Aris. But there is much to discuss."

"It can wait. It can wait! Father will return in the morning, and there will be ample time for talking politics then."

While Aris summoned someone from the household staff to prepare two of the guest rooms, Leo stood paralyzed. This wasn't happening. Perhaps if he squeezed his eyes shut tightly enough, the world would revert to the way things ought to be, with the girl he loved safely back in Pisa.

Elsa set her carpetbag on a padded bench at the foot of the freshly made bed. Her guest room here did not have all the useful accommodations of her rooms in Casa della Pazzia—no scriptological supplies in sight—but it had a similar degree of pointless lavishness to the decor. The sight alone exhausted her, all that carved wood and intricately patterned upholstery.

Though if she was being honest with herself, the room wasn't the problem. It stung worse than she'd thought it would, seeing Leo again like that. Even with all her mental preparation, it still felt as if someone had whacked her in the diaphragm with a walking stick, driving all the breath from her lungs with one quick slap of wood on skin.

A part of her wanted to believe what Faraz believed—that

Leo had been tricked into betraying them back in Nizza, and that Garibaldi had held him hostage in a prison worldbook ever since. But here was the evidence, as cold and unforgiving as the stony landscape outside: Leo, wandering unfettered through his father's stronghold, his beloved older brother at his side. He could have walked right out the front door anytime he wanted, but he chose to stay.

While Elsa banged her head against the problem of how to find the editbook, he chose to stay. While Faraz and Porzia tore into each other like starving wolves, he chose to stay. While Vincenzo deceived his superior, and in so doing possibly burned his connection to the Carbonari who meant everything to him, Leo chose to stay. After all that strife, to see the proof that Porzia was right . . . it was almost more than Elsa could bear.

She heard footsteps out in the hall, and Leo paused in her open doorway. *Think of the devil and he shall appear*, as Alek would say.

"Hello, Leo," she said, her voice tight with contained anger.

He stood by the door for a moment, uncertain, before crossing the room to her. He leaned close and lowered his voice. "You shouldn't have come," he hissed. "I can't keep you safe here."

Under her breath, Elsa replied, "I don't need you to protect me. I never asked for that."

"I forgot," he said bitterly. "Elsa the island, who never needs anything from anyone."

"Funny, then, how it was me who stuck with Faraz and Porzia when you abandoned them."

Leo's eyes widened and he leaned back, as if the words hit him like a slap. "I did it *for you*—"

"For me! Is that a terrible joke?" The hurt and rage she had worked so hard to lock away threatened to come bubbling to the surface, and Elsa had to squeeze her eyes shut for a moment to push it back down. "I don't. Want. To talk about this."

"Of course," he said tightly. "Stubborn as ever, I see."

"Mm, yes. I stubbornly persist in wanting to make my own decisions. How very unreasonable of me."

He sighed at the acidity in her tone. "I didn't come here to fight."

"And you're doing a bang-up job of that."

"Elsa, please, I—"

He reached for her arm, but she slipped out of reach and walked over to the door. She rested a hand on the knob suggestively. "I'm tired."

Leo cleared his throat. "Right. Good night, then." He retreated awkwardly out of the room. In the hall he turned to give her a searching look, but Elsa shut the door in his face.

This was hardly the time to fall to pieces, not now that she'd infiltrated her enemy's stronghold. It was Vincenzo's life on the line, too, if she let slip her true feelings. So, with grim determination, Elsa resolved to set all thoughts of Leo aside. She would get him out if she could, as per Rosalinda's wishes, but her one true mission was to retrieve the editbook.

It was already light out when Elsa woke, but the sun seemed to have forgotten to bring any warmth with it this morning. She threw on a dressing gown over her thin white shift and fished out her thickest pair of socks to ward against the chilly floors. Good thing she'd found the energy before bed to wash the road dust off her face; the water in her washbasin, which had been pleasantly warm before, had cooled overnight and was now frigid.

Elsa was still standing in front of her carpetbag, trying to decide whether she should properly unpack, when there was a knock on the door.

She opened the door to find Aris standing on the other side. His eyes raked down her frame, as if simultaneously shocked and pleased at her state of undress. Elsa yanked her robe closed over her nightgown and folded her arms angrily.

"Yes?" she prompted.

Aris leaned casually against her doorframe. "It's time for breakfast, if you eat that sort of thing."

"All right."

He didn't budge.

She said, "I'll just put on some proper clothes, then, shall I?"

"Oh, signorina, don't go to any trouble on my account," he replied with a smirk.

Elsa closed the door in his face. Apparently, this was becoming a habit with the Garibaldi boys.

A minute later, as she dressed, it occurred to her that she ought to have asked Aris for directions to the dining room before closing him out. Oh, well. She'd have to find her way on her own.

Her limited experience with large European estate houses got her as far as guessing that the dining room would be downstairs from the bedchambers. The house was eerily silent, which made her miss the constant whirr and clatter of Casa's house-bots and the periodic shrieking of children at play. Odd, how she'd filtered out the background noise at the time and only noticed it retroactively from its absence.

This place wasn't a home. It reminded her more of the graveyard in Paris, that night when they'd dug up the false remains of Charles Montaigne.

The quiet did, however, assist Elsa in discovering the location of the dining room. She caught the muffled sound of voices and followed it until she glimpsed Vincenzo through an open doorway.

Between Elsa and the dining room was a narrow butler's pantry where a young woman appeared to be working. She had pale skin and neatly tied mouse-brown hair, and she wore an apron over a plain dress. She was lifting a silver food tray out of a square hole in the wall, not unlike the trapdoor that Casa's food train emerged from. At Elsa's approach the poor girl jerked like a spooked animal, nearly fumbling the tray, and her eyes went wide as saucers. She quickly dropped her gaze to the floor and muttered, "Signorina," squeezing back against the wall to give Elsa room to pass.

For a second Elsa froze in place. She'd meant to say hello; with her friendly overture rebuffed before it had even begun, she couldn't think how to proceed. It seemed the girl wanted Elsa out of the way and in the dining room, so without a better idea of what to do, she complied.

Leo and Aris were already seated with Vincenzo at the table. There was only one place setting left unclaimed, so Elsa had no choice but to slide into the chair beside Leo. No Garibaldi yet, and if the number of plates was any indication, he did not plan to breakfast with them.

As soon as Elsa was settled, the girl came in through the side entrance, balancing the tray of food on one arm and carrying a carafe in the other hand.

"Who is that?" Elsa whispered to Leo as the girl set the carafe on the table and began serving them from the tray.

"Who?"

Elsa leaned away to give the young woman access to her plate, then waited for her to move on to the other side of the table. "*Her.*"

"Oh, I don't know," Leo said. "Part of the household staff."

His dismissiveness stunned her. While Elsa understood that an automated household like Casa was the exception rather than the rule here in Europe, she had little experience with servants and found the situation disquieting. Everyone pretended the girl who brought the food was invisible, or at least beneath their notice. It didn't seem right.

Elsa and Jumi were the closest Veldana came to royalty, on account of their scriptological talents, and they still tended their own vegetable garden and raised their own chickens and kept their own cottage. The concept of "lower" classes—people who did not matter—was a foreign one.

Elsa made herself push those thoughts aside to be mulled over later and focused on her breakfast instead. Her plate now held a stack of paper-thin brown pancakes, folded over. She prodded them gently with her fork and discovered melted cheese inside.

"Buckwheat crepes," Aris said from across the table. "They're French."

The group spoke of nothing in particular until the servant girl had finished her task and vanished from the room.

Aris commenced eating with a healthy appetite. "So, Signorina da Veldana," he said in between bites, "my father has an unfortunate history with you. What assurances do I have that you aren't here to stab us all to death in our sleep?"

Elsa nearly choked in surprise at his bluntness, and had to clear her throat with a mouthful of coffee. "Uh, well . . . for one thing, I'm no use with a blade."

Aris shrugged. "A well-timed laboratory explosion, then."

"Mm, that would seem more likely, wouldn't it?" Elsa agreed. "I can give you no assurances, because you can never be truly sure what lies in someone else's heart. Isn't that right, Leo?"

Leo's eyes widened and he swallowed heavily, as if he were shocked to find the verbal jousting suddenly aimed at him. He declined to answer.

Across the table, Vincenzo was watching her with a look that said, *Careful*, but Elsa had a feeling that careful wasn't going to get her anywhere. Trying to earn Aris's trust was like hunting a mythical beast that could never be caught. It seemed the only way to get him to shed his suspicion would be to make him intrigued instead.

Before Elsa had time to test her theory, their conversation was interrupted by the clomp of boots in the hall, and Garibaldi burst into the dining room.

Everyone except Aris froze with their forks in midair and stared at the sudden arrival. Garibaldi swept his gaze over them in a way that noted and quickly dismissed the presence of the guests. Instead, he turned his attention to his eldest son.

"I hire a cook who trained with the finest pastry chef in Marseilles, and this is what you waste her talents on."

"I'm partial to crepes," Aris said, still eating.

Garibaldi pulled out a chair and threw himself down at the head of the table, then he kicked up his dusty boots, uncaring of the diners. It was his house and his food, and he'd rest his boots on his table if he damn well wished, apparently.

"Elsa da Veldana," he said. "I wasn't expecting you."

"Surprise," said Elsa.

"I'm rather curious to know how you found us." He spread his hands, indicating the fortress around them. "The remote location was a selling point, not an accident."

Elsa opened her mouth to reply, but Vincenzo cut in. "That

would be my doing. Friends in low places. Information flows both ways through the Carbonari network, I'm afraid."

Garibaldi turned his attention upon Vincenzo with an apparent lack of recognition, so he introduced himself. "Vincenzo Cavallo. I studied with Rosalinda Scarpa, if you recall."

Garibaldi nodded once, his expression so closed off that Elsa couldn't tell whether he actually did recall. "Well," he said, "it is indeed a surprise. I can't imagine the Order is very pleased with this development."

Keep your lies close to the truth, Faraz had told her. So she said, "The Order of Archimedes never did anything for me. If you'd killed Jumi, they would have let out sighs of relief and taken consolation from her death. 'At least that troublesome woman is gone,' they'd have said." Elsa didn't have to fake the anger in her voice. "My mother taught me to use all my skills in defense of Veldana. Our philosophy is, I think, not so dissimilar from yours, when you get right down to it."

Garibaldi nodded. "They want to slap reins on us all. They're cowards, terrified to leave the sanctity of their laboratories and actually engage with the world."

His words sounded like old, well-worn rhetoric, not an opinion he'd put any effort into freshly considering.

"Losing the editbook puts my world in a precarious position. It was our trump card." Elsa slid her plate away, food half-eaten, and rested her elbows on the table. "In light of this, I am prepared to make what political alliances are necessary to ensure Veldana's independence. And given our . . . antagonistic relationship with European pazzerellones, I believe you are best positioned to shield us from the Order. I am prepared to overlook the past if our current needs require it."

"How practical of you," Garibaldi said. From his tone, Elsa

couldn't quite be sure if he was mocking or sincere. "Is the Veldana worldbook secure?"

"For the moment." Elsa allowed herself a quick glance at Leo; his gaze was on his plate, but the frown line between his brows told her he was listening. Listening and believing? Hard to tell. "The imperialist tendencies of European powers are a cause for concern, though. We have no army to defend our independence."

Garibaldi waved a hand, dismissing this concern. "Armies are of no consequence when you have science. Technology has the power to liberate more than just our minds, if you can find the courage to use it."

The serving girl reappeared with a fifth cup and a fresh carafe in order to pour a coffee for her master. Elsa could not help but marvel at Garibaldi's hypocrisy. Here he was expounding upon his own ideological superiority—the importance of an Italian republic run by and for the people—when he employed servants in his own house. Vincenzo had made it sound like the Carbonari were concerned with the welfare of common people, but who exactly did Garibaldi plan to liberate? Wealthy merchants and landowners?

Jumi had always impressed upon Elsa that European politics were a farce. And this conversation was not doing much to disabuse her of that notion.

"In any case," Garibaldi was saying, "even if the Order is content to leave you alone, I imagine the French will be after Veldana soon enough."

"The French," she echoed. "Really."

He took a folding knife from the breast pocket of his suit jacket and scraped beneath his fingernails with the tip of the blade. "Not officially, of course, but the Third Republic is quite the collector of pazzerellones and their creations. When they can get away with it."

"I've heard that warning before." When she'd first arrived on Earth after her mother's abduction, Alek had smuggled her off to Casa della Pazzia for that very reason: to keep her out of the hands of governments.

"Don't worry." Garibaldi put the knife away and kicked his boots off the table edge to stand. "Veldana will be the first official ally of the Republic of Italy. I'll render you untouchable."

Elsa leveled an impassive gaze at him, swallowing the sharp retort that so desperately wanted to bubble out of her. The French were the least of her worries; much worse were her fears about what would happen when Aris figured out how to use the edit-book. But if any flicker of her true feelings crossed her face, Garibaldi missed it. He was already walking away.

After breakfast, Elsa retreated to the solitude of her bedroom, needing time to shake off the disquiet that Garibaldi's words had set upon her. *Render* was not a verb one applied to one's allies and equals.

For this one moment, Elsa allowed herself to think of Veldana, to wish she could be home tending to her mother's health; perhaps they would walk down to the newly scribed shore together, if Jumi felt well enough. But home was in a worldbook back in Pisa, and she was here.

An empty writing desk stood in the corner of her room. Elsa had brought a few basic scriptological supplies with her, and the task of laying them out neatly atop the polished wood gave her some small comfort. The familiarity of ink bottle and fountain pen and clean white pages made her feel more in control of the situation.

"So how did you really find us?"

Elsa glanced up—it was Aris, leaning casually against the frame of her open doorway.

"What do you mean?" she said innocently, going back to the task of arranging her scriptological supplies on the writing desk.

"Oh, come now." He tilted his head to one side, watching her with those too-familiar amber eyes. "You are a polymath. You can't expect me to believe you'd stoop so low as to rely upon common spy-work to find us."

"I'm sure I don't know what you're implying."

He pushed away from the doorframe and sauntered closer, though his approach did not seem aggressive so much as curious. "I must know how you did it, how you circumvented the block I placed on tracking Leo." A grin pulled at the corner of his mouth. "I'm going to lose sleep over this, signorina. It's cruel to leave me in suspense."

"I didn't," she said in earnest.

Aris narrowed his eyes at her, suspicious of her apparent sincerity. Meeting his gaze, Elsa realized this was an opportunity to gain his confidence.

"I didn't," she said again. "I couldn't figure a way through your block, so I found a different target."

She went to the bench at the foot of the bed, where she'd set down her carpetbag. She reached inside and produced the plague doctor mask, holding it up for Aris to see.

His eyes went wide, and then he laughed. "Is that mine?"

"Leo had it, but the ownership points to you." She passed the mask to him. "Keep it—let it serve as a reminder."

"A reminder?" He arched an eyebrow at her. "Of what?"

Elsa made herself smile. "That you're far too clever for your own good."

He held the mask up to his face, looking at her through the round eyeholes. When he spoke, his voice echoed weirdly in the mask's long snout. "There is no such thing as being too clever, signorina. There is only not clever enough."

"Call me Elsa."

He pulled the mask away from his face and turned it over in his hands, running his fingertips over the slight imperfections where the cracks had sealed. After a moment he said, "Elsa," rolling the name around in his mouth in a fashion she didn't entirely appreciate. "It's a European name."

"A nickname, convenient for its familiarity in both worlds," she answered, keeping her tone carefully neutral. Her full name was Elsunani, but she wasn't about to give that away.

"Hmm." Aris went suddenly still and looked up from the mask, his gaze piercing. "Why are you here, Elsa?"

"I believe Italian unification would serve the political interests of Veldana."

Aris kept staring.

"Or perhaps I'm here for Leo," she offered.

He blinked once, slowly, his gaze unwavering.

"Or I want the editbook back," Elsa concluded. "It's certainly one of those three motivations."

"Yes," he agreed. "But which one?"

She shrugged. "You'll have to wait and see."

He laughed, and just like that the tension left him and he was in motion again, sauntering toward the door. "I think I'm going to enjoy this, Elsa da Veldana," he threw over his shoulder as he went.

When he was gone, Elsa let out a heavy breath. She hoped she had said enough to intrigue him, but nothing he would not already have thought of for himself. Rosalinda had been right: this was a dangerous game.

*　*　*

The grand ballroom's south-facing windows painted bright rhomboids of sunlight on the smooth wood floor. Or perhaps it should be renamed the dueling room, Leo thought, since fencing practice was the only activity for which he'd seen it used.

Vincenzo wrote letters in the air with the tip of his foil, warming up his wrist. "Have you been practicing with Rosalinda?"

Leo shot him a sidelong glance. "Not as much as I'd like. It can be hard to get away, you know." Was that an innocent question? Or was Vincenzo trying to remind him that they were both loyal to the same mentor?

"I don't get to Toscana much, myself. Spend too much time away on assignment."

"Nature of the job, I'd guess," said Leo. In the intervening years since Venezia, he'd heard nothing of Vincenzo from Rosalinda, but that was to be expected. Carbonari did not openly discuss the secret missions of their colleagues with outsiders.

"En garde?" Vincenzo proposed.

"Sure, why not." Leo stood opposite him and they began trading attacks.

Aris was supposed to be with them. He was not. Leo did not like to think what that might mean—what nefarious task might be delaying his brother.

As if summoned by Leo's thoughts, Aris entered the ballroom with an indignant declaration. "You started without me!"

"Well," Leo said between parries, "you're late."

Especially now that his brother was watching, Leo had to calculate his movements with the utmost care, calibrating his apparent skill level so as to beat Vincenzo narrowly. It was a precarious dance; years had passed since the last time they'd practiced together, and Leo had to feel him out with tentative forays. Step and lunge, parry and riposte, study his attacks and test his reactions. Aris would be displeased if Leo lost to Vincenzo, but Leo couldn't appear overly skilled either, not after feigning rustiness during their own bouts.

Vincenzo's arrival certainly did complicate things. Not the least of which was Elsa. Were they in on this together, whatever *this* turned out to be? Or did his help only extend as far as Ricciotti's cause, regardless of Elsa's true intentions? How much of an ally was he, and to whom? Leo would have to figure out where Vincenzo's true loyalties lay, and he'd have to get to the truth before Aris did.

Vincenzo landed a solid touch, thanks to Leo's distracted state of mind, and Aris snorted disappointment at his brother's weak performance. "Please do pull your head out of the clouds and pay attention, Leo. You're making us look bad."

"Very well," Leo said, dropping his guard. He pulled his fingers out of the rings in the grip and tossed the practice foil at Aris. "Show us how it's done."

Aris plucked the foil out of the air and flashed a wicked grin. "As you wish, little brother."

Aris and Vincenzo squared off against each other, saluted with their foils, and then stepped together in a sudden flurry of lunges and parries. Aris needed no time to feel out his opponent, having watched the previous match, and he was aggressive with his attacks.

Vincenzo held his own. A bead of sweat crawled down his temple onto his cheek, but he was grinning right back at Aris. They were well-matched in a duel, following each other like dancers, back and forth in synchronized steps. It almost seemed as if the *clack clack clack* of the foils against each other was actually the sound of electricity crackling between them.

Back in Venezia, Aris and Vincenzo had been good friends. Young Aris had been thirsty as a dry sponge for attention, and Vincenzo—only a couple of years older—had often accommodated that need. Leo had been too young to notice at the time, but in retrospect, he wondered if it had been something more than simple friendship. At least on Vincenzo's part.

Leo frowned. Was Vincenzo here for Elsa . . . or was he here for Aris?

There was a soft knock on the bedroom door, so soft that Elsa was not entirely certain she hadn't imagined it, but when she paused to listen, she thought she could hear someone shuffling nervously in the hall outside. Soft and nervous meant it almost certainly was not Aris again, so she opened the door. And indeed it wasn't Aris: it was the serving girl from that morning, the one who'd cowered against the wall to let Elsa pass.

"I am sorry to disturb, signorina . . ." The girl spoke with an accent Elsa couldn't place, and she seemed uncertain with her use of Italian. Or perhaps it was simply this situation making her nervous.

"It's no trouble," Elsa said, trying to sound patient and entirely undisturbed.

The girl wrung her hands together, and the words spilled quickly from her lips. "Signorina, I wanted to apologize for not attending you this morning. We have not welcomed any women guests in the time of my employ, and . . ."

"Attending?" Elsa interrupted, not sure what they were talking about.

"Assisting with your *toilette*. Your hair, your laces . . ."

For a moment Elsa simply stared, struggling to understand why anyone would think an apology was needed. The girl looked to be around the same age as Elsa, if not somewhat older. In Veldana, it was true her scriptological abilities afforded her a measure of respect from other villagers, but still—nobody came around to tie her laces for her in the mornings. Jumi had always taught her power meant responsibility, not pampering.

"That's really not necessary," said Elsa. "As you can see, I've quite given up on corsets." She was wearing a leather tunic over a cotton shirt and trousers tucked into tall boots.

"Your hair, then," the girl persisted.

This right here might win the contest for the strangest conversation Elsa had ever found herself a part of. "Let us begin anew, you and I. My name is Elsa."

The girl bobbed her head deferentially. She did not offer her own name.

"And you are . . . ?"

The girl's eyes widened slightly, as if she were edging onto uncertain ground, but she said, "Colette, signorina."

"Well, Colette—you know you don't have to call me 'signorina' when there's no one else around to hear. Up until a month ago, I'd lived my whole life in a cottage with a thatched roof. We kept a chicken coop and a vegetable garden, and the food didn't cook itself." Elsa offered her a tentative smile.

Colette returned it. "As you say . . . *Elsa*." She spoke the name as if it were a secret code of conspiracy between them.

A plan began to grow in Elsa's mind. Servants were invisible. They overheard conversations and glimpsed private activities. They could go anywhere in the house with the flimsiest of excuses. It seemed probable they would even have copies of all the keys.

Yes, this was how she would do it. She would befriend the servants. And then these people who mattered so little, who were treated like ghosts—*they* would be Garibaldi's downfall. What could be more fitting? He would be defeated by his own hypocrisy.

11

EVERY DAY IS A JOURNEY, AND THE JOURNEY ITSELF IS HOME.

—*Matsuo Basho*

For most of the distance the path hugged the side of the sea cliffs, staying relatively flat while the mountains rose on their right like a herd of ragged hunchbacked beasts. Porzia knew it was only a couple of kilometers to Manarola, and another couple after that from Manarola to Corniglia, but they all had luggage and supplies to carry, and most of them had not slept particularly well. Even if they'd been well rested and better prepared, they would still have had to set a slow pace on account of the younger children. Aldo was only eight and tiring quickly.

The sun crawled higher and the morning grew hot. Porzia felt grateful for the breeze off the water that cooled the sweat on the back of her neck. Revan was in the lead with her brother Sante, both of them seemingly indefatigable. Faraz had taken up the rear, making certain no one fell too far behind. Porzia found herself trudging along in relative solitude, which gave her time to agonize over the choices she'd made.

Where was Elsa now? She could be on Garibaldi's doorstep already, though she would still need to find and steal the edit-book. Surely that process would take longer than this hike along the Cinque Terre coastline. Porzia couldn't bring herself to abandon the children—not until they were safely tucked away in the Corniglia ruins, at least. But guilt and doubt gnawed at her.

The tops of a few cheerily painted buildings came into view, peering over the ridge that stood between them and Manarola. The path angled downward, closer to the sea, and circumnavigated around the base of the ridge, which jutted out into the water.

Revan was also focused on what lay ahead, though he seemed more disquieted about the curious looks their group was eliciting from the fishermen floating in their rowboats nearby than he was about the condition of the trail. He fell back to walk beside her. "Are we expecting trouble here?"

"No. Not from the locals, anyway," Porzia said.

He eyed her. "But from someone else, yes?"

She sighed. "I don't know how much Elsa told you."

"Next to nothing."

"Well, suffice it to say, now that Elsa and Leo are both gone, we're less likely to be of interest to anyone with ill intent."

By now the village was in full view, and Revan's attention focused like a searchlight on the details of Manarola.

"Why is the town so crowded and clumped together?" he said. "And the buildings so tall?"

Porzia laughed, surprised. Had he even stepped outside Casa della Pazzia to see the rest of Pisa? Were the isolated villages of Cinque Terre effectively his introduction to Earth? "Wait until you see a real city like Paris or Roma. This is nothing." After a pause, she asked, "Why are you still here, Revan? Why did you give the portal device to me instead of using it to go home?"

Revan showed her a lopsided grin. "Well you did seem hopelessly in need of assistance."

"We also seemed rude—which I'm sorry about—and our situation was not your problem, which remains true now."

"I love my home, but . . . Veldana is so small. We like to pretend the real world doesn't matter, that it can't touch us, but after Jumi's abduction we can't cling to that illusion anymore," he said. "If I'm to have any hope of keeping my people safe, I need to learn about Earth."

"Pazzerellones aren't exactly the safest company to keep, and if anything happens to you, Elsa won't be pleased with me."

"Elsa thinks it's all on her to protect Veldana." Revan snorted. "She's wrong. In a community, people protect each other."

Porzia wondered what it was like growing up with strong ties to one's village, with *Veldanese* the only aspect of identity that mattered. With no centuries-long familial legacy to live up to. Even imagining it felt like blasphemy.

Past Manarola, the trail ran beside the railway on the inland side of the tracks. Both trail and tracks stayed low near the water, relatively straight and flat. But Porzia knew what lay ahead. They still had to scale La Lardarina, the stairs that switchbacked up the side of a hundred-meter-high promontory, atop which perched the village of Corniglia.

By the time they reached the foot of the stairs, Faraz was carrying extra luggage and Revan had Aldo riding on his back. The fact that self-serious Aldo was tolerating this arrangement spoke volumes about Revan's skill at handling children. He might not be a pazzerellone, but right now he was helping in exactly the way Porzia needed.

Her feet were starting to hurt in a way that promised blisters. She was wearing her most sensible shoes—a pair of low-heeled ankle boots—but even these were not intended for rocky footpaths through the country. To add insult to injury, Sante had run ahead and was lounging on the bottom steps of La Lardarina, waiting for everyone else to catch up.

Porzia sighed and resigned herself to the inevitability of how sore she would feel tomorrow. She was breathing hard after only a minute on the tortuous stairs, and she was deeply glad she'd had the sense to pass on wearing her usual corset. Meanwhile, even with the added weight of Aldo on his back, Revan seemed to be deliberately slowing his pace out of consideration for the rest of them.

At the top of the promontory they crossed through the narrow streets of Corniglia, aiming for the opposite side of town. The locals stared at the bizarre procession of children, and Revan stared right back with naked curiosity. On the far side they picked their way through terraced vineyards, and then into the woodland where the ruins were hidden.

Porzia shut off the optical defenses, and the ancient, crumbling castle appeared out of nowhere. Revan gasped in awe; Sante ran ahead, excited to see a place he'd been allowed to visit only a few times before. Everyone else was too tired to muster much of a reaction.

Porzia pushed sweaty strands of hair out of her face, unable to remember the last time she had felt so disheveled. Nonetheless, she also felt a sense of accomplishment at having delivered the children to their new safe haven. She briskly ushered everyone inside.

The cavernous entryway was cool, musty, and dim. Dust motes floated through the filtered sunlight from the high windows, and the children's shuffling feet seemed loud in the sudden silence.

Aldo scowled. "Are there books? I bet there won't even be anything to *read* here," he said darkly, as if this were the most damning criticism anyone could possibly level at a place.

"Oh, come now," Porzia said with forced brightness. "We don't need stories—we've embarked on an adventure of our own. It's fun."

Olivia wrinkled her nose. "It's dusty, is what it is. I don't remember it being this dusty."

Privately, Porzia thought "dusty" was a generous understatement. When she spoke, her falsely bright tone started to turn brittle. "All right, everyone. Leave your things here for now, and let's get the bedrooms cleaned so we can set up sleeping arrangements."

The grand stairway in the entry hall ended halfway up in midair, above a pile of rubble. Instead, Porzia led them to the servants' stairwell in the rear—narrow, steep, and dark, but at least all the steps were intact. The rooms above were mostly unfurnished, and the children grumbled about the absence of mattresses.

Porzia asked Revan to coordinate the usage of brooms and mops, the bedrolls in need of arranging, and the blistered feet in need of doctoring. Then she snuck back downstairs to search the laboratories for a second portal device to replace the one Casa had stolen out of Elsa's escape kit.

By the time she found what she needed and returned to the entrance hall for Elsa's box, Faraz was coming to look for her. "What are you doing?"

"There's still an escape plan that needs to be set up in Trento, in case you've forgotten," she said, but she couldn't find the energy to put any heat into the words.

"I hadn't," Faraz said. "But are you up to it? The return portal will land you back in Riomaggiore, and you'll have to do the walk a second time today."

"I am well aware of how portals work, thank you."

Their nascent argument was interrupted by the sudden appearance of Simo, the middle-aged housekeeper, ambling into the entrance hall while humming tunelessly to himself. He carried a lit candle in a brass holder and was using the flame to light the wall sconces. It was the middle of the day, with hours left until nightfall, but Porzia didn't have the heart to point out his mistaken timing.

When Simo spotted them still standing by the door, he broke into a wide grin and called across the room, "Simo!"

"Hello, Simo." Though it pained her, Porzia forced herself to return the smile. Then he ambled onward, down another corridor, doggedly pursuing his pointless task. Simo had been textualized years ago, before Porzia was born; when a specific person got added to the text of a worldbook, it wrought terrible harm on their mental faculties, and some scriptologists even hypothesized that textualization impaired free will.

Porzia's siblings didn't know who Simo was—who Simo had been once—but Porzia had figured it out, and that knowledge felt like a briar grown around her heart, twisting its thorns into her. He was her uncle, her father's brother, and even worse than Simo's fate was the knowledge of how her own parents had dealt with it: sending him away, hiding him out of sight somewhere he could be conveniently forgotten. Telling the world he was dead. When Porzia thought about what they'd done, she choked on the shame of it.

Growing up was defined by the realization that one's parents were fallible, and Porzia never felt older than she did here. This was her parents' most egregious mistake, staring her in the face every hour.

"I hate this place," she confessed to Faraz.

"It's not so bad here. I've seen worse," he said.

"No, it's awful, being exiled from our own home to this horrid castle."

"You don't get it. You can't!" Faraz shouted, startling her.

"You have parents and siblings and cousins . . . you've lived your whole life in the same house where you were born, in a town where everyone speaks your language. You don't know the first thing about what it's like to have no family, no home—to be cast adrift on the world!"

Porzia felt as if she'd been slapped. She couldn't remember the last time Faraz had been truly furious with her, if such a time had ever happened. Raised voices were standard fare in the Pisano family, but tempers generally cooled as quickly as they flared. This was different—this was Faraz, who let nothing rattle him, who never raised his voice even when they argued. Faraz was supposed to be as steady and immovable as the sea. Who was this stranger wearing his face?

Her expression of shock did nothing to slow the torrent of his words. "You might miss him, but you don't *need* him. But me—he was all I had, Porzia! I told myself I could live without the parents I hardly ever knew, without the mentor who sent me away to a foreign country, because at least Leo and I had each other. Brothers by choice, forgetting the past and moving forward together. Hah! So much for that."

Tentatively, Porzia reached for his arm. "But . . . you *are* family to us . . ."

"Ugh!" he said, pulling away from her touch. "Save your propaganda for an Order meeting."

He stormed out of the entrance hall, leaving her alone. She spread her hands in the air, at a loss, and said to herself, "My God, do I not have time for this."

Porzia decided to go as far as Manarola before opening a portal with the doorbook, just to be safe, since they'd discovered Aris had invented the ability to track portals. Best to protect their location. So she descended those infernal stairs and took the seaside pathway, then hid behind a rise in the landscape so none of the locals would see her disappear.

The untested doorbook destination took her to Trento on the first try, and Porzia stepped through the portal into a broad piazza with an elaborate fountain and a Romanesque cathedral, all columns and arches and a large rose window. At right angles to the cathedral was a long building with a crenelated roofline that ended in a clock tower. It felt almost familiar from her research and scribing the destination with Elsa, and yet also disquietingly different—not exactly how she'd imagined it to be.

Porzia shrugged off the sensation, put on her best air of *I am definitely supposed to be here*, and snuck into the clock tower to hide the supplies for Elsa.

Alek's bad hip was already bothering him. The uphill hike from the village to the swirling Edgemist of Veldana felt steeper than it used to be, and the brief but intense cold of the portal worsened the ache. No way around it—he was getting old.

Stepping out of the portal, Alek arrived in the cavernous octagonal library of Casa della Pazzia. Except for a pair of Casa's bots standing idle, the library was empty, and the house sounded eerily quiet.

"Hello . . . ? Revan?" Alek called, and then immediately felt foolish. A whole day had passed since the boy's disappearance; of course Revan wasn't standing right beside the Veldana world-book, waiting for an adult to follow him out.

"Good evening, Signor de Vries." The house's disembodied voice echoed in the resonant hollow of the domed ceiling. "You have returned."

The pair of house-bots rolled up to greet him, one on either side, which Alek found a bit unnerving. "Good evening, Casa. Would you mind directing me—"

The bot on his right snatched the portal device away from him, leaving Alek to blink at his empty palm.

"I'm afraid I must confiscate that," Casa said. "This is for your own protection, you see."

Alek frowned. "What do you think you're doing?"

"I've lost so many," the house lamented. "They're out in the dangerous world, naked of my protection. I cannot bear to lose anyone else."

Alek ran a hand over his thinning hair, exasperated. This explained why Revan hadn't returned; he felt certain Elsa would have sent him back to Veldana if she could have. But why would Gia instruct the house to confiscate portal devices?

"Casa, take me to Gia, please—or Porzia, if her mother's occupied at the moment."

"They're gone, they're all gone," Casa bemoaned. "Everyone has abandoned me except the youngest of the squalling progeny. I am a failure."

Alek cleared his throat. "Uh, right." The true depth of his present dilemma was beginning to dawn on him.

The house said, "But at least I have you, now."

12

I DO NOT BELIEVE THAT THIS WOMAN EASILY FINDS HER
EQUAL IN THE SCIENCE IN WHICH SHE EXCELS.
—*Gottfried Liebniz, regarding Maria Kirchin*

In the afternoon, Aris insisted he had something to show Elsa, and Elsa alone. He led her through the house, his eyes alight with devious intent, and grudgingly she followed. They went up to the sleeping chambers and then kept climbing to the floor above that.

"Where exactly are we going?" said Elsa.

"I can't tell you, obviously. It's a surprise." On the landing, Aris grabbed the banister post and swung himself around in a fast arc, angling toward the next flight of stairs.

Up again, and they came to a long, narrow room tucked between the eaves. The walls were cut off by the sharp angle of the roofline, such that there was enough room to stand in the middle but not on either side. A track of clean floor was worn through the layer of dust, as if Aris frequented this route.

Dryly, Elsa said, "Ooh, an attic. You always take me to the nicest places."

Aris simply tossed her an inscrutable look and followed the length of the room to a door at one end.

"A closet in the attic," Elsa amended. "Thrilling."

But when he grabbed the knob, the door opened onto bright daylight. It was a dazzling afternoon, the air crisp and dry, the sky a cloudless dome of blue.

Aris stepped through, and for a moment Elsa expected him to fall to his death, but instead he stepped onto solid ground. She followed, thoroughly disoriented, and looked around. They were in an odd sort of courtyard cut into the bedrock so the stone bounded it on three sides. The last side abutted the house, though thanks to the dramatic slope of the mountainside, the ground was nearly level with the eaves.

In the center of the courtyard squatted an enormous machine. Elsa's gaze skirted over the aluminum frame and stretched canvas of the wings, and she knew it immediately for a flier, though it was the first she'd ever seen. It had a gasbag as well for additional lift, which seemed necessary given the probable mass— the main body of the craft was as long as a railcar and nearly twice as wide.

Aris swept his arms open, as if presenting the airship to her. "Do you like it? I've just finished hooking up the engine to the flight apparatus. I thought you might care to join me on its maiden voyage."

"Yours then, I take it?" Elsa asked.

"Of course mine. Leo's been too busy sulking to do any serious work, and there are no other mechanists about. Besides, I like to think my signature genius is evident in the design," he said, a manic glint in his eyes.

"Perhaps," Elsa allowed. "I'm afraid I don't know your work well enough to tell one way or the other."

"Then allow me to introduce you." He held out a hand as if asking her to dance.

Elsa hesitated, then kicked herself for it; she was supposed to be pretending they were allies. She swallowed her reluctance and quickly took his hand, letting him lead her up a ramp into the cabin of the airship.

The interior of the cabin was not set up for passengers, Elsa discovered. Instead the space was equipped as a mobile laboratory, with racks of well-secured tools and workbenches bolted to the floor. Toward the front hulked the steam engine, which reached up to the ceiling and down below the deck. Elsa walked up to the gap where the floorboards ended; upon closer inspection, it looked as if the wing mechanisms were located in a crawl space beneath the passenger cabin.

Aris slipped past her and through a narrow passageway that ran along the side of the engine. "Come on!"

Elsa followed and found herself in a small pilot's cabin, encircled on three sides with large windowpanes. The windows were angled to allow the pilot to lean out past the hull and see the ground below. In the center of the cabin stood a console covered in a complex assortment of levers and wheels and gauges.

Aris went immediately to the controls and fired up the engine. "Retract the wings," he said, pushing up on a large lever, "release the wheel lock . . . and we're good to go."

The airship rolled forward, ponderous and slow. Elsa looked out the front window and spotted a shallow ramp that wrapped around one side of the fortress, giving the courtyard an outlet to the valley.

"Ready for her maiden voyage?" Aris asked.

"Wait." Elsa threw him a glare. "You seriously haven't tested this thing before? Not at all?"

"There's a first time for everything." He grinned.

They hit the top of the ramp and picked up speed, gravity assisting the steam-driven wheels. The fortress blurred by, close on their left. Ahead the ramp simply ended in a sheer cliff.

Elsa frowned at the drop-off. "This is probably a terrible idea, isn't it?"

"Too late now!" Aris crowed.

With a lurch that sent butterflies through her stomach, they dropped into the sky above the valley floor. Aris yanked the large lever, extending the wings; pistons churned and the wings pumped up and down, *chuff chuff chuff*, and their altitude steadily rose.

Elsa squeezed into the space between the controls and the front windows so she could lean out over the slanted glass. She had never before seen the earth from a bird's-eye perspective, and she drank in the sight. "It's like how you picture a world in your mind's eye when you're scribing it, but . . . but to be able to actually *see* everything . . ."

She couldn't find the words for this. The mountains took her breath away. What had seemed merely impressive and aesthetically pleasing from the ground suddenly became something more when viewed from above: an ancient story written in the landscape, the incomprehensibly large forces of nature locked in a constant conflict, playing out over the eons.

"I want to add mountains," she said.

Aris quirked an eyebrow at her. "Add mountains?"

"To Veldana. We don't have any mountains." She'd never thought of that as a lack in need of correcting before.

Suddenly, the airship gave a shudder so strong it rattled her teeth, and the steady *chuff-chuff* of the wing mechanisms working beneath the floorboards ground to a halt. The engine promptly filled the unexpected quiet with a piercing whine of escaping steam.

Elsa clapped her hands over her ears and shouted, "What's happening?"

Aris glanced out a side window to confirm what he probably already knew. "The wings have jammed."

"Obviously! But why?"

"I don't know!" Aris dashed back to the instrument panel. "We're losing altitude."

Elsa did not like the screech of that steam. She looked at the instruments and pointed to the pressure gauge. "We've got pressure building in the steam chamber. If the engine blows, we'll lose our chance to fix the wings."

Aris yanked back on the acceleration lever, but the screech didn't stop. "If the engine blows, like as not the hydrogen in the gasbag will ignite, and we'll be too dead to worry about what happens when the ship goes down."

"Fair point," she said. "So let's not explode, shall we?"

"Let's not," Aris agreed. "I'm open to ideas for how to avoid a fiery demise."

Elsa's mind raced, formulating and discarding a long list of solutions that would have worked if only she'd brought her laboratory worldbook with her. But the lab book was safely hidden in Trento, where Aris couldn't access it. She'd outsmarted herself. "There's got to be a valve we can loosen, just to buy us some time."

"There's one on the workshop side," Aris said. He rushed back down the passageway, with Elsa following close on his heels. "I added it in case I needed to borrow some steam power for the laboratory equipment."

Aris shoved his hand into a thick leather glove, grabbed the valve handle, and loosened the valve just a little. Steam hissed into the cabin, turning the air hot and humid. The pitch of the escaping steam lowered and then the screech faded out altogether. Aris waited another few seconds before closing the valve.

"That should do it for now," he said, tossing the leather glove aside.

Elsa said, "Where's the access hatch for the crawl space?"

"Right here." Aris yanked up on the floor panels and a trapdoor opened.

Elsa lowered herself into the crawl space feet-first, ducking her head to squeeze below the floorboards. The air was hot and stuffy, difficult to breathe, and everything was dark except for the little sunlight that snuck in through the gaps in the hull where the mechanisms connected to the wings outside.

"Hand me a lantern!" she called up to Aris.

He passed one down to her. "There's a hook on the ceiling to hang it from. You see?"

"Yeah, found it." Elsa hung the lantern, then turned her attention back to the mechanical problem at hand. At least she could see the gears now.

First she checked for breakages, but no failure points were evident. Then she searched for obstructions in the mechanism, anything that might have gummed up the works, but found none. Instead, it looked like the friction of running at full steam had heated the gears and deformed the metal enough to make everything grind to a halt.

"I need a wrench!"

A leather satchel full of wrenches landed behind her with a muffled clang. Elsa dragged the satchel around and rifled through its contents, selecting the proper-size wrench. She fitted it to the component she wanted to loosen and heaved, but the wrench handle wouldn't budge.

She yelled up to Aris, "I can't decouple the drive shaft from the wing mechanism! The engine's applying too much strain."

"Can you fix it without decoupling?" Aris called down.

"Get me some lubricant!"

There was no hope of actually fixing the problem in the air with the engine running. The best Elsa could hope to do was get the wings pumping again and keep them aloft long enough to perform a controlled landing instead of a crash.

Aris leaned down through the gap in the floor to pass her an oil canister with a long, narrow snout. Elsa took the lubricant and crawled closer to the gears.

Somewhere in the back of her mind, she observed Aris's strange behavior. Helpful and compliant, almost deferential. It seemed out of character; maybe he'd dropped his usual act on account of the mortal danger they were in. She had no time to puzzle it out now, though.

Elsa squirted lubricant over the gear teeth and along any other point of friction she could find. The gears scraped and ground together, making a horrible noise as they grudgingly began to rotate. The jammed-up pistons struggled to push the deformed gears into motion. *Chug . . . chug, chug chug chug.* As the components began to move Elsa backed away, shielding her head with one arm, not entirely certain the mechanism could handle the strain. But no chunks of metal went flying, and the wings gradually began to *chuff* against the air again.

Elsa twisted around in the cramped space and pulled herself out through the trapdoor. "I got things moving down there, but we're nowhere near full power and it could break down any minute, even with the reduced drive."

Aris nodded. "We'll have to do an emergency landing. No

way we're getting back the elevation we've lost without the wings fully functional."

Elsa followed him back into the pilot's cabin. While Aris went to the front window to look for potential landing sites, Elsa checked the gauges. The needle on the altimeter was still going down, but much slower than before—a controlled descent, for now at least.

"Adjust our heading ten degrees to port," Aris said.

"Port?" Elsa had no experience with nautical terms.

"Left."

Elsa grabbed the wheel and gently eased it counterclockwise, adjusting their course.

"Good, just there," Aris said, still looking out the window at the section of the valley floor he'd selected as an emergency landing site.

Elsa was also thinking ahead to their landing, though she was more concerned with the possibility of the impact rupturing the engine and igniting the gasbag.

She said, "I'm assuming the coal feed is automated?"

"Yes, you can shut it off here," Aris said, pointing to a lever.

"How long does it take the engine to cool after you cut the coal?"

"The steam tank will stay pressurized for ten minutes or so— maybe less, since we released some of the pressure."

Elsa checked the progress of the altimeter. "We'll be on the ground sooner than that."

It was a calculated risk either way. Cutting off the fuel input would mean a harder landing, but also a less explosive engine. Elsa did some quick math in her head and flipped the lever.

As the ground rose toward them, Elsa stepped aside and gave the controls back to Aris in the hope that he had some experience with landing flying machines. There wasn't time to ask. He course-corrected a bit, then leveled them off and adjusted the wing angle for maximum lift.

"Brace yourself!" Aris said, grabbing the edge of the console.

Elsa pressed her body against the doorframe and held on as best she could. *Wham!* They hit the valley floor hard enough to rattle her teeth and bounced back up into the air for a few stomach-lurching seconds. They landed again and stayed down this time, skidding along the grass for several meters before coming to a stop.

Aris released his death grip on the console. He tugged on the front of his waistcoat, straightening his somewhat disheveled clothes. "Well, that could have gone worse."

Elsa exhaled. "At least we didn't explode."

Aris turned to face Elsa and swept an appraising look over her, then pulled a handkerchief from his pocket. "Hold still."

"What—" she started to say, but Aris was already reaching forward to wipe her cheek with the handkerchief. She froze under his touch, and her pulse thrummed in her ears.

He was the enemy, Elsa knew that deep down in her bones, but she had to pretend to like him. And there was an unexpected tenderness to the way he wiped the smear of lubricant off her cheek. Suddenly she didn't know how she should feel.

"There," he said, "that's better."

Elsa tucked away her confusion and reached for dry wit instead. "Oh good. Now that my face is clean, we can trudge all the way up the dusty road in the heat of the afternoon."

As they left the crash site and started the long walk back to the fortress, Elsa actually found the weather to be pleasantly cool. Before she came to Europe, she had spent many an afternoon hiking in the Veldanese heat, surveying her world. She didn't admit this to Aris, though; if he felt guilty about their situation, that would serve her purposes.

But instead of apologizing, Aris glanced at her with a look of evaluation. "You handled yourself fairly well, I have to admit."

Elsa wasn't sure whether to be more irritated with his grudging praise or with the fact that he felt entitled to judge her skills in the first place. "You, on the other hand, were hardly any use at all."

A wicked grin spread across his face, and Elsa realized he'd played her. The whole thing—the flight, the breakdown, the midair repairs—it was all a setup.

A flash of anger heated her cheeks, and she stopped dead in her tracks to glare at him. "You know it's rude to test someone without warning them first."

Aris gave an unapologetic shrug. "I am my father's son. Besides, it wouldn't have been much of a test if you were forewarned."

Elsa snorted and recommenced trudging up the path. After a few meters traversed in silence, she said, "I could have just as easily made the situation worse instead of fixing it. What were you planning to do then?"

"I was confident you'd perform well. And anyway, I wanted to see it for myself: Elsa in action."

Through gritted teeth, she said, "You gambled with our lives."

"As it turns out, you're a solid bet," he replied, that grin of his returning.

"And you're unbelievable."

Elsa picked up her pace, stalking away from him. She didn't have to feign her irritation now; it was all too real. Her heart hammered against her ribs not so much from the exertion as from the anxiety of realizing just how little control she had over her situation. Rosalinda had been right to warn her about the Garibaldis. They were all spiders.

Dinner was a tense affair, for Leo at least. Aris gave off his usual air of impermeable insouciance, Vincenzo settled in as if he'd never parted ways with Aris, and even Elsa seemed to be edging toward cautious comfort at her new situation. Leo fumed inside— betrayed by his father and the universe at large, his sacrifice transmuted into a meaningless gesture.

Leo suspected Ricciotti had never harbored any intention of honoring their deal. And even if he had, he certainly wasn't going to honor it now that Elsa had practically offered herself up to him. Good God, what a fool Leo had been to think he could prevent this. There was no shame like the shame of being rendered ineffective.

There must have been dinner conversation, but Leo heard none of it. He was too busy mentally calculating whether it would be better to confront his father later, in private, and what he could say to fix Elsa's precarious situation. There must be *something* he could do.

After dinner, Ricciotti retired to his study to attend to business. Leo stood in the hall outside the closed door, hesitating, his stomach a nervous knot that threatened to reject what little food he'd managed to put into it. But he had to face his father, man to man.

Leo rallied his courage, grabbed the doorknob, and let himself inside.

Ricciotti was seated at his desk, looking over a handwritten report. "Amazing," he said, "how quickly a situation can fall to the wolves. The French police are already tightening their grip on the port district. We've hardly been gone two weeks."

"What?" said Leo from the doorway. Per usual, his father had neatly knocked him off balance. Ricciotti had a way of expecting everyone to follow his train of thought, without the assistance of any stated context—and failure, of course, was a sign of intellectual incapacity.

"Nizza," Ricciotti said, in a tone full of disappointment at his son's slowness. He'd been running a base of operations there when Leo caught up to him. And Nizza was where Leo had betrayed his friends.

It sparked anger in Leo's chest, where the fuel was already dry and crisp for the kindling. "Why should I care anything for Nizza? You never even spoke of the city when we lived in Venezia."

Ricciotti shrugged. "You still thought our name was Trovatelli then; we had a false identity to maintain. But Nizza was your grandfather's childhood home, and he took it as a blow when the king treated with France and left the city under French rule. A wrong he did not live to correct."

Leo's jaw tightened as he tried not to shout. "I came to discuss Elsa."

"What of her?" Ricciotti said. "I thought you'd be pleased. You've been moping ever since you left Pisa, and now one of your friends has come to visit."

Leo ground his teeth together and managed not to say, *She isn't here to visit, she's here to take back what I stole from her.* "We had an agreement. You cannot keep her here."

Ricciotti's eyebrows rose haughtily. "I'm not *keeping* anyone."

"You promised to leave her out of this!" Leo fumed.

"She showed up at our doorstep like a lost puppy. What would you have me do, Leo—turn her out, to wander the countryside alone?"

Ricciotti's gaze upon him was so calm, so smug, it made Leo want to scream. He was powerless against his father, and Ricciotti reveled in his control. Leo could do nothing to protect Elsa; he could not even win a simple argument.

"I hate you," Leo said, and left the study.

He stalked through the empty halls like a loose grommet rattling around inside a massive machine, redundant and unnoticed.

If Elsa truly sought an alliance, there would be no convincing her to leave. But if she'd come for the editbook, as Leo suspected, then there was a way to get her away from here: he would have to steal back the very same book he'd once stolen for Ricciotti.

Leo did not appreciate the irony.

It required an unexpected effort for Elsa to ferret out the location of the servants' stairs down to the lower levels. Garibaldi's fortress was enormous, and until that moment Elsa hadn't realized how much she'd relied on Casa's assistance to navigate the maze of hallways back in Pisa. Now there were no house-bots to lead her, and she had to deduce the layout for herself.

Once down on the proper floor, Elsa found the kitchen largely from the leftover smells of cooking and the residual heat of the ovens. She snuck closer and heard the banging of pots and pans, and the sound of two voices. She risked a quick glance inside.

Colette was helping an older woman—presumably the cook—clean up the kitchen for the night. They spoke a Latinate language unfamiliar to Elsa. It sounded rather like the dialect she'd overheard in Nizza, but with stronger overtones of French pronunciation. Elsa tucked herself against the wall beside the doorway and listened, ears straining to parse the words. She knew French and Italian and Latin, so it wasn't long before this new language began to clarify in her mind.

As the sounds resolved into sentences that carried meaning, Elsa supposed she ought to feel ashamed for spying on Colette and the cook. They were innocent in all this. But the voice of Elsa's inner, stone-cold pragmatist overruled her guilt. Anything to get the editbook—the welfare of two worlds rode on her success.

She listened long enough to get a decent grasp of the language, and then she listened a little more. She would need to understand these people, understand their worldview as best she could. It was an analytical problem, not unlike studying the internal structure of a worldbook or the workings inside a machine. Though Elsa knew she lacked a natural instinct for people, she was determined to make up for it with a brute-force application of logic. Anything—or anyone—could be puzzled out like clockwork.

Colette and the cook spoke mostly of the minutiae of their work. They gossiped a bit about the mysterious new arrivals, but apparently none of the staff knew anything of consequence about Elsa and Vincenzo, which seemed to only heighten their interest.

Elsa made sure to leave her post outside the door before their tasks in the kitchen drew to a close. She had gleaned enough to think on, for the moment. Perhaps she could leverage their curiosity to get closer to them.

When she went back upstairs, Elsa discovered the door to her bedchamber was not quite all the way closed. There was a rustling inside, someone moving around. Silently, she pushed the door open, slid inside, and snuck up on Aris, who was absorbed in the task of rifling through her luggage.

"Find anything good?" Elsa said.

Aris jumped and whirled around, but his expression held no

trace of guilt. Instead, he flashed her an unapologetic grin. "Can't blame me for looking. I'm the curious sort."

"I didn't bring any worldbooks, if that's what you're searching for." Elsa raised her eyebrows. "Wouldn't want to make myself redundant, now would I?"

Aris gasped. "My dear signorina, how could you believe such a thing? You are unique and irreplaceable."

"Mm-hmm. And you're a scoundrel," she quipped, silently grateful that he didn't seem put off by her natural abrasiveness. It wasn't that she understood him, precisely, but she did find him surprisingly easy to spar with. "There's nothing here to help you figure out how to use the editbook."

"The 'how' is trivial, I'm sure," Aris said. "But there is the small matter of it being scribed in Veldanese—a language that literally no one in the world speaks."

"Except me, of course." And at the moment Revan, though she certainly wasn't about to mention that.

"Yes." The corner of his lips twitched. "Except you."

"Maybe all you have to do is ask nicely. I could explain the syntax to you—all we'd need is the editbook, of course."

He smirked. "Oh, of course. I'll just show you where it's hidden, then."

Elsa shrugged, doing her best to seem as if she didn't especially care one way or the other. "You'll have to eventually. If you want to learn to use it, anyway."

"Or you could teach me the language the old-fashioned Earth way: one word at a time."

"That would take forever," she said. "But I'm feeling generous at the moment so I'll give you a whole phrase, just to whet your appetite. *Patani jah nivereen.*"

Aris quirked an eyebrow, then repeated the phrase back to

her. He didn't quite manage to mimic the correct pronunciation of *jah*, but he came close enough. Not bad for someone who didn't have the inscribed Veldanese talent for learning languages, Elsa supposed.

"What does it mean?" he asked.

"Translated literally, it means 'high as birds.' The way new lovers feel." She paused, letting the unspoken suggestion hang in the air for a moment. "Or, you know, the elation of success when you complete a project. Or stop an airship from crashing."

"What's the phrase for when you let a pretty girl rob you blind?"

Elsa gave him her best look of innocence. "We don't have a phrase for that."

"Ah. That's just as well. I'm afraid it may be some time until we need that phrase. Father doesn't trust you yet—certainly not with the editbook."

"And that wounds me terribly," she said, her tone dry as a desert. "Now get out of my room."

Aris sauntered to the door. "Good night, Elsa da Veldana."

"Good night, Aris Garibaldi."

13

THE LIFE SO SHORT, THE CRAFT SO LONG TO LEARN.
—*Hippocrates*

Porzia had resolved to assume Elsa would succeed. If—no, *when*—Elsa returned with the editbook, they would need an ironclad plan for what to do with it. After all, they'd had it in their hands once before, only to lose it when Leo turned against them. The editbook couldn't be destroyed without risking damage to the real world, so they would need a way to contain it securely.

First Porzia needed to scribe a workshop, the way Elsa had scribed herself a laboratory world. This would allow her to create specialized scriptological materials that didn't exist in the real world—the first line of defense would be to make a worldbook that was itself difficult to use. Charles Montaigne may have gone entirely unhinged, but he was right about one thing: the value of nested security measures.

As Porzia added the finishing touches to her workshop world, she realized the one problem with her scheme: so far, she'd been exceptionally careful to keep hidden the location of the ruins by not opening any portals near Corniglia. But to use her workshop, she would have to go through a portal. Which meant she would have to go elsewhere to do so.

Porzia left her room and, reluctantly, went in search of Faraz. Someone needed to watch the children while she was away, so he'd just have to man up and put aside their argument.

After a few minutes of searching, she hadn't found Faraz, but she did find Olivia scrunched onto a narrow stone window seat with an enormous volume open in her lap.

"What are you reading?" Porzia asked, perching on the stone beside her sister.

Olivia tilted the cover up to let Porzia read the title. It was an anatomy textbook—the kind meant for university students studying to become doctors.

Porzia raised her eyebrows. "How dreadful. Where did you get such a thing?"

"I brought it with me from Pisa," the girl answered quietly.

Porzia blinked, baffled. Tiny twelve-year-old Olivia smuggled that enormous tome out of Casa della Pazzia and lugged it all the way here? All she could think to ask was, "Whatever for?"

Olivia finally looked up from the pages and gave her sister one of those impassive, older-than-her-years stares. "Faraz doesn't specialize in human anatomy. And we're going to need a doctor in this family."

Porzia sucked in a breath. It was a wonder her heart didn't shatter like glass when her sister said things like that. She wanted to protect her siblings from the whole horrible world, but there was one thing she couldn't protect them from: growing up.

"I thought you liked chemistry," Porzia said, and then dug deep to recall some of the relevant terms. "You know, esters and aldehydes and . . . turpentines . . . ?"

"Terpenes," Olivia corrected, her gaze drawn back down to the page.

"Yes, terpenes. What about those? Your perfumes."

She shrugged. "When Elsa was poisoned, she almost died because we don't have an alchemist who knows human medicine."

Porzia swallowed, her throat tight. She tucked a loose lock of Olivia's dark hair behind her ear. "I'm proud of you."

"You wanted something," her sister reminded her.

Porzia had nearly forgotten. "Oh, just wondering if you'd seen Faraz anywhere."

Olivia shook her head.

Porzia huffed. "What about Revan? Is he about?"

"He went outside with Sante."

"Well they better not have gone far." Porzia planted a quick kiss on the top of her sister's head and left Olivia to her study.

Someday, her siblings would no longer need their older sister; her duties to them were finite. And Casa della Pazzia, once the unbreakable stone foundation of their family, had become quicksand beneath their feet. The defining aspects of Porzia's life had turned suddenly ephemeral. Who was she, if not the responsible eldest sibling destined to marry a mechanist and raise another generation of pazzerellones within Casa's walls?

Was there room for her to want a different life for herself?

Porzia took the servants' stairs, which were frightfully narrow and steep yet still managed to improve upon the crumbled devastation that had once been the main stairs. She crossed through the dim-lit hollow of the entryway, grabbed a door handle, and leaned her weight back against the stiff hinges.

In the clearing outside the front doors, she discovered Revan and Sante standing together. Revan was holding a length of thin rope by both ends and saying something she couldn't quite hear to Sante. He lifted the rope and whirled it around so fast it blurred into a disk, then jerked his wrist and released one end. Something small—a pebble?—shot from the sling and hit a tree trunk, and even from so far away Porzia could hear the hollow thud of its impact.

Sante let out a delighted whoop, and Porzia found herself reluctant to interrupt. But she did have work to do, so she walked up behind them.

"What are you two up to?" she said.

Sante glanced back at her with a look of hero worship in his eyes. "Revan's showing me how to use a sling! It's *so awesome*."

Porzia smiled indulgently. If only he could muster that kind of enthusiasm for a scientific discipline—*any* scientific discipline. To Revan she said, "How kind of you."

He gave an easy shrug. "It's no trouble, we're having fun." And she could tell he meant it—that finding fun and sharing it with others came naturally to him, no matter the circumstances.

"Hah! You say no trouble now, but just you wait," Porzia joked. She raised a hand to ruffle Sante's hair, but he ducked deftly out of reach and gave her a perfect teenage glare. "I was hoping I could leave you in charge for a bit."

"Are you going somewhere?" The sun painted highlights on Revan's dark skin in a way Porzia found distracting.

She almost missed her cue to reply. "I, uh . . . I've got some work to do, and I'd rather not risk opening a portal near our secret stronghold."

"Sure, of course," he said, as if it were nothing. And Lord if she didn't feel grateful to have *someone* she could rely on.

"Thank you."

176

He nodded. "Stay safe."

"I will. And you," she said to Sante, "try not to set anything on fire."

Her brother rolled his eyes. "Killjoy. You're as bad as Mamma."

"Well I do try."

With that, Porzia went back inside to gather her scriptological supplies. Despite her tendency toward suspicion, she found it oddly easy to trust Revan. And after her blowup with Faraz, there was a profound sort of relief in finding a new ally.

Porzia had a tiny seed of resentment buried deep in her gut for Elsa, who had left her with all this responsibility, but she knew the feeling to be irrational. She refused to let it take root and grow. Instead, she chose to be grateful for Revan, and to do everything she could to prepare for Elsa's return with the editbook.

Alek had been rattling around the empty halls of Casa della Pazzia for a whole day now. Last night Casa had offered him the use of Elsa's bedroom—*Massimo's old bedroom*—as if it were a boon. What a cold sadist of a machine. Alek could hardly breathe in there, where the memories rose unbidden and the old familiar pain of Massimo's death became once again fresh and sharp. He declined curtly and insisted on taking up residence in one of the smaller guest chambers instead. He did not need the ghost of his dead lover scratching at his mind, on top of everything else.

In the morning he discovered the nursery was locked, with the young children still inside. Casa refused to allow him access. He discovered the dining hall doors were gone, nothing but empty hinges in the doorframe, and the scratched plaster on either side suggested the doors' removal had been a messy event. Inside, the hall was scrupulously clean; a single bot twirled like a dancer, polishing the floor, the picture of innocence.

What had happened here? Where had everyone gone? Casa spent the day demurely avoiding his questions and deflecting his attempts to investigate. It was enough to test even Alek's patience.

Then, much to Alek's surprise, a narrow access panel slid open and a grease-stained Gioconda Pisano climbed out of the wall.

"Gia! What—" Alex exclaimed at the same time that the house said, "Signora! You're here!"

"Of course I'm here, Casa, darling. I could never abandon you," Gia said. "Hello, Alek. I'm afraid you've chosen rather a poor moment for a visit."

"But signora," the house moaned. "You were gone. Everyone left me!"

"I just popped out for a bit to check on the children for you. I knew you'd be worried about them. They're quite all right, but they miss you terribly."

There was a heavy silence as the house pondered this. "Are they coming home?"

"Not yet, Casa, but soon I hope."

Alek frowned. He recognized that soothing tone of Gia's— the tone that meant she was handling someone difficult by whatever means necessary. She met his gaze and shook her head ever so slightly, warning him off any indelicate questions.

Even Gioconda Pisano, master engineer, worried about what Casa might do. Good Lord, what had Alek blundered into?

"You're back, then."

Porzia looked up, startled. She hadn't heard Revan enter the dining hall. "Yes, sorry—I should've found you to let you know you're off duty."

He waved a hand, dismissing this consideration as if it were nothing. "Good to know you made it back safely, that's all." He helped himself to a chair on the opposite side of the long table and surveyed the loose pages and reference books scattered across the surface. "What is all this?"

Porzia sighed. "Notes and such, for the next phase of the project I'm working on."

He lifted a sheet of paper, glanced at it—upside down—and then put it back. With a little shock, Porzia realized that despite his inborn Veldanese talent for languages, Revan could not read.

His lips parted in a teasing smile. "Does this project of yours involve burying yourself in paper?"

"I just want to be ready," she snapped, before reminding herself to lower her hackles. "When Elsa returns with the editbook, we'll need a way to store it. Something well protected."

Revan seemed unfazed by her momentary sharpness. "I meant it seems like maybe you're focusing on this as a distraction."

Porzia shrugged, fussed with rearranging the papers, avoided thinking about what he was implying.

"Also seems like Faraz is making himself scarce whenever you're around," Revan observed.

She froze, then set aside the papers. If she'd been asked a moment earlier, Porzia would have thought she didn't want to talk about it. But beneath Revan's steady, nonjudgmental gaze, she found the words. "It's hard, you know? For so long it was me and Faraz and Leo against the world. Now, when I'm with Faraz, all I can feel is Leo's absence. I think we're both just tired of the constant reminder."

Revan nodded. "Leo has become a wedge between you."

"Yes," she agreed. "He's the wedge."

"Elsa and I were close when we were young," he offered. "We

were the two oldest children in Veldana, so I suppose we naturally gravitated toward each other."

Softly, Porzia said, "What happened?"

Revan splayed his hands open, holding palmfuls of empty air. A helpless gesture. "Elsa had this whole other world I couldn't touch. She was always right there, but also unreachable, as if there were a wall of glass between us, and with time the glass just got thicker and thicker until we couldn't even hear each other through it. I would only see her silhouette passing in front of the light, and wonder who it was. Does that make sense?"

Porzia watched him curiously. For someone who couldn't read, there was an odd sort of poetry to his words. "Perfect sense," she said.

A pained smile flashed across his face, then vanished just as quickly as it came. "And now she's left me behind. Again."

"At least she's coming back."

"Is she? I never know." It would have been easy to say those words resentfully, but to Porzia's ears he simply sounded sad.

In that moment she couldn't help but feel a little disappointed in Elsa, who ought to have been a better friend to Revan. And quick on the heels of that thought, she felt foolish and childish and disappointed with herself, because they all had much greater concerns than these.

Porzia needed to close the rift between Faraz and herself—now, while they had time. Who knew what storm would follow on Elsa's heels when she returned with the editbook? They had to be ready.

The next morning she rose early, hoping to get some work done in the predawn silence, when it was easy to concentrate. The children were still piled together in a sea of warm blankets, its surface softly undulating with their deep, even breaths.

In the middle of scribing a sentence, Porzia glanced up at the unexpected sound of footsteps shuffling down the hall. She rose and peered out of her room, but the guilty feet were already descending the stairs. With an annoyed glance back at her unfinished work, Porzia decided she ought to follow and discover who was sneaking out at such an hour.

Downstairs, she heard the creak of hinges echoing in the entry hall, and she pursued the sound through the castle and out the front doors. Dawn paled the eastern sky, though the sun had yet to crest the hills, so the world outside was lit with a soft, eerie, directionless glow.

She did not spot anyone at first. Porzia tilted her head, listening, and beneath the twilight trilling of birds she thought she heard footfalls moving up the path toward the ancient, half-wild lemon grove. Centuries past, one of Porzia's ancestors must have planned and planted the grove, though none of those original trees remained. Over time the grove reseeded itself, new trees replacing the dying ones until all traces of the once-neat orchard rows were gone.

Porzia followed the path. There was someone up ahead, at the edge of the grove; after a moment she recognized the lanky figure as Faraz. He had a prayer rug unrolled over a flat slab of stone, and he was kneeling on it facing southeast. Porzia stood still, listening, and caught the drone of recited Arabic carried on the early morning breeze. Quietly, she turned and backtracked, giving him some privacy.

From her pocket she took out a small cloth bag—one of several items she liked to carry with her everywhere, along with a pen and a bit of paper—and she busied herself picking lemons.

She waited a few minutes before proceeding deeper into the grove again. This time it was quiet; Faraz must have finished his morning prayer.

She rounded a bend in the path and got a closer look at Faraz. He was wearing a long gray tunic instead of his usual European-style button-up shirt; Porzia had no idea where or when he might have purchased the garment.

"Morning," Porzia called out to announce her presence.

Faraz glanced over his shoulder, startled, but thankfully he didn't seem displeased to see her. "Hello."

"I didn't know you had one of those," she said, indicating the prayer rug.

"My old teacher in Tunis felt it was superstitious, unbecoming for a scientist's apprentice." As he spoke, he focused on the task of carefully rolling the rug.

"So . . . you've been doing this for a while, then? Getting up early to pray, I mean."

He nodded. "Sometimes in the courtyard when the weather's agreeable. It's nice to get outside in the morning."

Porzia swallowed hard. Why would he keep this a secret? How could she not have known? Faraz had always been the unassuming type, not inclined to draw attention to himself, but Porzia made it her business to know people. Apparently she was not so accomplished at this task as she'd thought.

Faraz looked up at her and quipped, "I see you've fully transformed into a schoolmarm."

"What? Oh, yes, I suppose I have." She had fallen asleep last night still wearing her plain gray dress, so now it was rumpled in addition to being terribly unstylish. Fashion fell low on her priority list these days.

Movement in a nearby tree caught Porzia's eye, and the shape clinging to a low branch resolved into Faraz's favorite pet. Apparently even the tentacle monster knew about his morning prayers.

Faraz followed her gaze and said, "Time to go, buddy."

Ignoring him, Skandar plucked a small, underripe lemon from the tree branch and made it disappear. Porzia wasn't exactly sure what the beast had by way of a mouth and had no desire whatsoever to find out. She also didn't know, when the beast squeezed its one enormous eye shut, whether this was an expression of pleasure or of shock at the lemon's tartness.

Faraz lifted his prayer rug and carried it under one arm. "Are you headed back to the ruins?" he said.

It was an olive branch, and she took it. "Yes, let's go."

Faraz fell into step beside her and whistled through his teeth at Skandar. The beast opened its membranous wings, flopped off the branch into the air, and glided down the path to latch onto Faraz's shoulder.

The sight of those tentacles wrapping around him—even around his *neck*—was so grotesque as to be downright nauseating. But in the interest of making peace, Porzia held her tongue. If her silence on the matter of tentacle monsters was the cost of repairing their friendship, she was prepared to pay it.

They followed the path back to the ruins, and for the first time in a while, the silence between them felt light.

14

SHE KNOWS TOO MUCH FOR ME.

—*Charles de Brosses, regarding Maria Gaetana Agnesi*

Once again, Aris did not show up for their morning fencing practice, and Leo was left to worry over what trouble his brother might be stirring up instead.

Leo squared up against Vincenzo and traded parries, but his heart wasn't in it. How could he maintain a normal routine as if nothing had changed, when in fact *everything* had changed? Ricciotti would dig his claws into Elsa, and Leo was powerless to stop him. Vincenzo claimed to be assisting her, but he was obviously preoccupied with Aris. Even now as they dueled, Vincenzo's eyes kept flicking toward the doorway as if he was hoping to spot Aris there.

Leo sighed and used his opponent's distraction to land a touch. The blunted end of the foil hit Vincenzo's gut rather harder than Leo had intended, making his opponent grunt.

"All right, all right. I yield," Vincenzo said, holding up his free hand in joking submission. "You're in a foul mood today—what's bothering you?"

"Nothing," Leo said, too quickly.

Vincenzo raised a skeptical eyebrow. "You're scowling at me like I stole your favorite wrench."

Leo pressed his lips together, considering. "If you really want to know, I'll tell you: it's Aris that worries me. In particular, Aris and you."

"I'm sure I don't know what you mean." Vincenzo let his gaze drift away, avoiding eye contact.

"I'm serious about this, deadly serious," Leo insisted. "You're nothing to him. He finds you an amusing diversion—that's all. I know my brother, and he'll play with you until you break, then throw you away without a second thought and find a new toy to entertain him."

Vincenzo pressed a hand to his chest mockingly. "Your concern for my welfare touches me deeply, truly it does. I never expected to find such an ardent protector among this nest of vipers."

Leo felt his jaw tighten. "Fine, get yourself killed. See if I care." He spun on his heel and made for the exit.

"No, no—wait!" Vincenzo called after him. "Aren't you going to offer to duel with him in defense of my honor? That would surely have me swooning . . ."

Leo paused in the doorway. He swished his foil through the air, frustrated, searching for the right words. No one ever listened to him, anyway. Still, he had to try. "I may not have all the worldly experience of a Carbonari agent such as yourself, but I do know this: my brother is a dangerous person to love."

Vincenzo swallowed hard, the jesting grin falling from his face. "I know," he said. "I know."

Leo gave a nod. "That's good." Because if Vincenzo didn't, he was in for an unpleasant surprise.

And then Elsa would find herself with a shortage of allies.

"Where are you taking me this time?" Elsa said. "I'm not in the mood for more of your tests."

At least they weren't climbing any stairs. Still, Aris had that devious glint in his eye, the one that promised he was up to something. Or perhaps the glint was simply a permanent fixture in his expressive repertoire. Because he was always, perpetually and repeatedly, plotting something or other.

"Oh, nothing like that," Aris said. "I want to show you something. Consider it my apology for vexing you yesterday."

They stopped partway down the hall at a closed door. Aris tried the knob as if expecting it might be locked, but it was not, and he ushered Elsa inside.

It was a parlor of sorts, or perhaps an office, with a desk and bookshelves at one end and armchairs set in front of a hearth at the other.

"Over here," Aris said, leading her toward the banked fireplace.

Above the mantel hung an oil painting, a portrait depicting a figure seated on a horse. Because of the men's clothes and the military saber belted to one hip, Elsa initially thought it was a man, but no—there was a distinctly feminine cast to the rider's body shape beneath the bulky clothing, and her cheeks were smooth. Unsmiling, she stared out of the portrait with an expression that seemed to say she'd seen it all and was unimpressed. Elsa liked her immediately.

"Anita Garibaldi," Aris breathed, as if it were a prayer. "My grandmother."

"She looks . . . fierce."

"I never knew her—she died when Father was just two years old—but I know all the stories." There was an unexpected reverence in his voice; it reminded Elsa that, despite all his brash confidence, Aris had been a boy once, young and impressionable. As he stared up at the painting, his eyes shone with the red glow of the embers. "Anita's a legend in South America, and they'll be telling tales of her for centuries to come. She was a master horsewoman, and just as skilled with a sword. No man could match her courage and fortitude."

Elsa said, "I think I would've liked to meet her."

His gaze shifted away from the painting and onto Elsa. "Do you know what my grandfather said when they met?"

"What?" she said.

Aris leaned closer, his eyes locked on hers, his voice dropping an octave. "*You must be mine.*"

Elsa resisted the urge to lean away. This was it—this was her opportunity to get in closer with Aris. She'd never get near to the editbook unless he trusted her completely. And here he was at his most vulnerable, giving her the opening she needed.

Elsa stood on her toes, erasing the distance between them, and pressed her lips to his.

For a moment he froze in surprise, as if he hadn't really believed she'd fall for his not-so-subtle insinuations. Then he kissed her back—he kissed her like a starved man, like he wanted to consume every bit of her in the bright white flame of his hunger. His hands found their way into her hair and held her in the kiss, as if afraid she might try to escape. Elsa hooked her fingers around his belt and pulled his body against hers, felt the heat of him even through his thick brocade waistcoat.

He pulled away just far enough to speak. "Oh, Elsa . . ." He stared at her in wonderment, with those horribly familiar amber eyes. "I never thought I'd find someone who could match me, not in a thousand years."

"We mustn't," Elsa breathed, and she didn't have to falsify the guilt in her tone.

"Because of Leo?" Aris said. He ran his hands up and down her arms soothingly. "The heart wants what the heart wants. My brother will understand that."

Elsa shook her head, mute, wearing her doubt and confusion openly on her face. She wanted Aris to work for it; she needed him to believe that *he* had seduced *her*, and not the other way around.

"You and I are the only two polymaths in the world," Aris said. "Don't you see? We were made for each other."

"I *am* a polymath," Elsa said, "so what can you offer me that I cannot already do for myself?"

A grin pulled at the corner of his mouth. "I can promise never to be boring."

Elsa let herself smile at that. "I believe you."

Then her lips found his again, and the analytics of the situation faded into the background. There was no room for rational thought in the heat of the moment, with his hand tracing the length of her spine and his tongue searching for hers.

The latch on the door clicked, and Elsa sprang away from Aris, startled at the sound. She turned to see who had caught them.

Leo stood in the doorway.

"Ah, brother," Aris said. "We have something to tell you."

Contrary to Aris's reassuring tone, it did not look at all as if Leo would understand. Rather, he looked as if Elsa had driven an invisible spear through his rib cage, and his collapsed lungs would never again draw breath.

His eyes held her gaze for a long moment. His face went blank, as if the life were draining out of him. Then, without uttering a word, he turned and left.

Elsa moved as if to follow, but Aris caught her arm and held her back. "Let him go. It's better if you let him go, when he's in a mood. He'll come around."

She shook off his hand, annoyed with him and disgusted with herself. "How easily you dismiss his feelings. Has it never once in your life occurred to you to think of Leo's happiness before your own?"

Aris laughed. "Don't be ridiculous, of course he's happy now. He's home with his family." Then, as the question sank in, he frowned and looked away. "He will be, at least. He only needs time to adjust."

Aris hunched his shoulders, angry and wounded at the thought of his brother's dissatisfaction. In that moment he seemed so raw and young, and Elsa realized that Aris did not understand people—did not understand them at all. He could be brilliant with machines, with chemicals, with words, but the complexities of human psychology were beyond his ken.

He knew his own blindness, and he hated it.

Elsa felt an unexpected swell of genuine sympathy, and she went up on her toes to peck his cheek. "It's fine. I'll fix it, it'll be fine."

Elsa checked the ballroom and the dining room and searched the sleeping quarters on the floor above, but nowhere did she find Leo. The laboratory doors on the main floor were locked. Where else might he be?

She decided to take the servants' stairs down. Leo was Italian, and the Italians were excessively preoccupied with food, so maybe he'd sought comfort in the kitchen.

It was a long shot, so Elsa wasn't terribly surprised to find an absence of Garibaldi boys on the servants' floor. But she did find Colette, kneading dough on the scarred wood of the old table in the center of the kitchen. Flour powdered her arms and apron, and as she worked the dough, fine particles rose in the air, floating like dust. She glanced up with a questioning look at the sound of Elsa's entrance.

"Excuse the disturbance," Elsa said, in a somewhat stilted version of the language she'd overheard Colette speaking with the cook.

Colette's eyes lit up and she paused in her work. "You speak Provençal?"

"Oh, only a little. I spent some time in France," Elsa said, which was not exactly untrue. "Where's the cook?" she asked in a tone of mild curiosity. She wanted to know if anyone was in the pantry or the root cellar—anywhere out of sight but close enough to overhear.

Colette brushed a sweaty strand of hair from her face with the back of one hand. "She went to her room for a bit of rest. Her feet bother her sometimes," she said, then added as an afterthought, "Best not to tell anyone."

"Of course," said Elsa. From the girl's tone, she guessed such an infirmity, if revealed, might be grounds for dismissal.

Colette wiped her hands on her apron and stepped around the table. "Did you need her for something?"

"The cook? No, sorry—I was looking for Leo. Searching the whole house, actually. I don't suppose he's been down here?"

Colette gave Elsa a look that seemed to question her mental soundness. "The young masters don't grace us with their presence in the kitchen. It wouldn't be at all proper."

"Right. Of course. Very improper." Elsa wondered if she would ever understand these status-obsessed Europeans.

"Have you tried the solarium?" Colette leaned in and lowered her voice confidentially. "It's abandoned, but lately I've seen him sneaking up there for some privacy."

Elsa blinked. "No, I didn't even know there was a solarium."

"Southeast corner of the house, all the way at the top."

"Thank you."

"Anytime. Elsa." On Colette's lips, the name still sounded like a shared conspiracy, and her smile managed to be at once tentative and sly.

As Elsa climbed the stairs again, the thought of Leo needing a hiding place gave her an odd, queasy feeling. She'd been too angry to wonder how he was, how his choices had affected him. She'd assumed this was a homecoming, but perhaps Leo saw it more as a self-imposed exile.

She followed Colette's directions and found Leo in the solarium. The sky outside was overcast, bathing the whole room in bleak, pale light. He sat facing away from the door, tension written in the angle of his shoulders.

At the sound of her entrance, Leo shifted on the stone bench, but he did not turn. Elsa hesitated in the open doorway, reluctant to intrude upon his solitude. Softly she said, "Hello, Leo."

He took a deep breath and let it out. Silence stretched between them. Then he said, "When we were little, Aris would catch swallowtail butterflies in the courtyard and set their wings afire. He liked to watch them flutter through the air, smoking and dying. I think Mother told him to stop, but he never listened."

Elsa stepped tentatively into the room, moving slow and quiet like she would if she were trying not to spook a wild animal. "You've never said anything about your mother before."

Leo shrugged. "There's not much to say. I don't remember

her well—she died a year or so after Pasca was born. She was . . . very tired. I have this one strong memory of her damp palm pressing against my cheek, and I can recall her face quite clearly. Dark circles under her eyes like bruises." He sucked in a ragged breath. "Though now I know even that was a deception. My real mother died when I was born, or sometime thereafter, just as Pasca's mother did, and Aris's mother before them. Garibaldi's experiments killed them all."

Elsa felt the horror of it deep in her chest, like a vacuum sucking out all the air. She managed a single syllable. "Why?"

"He cared only about producing polymaths. The host need only survive long enough to carry the infant to term. After that, their welfare became irrelevant to him." Leo fell silent for a moment, then let out a harsh laugh. "Joke's on him. All that effort, just to have Pasca die and me turn out a simple mechanist."

Elsa stepped closer, reached out to put a comforting hand on his shoulder but hesitated, her hand hovering uncertainly in the air before she pulled it back. "I'm so sorry, Leo."

He finally looked at her then, and his gaze hit her like a throwing knife. "I don't tell you this to garner your pity. I'm trying to warn you about my family. I'd have thought it would be enough that they abducted your mother and ransomed her for the editbook, but apparently not."

"You know why I came," she said. In the safety of her mind, she begged him to understand the words she could not risk saying aloud. Even here in the derelict solarium, they might be under surveillance.

"Do I?" said Leo doubtfully. "Tell me, Elsa: Are you manipulating Aris, or is he manipulating you?"

She pressed her lips together, unsure how to answer. "Does it have to be one or the other?"

"Yes. Always."

"I understand why you're angry . . ."

"Angry?" He let out another bark of harsh laughter. "You'll do whatever you like, and there's nothing I can do to stop you. I have learned that lesson well."

She could think of no reply, and so kept silent.

"Tell me you have no feelings for him." He looked away, as if he could not bear to see her face when she answered.

Elsa swallowed, her throat gone dry. Even if she'd felt nothing when Aris had kissed her, she could not say so now—she could not admit her deception. The ruse must be maintained.

When her silence stretched too long, Leo heaved a resigned sigh. "For the record, this isn't anger. It's despair."

Leo stayed in the solarium long enough that he had no choice but to admit to himself the truth: he was sulking, and this self-indulgence was not very mature of him. He suspected Porzia would have given him a brisk, stern talking-to. If she were here, which she was not. God, he hadn't known it was possible to feel so alone.

How had everything gone so wrong? He'd started with the best of intentions; all he'd wanted to do was protect Elsa and her mother.

Elsa had never lost anyone, not permanently. Death barely touched her young world. She'd understood the danger to Jumi only in a distant, theoretical sense—she had not truly internalized the reality that Jumi would have died if the situation had been mishandled. Elsa was brave and clever and mature in many ways, but she still retained a child's faith in the immortality of her loved ones. Losing Jumi would have crushed her, the way Leo had been crushed when he believed his own family dead.

Elsa just didn't understand. She couldn't. Now here she was again, this time underestimating the danger to herself. And Leo was powerless to protect her.

Enough. No more wallowing in self-pity; Ricciotti was never going to *give* Leo his agency or his independence. He must reclaim it for himself. It was up to Leo to undo the disastrous choice that had led Elsa here, into the clutches of the Garibaldi family. He knew Elsa would not leave without the editbook, so the solution was obvious: Leo would have to find it and steal it back.

The editbook would be somewhere Aris could access it easily. Ricciotti himself couldn't scribe, so he'd be relying on Aris to figure out how to use the book. But where would Aris hide it? Not in his scriptology study, certainly—much too obvious.

Well, two could play at the surveillance game. A plan formed in his mind.

He glanced around the solarium; in the corners, dead leaves had collected like snowdrifts. Leo picked up a few, examining them. They were brittle with age but just the right thickness. Satisfied, he tucked the leaves into his waistcoat pocket.

Then he left the solarium to stroll the halls, pausing at those doors he knew to be locked. For each locked room, he broke off a small piece of leaf and wedged it into the doorframe. If the leaf remained undisturbed, he would know the room wasn't in use and could be eliminated.

Leo remembered enough about his father's rigorous expectations and lack of patience to know that Aris would be studying the editbook every day. Ricciotti would demand nothing less. So all Leo had to do was figure out which places Aris frequented.

When he finished laying his tiny, innocuous traps, Leo retreated to his bedchamber to wait.

He woke with a start some time later, unsure whether there

had been a sound or if he had dreamed it. The room was dark, the house silent. He fumbled at the bedside to light a candle, then checked his pocket watch: half past midnight.

He'd fallen asleep with his clothes on, his boots still laced. Not his intention, but it didn't matter now—he was up, and the rest of the house was not. Time to go hunting for the right door.

He crept down the stairs and began checking for signs of opened doors. His eyes strained against the dim light, searching the floor of the hallway for dislodged leaf fragments. There— he crouched and picked up a piece, dry and crisp between his fingers. It had fallen from the doorframe of Aris's mechanics laboratory.

The door was locked, but Leo's lockpicks made short work of that problem. The lab looked unchanged from the last time Leo had let himself in, though that didn't necessarily mean anything. Aris was the neat one—he could have built an army of bots in here, and then returned every piece of equipment to its exact pre-ferred location.

Leo walked a slow circuit around the room, searching for any signs of scriptological activities, but the ink he found beside the drafting table was an ordinary black, not the shimmering mid-night blue of the special ink used for scribing. No books of any kind were in evidence.

But wait—that didn't make sense. He'd seen the mysterious clockwork creature open a portal in this very laboratory, and a portal implied a destination. There had to be worldbooks nearby.

If Aris was going to construct a secret door or hidden com-partment, where would he put the trigger mechanism? Leo went to the workbench and ran his hands along the edges, feeling the underside for buttons or switches. Nothing.

Leo didn't know exactly what he planned to do if he found any worldbooks. He could operate a portal device well enough—that was a simple matter of numbers and dials. But interpreting the nonsense that scriptologists wrote upon those pages was beyond him. He found it truly astounding that anything could at once be so dull and so complex. Let alone that it actually *worked*. Building something out of pistons and joints and gears made sense; building something real out of nothing but intangible words still seemed the height of absurdity. Words! The very idea was mad.

Best not admit that to Elsa, he thought, his mind drawn automatically to her, like a compass needle finding magnetic north. Love wasn't just a feeling, it was a paradigm shift—a new context for everything. He could not help but imagine what Elsa would think, how she would respond. Even now he couldn't stop, even knowing it was over between them.

Leo walked the circumference of the lab, running his fingertips across the walls to check for telltale hairline cracks. On the back wall he felt a tiny groove, invisible in the low light, and his pulse jumped. He followed the line by touch, and it described a panel three feet tall by four feet wide. Aris *was* hiding something; but how to open it?

Experimentally, Leo pushed against the panel, then against the wall surrounding it in several places. Nothing. An idea struck him: he held his candle up to the unlit wall sconce nearest the panel and pressed his cheek against the wall to examine it from the proper angle.

Leo grinned. "Always got to go for the high drama, eh, brother?"

He hooked a finger around the brass pipe of the sconce and pulled down; it levered away from the wall, and with a loud *click*, the panel slid open. Built into the wall was a hidden bookcase.

Leo set his hands on his hips and surveyed the spoils of his investigation. Aris thought he was so clever, but Leo was onto him now.

15

A t last Porzia had reached the most delicate and challeng-
ing part of scribing the worldbook that would, someday
soon, store and protect the editbook.

If only they hadn't needed to abandon Casa della Pazzia, she
could have taken a portal to Veldana and asked Jumi and Alek for
advice. Jumi was an expert in this sort of thing; she was the one
who'd scribed the Veldanese linguistic talent into the Veldana
worldbook. But they were out of reach, so Porzia had to do her
best and pray it was good enough. The pen in her hand felt heavy
with the invisible weight of responsibility.

These last few lines were the dangerous part, where she had to
balance specificity with the perfect amount of vagueness. Too
vague, and the worldbook would provide little security; too specific, and she could end up accidentally textualizing someone,
addling their wits like what happened to Simo. For the conditional

statement, Porzia decided on *born in a scribed world*, which was broader than she wanted but erred on the safe side.

When the worldbook was finally done, Porzia sought out two very particular test subjects to help her evaluate it. Little Aldo would serve as an independent scriptologist, and Revan would represent the Veldanese. Feeling giddy at the prospect of success, she gathered them together in the relative privacy of her room.

Porzia opened the worldbook to the first page and held it out to Revan. "Tell me what you see."

He gave her a confused look, as if wondering whether it was a trick question. "Uh . . . a book? Paper?"

"Yes, but what's inside?"

"Nothing. It's blank."

"Excellent." Then Porzia held the same page open for Aldo. "Could you read the coordinates for me, please?"

"Of course I can," Aldo said, affronted at the suggestion that he might not be able to. His hands were still too small to comfortably work an adult-size portal device, but he had no trouble reading the coordinates off the page.

Revan said, "Wait—huh?"

Porzia grinned. "The ink is visible only to scriptologists of the Pisano bloodline."

"But . . . how?"

"The materials I used to make this worldbook are themselves the products of another worldbook—a laboratory where I can design custom inks and papers that can't be made in the real world," Porzia explained. "Thank you, Aldo, that was very helpful. Why don't you go find Faraz now?"

"But I want to go in the world with you!" He stomped his foot and scowled at her.

"Next time," Porzia promised. "No portals in the castle, remember?"

Aldo was not happy with this answer, and Porzia suspected he'd spend the rest of the day sulking about it if he didn't get his way. That boy could hold a grudge.

She sighed. "All right, fine. But no complaining about how far we have to walk—that's the deal."

Aldo's scowl vanished, instantly replaced with a beaming smile. "I can do it," he said, full of determination.

So Porzia had an escort of two as she left the ruins with her new worldbook in hand. They walked most of the way to Manarola, and though Aldo certainly did slow their pace, he kept his promise and did not complain even once.

Porzia selected an out-of-sight nook along the path and let Aldo read the coordinates off the page for her. Then she led them through the brief darkness of the portal and stepped into her new world for the first time.

They stood inside a square pavilion of classical design, caged in by Corinthian columns on all sides. Beyond the edges of the pavilion floor, sheer stone cliffs dropped into a sea of Edgemist. It was not a large world, nor an especially welcoming one. Even the air felt chilly against Porzia's bare forearms.

In the center of the pavilion sat a broad stone pedestal topped with a transparent blue sphere about the size of the globe in the library back in Pisa. Electricity sparked across the sphere's glassy surface.

"What's that for?" Aldo said, standing on tiptoes to get a better look.

"Careful—don't touch," Porzia warned.

Revan walked a slow circuit of the pavilion, looking around. He whistled through his teeth. "You made all this, just in the few days we've been in Corniglia?"

"I thought you'd be used to this sort of thing," she said.

"Sure, Jumi adds new areas to Veldana all the time, but that's just expanding something that already exists," he said. "I guess it seems different, making a whole new world from scratch whenever you like."

"Actually, what Jumi does requires a fair bit more finesse. If you scribe a new world and muck it up, you lose some time and effort and materials, but you don't risk killing off your entire nation."

Revan blinked. "Never thought of it that way."

"Anyway. Here you go," Porzia said, handing Revan her pen. "Put this inside the sphere."

"You want me to touch that thing? It looks dangerous."

"It shouldn't be dangerous to you. I scribed it specifically for this purpose. Go on."

Revan squinted at her. "What do you mean, 'shouldn't be'?"

"Ooh!" said Aldo. "I'll do it! I'll do it! Can I do it?"

"No, you may not," Porzia told her little brother. Then to Revan she said, "Obviously it hasn't been tested yet. That's what you're here for—to make sure everything works properly."

"I don't know." Revan eyed the sphere skeptically. "How am I supposed to put something inside, anyway? It looks solid."

"Of course it looks solid. It *is* solid, for anyone born on Earth. But not for you." When he still hesitated, Porzia huffed, "Do you trust me or not?"

Revan pressed his lips together, hardening his resolve, and held the pen out in front of him. Slowly, he eased the pen toward the sphere. An arc of blue electricity licked outward as if exploring the object, but Revan didn't jump. The pen touched the sphere and passed through as if no barrier existed. Porzia watched Revan's face as he dipped his hand through the surface; his eyebrows rose in surprise, but there was no sign of pain.

"How does it feel?" she asked.

Revan set the pen down on the pedestal inside the sphere and pulled his hand back out. "It doesn't," he replied while he scrutinized his palm and the back of his hand. "There's no sensation at all, as if it's nothing but an illusion."

Porzia tapped one finger against the surface of the sphere. The electricity swarmed toward her with an audible *zap*, and even though she pulled away quickly, her whole hand cramped with a bone-deep ache.

She massaged her fingers with her other hand and shot Revan a rueful glance. "No, it is definitely not an illusion."

Revan looked distressed at her pain. "Why did you do that? Are you badly hurt?"

Porzia shook the rest of the stiffness from her hand and said briskly, "I told you—we came here to test it out. Now it's properly tested."

His eyes widened. "You're mad."

"Thank you," she replied with a smile.

"That wasn't a compliment."

"Then you're saying it wrong," Porzia quipped. "'Mad' is always a compliment."

He was watching her with an intensity that made heat rise in her cheeks. He reached out and took her hand in his, gently examining it for injury. The touch of his calloused fingers against her palm sent a shiver through her.

Porzia cleared her throat. "My pen?"

Revan quickly dropped her hand and reached into the sphere to retrieve the pen. "Right, here it is."

He hesitated, dark eyes meeting her gaze. Instead of handing the pen to Porzia, he leaned forward and kissed her.

His lips were soft and full, and the kiss buzzed in her brain like static, obscuring rational thought. There were practical matters she ought to consider before engaging in such behavior, but for the life of her Porzia could not remember what they were. For now, it was enough to know that this kind, guileless boy wanted to kiss her, and that she wanted to kiss him back.

"Ew!" Aldo declared.

Porzia startled out of the kiss, pulling back from Revan and raising a hand to cover her lips. For a moment she'd forgotten they weren't alone.

She turned to Aldo and ran her hands down the front of her dress, trying to smooth out the flustered sensation. "Well," she said with forced brightness, "we'd best get back. I wonder if Simo's been up to anything fun—what do you think?"

Aldo looked deeply skeptical at her deflection. Fantastic: now even her youngest sibling could see right through her. But then Aldo said, "Simo's boring. He doesn't have *any* books at all."

"Still, you must be nice to him. Like he's part of the family, remember?"

Aldo heaved a dramatic, eight-year-old sigh. "I know, you said."

She risked a quick glance at Revan; a smile flickered across his lips in answer. He looked at ease, neither embarrassed nor smug. What a strange culture the Veldanese must have, with their guiltless kissing. She supposed they did not even have the phrase *to steal a kiss*, since you could not steal something freely given.

Porzia opened a portal back to Cinque Terre and waved them through. Then she followed, working hard to wrestle down a giddy smile.

* * *

Alek wasn't much help with mechanical repairs. Give him a syntactical challenge any day, but scriptology was not going to solve the problem with Casa. He played assistant to Gia as best he could, though all the tools looked the same to him and he had no idea what she was trying to accomplish.

Burak was still hidden in the walls, working in secret thanks to some sort of blind-spot device. Alek helped by running messages to him; Casa watched Gia's every move with intense scrutiny, so Gia and Burak could not risk a direct meeting.

Alek took the basement stairs as fast as he could, leaning heavily on the railing every other step. He'd been up and down five times already, and his bad hip was screeching in protest. At the bottom, the generator room provided little relief—it was hot as a Veldanese afternoon in there, and stuffy to boot.

"How's it looking?" Alek said.

Gia squeezed out of the narrow space behind one of the huge, hulking generators. "Well . . . I have a few minor concerns . . ."

Casa's disembodied voice bellowed, "You do?!" They had told the house that Gia was working to shore up security, which at the time seemed like a good way to trick Casa into giving her access to the systems. But now the house was excessively anxious over her progress.

Gia sighed. "*Minor* security concerns, I said *minor*. Don't worry so much—it shouldn't take long to make the necessary adjustments."

She threw Alek a look that was equal parts exasperation and exhaustion. Alek drew back a corner of his mouth in sympathetic agreement.

A deep, resonant chime sounded somewhere in the house, making Alek jump. He said, "Was that the doorbell?"

Gia closed her eyes, as if praying for patience. "Casa, please don't admit anyone into the house right now."

"No need to worry, Signora," Casa replied. "I am quite capable of keeping you safe."

"That's precisely what I'm afraid of," Gia muttered.

"Signor Pisano is with the group at the door. Should I not welcome him home?"

"No!" Gia yelped. It took her visible effort to steady her voice. "We'll go up and speak with them. Please wait for us, Casa."

She took the basement stairs at an undignified run, and Alek followed as fast as his bad hip would let him. As they rushed down the hallway to the foyer, Casa said, "Signor Pisano is being most insistent . . ."

Alek's heart stuttered in his chest when he looked up and saw the front doors cracking open. Gia dived for the doors and grabbed them, blocking the entrance with her own bulk just barely in time. Alek came to a stop behind her and pressed his palm against his ribs; he was too old for this sort of excitement.

He peered over Gia's shoulder and through the crack to spot Filippo—husband to Gia and head of the Pisano family ever since his brother Massimo died—who stood on the stoop, wringing his hands anxiously. Beside him was Augusto Righi, a portly mustachioed man who served as the current elected leader of the Order of Archimedes. With them were two other pazzerellones: the council secretary, a Signor Papone if Alek recalled correctly, and a German representative whose name vanished from his memory. And behind them stood a pair of seven-foot-tall enforcer automatons, not unlike the ones designed to guard Montaigne's prison.

This was all highly unusual, and made Alek's skin feel hot with nerves.

Gia cast Alek a worried look over her shoulder and said, "I'm afraid you really, truly cannot come in just now."

"Move aside, Gia," Righi said.

Filippo looked miserable. "We have to let them in, my love."

"No," Alek said, "Filippo, you don't understand. The house——"

But Righi motioned the enforcers forward, and they pushed their way inside so roughly that Alek had to catch and steady Gia. She made a surprised, indignant noise, and Filippo came immediately to her side as if to declare his allegiance against the machines' rudeness.

Righi cleared his throat. "Now. As I'm sure you are aware, the individual known as Elsunani di Jumi da Veldana no longer qualifies for asylum here."

Gia rested a hand on her husband's arm, but her frown was all for Righi. "What in the world are you going on about, Augusto?"

"Montaigne has escaped—not two days after we hear, from your very own daughter, that the Veldanese girl has sided with Garibaldi. Someone broke him out. As coincidences go, it stretches the imagination."

"Hold on, hold on." Alek held up his hands at the absurdity of this accusation. "There is no love lost between Montaigne and Elsa. I simply cannot imagine any reason she would want him free. We wouldn't have even had him in custody in the first place were it not for her."

Alek glanced at Filippo for support, but the head of the Pisano family just gave him a helpless look, as if this battle had been lost before they'd left Firenze.

"I'm of course willing to consider the possibility of a misunderstanding," Righi said magnanimously. "But we cannot ignore such a potential threat to the integrity of the Order. Until we determine the truth, the Veldanese girl is to be taken into custody at a more secure location, so if you have any knowledge of her whereabouts——"

The double doors slammed shut behind them, making everyone jump. In the silence that followed, Gia and Alek exchanged a despairing look.

"Oh, Augusto, you old fool. You shouldn't have said that," Gia said.

Righi bristled. "What exactly is going on here? What have you done?"

Casa's voice seemed to enter the room slowly, as if it were oozing down the stairs or seeping up through the cracks between the floor tiles. "It is not what *they* have done." Low and soft, menacing. "It is what *you* have done."

In six places around the room, spiderweb cracks appeared in the plaster. There was a muted whirring noise, and all six patches of plaster buckled at once, filling the room with dry white dust. Alek coughed, squinting, trying to make out what Casa was doing. At his elbow, Gia let out a cry of dismay, as if she already knew.

"The children belong to me," the house growled. "You will not have them."

When the plaster dust settled, Alek saw they were surrounded by six mechanical arms protruding from the walls, each one aiming some sort of long-muzzled rifle at them. Gia clung to Filippo, burying her face in his shoulder.

"Wheat from the chaff," the house said, and fired.

16

As she left her chamber for the dining hall, Elsa felt trepidation settle heavily in her gut, leaving no room for food. She knew from Colette that Garibaldi, who had been mysteriously absent yesterday, was due back for lunch. Surely both his sons would be expected to attend him, and she dreaded what might happen with the Garibaldi boys together in the same room.

At the door, Elsa discovered she was only the second to arrive, and she took a chair across the table from Vincenzo. She sat with her spine straight and her shoulders stiff, incapable of relaxing.

Vincenzo said, "So how's the alliance going?"

Elsa searched his expression, wondering if he was making a coded request for information about their true mission, or simply making small talk. His face gave no hint either way. "Well enough, I suppose," she said. "This is Veldana's first political alliance, so it's not as if we have much to compare it to."

"You ought to draft a formal document. That's what governments do."

"Garibaldi isn't a government—at least not yet."

One corner of Vincenzo's mouth drew up into a lopsided grin. "I wouldn't tell *him* that, if I were you."

Then Aris sauntered in, wearing an easy smile. He nodded a greeting to them both. "Vico, Elsa."

He pulled out a chair next to Elsa and sat down so close beside her that their arms touched. Elsa froze. Vincenzo started to frown but caught himself and wiped away the expression. The air seemed to ring with a tension she didn't quite understand the source of.

With feigned innocence, Aris asked, "Are you feeling quite well, Vico?"

Vincenzo showed him a lazy, unbothered smile. "I don't know what you mean."

Aris shifted his arm to rest on the back of Elsa's chair, and she felt sick. He was not touching her like a person craving contact with another person; he was touching her like an owner showing off a new toy. A muscle in Vincenzo's cheek twitched, which seemed to delight Aris.

Elsa wasn't sure exactly what was going on, but instinct told her Aris was acting deliberately horrible, and it made her skin crawl. The sympathy she'd felt for him yesterday evaporated. She was struggling to stop herself from pushing his arm away when Garibaldi came striding in, breaking the tension; Aris dropped his arm from her chair as quickly as he dropped whatever game he'd been playing, his attention instantly drawn to his father.

Elsa felt a swell of relief, and at that she needed to stifle a laugh. Relieved at the arrival of Ricciotti Garibaldi—who would have thought it possible?

Colette immediately appeared and served plates of small

spinach dumplings swimming in melted butter. A ghost of a smile crossed her face, timed carefully so only Elsa would see.

Bolstered by her new conspirator, Elsa turned to Garibaldi. "I know your business keeps you quite occupied, but perhaps it's time to discuss the terms of our alliance."

She forked a pair of dumplings into her mouth, hoping to project an air of calm. There was cheese cooked into them as well, she discovered, and the butter was flavored with sage, and the intense strangeness of the food threatened to distract her from the conversation.

She barely heard Garibaldi reply, "There are those who consider it distasteful to discuss politics over a meal. But for you, signorina, I think we can make an exception." He smiled as if he were doing her a favor. "So tell us: what can we do for Veldana?"

She swallowed. "What I want is a powerful ally willing to support Veldana's independence if it ever comes under threat. I thought the Order of Archimedes would be that ally, but now I fear they're more likely to try to control us than they are to support us."

Garibaldi nodded. "Pazzerellones have such potential to be a force for change in the world. Instead, the Order ensures we hide ourselves away, *dans une tour d'ivoire*, removed from society. I have no doubt they are afraid of what you might do if you remain beyond their influence."

Elsa paused, planning her words with care. "In return for your support, I am prepared to offer this: I will personally scribe the changes you wish into the editbook."

He shook his head. "That won't be sufficient. I need you to instruct Aris in Veldanese scriptological technique."

"I'm afraid I cannot agree to help unless you allow me at the very least to supervise the editing process," she insisted. "The

Veldana worldbook exists on Earth; if you were to deal catastrophic damage to the real world, it could in turn affect Veldana."

"But surely you don't believe our goal is to destroy reality. We do, after all, live in it."

"Your *goal*? No. But I do believe you might destabilize the world by accident." She turned to Aris. "No offense."

"Absolute offense." He bristled. "I'm a polymath—I do not make errors when I scribe."

"Veldanese grammar is full of subtleties and variations, and so to scribe in Veldanese requires syntactical precision. I cannot teach it to you in a day." This was entirely true; it was also a convenient excuse to demand access to the editbook.

Garibaldi chewed thoughtfully and swallowed. "I will consider your proposal," was the best he would allow.

Leo never joined them. Colette made the empty plates disappear and replaced them with a second course of thinly sliced liver and onions. Elsa made herself eat, Aris's sidelong glances weighing heavily on her, as if he intended to read her secrets by sheer force of will. Across the table Vincenzo was the opposite, refusing to meet her gaze. He excused himself early and fled the dining room.

Elsa envied his rudeness but didn't dare emulate it, needing as she did to ingratiate herself to Garibaldi. So she waited until the meal was over, and only then pursued Vincenzo up the stairs to his guest chamber. She could use some advice on how to proceed, and sulking Leo didn't seem a likely source.

Vincenzo's door stood open, so Elsa started to say, "What did you think of—"

She stopped short in the doorway, taken aback at what she saw inside: Vincenzo was packing his things. He glanced up at her, raw hurt in his eyes.

"Where are you going?"

He shrugged, looking away. "When you need me, I'll be there."

"What are you talking about? You're needed now. Continuously," Elsa said. "Is this about Aris?"

She was so accustomed to Vincenzo's devil-may-care bravado that the wounded look now crossing his face gave her a profound sense of disorientation. He could laugh at the prospect of death, but shied away from subterfuge? Wasn't he supposed to be a *spy*? Elsa stared at him, baffled.

"You can't expect me to stay here and watch"—he waved a hand vaguely at her—"*this* happening."

The muscle in his jaw clenched, and understanding finally dawned on her. Vincenzo saw Aris as more than a childhood friend. "Oh," was all she managed to say.

"I'm not asking you to stop," he said. "So please don't ask me to stay."

Elsa wanted to tell him that whatever happened between herself and Aris, it was only a game—an elaborate chess match of emotions and truths and lies. A game she would happily quit, if they weren't playing for such an important prize. She wanted to say she was glad Aris had shown an interest in her instead of Vincenzo; whoever got close to Aris would eventually have to stab him in the back—metaphorically, if not literally—and better it was Elsa who carried that burden.

She couldn't risk saying any of that aloud, though, in case their conversation was being monitored. Instead, she simply rested her hand on his arm. "I am sorry if I've hurt you. It was not my intention."

"I know." Vincenzo quickly turned his attention back to his bag, pulling the strings tight with more force than was strictly necessary.

"Wait here a minute before you go—I have something you should take with you." This was an opportunity, at least, to get the fake portal device away from Aris's prying eyes. She'd already caught him going through her bags once, and the last thing she needed was Aris getting his hands on the doorbook.

Vincenzo threw her a quizzical look, but said, "As you like."

Elsa ran to her room to grab the receiver, but when she returned, she overheard arguing in his chamber.

"Vico, you're overreacting. Wait." Aris's voice. Elsa pressed herself against the wall of the corridor.

"Wait? Wait for what, exactly—for you to just once in your life discover a shred of sympathy? I'll hold my breath, and die suffocating."

"I was *trying* to make you jealous. Isn't it obvious?"

"I shouldn't be surprised that Garibaldi's son can't tell the difference between loving people and toying with them."

"But you're the one I really want," Aris said, a sulky undertone to his words.

Elsa felt like the breath had been knocked out of her. There were times when getting close to Aris felt easy, but what if it was foolish to even attempt to sway him? What if there was no goodness inside Aris to appeal to, no room left for a conscience amongst all that possessiveness and raw need?

"I know this is going to come as a shock," Vincenzo said, "but the world doesn't revolve around what *you* want."

Aris snorted. "I beg to differ."

Elsa retreated to the empty room across the hall and waited there, hidden, watching as Aris stalked angrily out of Vincenzo's room. When the sound of his footsteps faded, she rejoined Vincenzo.

"Here," she said, passing him the receiver disguised as a portal device. "Can you hold on to this for me?"

"I'll protect it with my life," Vincenzo said. She wasn't sure if he was being gallant or ironic.

Elsa turned to go, but then reconsidered. "I haven't forgotten why I'm here, you must know that," she said earnestly.

"I believe you." He waved a hand at his packed bag and added, "This is a . . . a self-preservation thing. You pazzerellones wouldn't understand."

His crooked smile landed on her like a slap. Was it true that pazzerellones played with hearts as casually as they played with volatile chemicals? Was she that sort of person now?

Elsa didn't know the answer.

Alek de Vries was still in one piece, but the same could not be said of everyone.

Filippo had neared hysterics at the sight of the blood and the broken bodies, the stench of spilt viscera, the enforcer bots reduced to smoking piles of shattered gears. Gia, grim-faced and determined, had asked Alek to draw him away. He had led Filippo to the sitting room in the front of the house, primarily because he'd anticipated it would be an easy place to locate alcohol.

There was something morbidly funny about the menfolk withdrawing to the parlor while the lady of the house saw to the carnage, and Alek did not like himself very much for being amused at that particular moment. Though perhaps it was the best way to cope—he also did not like to think too closely on what they'd lost. Righi, head of the Order, plus two other regular members of the council. It was a terrible blow, which could weaken their influence not just in the Kingdom of Sardinia but across Europe.

Alek poured Filippo another glass of grappa, on account of how he'd downed the first like a shot of whiskey. He wrapped

Filippo's shaking fingers around the stem of the tulip-shaped glass and resumed his seat beside his shocked friend.

"Righi had an apprentice, did he not?" Alek had some vague memory to that effect—an apprentice not much older than Elsa. When his question met with no reply, Alek said, "Filippo?"

"Eh? Oh, yes, he does—did. *Did*," Filippo said again, as if to cement the past tense in his mind.

"There's a blessing, at least." Thank God the boy had not been dragged along on his master's last fateful errand. "We should send word to Bologna. Will the boy come here, do you think? Or does he have family?"

"He can't come *here*," Filippo said, aghast.

"No, of course not . . . I didn't mean now." Alek marveled at himself, at what an irredeemable pazzerellone he could be. He was already thinking ahead to a time when all this was fixed; his automatic assumption was that science would prevail, and Gia would effect the repairs, and everything would return to normal.

In truth, there was no guarantee. Alek and the Pisanos knew this better than most, or at least they should, after the terrible loss of Filippo's brother Massimo.

Alek sighed. "We should send word to Firenze—the Order needs to know what happened."

"The wireless telegraphy machine is off-limits," Casa snapped, the house's voice making Filippo jerk in surprise.

"You don't want any further intrusions, do you?" Alek said. "If you allow me access to the wireless, I'll warn them away, and then no one will try to take your children. Won't that be good?"

Grudgingly, the house admitted, "I suppose that would be preferable to making another mess in the foyer. Very well, Signor de Vries."

Alek levered himself out of the armchair and gave Filippo's shoulder a comforting squeeze. He hated feeling useless; at least sending a wireless message was something constructive to do. Something to distract himself from the obvious fact that everything was falling apart.

Leo had taken the lunch hour to check and reset all the leaf pieces in the doorframes. He wanted to confirm which rooms were in frequent use before involving Elsa in the search. It felt oddly satisfying to act in defiance of his family, and he almost wished he would get caught. He wanted them to hurt the way he hurt. But he finished checking the doors without incident, his success both a relief and a disappointment.

He returned to his room and stopped short at what he saw within—Ricciotti was seated in his reading chair.

"Father," Leo said cautiously. He couldn't help shifting his eyes around the bedchamber, checking for signs of a trap. Maybe he had not gotten away with all that sneaking, after all.

Ricciotti said, "We need to talk."

"So I gathered." Leo swallowed. "Regarding what, exactly?"

"Aris has always been a selfish boy . . . ," Ricciotti began.

Though Leo might have said those exact words himself, when his father said them he felt an irrational urge to rush to Aris's defense.

"It's not fair, I know," Ricciotti continued. "But he only wants what's yours because he wants to feel close to you. You can see that, can't you, Leo?"

Leo shook his head, stunned. Were they really discussing his romantic life? "What I can't do is believe we're having this conversation."

"I expect much of your brother—perhaps too much, sometimes. But do not interpret that to mean I can't *see* him." Ricciotti leaned forward, elbows on knees. "You are my sons, and I do love you both, and I want what's best for you."

Leo stared. This could be a manipulation; Ricciotti was certainly capable of that. But it terrified Leo more that it might be sincere.

Slowly, he said, "So . . . you're saying you want me to remove myself as an obstacle to Aris's happiness?"

Ricciotti waved a hand, dismissing this idea. "Not at all. A little healthy competition between brothers is a fine thing, so long as it doesn't turn to animosity. I'm simply hoping you won't let that girl become a wedge between yourself and Aris. He . . . may not have the sense to drop the bone, so to speak."

Leo was too bemused at the conversation as a whole to take offense at his feelings for Elsa being likened to a dog fighting over table scraps. "I'll keep that in mind," he said.

Seemingly satisfied, Ricciotti rose from the armchair. He loomed close to Leo, his presence almost gravitational, and he clapped a hand on Leo's shoulder. "Aris may be the elder, but sometimes you must be the mature one, understand?"

"Yes, Father," he answered automatically, as if his body were responding to Ricciotti's paternal authority whether he liked it or not.

Ricciotti gave a satisfied nod, patted his shoulder again, and left. Leo searched desperately inside himself for the resentment that Ricciotti usually instilled, but he could not find it anywhere. He rubbed his shoulder, trying to erase the feel of his father's touch.

I do love you both. The worst part was, Leo believed it.

That night Elsa woke with a start from a light sleep, unsure of what had roused her. A sound? A dream? Then the knock came again.

Blinking away the daze of sleep, she slid out of bed and fumbled in the dark for her dressing gown. The air was unpleasantly chilly, the floorboards cold against her bare feet. She answered the door to find a certain blond boy standing in the hall.

"Leo?" she said blearily. "What are you doing?"

He carried a small kerosene lantern, the light turned down so low it was barely enough to see by, and left his face in shadow. "May I come in?" he said, his tone carefully neutral.

Elsa considered him, trying to glean a hint of his intentions from his stance or the angle of his shoulders. He held himself stiff, collected, ready for battle. Perhaps this was to be expected, after how they'd left things in the solarium. Though why he thought he needed the rapier that was at this moment strapped to his hip, she couldn't imagine. Was there danger afoot? Elsa held the door wide, then closed it behind him.

"It's late," she said. "I don't fancy another argument right now, if that's what you're here for."

"I'm not here to talk about us." He turned up the wick and let the lantern brighten the room. His gaze swept around, as if scanning for spies.

So the late-night visit was indeed about more than her reckless behavior. "What, then?"

"I found something." Leo leaned close, lowering his voice so she could barely hear him. "Aris has a secret stash of worldbooks in the mechanics laboratory. I don't know for sure that he's hidden the editbook inside one of them, but I think this is our best chance to get it back."

For a moment Elsa didn't reply, taken aback at Leo's sudden interest in recovering the very book he'd stolen from her. A flash of anger made her want to give him a cutting reply, but logic won out; everything that had happened between them paled in importance when compared against finding the editbook.

"You have my interest," she admitted. "Thank you for bringing this to my attention."

He nodded, visibly relieved at her acceptance of his olive branch. "All right then, let's go."

"Now? What if you're wrong and the editbook isn't there?" Elsa shook her head. "We should bide our time and gather more information."

"If we wait, we risk Aris figuring out that we know about the hidden worldbooks."

Elsa fervently wished Vincenzo were still here to give her advice about how to proceed. Another bridge burned—apparently she'd developed a talent for that. She made a frustrated noise in the back of her throat. "Fine, we'll do it your way."

She threw off the dressing gown and jammed her feet into the legs of her trousers. Leo flushed scarlet and turned to face away while she dressed. Elsa hadn't meant to offend his modesty, though it did give her a certain petty satisfaction all the same.

She buckled her leather bustier over a linen shirt. "We'll need a portal device."

"I think I saw one there," Leo answered without turning around. "But where's yours?"

"Not here."

"How specific."

"It's a long story." And not one she was inclined to share with a person of questionable loyalties. She finished lacing her boots and stood. "Let's get this done."

Leo turned the lantern down again and slipped out into the hall, moving stealthily in the dim light. Elsa followed his lead, trusting his instincts when it came to the matter of sneaking. That much, at least, she could trust.

The mechanics laboratory was clean and organized despite signs of recent use. Discarded off to one side was a pile of warped

219

gears Elsa recognized as belonging to the airship transmission; Aris must have gutted the mechanism since the unfortunate maiden voyage.

Leo led her through the lab to the back wall, explaining, "I knew there had to be a worldbook in here somewhere, because I saw someone open a portal right over there."

"Someone?" Elsa said.

"Well, 'someone' in the loose sense. She was this automaton-monster sort of construct. Aris's creation, I'd assume, from the admixture of mechanics and alchemy. I think she's been watching me, although she was weirdly skittish when I caught her in here."

"If she was spying on you, she probably wasn't supposed to get caught doing it."

"Maybe," Leo said. "Or perhaps she's supposed to be guarding the editbook instead." He pulled down on a wall sconce, and a panel opened to reveal a hidden bookcase.

"That's not at all suspicious," Elsa said dryly.

"What do you think? See anything promising?"

She ran her fingertips across the spines, feeling for the steady thrum of finished worldbooks. Several of Aris's books had the tentative vibration of works in progress, and Elsa found it curious that he would have so many incomplete projects at once. Perhaps he was the type to abandon a worldbook partway through, if it wasn't working exactly as he intended.

She pulled out the first of the finished worldbooks and opened it to scan the text. "This one's an alchemy laboratory. See here? He's altered the basic principles of chemistry." Apparently Elsa was not the only polymath using scriptology to get around the physical laws of the real world.

Leo didn't bother looking. "I'll have to take your word for it, I'm afraid."

Elsa shelved the alchemy lab and found another complete worldbook. After reading for a minute, she said, "Huh . . ."

"Tell me that's a good 'huh,'" Leo said hopefully.

"This one's another lab, I think, but it has alterations to linguistic properties." Her interest was piqued—Veldana had special language properties too—but there wasn't time to study this text in depth and figure out what Aris had designed it for. She replaced it and opened the next book.

"Oh! This one looks promising," Elsa said. "It's a maze world. Well . . . sort of. Anyway, it's the only worldbook here that seems to have anything I'd call security measures. Shall we go?" She reached for the portal device that was stashed on the shelf above the books.

Leo pressed his lips together, considering. "As much as I'm loath to serve as the voice of reason, I feel obligated to point out that the last time we recovered the editbook from a maze world, we needed Faraz and Porzia's assistance to complete the task."

Elsa gave him an appraising look. "You're right: caution really doesn't become you."

He scrunched his face distastefully, as if he wore the caution like an unfortunate fashion choice. "Somebody ought to keep us in check, and Faraz isn't here."

"How very sensible of you," she said in a mollifying tone, with only a hint of mockery. "Now are we going to dive blindly into to danger, or what?"

"Oh God yes." He grinned.

It seemed like forever since she'd last seen him smile; it hit Elsa like a hatpin to the heart. She quickly looked away and busied herself with setting the coordinates. The black maw of a portal yawned open for them.

They stepped through the portal into a vertiginous puzzle of paths and stairs that changed angles and twisted back on themselves in defiance of gravity and geometry. There was an open doorway on the ceiling—or rather, on the path above Elsa and Leo—and just out of reach on their left was a set of stairs tipped ninety degrees to lie on its side. There were no structural supports in sight, just a maze of stone pathways hanging in the air like a massive spider's web. In the empty spaces between, there was only the distant purple glow of Edgemist.

Leo said, "What the . . ."

Elsa laughed, but she wasn't entirely sure whether it was from delight or dismay. "One thing I can say for Aris: He does have a certain flair, doesn't he?"

Leo muttered under his breath, "Yes, let's swoon over how brilliant my brother is."

Elsa caught the words. Dryly, she replied, "And after that, can we argue about whose property I am?"

Leo gave her one of his inscrutable looks, some warring combination of woundedness and guilt. Then he shook it off and said, "In any case, this place is deranged."

He edged over to look below the path they stood on. There were no handrails anywhere in sight, no safety precautions whatsoever. Elsa guessed this was not an oversight, but an intentional feature.

Leo whistled. "There's no ground or anything—it's just Edgemist down there beyond the maze."

Elsa looked both ways along the path they were on. In one direction, the path ended where it curved abruptly upward at a ninety-degree angle and became a wall; in the other direction it became a stairway.

"Well, we're not exactly spoiled for choices. Let's go," she said, and headed off to climb the stairs, with Leo following a few steps behind.

At the top, the staircase ended in a round landing twice the width of the path they'd been following. Elsa stepped into the center and her stomach lurched with the sudden sensation of gravity abandoning her. Her boots lifted off the floor and she began falling up.

Leo lunged for her, his fingers closing around her ankle, and he dragged her back down. Her stomach twisted as gravity flipped again, and she fell into his arms, too disoriented to try for a neat landing.

Elsa's pulse leapt in her throat, and not just from her narrowly averted fall. Leo's hands lingered, reluctant to let her go, and his touch called up a sharp memory of their last embrace. Sharp like broken glass, because in hindsight she knew he had already been planning to betray her when they'd kissed—and because a part of her wanted to kiss him again, no matter what he'd done.

She pulled back, irritated with Leo for that yearning look he was giving her, and with herself for warming to him despite everything.

"You all right?" he said.

"Localized gravity fields. So no, we're not all right, we're navigating through a death trap."

If only she had her laboratory worldbook with her, she could build a gravitometer to detect the fluctuations before they blundered right into them. But of course she'd scribed her lab book in Veldanese, which meant she couldn't have risked bringing it to Garibaldi's stronghold.

Leo was staring up at the path above them, a strip of gray stone running parallel to the one they'd been following. It hung much lower over their heads now that they'd climbed the stairs.

Elsa rubbed her forehead. "Please don't tell me you're thinking what I think you're thinking."

By way of an answer, Leo lined himself up and stepped deliberately forward into the gravity well. He fell upward, twisting head over heels in midair, and landed neatly—feet-first and upside down—on the path above.

He held his arms out, proud of his demonstration. "It's not a trap, Elsa—it's the way through!"

"Through to where? There are doors scattered all over the place, but they don't look like they lead anywhere."

She had reservations about the idea of using the gravity fields to their advantage. But at the very least it was admittedly disorienting trying to converse with someone who was standing upside down relative to her own perspective. So Elsa took a deep breath, then edged carefully across the gravity transition.

The stone path dropped away, and the world spun around her—an enormous, nonsensical web of stone ribbons momentarily devoid of directionality. The new path came up beneath her and she caught it with the soles of her boots, stumbling two steps forward before her inner ear became entirely convinced of which direction now claimed the mantle of "down."

She straightened cautiously and glanced around to get her bearings. "So what do we do now?"

"We'll just have to follow the gravity pockets until they lead us somewhere useful," Leo said, with a self-assurance that did not seem especially well-earned to Elsa. She still suspected this world was designed to punish any misstep with a rapid demise—specifically, the rapid demise of falling into the Edgemist and ceasing to exist. Not that Leo's confidence would falter over such a petty matter as imminent mortal danger.

"Wonderful," she grumbled. "Here we are again in the land of Leo Knows Best."

He frowned. "What's that supposed to mean?"

"You know exactly what it means," Elsa snapped.

Leo folded his arms. "Are we arguing about the editbook, or about my brother, now? I've lost track."

Elsa felt a hot pressure growing in her chest, restless for release. Back in Pisa she'd been so careful not to vent her feelings, since Faraz and Porzia were struggling enough without the added burden of her hurt. And in Garibaldi's stronghold there was no room for error, no room for honest emotion. But here, in this moment, there was only her and Leo and the dense pain of what they'd done to each other.

"You took my choice away!" The dam inside her breached, and all her bottled-up anger came flowing out. "It was *my* decision, *my* responsibility, and you literally stole it *right out of my hands!*"

"I was trying to protect you!" he shouted back.

"Why couldn't you try to *respect* me, instead? I loved you, and you treated me like a child!"

Leo froze, stunned, and it took Elsa a moment to replay those last words and discover the cause. "You loved me?" he echoed, barely above a whisper. "Is that . . . past tense?"

She took a deep breath and let it out.

"Ask me again when this is over." She turned away, feeling drained and hollowed out, and not wanting to watch his face as he processed what she'd said.

He was silent for long enough that she almost wondered if he'd mysteriously vanished. When he finally spoke, his voice came out carefully measured and controlled. "All right, let's find the editbook."

They started moving again, in the same general direction but upside down from their previous orientation. Leo stalked ahead, managing somehow to keep a lid on his mood. Elsa didn't know whether to feel relieved that the argument had been set aside, or annoyed at his ability to compartmentalize.

At the next gravity shift, it was Leo who began to float away, and Elsa who frantically grabbed the back of his waistcoat to pull him back down to safety. This time there was no path above them to aim for—just empty air and, eventually, the oblivion of Edgemist. So they turned around and went back in the direction from which they'd come.

Soon they reached the open doorway in the floor—the one Elsa had noticed on the ceiling when they'd first arrived—and Leo crouched beside the rectangular hole to investigate.

"We can walk around it," Elsa pointed out, exasperated.

"Sure," he said, "but does that seem like the cleverest possible solution? We need to think like Aris."

Leo pressed his palms against the stone, right on the edge, and deliberately tipped forward. Still holding on to the frame, he swung headfirst into the doorway, and then climbed all the way through to stand on the opposite surface of the same path.

Elsa stepped up to the edge and looked through, only to see Leo looking back at her like a reflection in a pool of water. "You've got to be joking."

He crouched and reached a hand through the doorway. "It's fine, I'll pull you through."

She also crouched and grabbed his hand. After a childhood spent scrambling over the wild terrain of Veldana, Elsa considered herself quite physically competent, but this world presented a whole new challenge. She was not too proud to accept assistance if it meant not falling to her death.

Leo pulled her down until the gravity flipped and down became up, and she was scrambling to get all four of her limbs onto the path.

Elsa felt Leo suddenly tense beside her. "Did you see that?" he said, fast and hushed.

Elsa almost asked, *What?* but when she looked around the motion caught her eye—something large and winged and green-skinned, moving with easy confidence through the maze. It leapt, twisted, and fell, landed as sure-footed as a cat, and moved on through the next gravity shift. Even at a distance, the creature's grace was mesmerizing to behold.

At last, the creature ducked out of sight behind a stone stairway. Elsa waited to catch sight of it emerging somewhere, but it did not reappear.

"There," said Leo, as if this were a victory. "That's where we need to go."

His self-assurance was definitely starting to grate on Elsa's nerves. "And how did you leap to that particular conclusion?"

"Unless she literally vanished, there's something over there— something that merits building a big, scary, taloned construct to protect it. What could it be, except the editbook?"

"For all I know, Aris built a big scary construct to guard his extensive collection of big scary constructs," she retorted.

"Do you have a better idea of where to look?" he huffed.

Elsa admitted that she did not, and so Leo began planning out a route through the gravity maze. She let him take the lead, mostly because they'd already wasted enough time and energy on arguing. They jumped and climbed and slid, fell in all sorts of directions, backtracked when they reached a dead end, and did it all over again.

It was strange being able to see their destination, see all the various paths that converged there, and yet still need to rely on trial and error to approach it. At a distance there was no way to judge the orientations—did a particular section of path or set of stairs have gravity on one side or the other, or both, or neither?

Even having seen the clockwork creature move through the maze proved to be of little use. Leo tried to lead them along the route the creature had taken, but upon closer inspection, some of the leaps would be dangerous at best for anyone who lacked wings.

They got stuck on a long stairway, which ran parallel to the path they wanted. Leo paced, looking for a solution; in the middle of the stairway the gravity shifted ninety degrees, so climbing down became climbing up, which made pacing a rather dizzying prospect.

Their target path ran parallel to the stairway but was angled such that it looked like a wall from their current perspective. Elsa tilted her head, pondering the gravity vectors.

"We jump from the middle of the stairs," she suddenly declared.

"What?" Leo called, returning from the far end of the stairway.

Elsa walked down to the transition point, where the stairs had two equally useless surfaces and moving in either direction would mean climbing up. "The two gravity vectors are mostly canceling each other out in the middle. Can't you feel it? The pull is weakest here."

Leo folded his arms. "If you're hoping I'm going to tell you not to try it, I should warn you I've already used up my daily allotment of caution."

She ignored him and lay down on her side, wedged between two stairs with her legs hanging off the edge of the staircase. "Grab my arm," she insisted.

He crouched and locked arms with her. Holding her legs straight out to the side as best she could, Elsa slid off the stairs into empty air. Her stomach lurched as the gravity of the path beneath her feet caught ahold of her.

"Okay, let go!"

Leo released her arm, and she fell onto the path with a thud that jarred her knees. She stepped away to make room for Leo to follow, and he landed behind her with a bit more grace. They'd finally done it—this path ran directly behind the wide stairway where they'd seen the clockwork creature vanish.

Elsa peered ahead, looking for details of their destination through the web of paths obstructing her view. "Is that a wall? As in a *real* wall?"

"I told you there was something hidden over there," said Leo.

Elsa did an eye roll that would've made Porzia proud. "Fair warning: if this turns out to be Aris's collection of disembodied heads preserved in jars, I'll be severely disappointed."

Behind the stairs was a wide wall with a door set into it—not one of Aris's rectangular holes, but a real door. Elsa didn't protest when Leo squeezed past her to take the lead, since he had his rapier on him and she was still without her revolver. He turned the knob quickly and ducked through.

At last on the other side was a proper room, with a floor, a ceiling, four walls, and a couple of doorways leading into farther chambers. It was furnished like a parlor and even had a fireplace. Elsa had never in her life felt so relieved to be enclosed.

Seated on the floor, leaning his back against an armchair, was a strange boy. Or perhaps it was a boy-shaped construct—the integration of flesh and machine was so extensive as to make Elsa unsure of her determination. No, she decided, changing her mind again: he was a boy. Mostly a boy.

The right half of his skull had been replaced with glass, through which the pulsing veins of his brain were visible. His right eye socket was brass from the brow ridge to the cheekbone, with a mechanical eye like a glowing red monocle set within. Two fingers on his left hand were mechanical replacements as well as the entire right hand, and from the flash of brass visible through his open shirt collar, Elsa guessed the replacement went all the way up the arm and over the shoulder.

He looked pale and delicate, about the size of Porzia's sister Olivia, but something about his expression made her think he was older than he looked. His hair, where he had any, was an indeterminate dusty blond-brown. There was almost nothing familiar about him—almost.

For the half-metal boy was staring at them, eyes wide, and his organic left eye was an unmistakable shade of amber.

Beside Elsa, Leo stood as frozen as a statue. He did not even seem to breathe.

"Pasca?" Leo said, choking on the name.

17

BEING DEEPLY LOVED BY SOMEONE GIVES YOU STRENGTH,
WHILE LOVING SOMEONE DEEPLY GIVES YOU COURAGE.
—*Lao Tzu*

L eo stared into his little brother's face and the ground seemed to shift beneath his feet. A reorientation of tectonic proportions. Pasca was alive—this changed everything.

Pasca clambered to his feet, and though he said nothing, Leo could swear there was recognition on his face. Even after so long apart, and whatever horrors had befallen him, they knew each other instinctually, blood calling to blood.

Leo felt as if he'd had a metal chip wedged into the gears in his heart, wedged so tight between the teeth and for so long that he'd forgotten they were supposed to turn at all. Now, suddenly, the blockage came loose and his mainspring could finally unwind the tension he'd carried for seven years.

He moved to close the distance between them, but the clockwork creature bolted in through another door and stepped in front of Pasca. She loomed menacingly over the interlopers and growled deep in her throat. Pasca reached up and placed a hand on her elbow, calming her.

The creature made some intricate gesture at Pasca, the bronze tips of her long fingers clacking together. Pasca responded with a brief but very specific gesture of his own.

"It's a language," Elsa said, her voice bright with fascination, "a visual language, composed of hand shape and position and movement. Do you see?"

"I . . . what?" Leo was too stunned by Pasca's mere physical existence to be making inferences.

Elsa imitated their gestures as they silently conversed, and when the creature noticed what Elsa was doing, she stopped mid-sentence and stared. In that infuriatingly easy way of hers, Elsa began communicating with the creature.

Leo couldn't wait any longer, and he fell upon Pasca with an embrace that nearly knocked the boy off his feet. Pasca was older now and taller and hard metal in places that used to be flesh over bone, but he felt solid and real, so real, and after a moment of surprise he was hugging Leo back. Nothing else in the universe mattered.

But Leo's talent for analysis was gradually returning, and as the objective part of his mind began observing and cataloging the facts, it felt more like a curse than a gift. Fact: Pasca was trapped in a worldbook with a construct for his only companion. Which meant he may have lived in near-total isolation for half his childhood. Fact: Leo had never heard of a person with such extensive body modifications. The procedures must have been intensive and excruciating; it was a miracle of science that he'd recovered at all. And Pasca had not spoken aloud, nor responded to the words spoken in his presence.

Leo relaxed his embrace and held Pasca at arm's length

instead, hands on his shoulders. He looked pallid—from struggling health or lack of sun or both—but there was alertness in his eye. In the organic one, at least; the mechanical replacement had an uncanny gaze.

"Little brother, what happened to you?"

Pasca shook his head, though Leo wasn't sure if he meant he didn't know the answer or couldn't understand the question. There was no time to work it out, though, because the door behind Leo banged open.

He spun around to see a furious Aris. "You're not supposed to be in here, brother. And you're definitely not supposed to bring guests," he said, with a glance at Elsa.

Leo stared, momentarily speechless. "Is there *nothing* you won't lie about?"

Aris ignored the question. He made a precise, impatient hand gesture at the clockwork creature, who bowed her head contritely in response. Then he said, "Come along, you two," to Leo and Elsa, as if they were naughty children.

Elsa protested, "We most certainly will not."

Leo scrubbed his face with both hands. "Oh, Aris, what have you done to Pasca?"

"What would you have done? I couldn't very well let him die. He's my *brother*," Aris said, as if that should be explanation enough.

"Of course not. Not *your* brother," Leo replied acidly.

"What is that supposed to mean?"

"You turned Pasca into an experiment! We're not your playthings, Aris—you don't own us. Did you even ask him what he wanted first, before implanting all these mechanical body parts?"

Aris smirked. "We are, all three of us, experiments. You know that as well as I."

"Look at what you have done. You tortured him."

"I tried to fix him. I'm still trying! This is your fault, anyway—if you'd kept better track of him, Rosalinda would have gotten him out safely, and he never would've been trapped in the fire." Aris made a guttural noise of frustration. "I can't believe we're arguing about this, of all things. I thought you'd be happy he's alive."

"Then why didn't you tell me? Why did you keep him hidden?"

Aris tossed his hands in the air. "I was worried you'd over-react. Oh, look, I was right."

"Because you kept him locked away like a prisoner!" Leo said.

"To protect him!"

"From what?"

"From Father!" Aris bellowed.

Leo stared at him, their gazes locked. The very air between them seemed to carry an electric charge. Could it be true that Aris had found something he wanted more than Ricciotti's approval? That his loyalty to his brothers outweighed his loyalty to their father? Leo felt as if a fist were squeezing his heart, a painful twinge of hope in his chest.

No, he could not afford to indulge in it. "I'm taking Pasca away from here," he decided. "As you should have, if you'd any sense."

"I don't think so." Aris clutched his portal device and dialed madly. An odd little portal no larger than a dinner plate opened beside him, the black disk lying horizontally instead of standing up in the proper orientation. He reached in with one hand and withdrew a rapier.

Leo unsheathed his own, but before he could face off against his elder brother, Elsa yanked out a pocket watch and said, "We hardly have time for this again." Then she threw something small that shattered against Aris's hand.

Aris's eyelids drooped and his grip loosened, letting the weapon fall to the floor, and he followed it down a moment later.

"Faraz's sleeping potion," Elsa explained.

"Nice throw," said Leo.

"I was aiming for his face, but I'll take what I can get." She tucked the empty watch casing back into her pocket with an efficient, practical motion that was so very . . . *Elsa*, that he almost leaned in to kiss her before he remembered. "So," she said, "are we rescuing your little brother, or what?"

Elsa tried not to dwell on what a catastrophe this was. All her careful deceptions, the progress she'd made toward earning Aris's trust . . . her whole plan up in smoke.

Leo hovered in the doorway leading out into the gravity maze, trying to convince his brother to follow with an emphatic wave of his hand. Pasca hesitated, his brows knotted with worry as he stared down at Aris's unconscious form. His weight shifted from foot to foot, as if a part of him wanted to follow, yet another part was tied to Aris with an invisible string.

Elsa touched his shoulder to draw the boy's attention and inclined her head toward the door.

Aris doesn't like it when I go out in the maze, Pasca signed. *It's dangerous.*

The language was still new to her, but Elsa stumbled her way through an explanation. *Leo wants to bring you to the people who took care of him. There will be other children your age, and you won't have to hide.*

"What's wrong? We have to move!" Leo said desperately.

Elsa replied aloud, "He has to choose this for himself, Leo. Otherwise we're no better than Aris." Then she signed to Pasca, *I know leaving is scary, and I know Aris cared for you as best he knew how. But you can't spend your whole life locked away.*

Pasca stared at Leo, as if to search for something in his brother's eyes. After a breathless moment, he nodded. *Okay.*

They made their way back through the gravity maze, the clockwork creature in the lead with Pasca carried in her arms. When they arrived back in Aris's lab, Elsa paused by the formerly hidden bookshelves. "Hold on a minute," she said, and ran her hands across the spines, this time pulling out the volumes that *didn't* feel like worldbooks.

Leo paced back to her side with nervous energy. "What are you looking for?"

"Someone who keeps his lab this neat is probably a meticulous note taker. And if Aris kept detailed medical records on Pasca, the records should leave with him. Might need them later."

She flipped through the journals and notebooks until she found one with design sketches for a child-size mechanical hand. "Here," she said, passing it to Leo. "Let's go."

The clockwork creature set Pasca on his own two feet now that they were through the difficulty of the maze, and everyone poured out into the hallway.

Leo turned automatically in the direction of the ballroom, but Elsa hissed, "Not that way. There are always guards watching the front door."

"Where then?" Leo hissed back.

Elsa's mind raced, considering the possibilities. The only other exit she knew about was the attic door leading to the airship courtyard. But there were people who knew the fortress better than she did.

She turned to the clockwork creature and signed, *You go out a window. Wait for us outside, we'll meet you.*

Elsa's signing was still awkward and clunky with the newness of the language, but the creature seemed to understand. She turned to Pasca first—not quite asking permission, but confirming that he was comfortable with this plan—and then she departed, moving much more stealthily than her size would suggest possible.

"Now," Elsa whispered, "where are the servants' quarters, do you know?"

Leo nodded. "I can find them."

On the bottom floor in the back of the house was a narrow, windowless corridor off which the servants slept. Elsa and Leo had to—very quietly—check several rooms before finding Colette asleep on her small cot.

Elsa shook the girl awake and switched to Provençal. "I'm sorry to disturb you, but it's urgent."

Colette blinked sleepily. "Yes? What's happening?"

"This is important." Elsa held the girl's gaze, her tone low and intense. "Can you sneak us out of the house?"

Colette hesitated, looking past Elsa and taking in the unfamiliar sight of Pasca.

"Colette?" Elsa prompted.

She saw the decision in the girl's eyes, like the flip of a switch, commitment replacing doubt.

"There's a side door off the kitchen for unloading deliveries," Colette said. "It's kept locked, so it won't be watched, but I can get the key."

She threw a robe atop her nightgown and led the way. From

an office near the kitchen, she stole a large iron key, then led them past the counters and stoves and through the pantry to the supply entrance.

Colette lit a hooded outdoor lantern that she found hanging on a peg beside the door and traded it for Leo's. "It's brighter," she explained, "and aims in one direction . . ."

Leo nodded. "So it's harder to spot from the house. Thank you."

Colette simply dipped her head in that deferential manner servants used with their employers. She fitted the large key into the lock and flipped the heavy dead bolt; it unlocked with a metallic *thunk*, loud against the silence of the house, making Elsa wince.

Leo and Pasca went through first, out into the night where the clockwork creature waited for them. But Elsa stopped short, her hand on the doorframe. If she let go now to follow Leo, the door would be locked to her forever after. She'd never get back into the house, or back into Aris's confidence.

Leo looked over his shoulder and paused, waving at her urgently. "What are you doing? Come on, we have to move!"

Her feet stayed rooted in the open doorway. "I can't leave without the editbook."

"What—Elsa, I need you!" His voice rose in desperation. "How am I supposed to get Pasca back to Pisa without you?"

"Vincenzo will find you—he promised he'd stay nearby in case we needed him," she said, trying to sound more confident than she felt. "He has a receiver disguised as a portal device that will lead you to where the doorbook's hidden in Trento."

Leo tossed his hands in the air. "I can't use the doorbook, I'm not a scriptologist!"

"All you have to do is read the coordinates, it's not that difficult. You'll figure it out." Behind her, Colette shifted her weight nervously, so Elsa told the girl, "It's fine, we're done here."

"Wait! Elsa—" Leo called, but she was already ducking inside. The heavy door closed, cutting off his words.

As Colette turned the key and the dead bolt clacked into position, Elsa leaned against the wall. She slid down until she was crouched on the floor in the shadows.

The guilt she could bear. But worse, there was part of her that felt some grim satisfaction at the act of turning away from Leo in his hour of need—eye for an eye, betrayal for a betrayal. Elsa did not like that ugly part of herself very much.

Colette's soft-soled slippers whispered against the slate floor as she moved to the end of the hall. She peered around the corner, checking the kitchen, then returned to Elsa's side, bringing with her the lantern's circle of light.

"Are you well, Elsa?"

Elsa cast the other girl a wry look. "You mean aside from being a terrible person?"

Colette paused, as if uncertain how to respond. "We should go. It wouldn't do to get caught at the door in the middle of the night."

"You're right." Elsa pushed to her feet, resigned to the course she had chosen. She was staying, so she'd better do it thoroughly.

She headed back to the mechanics laboratory, and the gravity maze, and Aris.

Elsa sat cross-legged on the floor of Pasca's plush prison and waited for Aris to regain consciousness. At first she'd tried to move him to the divan, but his limp weight proved too much for her alone. So the carpet it was for them both. She dabbed at his forehead with a damp cloth, which probably wasn't doing anything useful but nonetheless seemed appropriate.

Eventually he stirred, and when his eyes opened, he blinked blearily up at her.

"There you are," she said. "Welcome back to the land of the conscious."

He slurred, "Wha did you . . ."

"Sorry about all that," she said, setting aside the damp cloth. "I have a weak spot for Leo, as you well know."

"Leo? Where—"

"He left with Pasca." At this Aris attempted to sit up, agitated, but Elsa pushed him back down. "Relax, there's no point. He has a five-hour head start—they could be anywhere by now." She hadn't expected Aris to stay asleep so long; Faraz must have gotten a bit overenthusiastic with the potency.

"You knocked me out," Aris said indignantly, just now piecing together the memories.

"Mm, and I'm sure this violation of your trust comes as a terrible shock, given that you never trusted me in the first place," she said. "Besides, I owed you one for that time your sleeping gas knocked me out."

"When we took your mother? That was a lifetime ago," he scoffed. "I thought you came here to bury the hatchet."

"That was last month, and don't pretend you didn't know I came here for Leo. But now that I've discharged my duties to him, I am . . . free." Even Elsa could no longer tell where the truth ended and the lies began. She had sent Leo back home to Faraz and Rosalinda, as promised. And if the implication was, *free to be with Aris*, was that not also technically accurate?

Aris propped himself up, with more care and deliberation this time. "'Free' is such a delicious word, don't you think? How do you say it in Veldanese?"

"Hmm . . . there's no exact word, though the phrase *weh iket-nenu veralsa* comes close in practical usage."

"*Weh iket-nenu veralsa*," Aris repeated. "What's the literal translation?"

Elsa just smiled. It meant, *Never is the white guy coming back.*

18

To understand is to forgive.

—*Blaise Pascal*

Leo stepped out of the portal onto the train platform in Riomaggiore and heaved a sigh of relief.

Vincenzo had met up with them almost immediately—he must have been hiding in the valley, keeping an eye on the fortress—and gave Leo a receiver cleverly disguised as a portal device. After the long walk into town, Leo had used the receiver to home in on Elsa's supplies, hidden behind a crate in a storage area inside the clock tower. He'd opened the portal using coordinates from the doorbook, but the doorbook itself needed to stay behind in Trento with Vincenzo—otherwise Elsa would've been stranded in the Austrian Empire.

Which meant that if this portal hadn't worked, Leo and Pasca would've been the stranded ones.

A cool breeze off the water brought the salt-scent of the sea, and Leo watched his brother breathe deep of it. Riomaggiore was still cloaked in night, but the sky behind the rough hills to the east was starting to pale. The clockwork creature stuck to Pasca's side protectively, though she looked around in wonder at everything, equally impressed with the vast ocean and the quaint little village.

Leo checked his clothes and discovered a bit of luck: the bills stuffed forgotten in his trouser pocket were Sardinian currency. He'd never spent enough time in Trento to bother exchanging them for Austrian money.

"We can get some breakfast in town and then take the morning train to Corniglia." Porzia had left a note with the doorbook instructing Elsa not to return to Casa della Pazzia under any circumstances. "You must be exhausted after all that hiking around the Trentino countryside, yeah?"

Pasca did not reply. Leo realized his brother had his eyes closed, facing into the sea breeze, and did not even know Leo had spoken. Pasca was deaf.

The clockwork creature had heard him, though, and while she did not seem to comprehend, she nonetheless touched Pasca's shoulder to catch his attention. Pasca glanced up at her, then turned an expectant gaze upon Leo.

In that moment, Leo would have traded a limb for the Veldanese talent at languages. To get his little brother back from the jaws of death, physically here and yet unable to communicate . . . it made Leo feel as if he'd swallowed ground glass.

Pasca had been only seven years old the last time Leo had laid eyes upon him. He didn't look fourteen now, though simple math insisted he must be. Perhaps the stasis chamber—the one Ricciotti had used on Jumi—was originally invented with someone else in mind. Either way, it was clear Pasca had been through hell, and Leo could not even ask him what he needed.

He decided he'd better at least try to let Pasca know his plan for their immediate future. He pointed at his mouth, then gestured at the train tracks.

Pasca narrowed his eyes, confused.

Leo suppressed a sigh and tried again, holding up a finger to indicate *first, food* and two fingers for *second, train ride.*

Pasca's expression opened with comprehension, and he nodded.

That was something; that was a start at least. Now that Leo had liberated Pasca from Aris's custody, there was no choice but to make this work. His little brother would be his whole world now.

Leo couldn't admit how terrified he was to return until he found himself in the grand hall surrounded by a cluster of excited children shouting questions. He spotted Faraz the instant his best friend entered the room, and as Faraz's long strides ate up the distance between them, a small part of Leo wanted to freeze time, his dread at what would come next too intense to face. But then those familiar lanky arms were embracing him, and Leo's throat tightened. He hadn't ruined his closest friendship, after all.

"Leonardo Garibaldi!" A voice echoed in the deep, shadowed recesses of the entrance hall. Faraz let go of him, the children fell silent, and all eyes turned to the archway where Porzia stood, fists against hips.

Porzia crossed the expanse of floor as if her fury were like the pressure in a steam chamber, powering her. "How dare you. How *dare* you!" Leo stiffened, and Faraz pulled back from him a step, as if instinct demanded he withdraw out of range of her ire.

"Don't call me Garibaldi," Leo growled.

She arched an eyebrow. "What should I call you then?"

"'Trovatelli' will do just fine," he said, with a raw finality in his voice. The surname Trovatelli meant *foundling*. *Orphan*. It was the alias he'd grown up using before he knew his father's real identity; to reclaim it now had layers of meaning he hoped she'd understand.

Porzia sniffed, determined not to soften so easily. "Don't think this is over—I'm not done with you yet." She turned her gaze upon his traveling companions. "Where is Elsa?"

Leo winced. "She stayed behind."

"You're saying you left Elsa there," Porzia said flatly. "Alone with your megalomaniacal father."

Guilt bloomed in his chest, but he said, "Vincenzo's keeping an eye on things. And anyway, it was her decision."

"Unbelievable," Porzia muttered.

Faraz pointed out, "She did promise to pursue the editbook, first and foremost."

"Faraz, I'm shocked—*shocked*, I say—that you're rushing to his defense," Porzia answered, voice dripping with sarcasm. She looked again at the clockwork creature and at Pasca, as if truly noticing him for the first time. "Leo . . . who is this?"

Leo's mouth pressed into a thin line. The words didn't want to come out. Finally he managed to say, "This is my brother, Pasca."

Porzia stared, stunned. Beneath all his gruesome modifications, Pasca looked pale and tired, and something in Porzia's expression softened. "Olivia?" she called.

The girl seemed to appear at Porzia's elbow as soon as her name was spoken. "Yes?"

"Will you please take Leo's brother upstairs and find him a quiet place to rest?"

Leo twitched at the word *quiet* but decided it wouldn't be prudent to correct her on the irrelevancy of quiet to a boy who could not hear. Olivia gently coaxed Pasca and the creature to follow her, taking the boy by his mechanical hand and smiling at him. Leo felt relieved at the thought of having help taking care of Pasca . . . followed immediately by deep shame at his own relief.

As Pasca and company left the hall, a dark-skinned stranger passed them; the clockwork creature leaned curiously toward the young man, who squeezed against the wall to give her a wide berth. Porzia peeled away to intercept him, and from her gestures she was explaining the situation to the new boy.

Leo frowned and asked Faraz, "Who's that?"

"Elsa's friend, Revan," Faraz said.

"Elsa doesn't have any other friends—we're literally the only people she knows on the planet."

"From Veldana," Faraz explained, giving Leo a quizzical look. "Where has your deductive genius gone? Is this the real Leo, or an automaton replacement?"

"Oh," Leo said, feeling stupid. "In my defense, he doesn't have the eyes."

"Why would you assume all Veldanese have green eyes?"

Leo shrugged off the question, too busy trying to remember. Hadn't Elsa said something about how Leo wasn't the first boy she'd seen with his shirt off? His scowl deepened. "So . . . wait. Define 'friend.'"

Faraz laughed. "Sorry for doubting you—you're *definitely* our Leo."

After Pasca had rested, they took over the long table in the dining room and spent the afternoon on the difficult task of establishing communications. Pasca's mechanical right hand seemed quite dexterous when he signed, but it lacked the muscle memory for writing, so he could only write in the jerky fashion of a child first learning to hold a pen. That was sufficient, at least, to write a word in big, blocky letters, and then sign the same word, teaching Leo the visual language he now relied upon.

Leo was not a fast learner; language had never been his strength. And though hope crested like a wave when he learned Pasca could still speak aloud, that same hope came crashing down as he realized his brother was painfully self-conscious of speaking words he could not hear.

Leo had been an older brother again for mere hours, and already it overwhelmed him. How was he supposed to take care of this child who felt like a stranger, with whom he couldn't even speak?

He rose and left the table, needing a moment to himself, but Porzia followed him out into the empty entrance hall.

She folded her arms tight over her ribs. "You haven't explained why you turned on us yet."

"It was a deal to protect Elsa—a foolish deal." Leo scuffed the toe of his boot against the floor. "Your note didn't have any details about what happened at Casa della Pazzia. Is everyone safe?"

"Do you care, one way or the other?" Porzia gibed.

"Of course I do."

"The younger children are locked in the nursery, and Mamma and Burak stayed behind. We've had no word from them."

"Well, thank you for taking in my brother and me, despite the terrible timing."

Porzia gave him a glacial stare. "Pasca is welcome to stay with us. I haven't decided about *you* yet."

Leo let the threat go. He knew her too well; if she were going to throw him out, she wouldn't have hesitated so long. "I don't know what to do for Pasca. He's been locked away and experimented on for half his life—is that something a person can ever recover from?"

"He's safe here for now." She sighed. "The rest we'll figure out in time."

Would they, though? Was any amount of care and patience enough to erase the horrors of the past? Not in Leo's experience. Listlessly, he said, "It might have been better if Aris had let him die."

Porzia's eyes went wide with shock, and then she slapped him across the cheek. "Don't you dare say that, not ever! No matter what's happened to his body, your brother is still in there."

Leo raised a hand to rub his stinging cheek. "He used to love scriptology. Now he can't even hear, let alone write cleanly enough to scribe. What sort of a life is that?"

"Are you so blinded by your father as to think a person's worth can only be measured in madness? That to be silent is to be less than whole? Olivia knows that is not so, and she's only twelve. Grow up, Leo."

Leo didn't have time to formulate a response, because at that moment Sante burst in through the front doors, his eyes wild with excitement. "There's an airship coming over the mountains!"

"An airship!" Porzia said sharply. Airships did not visit tiny, remote villages like Corniglia. "We have to get the children inside."

Leo grabbed his rapier from where he'd left it by the front doors and bolted outside, a step behind the others. Porzia was yelling at Sante to stay, and Sante was rushing to keep up with her, yelling back that he could help.

And then Leo caught sight of it: the airship skimmed close over the rolling peaks of the Apennines, the landscape seeming to dwarf it at first, but it grew larger and larger as it aimed straight for the ruins. Great mechanical wings extended out from the sides of the gondola, sailcloth stretched over jointed metal frames, and cold panic flooded Leo like ice water in his veins. *Aris's* airship.

Hovering above the clearing where the children had been playing, the airship opened its belly and let down half a dozen ropes like tentacles reaching for the earth. Black-clad soldiers rappelled to the ground below, armed with rapiers and military sabers, moving with the precision of Carbonari training.

At least they didn't have guns. Was that a sign Aris didn't want his men using lethal force? Or simply a sign of his hubris?

Leo spotted Revan near the trees north of the ruins, swinging his sling in a blur of gathering momentum, and he couldn't help but grin. If the Veldanese kid was as competent as he looked with that thing, the invaders were going to be sorry they didn't bring ranged weapons. Leo, on the other hand, ran to intercept them head-on, buying Porzia the time to frantically herd the children inside.

He met the nearest soldier sword-to-sword, and after only three parries he made an opening in his opponent's defense. Leo ran him through and left him coughing blood and dying in the dirt. He couldn't afford to dwell on what he'd done; for now he was nothing but the weapon Rosalinda had trained him to be. So he followed the song of adrenaline in his ears and moved on to his next target.

Leo dispatched another enemy, then looked up for the next. Halfway across the clearing, he spotted Sante closing in on an attacker with a rapier he'd stolen off a corpse. God, what was the boy thinking? Leo's feet moved, trying desperately to close the distance even as his brain worked out the cold calculation of how long it would take a Carbonari-trained fighter to disarm a thirteen-year-old.

Sunlight glinted off Sante's weapon as it spun out of his hand, and the boy went down in a splash of red. Stabbing the attacker in the back was almost an afterthought for Leo; all that mattered was the deep gash the man's saber had sliced across Sante's torso.

Leo dropped his rapier and fell to his knees beside Sante. He pressed his handkerchief to the wound, but the cloth was too small and soaked through in seconds; Sante made awful groaning sounds, eyes glassy with shock.

How was it possible to feel this helpless? Where was Porzia, or Faraz, or anyone? Suddenly Leo was sweating and shaking, and he was eleven years old again in a house on fire, pulling the pocket watch off his father's corpse, or so he'd believed. He gulped quick, deep breaths, desperate to banish the memory and cling to the present.

"Porzia," he tried to shout, but he could find no air.

Porzia scanned the clearing in front of the ruins for wayward children, but the frantic racing of her heart made it difficult to focus. The resonant growl of the airship engine and the enormous wings buffeting the earth added to the chaos. There were men on the ground—dead or incapacitated thanks to Revan and Leo—but a second wave of attackers followed the first few men, and these wore bulky contraptions over their faces, obscuring their features.

One of the soldiers threw a metal canister at Revan; it landed at his feet, and he looked down at it, confused. Porzia stared as a horrible realization dawned on her: the contraptions worn by the soldiers weren't masks, they were some kind of respirators, like the ones Elsa had built in the labyrinth world.

"Revan!" she screamed. "Kick it away! Cover your mouth!"

Instead of following her instructions, Revan looked up at her, as if he wasn't sure he'd heard her correctly. Then the canister began to spray gas in all directions, enveloping him in a gray cloud, and his expression of surprise quickly went slack. Revan collapsed, unconscious.

Or dead, Porzia thought to herself as she whipped out a handkerchief to cover her nose and mouth. At least the gas was dissipating quickly, carried away on the wind created by the powerful wing strokes of the airship. Porzia was grateful they'd met the assault outside instead of holing up within the ruins. In a confined space, one or two canisters would be enough to knock out all of them.

As soon as she dared, Porzia ran to Revan's side, still holding the handkerchief over her face against any traces of gas that remained. With her free hand, she scrambled to find his pulse— he had one, slow but strong, and relief flooded through her like cool water in her veins. Then the hard sole of a boot landed on her shoulder and shoved her aside, sending her sprawling in the grass, the back of her head hitting the ground with enough force to make stars burst in her vision.

She scrambled to find her feet, but her sense of balance listed wildly, and by the time her head cleared, two of the attackers were dragging Revan away toward the airship.

"Stop!" she shouted uselessly, but she got her feet under her and bolted after them as fast as her skirts would allow.

As if Revan's capture had been a signal, all the remaining soldiers ran back to the airship and grabbed ahold of the ropes. The soldiers climbed, while Revan's limp form—now trapped in a rope harness—was reeled in from above. Porzia reached the ground below the airship just as Revan disappeared into the belly of the mechanical beast.

But they'd arrived with more men than were now in condition to retreat . . . which meant there were a few ropes free and empty, still brushing the ground.

"Porzia, no! Don't!" Leo shouted.

She glanced over her shoulder; he was crouched over something on the ground, she couldn't see what. It didn't matter. Someone had to go after Revan—they couldn't just let the soldiers kidnap him.

Porzia grabbed the rope in both hands, and it lifted her off her feet. For a terrifying second she struggled with her skirts, then managed to pinch the rope between her knees, securing her hold. The ground dropped away beneath her.

"Not your best-laid plan, Porzia," she muttered to herself, clinging to the rope as the airship rose into the sky.

19

IT IS NOT ALWAYS THE SAME THING TO BE A GOOD MAN
AND A GOOD CITIZEN.
—*Aristotle*

Elsa hadn't seen Aris all morning, and she couldn't find him anywhere. After a fruitless search of the fortress—or at least a search of all the unlocked rooms—she gave up and sat in her room, defeated and worried.

It seemed an ominous sign for Aris to vanish like this. She imagined him locking himself away in a scribed world, determined not to eat or sleep until he deciphered the editbook.

When a knock came, she assumed it must be Aris, done pouting about Leo's departure and ready for some verbal sparring. But when she opened the door it was Garibaldi who strode in.

"Signor," she said cautiously. "To what do I owe the honor . . . ?"

"We must speak," he declared. "Come, sit."

Garibaldi took the chair that went with the writing desk, and Elsa perched on the edge of the bed, reminding herself not to act nervous.

"Both my sons seem quite taken with you," he began. Elsa didn't know what to say to that. Apologize? Deny it? But Garibaldi continued, sparing her from the need to choose a response. "I, however, can't say I see what all the fuss is about, if we're to be frank."

"Excuse me?" Elsa raised her eyebrows in disbelief.

"I'm disappointed in you, Elsa—you've been putting on airs, leading Aris to believe you're a unique commodity. I'll reluctantly admit it's been a source of some friction between us." Garibaldi pinned her with his gaze. "But you're not the only Veldanese speaker on Earth, are you?"

Elsa went cold. Revan. How could Garibaldi possibly know about him? She tried to keep her expression mild, to prevent her fear from giving anything away. "I suppose Charles Montaigne knows a few phrases—he did scribe my world, after all—but he's hardly fluent enough to understand the editbook."

"Oh no, not him," Garibaldi said. "We did take Montaigne off the Order's hands, but you're right that he proved of little use."

"Who, then?"

Garibaldi showed her a horrible, gloating smile. Elsa felt sick to her stomach.

He stood without another word and left, pulling the door closed behind him. Terror sharp in her veins, Elsa darted for the door, but there was a mechanical whirring sound on the other side, and when she yanked the knob it did not open. She pressed her eye close to the crack—they'd attached some kind of locking mechanism to the outside of the door.

She was trapped, and Garibaldi was going after Revan.

It was difficult to say how many hours passed. Elsa didn't have a real watch, just the empty casing Faraz had given her, which had worked well as a potion-hiding place but helped not at all with telling the time. The sky outside was a thick slate gray, so not even the angle of the sun could give her a hint.

Eventually, Elsa heard the *click-whir* of the locking mechanism. The door opened just far enough to admit Colette, then the guard in the hall closed it again.

"I've brought you an early dinner, signorina," the girl said, holding up a silver service tray with a domed lid.

Elsa looked away, disheartened. "Thank you, Colette, but my appetite's abandoned me." Her stomach twisted into anxious knots every time she wondered what Aris was up to, and that thought was never far from her mind.

"No, signorina," Colette said significantly. "I'm sure you'll want this meal."

Elsa turned her attention back, her eyes widening as understanding dawned. Colette gave a small, conspiratorial smile, and lifted the lid.

There was no food. Upon the tray sat two enormous kitchen knives.

"On second thought, you're probably right. I should take the tray," Elsa said.

Colette set it down on the desk, and they each quietly lifted one of the knives. Elsa positioned herself behind the door, out of the line of sight, while Colette knocked to signal the guard to let her out.

The door opened just wide enough to let Colette slip through the opening, but she came out brandishing her knife at the guard's face, with Elsa ready to follow right behind. The guard was much larger than either of them, but he didn't have a weapon out because he needed both hands free to operate the locking mechanism and the door handle. He flinched in surprise, then plucked the knife from Colette's grip and backhanded her hard enough to knock her to the ground. In those precious seconds of distraction, Elsa rushed to close the distance.

The guard pulled his foot back as if to kick Colette, but Elsa growled, "Don't," pressing the pointed tip of her carving knife into his lower back. "A stab wound to the kidney is a fast way to bleed out."

The guard froze, then dropped Colette's knife and held his hands up in surrender. Gruffly, he said, "Haven't thought this through, have you, signorina? Unless you're prepared to commit murder."

"That's a tempting offer, given how hard you hit my friend. But instead, you're going to turn—slowly!—and get inside the room."

Elsa kept her knife on him as he followed her instructions. When he'd moved all the way through the door, she withdrew quickly, pulling the door shut and flipping the lock.

As soon as the locking mechanism clicked into place, Elsa rushed to Colette's side and helped her stand. "Are you hurt?"

A livid mark rose across her cheek; she raised a hand to press against it, wincing. "I don't think I'll lose any teeth, so that's something."

"I'm so sorry, this is all my fault," Elsa said miserably. When she'd set out to befriend the servants, she hadn't thought anyone would get hurt.

Colette stretched her neck as if the blow had wrenched a muscle. "I knew what I was getting myself into when I brought that tray."

Elsa smiled. "Of course. And thank you."

Colette inclined her head in acknowledgment. "Now, we'd better get out of here before we're seen."

Elsa followed as the other girl strode down the hall. "Do you still have the key for the kitchen door?"

Colette shook her head. "Not that way—there's a guard posted there now, and I wouldn't care to try our luck with the knives again."

Instead of leading her down into the warren of servants' corridors, Colette took the stairs up and up—headed for the high courtyard where Aris parked his airship. As they climbed, Elsa worried about Colette's involvement.

"Are you sure you should be helping me so openly? Do you have anyone Garibaldi might retaliate against?" He did have a nasty habit of controlling people through their loved ones.

Colette glanced at her with wide-eyed surprise. "Oh, I shouldn't worry about that, I don't think. I'm not nearly important enough to merit Signor Garibaldi's vengeance."

Elsa shook her head, bemused. "I will never understand you Europeans."

They emerged from the attic onto the airship field, which proved startlingly vacant. Colette led the way to a hidden path that angled sharply down toward the valley floor below.

"Halt!" someone called out behind them.

Elsa and Colette did not halt; indeed they did quite the opposite. They flew down the mountainside, careening around the switchbacks and half sliding down the slopes. When the path leveled out into a shallow, grassy glen, they leaned into a desperate sprint.

Elsa glanced over her shoulder and spotted a pair of guards, not quite on top of them yet but closing in. Fear kicked in her chest.

But then Vincenzo appeared out of nowhere, dashing full-tilt at the first guard and knocking him down. The second guard swung around, pistol in hand. A gunshot echoed off the valley walls, but Vincenzo was no longer where the shooter had aimed. He moved like a wildcat, dodging and then closing in, twisting and hitting until the second guard was moaning on the ground.

By this time, the first had found his feet again, but Vincenzo had found the second guard's pistol. *Bang, bang*—and the first guard crumpled.

The second guard was still down, breathing but unmoving. Vincenzo turned the gun upon him and shot him in the head.

Colette yelped and covered her mouth with both hands.

Shocked, Elsa said, "You killed them."

"Dead men tell no tales," Vincenzo answered casually, as he retrieved the other pistol from the grass. But then he looked up and saw her distress at his cavalier display of violence. "Elsa, we are at war. Don't think for a second that Garibaldi isn't prepared to kill to get what he wants."

"But . . . they're former Carbonari. They were your own people, once."

"These *scecchi*? Nah, they're mercenaries. Besides, it's not as if I'm close personal friends with every member of the Carbonari; we operate in isolated cells." Vincenzo held out the spare pistol to Elsa, and when she didn't immediately take it, he tucked it into her empty gun holster himself. "I don't even want to know how Garibaldi got his hands on state-of-the-art Austrian firearms, but let's not waste them."

Colette wrung her hands together. "I don't . . ." She paused and glanced uncertainly at Elsa, as if unsure of her right to speak. "I don't understand. The Carbonari want a unified Italian state, yes? And so does Garibaldi. Why are you enemies?"

Vincenzo shook his head, amused at her naïveté. "Sweetheart—if you think Garibaldi's 'rule of the people' would be the same as the Carbonari's, you're in for a sore surprise. When he says 'the people,' he means pazzerellones, not the likes of you and me."

Elsa pressed her hands to the sides of her face. "Let's save the political nuances for a later discussion. We just need to get away from here now. Please tell me Leo left my escape kit intact."

"Huh? Oh yeah, the portal-making stuff. He opened a portal with it, but left all the gadgets behind for you." He strode off into the bushes and retrieved a canvas satchel. "I brought everything along—figured we might need a quick getaway."

Elsa exhaled heavily with relief. "Let's get ourselves back to Pisa, then."

"Yeah . . . about that," Vincenzo said. "There's some news you haven't heard yet, regarding Casa della Pazzia. Porzia left us a note. We're headed to Cinque Terre instead."

Faraz arrived like an angel of mercy to save Leo from drowning in blood and memories. They lifted Sante between them and rushed him inside, Faraz immediately taking charge.

"Clear the dining table!" he commanded the children, who were gathered in the entry hall. "I need a clean sheet on it now. Olivia, fetch my alchemy kit. You, find Simo—he'll know where the alcohol is. Distilled, as strong as you can get."

Leo could hardly process the words through Sante's strangled screaming. The boy's eyelids scrunched shut with pain. They tried to lay him out flat on the table, but he stayed half-curled around his wound, the muscles in his limbs tensed. Leo had given up on the handkerchief and stripped off his linen shirt to use as a makeshift bandage, but even that was soaked through now.

Olivia rushed in, carrying Faraz's black leather kit. "What do we need first?"

"Glass vial, purple liquid," ordered Faraz. She fished it out and handed it over, and he poured the sleeping potion onto Sante's neck, so it could absorb through the skin.

Finally, the boy stopped keening and relaxed into unconsciousness. Leo took a step away, giving them room to work.

Faraz lifted the linen shirt for a peek. "Bleeding's not too bad, considering."

"You call that 'not too bad'?" Leo croaked. His own throat felt raw, as if he'd been the one screaming instead of Sante.

Simo arrived with a brown glass jug. Faraz doused his hands with clear liquid and passed the jug to Olivia so she could do the same, and the air filled with the sharp smell of distilled grain alcohol.

To Olivia, Faraz explained, "We've got to pack it with cotton so we can actually see and assess the damage. Looks like he took the worst of it over the ribs, and if we're lucky the sword didn't penetrate the abdominal wall."

Leo crossed his arms awkwardly over his bare chest, trying not to touch anything with his blood-covered hands. Between the alcohol fumes and the sight of Faraz peeling back the linen to expose the gaping wound, Leo was edging toward nausea. He wondered if he oughtn't take young Olivia out of the room, but the girl seemed to be handling the situation fine. Underneath her solemn expression, she seemed more interested than disgusted.

Leo, on the other hand, possessed the stomach of a mechanist. He'd seen dead people before, but the knowledge that the wound belonged to Porzia's still-living little brother somehow made it infinitely worse. When Faraz glanced up, he noticed. "You're looking green, Leo; if you're going to be sick, do so outside."

Since Faraz and Olivia had a hold on things there, Leo let his woozy and useless self out of the room in search of fresher air. He sat on the lowest step of the collapsed main stairway and gulped a few breaths.

God, Porzia was gone. She and that Revan fellow both captured. He should do . . . *something*, surely, but a vague desperation was as far as his brain managed to go. With everything that had happened in the last twenty-four hours, Leo felt as if his soul had been wrung out like a wet rag. It was too much to process.

His cheek itched; he rubbed it with the back of his wrist and discovered another smear of blood. Wash up—that was the first step. And then maybe he could come up with a plan.

Leo was still trying to scrub the blood out from under his fingernails when serious little Aldo found him to report that someone was approaching on foot. As he ran for the entrance, his body made a weak attempt at scrounging up some adrenaline, but there really was none left to give.

Luckily, these intruders proved to be Elsa and Vincenzo. "Good Lord, am I glad to see you two," he said, and then corrected himself. "Uh . . . three?" They had that servant girl in tow; the one who'd unlocked the kitchen door.

Vincenzo said, "It looks like a battle zone out there. What happened?"

"It *was* a battle zone out there," said Leo. "They kidnapped Revan and Porzia."

"What!" Elsa said. "How long ago?"

"I don't know, an hour? Two?"

"And you haven't gone after her yet?"

"How? Aris has a functional airship, and all we have is a poorly stocked pile of rubble." Leo gestured angrily at their surroundings.

Elsa said, "Did Porzia bring the tracking worldbook with her when they left Casa della Pazzia?"

Leo grabbed the sides of his head in both hands. "I don't know! I know nothing of use, all right?"

And then, against all reason, Elsa hugged him. "It's going to be okay. We'll figure it out."

Before he could really process her touch, she let go, intent on finding Porzia's bags and rifling through them for whatever worldbooks might have been smuggled out of Pisa.

Vincenzo took one look at his expression and laughed. "For someone so smart, you really are an idiot, aren't you?"

Once Elsa finished ransacking Porzia's bags, they all met up with Faraz to formulate a plan. Faraz looked tired and harried, but reported that Sante was stable. Elsa took a quick trip into her lab world to replenish their medical supplies, and then they got down to business.

"We have the tracking book," she said. "So long as Porzia and Revan are still on-world, we should be able to locate them."

Leo said, "The main question is, how do we mount a rescue after we find them?"

Vincenzo nodded. "Crashing an airship is easy, assuming you don't care about the health of the passengers. But boarding an airship is ridiculously difficult."

"Let's look at this from the other direction. What resources do we have?" Elsa said. "We can build weapons, but we still have only four people to operate them—five, if we can talk Colette into helping."

"Who's Colette?" said Faraz.

Leo frowned. "*Where's* Colette?" The girl had vanished from their company, but he couldn't recall when or why.

Vincenzo looked at Faraz and Leo like they were scum on his boot. "Sometimes you pazzerellones really are unbelievable."

"Let's put the class war on the back burner until Garibaldi's stopped, all right?" Elsa said. "How's our supply of knockout potion?"

"Gone," answered Faraz. "I didn't have any anesthetic, so I had to use my last dose on Sante."

"Could you synthesize more sleeping potion in my lab?" she asked.

"I could start, but one of the steps needs to incubate at thirty-seven degrees for fourteen hours. You can't rush chemistry."

"Hm." Elsa chewed her lip, which Leo found distracting. "Where's Skandar?"

"I don't know, hiding somewhere." Faraz shrugged. "Skandar's funny that way—doesn't blink in the face of a slavering monster, but someone familiar gets hurt and the poor beast crawls under a piece of furniture. Why?"

Leo interjected, "Because even I can admit your little monster has come in handy in the past."

"Hold on," Vincenzo said. "There are questions we haven't asked yet. How did they know about Revan, and how did they know to find him here?"

Faraz's eyes widened. "You're right—Porzia's been very careful not to open portals near the ruins, so Aris can't have traced her portal activity."

Leo got a cold feeling in his stomach. They'd been safely hidden here . . . until he showed up with his brother and a half-mechanical construct built by Aris. Aris, who could fit miniature transmitters inside brass bugs no larger than the palm of a hand, like those he'd infected Casa with last month.

"Where is the creature right now?" he said urgently.

Faraz said, "Skandar? I told—"

"No! Pasca's companion, the clockwork creature. We have to find her."

Elsa's eyes widened. "You think . . . ?"

"That I hand-delivered Aris's spy right into our midst?" Leo spat, furious with himself. "Yes, that seems probable."

After a few frantic minutes of searching, they found the clock-work creature in an unexpected place: the bedroom to which Faraz had moved Sante for recovery. The creature loomed over the bed and the unconscious form laid upon it, emitting a soft, wordless keening.

"What are you doing?" Leo said, keeping his voice calm and even.

Her head jerked up like an animal scenting a predator, except no—that wasn't fear on her face. Those dark, glassy eyes locked on Elsa, her features twisted with a horrible realization. She began to sign emphatically, almost desperately.

Faraz said, "What's she saying?"

Elsa translated, "'It was me, the mad boy followed me. I didn't know. It is my fault, my most grievous fault.'"

The clockwork creature relaxed her hands, let them fall to her sides. There seemed to be something final about the gesture, even to Leo, who understood so little of her language. Then she turned and dove at the window, shattering the glass and spilling out into the night.

Leo rushed to the window frame, shouting at her, "Wait!" but it was no use. He spotted a silhouette of wings against the moon-light reflected on the sea, and then the creature was gone.

20

Porzia came back to consciousness in a cage. The knockout potion they'd used on her when she came aboard left her with a pulsing headache and a slow, fuzzy sensation that made it difficult to orient herself. Cage bars and . . . someone in another cage beside hers . . . a round room, laboratory equipment, no doors—no doors! No doors and no rumbling vibration of an engine meant they were in a scribed world, not on the airship anymore.

"Look here! Our surprise guest has decided to join us." A dark-haired young man with Leo's eyes came into focus on the other side of the bars. "And who might you be?"

Porzia did her best to glare but doubted the look's effectiveness, given that she was only just now managing to get her hands and knees under her.

"Wait! Don't tell me," said Aris, despite the fact that she

obviously had no intention of telling him anything. "You must be the legacy brat. Eldest of a prestigious line, guaranteed a seat at the table no matter how incompetent you turn out to be. She who buys all her friends at a discount, when they're homeless and alone and desperate enough to trust any pretty face. Leo told me about you, Porzia."

She tried hard not to flinch, though the words stung. Surely Leo, even at his lowest, would not have made such nasty claims about her. But in the manner of all great insults, it hurt not because of its patent falsity but because of the grain of truth she recognized within. She *was* privileged. She *had* taken her friends for granted.

Porzia grabbed the bars, pulled herself to her feet, and dialed her raised-eyebrows haughtiness all the way up. "As evil masterminds go, I can't say I'm impressed."

"Oh, really?" Aris said, looking more amused than annoyed. "By all means, please do illustrate my failings."

"Well, you're not especially creative. First Jumi, then Leo, now Revan. Isn't the whole kidnapping routine getting a bit old? You really ought to branch out. Rob some banks, steal some horses . . ."

Aris laughed. "I suppose now I know where Leo picked up that attitude of his."

"Leo is perfectly capable of scorning you without any assistance from me." Porzia might have found more vitriol to sling at him, but that was when she realized the man in the cage next to her was not Revan, but Charles Montaigne—the original creator of Veldana and one-time thief of the editbook, who was supposed to be imprisoned by the Order. But if Montaigne was there, then where was . . .

Porzia's heart leapt in her throat. Revan was strapped into a device like some horrid combination of a gurney and a medician's chair, standing but tipped back at an angle. An elaborate mass of wires encircled his skull, and he had a gag—no, a wooden mouth guard—between his teeth, to keep him from biting off his tongue.

"What is this? What are you doing to him?"

"Here's the thing about scriptology, Porzia," Aris said. "By itself, it's an entertaining yet ultimately trivial endeavor. But when you scribe special physical conditions as the groundwork for alchemy and mechanics . . . well, *then* the possibilities are endless. As you were so quick to point out, creativity is everything. Like, say, a world where languages are neural imprints that can be taken out of one brain and transferred into another."

Porzia's knuckles whitened as she gripped the bars tighter, and nausea threatened her stomach. "Stop. Don't hurt him."

"I scribed and built all this to cure Pasca, but desperate times call for repurposed worlds." Aris shrugged. "Don't worry, it won't kill him. I tested the procedure on that French nuisance first, and see? Still breathing."

Montaigne spat out a rapid string of words, most of which Porzia failed to catch. Her French was not as strong as her German or Latin. Montaigne's tone, however, was quite obviously uncomplimentary.

Aris ignored the Frenchman's insults and kept talking to Porzia as if he weren't present. "Unfortunately, his grasp of the Veldanese language was rather less sophisticated than I was hoping for. Hence, the necessity of your friend." Aris turned to Revan. "I do hope you've been applying yourself when it comes to your Italian language studies, though. I'm afraid the machine will strip you of Veldanese. Terribly inconvenient, I know, but what's to be done? I may be the smartest person alive, but even

I'm not flawless, and the last stage of construction was a bit rushed."

Revan's eyes went wide and his face turned ashen, but he could only make muffled noises with the guard wedged between his teeth.

"You are sick," Porzia spat. "There is something deeply wrong with you, and that's why Leo took Pasca and ran away."

Aris froze; the smug superiority vanished. He slowly turned back to face her, and cold hatred shone in his eyes.

"Your own brothers couldn't get away from you fast enough because they saw you for what you really are!"

"Shut your mouth!" he screamed. "You will shut it yourself or I will sew it shut for you!"

Aris clenched his fists, took two forced breaths, and reined his temper back in. Then he spun away from her and went to Revan's side, where he began fitting a matching cap of electrodes onto his own head, his hands working in quick, angry, purposeful motions.

"No no no wait, I'm sorry, I didn't mean it," Porzia babbled, desperate to keep his attention on her. "It's not too late to get your brothers back, you haven't done anything you can't undo yet. I can talk to Leo! I can help you!"

Aris ignored her. He climbed onto a second gurney and bit down on a mouth guard. Then he reached out a hand and flipped a switch.

For long minutes afterward, Porzia couldn't tell whether Revan was breathing.

Aris took what he wanted from Revan's mind and then simply left him there, hanging against the straps like a forgotten rag doll. He did not so much as check Revan's pulse before opening a portal back to the real world. But even through her horror, Porzia had the sense to watch Aris's hands as he dialed the settings.

Aris's goons hadn't thought to search her pockets. In Porzia's experience, most men had no concept of how much a woman could hide beneath full skirts—including but not limited to her portal device.

But first she had to check on Revan, which meant she needed to get out of her cage somehow. Porzia reached inside her over-skirt to access her hidden pockets and pulled out a fountain pen and a thin volume of blank scriptology paper. It was more a pam-phlet than a book—only a few sheets folded in half and stitched together—though given the constraints of their current predica-ment, she was equally worried she'd run out of ink before she ran out of space on which to scribble it.

Could she scribe a doorbook with this? No, even if she under-stood Elsa's doorbook well enough to replicate it, she'd run out of materials.

Materials . . . this scriptology paper and ink weren't just a way to define the properties of a new world, they were objects with their own material properties. She needed to think like an alchemist—what could Faraz and Elsa do with just this, if they were here?

There existed certain syntactical constructions that every young scriptologist was taught to avoid. Recursive, self-referential text causes the ink to heat up and destabilize. Could Porzia amplify that effect somehow, so the paper would do more than smolder?

She tore off a scrap of paper, and in tiny, tight lettering she scribed three lines of recursive text. Atop those lines she then overwrote another self-referential construction that directly con-tradicted the first. And so on and so on, layers of bad text building up until the paper was soaked through with ink and turning hot in her hands. She quickly folded the scrap of paper into a tight little wedge and, reaching through the bars, jammed it into the keyhole. She pulled her hand away just in time to avoid the fizzle and pop and rain of white sparks that shot out of the lock.

"'Smartest person alive' my ass," Porzia grumbled. She grabbed ahold of the bars and gave the cage door a sharp shove, and the abused lock gave way.

Montaigne tried to grab her through the bars, saying something about *help* in French, but Porzia threw him a withering look and dashed to Revan's side instead. She patted his cheeks, desperate to revive him. "Revan, can you hear me? Wake up!" His chest rose and fell, but that didn't necessarily mean there was still a person inside. She fumbled with the buckle at the back of his neck and took the guard out of his mouth.

Revan's eyelids fluttered open. For a moment he stared, dazed and unseeing, but then his gaze focused on her face and his brow scrunched in confusion rapidly transitioning into panic, and Porzia felt sick with relief that at least there was a mind left to be confused.

"Can you understand me?" she asked, over-enunciating the words.

"Yes," he croaked, coughed to clear his throat, then said it again. "Yes . . . in Italian, I can."

"I'm so sorry I couldn't stop him." Porzia busied herself unbuckling straps, so she wouldn't have to see his face as he processed what he'd lost. "But I watched Aris dial a portal back to Earth; he scribed this laboratory using the German Standard for return coordinates. I can get us out now."

Revan rubbed his wrists where he'd pulled against the restraints. "But even if we get out of this world, won't we just be stuck on an airship instead? With that maniac for company, to boot."

Porzia helped him off the gurney and, given how shaky he was on his feet, onto a wooden chair. "Do you trust me?"

"Of course."

"Then rest here and leave the escape plan to me. I'll see you again in a moment."

She pulled out the portal device, set the coordinates to return to Earth, and flipped the switch. There was no time to consider what might be waiting on the other side; portals returning to Earth always deposited the traveler near the physical location of the worldbook, and that was all she counted on.

The portal spat her out into the belly of the airship, an open room with access to the cockpit in front and another chamber at the rear. She could hear movements and voices, but this area at this moment was miraculously unoccupied.

The horrid worldbook from which she'd just escaped sat close at hand on a table secured to one wall. Porzia snatched it up, read the coordinates out of the front, and reset her portal device. Then she checked the view out the window.

Even if she could find a parachute without someone catching her first, she didn't know how to operate one. But books were excellent at falling; all she would have to do was get back inside while it fell. The round little window creaked on its hinge when she opened it.

Porzia held the worldbook out the window with one hand and flipped the switch on the device with the other, opening a portal. She would need to time this perfectly—as the book fell away and the distance increased, the portal would lose its connection to the scribed world, and if Porzia wasn't all the way through she could get stuck in the frozen limbo between worlds.

She took a deep breath and bent her knees, readying to sprint.

Just as she was about to go through with it, Aris dashed in from the cockpit. "What are you doing? Stop!"

"How's this for creativity?" Porzia quipped, then she let go of the book and dove into the portal.

The cold nothingness between worlds lasted two seconds longer than usual, long enough to give Porzia a spike of terror, but then she made it through into Aris's lab world.

"Hah! I knew it would work," she said, giddy with the success of narrowly avoiding oblivion. "I don't suppose you know the air resistance of a falling book?" She could work out the Newtonian mechanics if she had the variables, but there'd been no chance to sneak a look at the altimeter, so any calculation would be educated guesswork at best.

"Falling book?" Revan held up a hand and half rose from his chair. "Wait—are you saying . . ."

"Yes, I dropped us out the airship window. The fall would kill a person of course, but since we're flying low and not over the water, it won't destroy a worldbook." Porzia took in his expression; he looked like he might be ill. "So we'll just wait here a while until the falling part has finished. Err on the side of caution, shall we?"

Revan gave a weak nod and collapsed back into his seat. "Please."

The airship had been idling low and hidden amongst the rugged hills inland of Cinque Terre, not having traveled especially far from Corniglia. Even so, it took Revan and Porzia several hours to make their way through the treacherous countryside with nothing but moonlight to help them. Porzia counted it as a minor miracle that they managed to navigate their way back to the ruins at all.

No one greeted them at the door, but she followed the muffled sound of argument and discovered the whole crew camped out around the dining room table. It was looking more like a war room than an eating area, with maps and diagrams and worldbooks scattered everywhere.

"Thanks so much for the daring rescue," Porzia announced.

They all finally looked up, noticing her and Revan in the doorway. There was a flurry of questions and explanations and embraces. Porzia did the talking, sensing that Revan wasn't ready to discuss what had happened to him; she would've preferred to keep silent about it until he was, but necessity was a merciless mistress. Everyone needed to know that Aris now possessed the linguistic knowledge to use the editbook.

She was about to explain their gravity-assisted escape when her eyes fell on a bin of bloody bandages shoved in the corner. "What happened?"

Leo said, "It's . . . it's Sante."

Porzia felt suddenly cold inside, as if her guts had been replaced with the emptiness between portals. "Where is he?"

Faraz said, "He'll live, Porzia—he'll be all right."

"*Where is he*?!" she screamed, and then she was racing for the stairs, with Faraz trailing behind her.

She stopped short in the bedroom doorway; the sight of Sante lying in the bed, so pale and still, felt like a stiletto between her ribs.

"It's not as serious as it looks." Faraz squeezed her shoulder. "We were actually quite lucky."

She knew he meant well, but it was cold comfort. Sante had been hurt. It was her job to take care of her siblings, but while her brother lay bleeding in the grass she'd been chasing after Revan, who was practically a stranger by comparison. Porzia had failed—failed spectacularly—at the one task that mattered the most.

Who needed an editbook, anyway? This right here was what it felt like for her whole world to fall apart. Shattered like an inkwell dropped from the ruins' highest tower.

Alek descended the stairs into the subbasement of Casa della Pazzia, a leather medician's satchel in one hand, his heart hammering from more than exertion.

Burak was waiting for him in a side corridor at an access panel, his eyes wide with a youthful excitement that Alek envied. "Did it work?"

Alek squeezed the boy's shoulder with his free hand. "An old scriptologist puttering around an alchemy lab isn't much of a threat, it seems."

Burak grinned. "Come on, they're almost ready."

The boy slipped through the access panel into the narrow space between the walls, and Alek ducked to follow him. Burak had become irritatingly adept at navigating these hidden passageways, but Alek still found them awkward, wood lathing close on his left and pipes crowding in on his right.

They emerged into a large round room, the secret heart of the house, full of humming machinery and the gurgle of fluid through massive tubes. Gia and Filippo had their heads together, discussing the readings from a set of gauges—gauges on the side of an enormous glass tank that occupied the center of the room.

Alek stepped closer, peering through the distortion of the thick glass and the murky water within. Something large floated in the tank, almost the size of a horse, but with a sort of amorphous shape, wrinkled and folded. "Is that—is that a giant brain?"

Burak bounced on the balls of his feet. "Isn't it the best? I can't wait to tell Leo that *I* got to see it."

Gia said, "Indeed—the great Pisano secret to creating an intelligent mechanical house is to use more than just mechanics." To her husband, she added, "Are you ready, darling?"

Filippo scribbled in a small notebook. "Yes . . . just finishing the dosage calculations."

Alek handed the leather satchel to him. "I managed to retrieve all the chemicals on your list. Casa was suspicious, but I suppose I appear convincingly harmless."

A smile flitted across Filippo's face but didn't last long; the gravity of what they were about to do weighed too heavily on him. As he checked the bottles of chemicals, he said, "I don't know how long I'll be able to keep Casa under, so the rest of you will have to work fast. We're invisible—or, rather, inaudible—in here, but the effects of what we do will be quite apparent."

Gia led Alek and Burak over to a wall panel that resembled a switchboard, but with a black cord plugged into every single jack. Alek looked up, tracing the cords across the ceiling and down into the tank. Gia explained, "Casa was never designed to be disconnected from the house systems, so we have to pull the neural connectors out individually—all two hundred and twelve of them."

Filippo mixed the chemicals in a tin bucket. "Ready?"

"Go ahead," Gia replied.

He climbed a stepladder and poured the chemical mixture into the tank. "Flooding the chamber now."

Alek glanced at Gia for guidance, but she held up a hand, forestalling him. Filippo clattered down the steps and rushed back to the gauges. "And . . . there it is, brain waves are dampened. Go!"

Squeezing in between Gia and Burak, Alek began madly yanking connectors out. The mechanists were fast and dexterous, but even so, each connector required two hands to simultaneously unlock the release and pull. And if Casa regained consciousness and realized what they were doing, Alek shuddered to think what their fate would be.

"Brain activity is starting to rebound . . . ," Filippo called, anxiety thick in his voice.

"Almost there!" said Gia, finishing with her rows and moving over to help with Alek's last connectors—209, 210, 211 . . . done!

"We did it!" Burak crowed, and Alek let out a giddy, relieved laugh. But Gia pressed the back of her wrist against her mouth, her eyes moist with tears.

"I apologize," said Alek. "This is no cause for celebration."

"Casa has never been isolated from all stimuli before—I dread the harm it will do to an already unstable mind. In doing this, we may be killing Casa," she said.

Filippo smothered her in a tight embrace, then pulled away to say, "I'm so sorry, darling, but Alek and I must get to Firenze posthaste."

"I know, I know," Gia said, dabbing at her eyes with her sleeve. "Garibaldi on the loose, and the Order without a leader."

Alek kissed her goodbye on her damp cheeks, in the Italian fashion. "Keep your spirits up, Gia. There's work still to be done."

21

IN GOD'S NAME I HAVE RECORDED THE WEATHER DAILY AND
WITH DILIGENT ATTENTION, AND IN ORDER TO SEE FROM WHICH
ASPECTS THE CHANGES OF WEATHER MAY COME.
—*Maria Margaretha Kirchin*

Elsa let Faraz go after Porzia and stayed behind with Revan. He looked dazed and calm in a manner suggestive of shock, and she hadn't the first clue what to do for him.

"Revan, I . . . I'm so sorry, I never should have let you stay on Earth." Speaking Italian with him felt like one more nail in the coffin of their old friendship.

"Nobody 'let' me," he said. Then, as if unsure what else to do, he offered her the somewhat battered worldbook he was holding. "There's some old white guy still locked up in here."

Elsa took the worldbook from him and turned it over in her hands. Usually worldbooks felt inviting to the touch, vibrating like the purr of a contented cat, but she recognized this one as the linguistic laboratory from Aris's hidden bookshelves. A hot wave of nausea rolled through her; she had *kissed* the person who'd then turned around and performed this horrific violation upon her oldest friend. The memory of her flirtation with Aris, however brief, felt like a putrescence she needed to purge from her body.

She almost confessed all this to Revan, but decided against it. How could it possibly help for her to unload her guilt onto him?

Instead, she said, "We were too young to remember this, but there was a time when Veldanese was stolen from all of us. Our world was rewritten to make us speak French. Once Jumi wrested control of our worldbook, she had to reconstruct our language from memory—no, not even from memory, more like from the silhouette shapes where the memories had been."

"So you think I can relearn it." His voice held no hint of hope, and if she were being brutally honest, Elsa would admit she couldn't guess whether Aris's machine had done permanent damage without first examining it.

Nevertheless, she said, "When you're ready to try, I believe you can. For now, just rest." She raised her voice to address the others. "We should all get some sleep while we still can."

Leo snorted. "You think my brother is sleeping tonight?"

"I think Aris has hours of studying to do before he'll be prepared to actually use the editbook. Reading Veldanese is just the first step."

Vincenzo's mouth twisted into a grim line. "Besides, they could be anywhere. It's a bit hard to run off to battle if we don't even know where the battlefield is."

"We have one of Aris's worldbooks," Leo protested. "We should at least try using the tracking map."

Elsa tossed the worldbook on the table. "Aris knows I used his carnevale mask to track him to Trento—he won't make the same mistake again. If we get a location off this book, it'll be a diversion, or a trap, or some nasty combination of the two. We're going to need fresh ideas."

So she went upstairs to find a bedroll and a spare patch of floor—for the few hours of night that were left, at least.

Someone shook Elsa awake mere moments after she lay down. Or it seemed that way, until she peeled her eyelids open to see the glow of early morning through the window glass.

Leo hissed in her ear, "I think I have it! Come on!"

Blearily, Elsa shrugged on her leather vest and shoved her feet into her boots and—without properly tightening the laces on either—picked her way around the sleeping children to follow Leo. He'd roused Faraz, too, who joined them in the hall, running a hand over his mess of sleep-matted curls.

As Leo led them down the narrow stairs, he kept glancing over his shoulder with a wild look in his eyes. Elsa couldn't tell whether it was excitement or exhaustion. "Napolitano weather reports!" he announced. "I finally remembered."

Elsa exchanged a look with Faraz, but he seemed equally mystified. She said, "Are we . . . supposed to know what that means?"

"*My father*," Leo said impatiently. "He's been receiving weather reports from Napoli. I found them in his study—didn't think much of it at the time."

"And now you do think much of it?" Elsa rubbed the sleep from her eyes.

Leo explained, "Napoli is the seat of power for the Kingdom of Two Sicilies—the kingdom my grandfather and uncle died fighting against."

"So it's on Garibaldi's vengeance list," Faraz concluded.

Leo nodded. "Right at the top."

They arrived at the former dining hall, now more of a strategic center, where Vincenzo was scowling over a half-sketched map.

"Everybody here now? Good," Vincenzo said. "I'm trying to work out the lines of sight from memory, but I can't be sure."

At Elsa's blank look, Leo said, "Weather reports. You need direct sunlight to operate Archimedes mirrors."

"Are there mirrors in Napoli?" Elsa asked, trying to keep up.

"Only the largest array ever built," Vincenzo said sourly. "They're set up to face the bay, to light enemy ships on fire, but if Garibaldi gets control of them he could turn the mirrors on the city itself. He'd be able to target both the royal palace and the garrison."

Elsa chewed her lip. "I don't know . . . If his plan is to use the Archimedes mirrors, what does he need the editbook for?"

"Maybe to take control of them?" Vincenzo said. "The mirror towers are well secured."

Faraz said, "Wait—if Aris can change *anything* with the editbook, why doesn't he just scribe his father onto the throne of a unified Italy?"

Elsa shook her head. "Not worth the risk. If he were too specific, he could accidentally textualize Garibaldi, damaging his father's mind like what happened to Simo. And not specific enough would mean someone else received the instant promotion to monarch. Anyway, the editbook doesn't change memories of the past; how long do you think the new regime would last with everyone remembering it wasn't supposed to exist?"

Leo said, "A show of power, though, forces the people to relinquish control more or less of their own will. War is familiar and therefore yields predictable results. And what would be more fitting than toppling the Kingdom of Two Sicilies with Archimedes mirrors—the same kind of weapon that sank my grandfather's ships?" He winced, as if it pained him to get inside his father's logic. "If there's even a small probability that we'll be able to intercept them, we have to go to Napoli."

Vincenzo jabbed his finger at a place on the city map he'd been sketching. "I should be able to get us into this tower. From there we can figure out how exactly Garibaldi plans to use the mirrors."

"All right, I'll get the doorbook. But what about Porzia?" Elsa didn't like the thought of going into battle with their team incomplete.

Faraz shook his head. "I don't think we could pry Porzia away from Sante's side for the end of the world. And I mean that literally."

They came through the portal into an open space that might have once been a courtyard or piazza, though to Elsa's eyes it looked as if the city had cannibalized it. The back sides of newer buildings encroaching on an incomplete remnant of the old city walls. A round stone tower loomed large, built into the wall as a guard tower and later heightened and repurposed. The mirror tower's door looked fortress-thick and was flanked by a pair of guards.

Vincenzo approached the guard on the left and recited a code phrase that Elsa didn't quite catch because he spoke it in Napolitano dialect. The guard on the right shouted at them to leave, and the guard on the left unholstered his sidearm and shot his partner in the chest. The gun's loud report kicked Elsa's heart into high gear, and Faraz muffled a yelp of surprise.

Elsa was starting to get a handle on the differences in phonology and grammar, so she understood when the guard said, "It took me two years to build the cover I've just blown. You better be right about this."

Vincenzo patted down the dead guard's body, retrieving a set of keys, and then he and the Carbonaro unlocked the door's two-key system together.

Vincenzo tossed his set of keys to Leo and waved them

through. "I'm right behind you—just need to stash the body out of sight."

Inside the tower was a staircase, dimly lit by small square windows. The original structure was maybe three or four stories high, and the newer construction doubled its height. At the top was a locked hatch, but apparently one key was sufficient now, since Leo got them through. They climbed out onto the exposed tower top.

An enormous metal hutch dominated the center of the tower; from the hinges, Elsa could tell it was built to fold down, presumably to reveal the mirror hidden within. Immediately below them to the south, a broad bay glittered with reflected sunlight. The choked streets wound up away from the water into hill country to the north, and on the eastern horizon loomed a conical mountain with two peaks.

Leo produced a telescoping spyglass and held it to his eye, examining the other towers arrayed around the bay. "No activity."

"Perhaps we've arrived before them?" Faraz offered.

Elsa shook her head. "Aris doesn't require physical proximity to use the editbook. In fact, he must be off-world in order to scribe changes to this world."

Leo said, "Ricciotti will want to observe the fall of Napoli firsthand, but even assuming Aris took the airship back to Trento to get him, they had several hours' head start."

"The sunlight's less intense in the morning," Faraz said. "It has to pass through too much atmosphere. They could be waiting for a better angle of incidence."

Vincenzo emerged from the hatch behind them. "Any sign of them yet?"

Leo shook his head. "Nothing out of the ordinary that I can see."

They waited in tense silence for several minutes. Leo scanned the city with his spyglass; Vincenzo paced around the tower top.

Elsa familiarized herself with the layout of Napoli as best she could from their vantage point, in case she would need that knowledge later; the city was difficult to discern from above, a jumble of red-tile roofs swallowing the streets.

Vincenzo's hands tightened on his weapons belt, and he finally said what they were all thinking. "Pig of a god! We've gambled on the wrong city."

But just as he finished speaking, a tremor shook the tower beneath their feet. Elsa held out her arms and bent her knees, like keeping balance on a moving train. She had no context for what the quake could mean, but she followed Faraz's gaze: a great billowing mass of gray was pouring into the sky from the mountain's highest peak.

"What . . . what's happening?" Elsa breathed.

"That," said Faraz, "is a Plinian volcanic eruption. They're using the editbook to trigger a natural disaster."

Vincenzo stared in horror. "The prevailing wind is supposed to come from the west."

For a second Elsa didn't catch his meaning, until she realized they were all looking east toward the mountain, and the wind was in their faces. The anomalous wind would carry that massive cloud of suffocating hot ash straight to the city.

Grimly, Leo said, "Weather reports for Napoli. They were never about the mirrors."

On ground level below them, panic was already spreading. People flooded through the narrow streets, fighting their way toward the port. Elsa's view of the docks was partially obscured from where they stood, but she was willing to bet there weren't near enough boats to carry the entire population of Napoli out of danger.

She said, "What do we do?"

Leo shielded his eyes with one hand. "Judging from the wind

direction, I believe our options are to run home and save our own hides, or stay here and get buried in hot ash along with the whole city of Napoli."

"There has to be something we can do." Elsa pulled out her laboratory book and portal device. "We'll . . . I don't know, change the winds, if we have to."

"Elsa, it's one thing to stick a nozzle on a canister of liquid nitrogen. That was merely impressive. This," Leo said, gesturing wildly, "this is impossible! It could take days to design a functional weather machine."

To her surprise, Faraz—reserved, practical Faraz—was the one who said, "Then there's hardly time to argue about it, is there? We have to *try*."

Elsa passed the lab book to Vincenzo to guard. He took it but protested, "I can't just stand here doing nothing."

"Then stand here making sure the world we're inside of doesn't get destroyed by fire raining from the sky," she said. "Good enough?"

He reluctantly acquiesced, and Elsa took Faraz and Leo through a portal into her laboratory. As soon as they arrived, she began to delegate. "Leo, start designing a power source; regardless of the specifics, a machine that can alter the weather will require a great deal of power. Faraz, walk me through the atmospheric chemistry."

Faraz nodded. "We need to create a high-pressure system over the city, so the surface air currents are redirected away from the most heavily populated area."

"So essentially, we have to pull down on a very large pocket of atmosphere." Elsa felt a nascent grin tugging at her lips, because Aris had already given them the solution in his maze world. "How do you boys feel about a directional gravity generator?"

Faraz's brow knit together. "Is . . . is that a thing?"

"It is now."

"Completely impossible idea," Leo added. "I love it."

They rolled the weather machine through the portal in pieces, needing three separate trips to transport all the components to Earth. To complete it, they repurposed the Archimedes mirror into a parabolic dish, though it was so heavy Leo had to rig a small crane to detach it from its mounting and position it to face upward.

The final stage of assembly atop the mirror tower was a race against time. Elsa checked the sky with Leo's spyglass and fought against the shock of panic beneath her sternum. The volcanic ash cloud rose in a straight column for an incredible height and then spread out, as if intending to blanket the landscape. Lightning flashed around the column, and Elsa could make out red streaks falling in long arcs around the peak—masses of still-glowing lava ejected high into the sky, and cooling into hard rock as they fell.

Veldana had no natural disasters. Witnessing one of Earth's, it seemed impossible to Elsa that this wasn't the end of the whole world.

"We're ready!" Leo called, as he climbed down off the machine, the last bolts tightened and the wrench tucked into his belt. It was a mad creation, cobbled together from whatever components they could think of, without any testing or time to double-check their calculations. *Ready* was a relative term.

"Right." Elsa tore her gaze away from the death-cloud and focused on the control panel. She flipped a switch and gradually moved a lever. "Powering up the coils now. How are we looking?"

Leo checked the gauges. "Levels holding steady."

The fine hairs on her arms stood on end as the electromagnetic charge built up. "Here's hoping we don't blow ourselves up," she said, and flipped the switch to initiate the gravity field.

The machine gave off a massive, subsonic *whomp*, and Elsa could feel the pressure change inside her ears—an unfamiliar and bizarre sensation.

The easterly wind flagged as the atmosphere high above them began to blow directly downward upon the city, the air spreading out in all directions as it met the ground. Elsa traded grins with Leo and Faraz; their weather machine was working, and she felt high as birds. They could protect this city from Aris, editbook be damned.

Faraz borrow Leo's spyglass to examine the ash cloud. "I think it's starting to work—looks like the wind is redirecting the ash away from the city now."

"Whew!" Vincenzo bent over, hands braced above his knees as if relief might knock him down. "Damn, that was a close one."

But then the weather machine seemed to waver, as if Elsa were looking at it through distorted glass. The power flagged and the air pressure dropped. Leo moved to check the gauges.

"No, don't touch it!" Elsa yelled at him, gut instinct telling her something was very wrong. "Everyone get back!"

The wavering intensified until the machine's metal siding seemed to be rolling like the ocean, and the air around it vibrated in a way that sent an involuntary shiver through Elsa's body. Leo quickly backed away, and just in time: the machine folded in on itself and vanished from existence with a resonant *pop*.

"*Mingia!*" Vincenzo swore. "What—what the—"

"He erased it." Elsa had seen this sort of vanishing before, but always in a worldbook and never done intentionally. "Aris edited our weather machine right off the Earth."

Leo threw his hands in the air, infuriated. "How did he even know about it?!"

"He must be observing the progress of the eruption and deduced what we were doing," she said.

Faraz stared, eyes wide. "We're out of time. The machine bought us a few minutes more, but not nearly enough to build a replacement."

Vincenzo recovered quickly from his shock, his lips pressing together with grim determination. "We can still save some people. Use that—that 'doorbook' to get them through a portal."

Elsa threw up her hands in defeat. "*Some* people, maybe, but not a whole city's worth. That would take hours."

"Please, Elsa." He swallowed like the next words threatened to choke him. "I have friends here. I know it's selfish, but—"

"Yes, of course we'll help," Elsa agreed. After everything Vincenzo had done for her, the least she could do was save his compatriots from being buried alive and suffocated in ash.

They rushed from the Archimedes tower, following Vincenzo's lead. It felt like a retreat.

22

EVERY DAY WE ARE CHANGING, EVERY DAY WE ARE DYING,
AND YET WE FANCY OURSELVES ETERNAL.
—*St. Jerome*

Standing on the grass beside the cathedral and the Leaning Tower, Elsa surveyed the refugees from Napoli: hundreds of them crowded together, easily more than the entire population of Veldana, and yet a tiny fraction of the city's people. There were Carbonari and friends of Carbonari, but also a wide selection of random citizens off the streets—whoever was close by and could be convinced to jump through a hole in existence, with nothing but the word of some strange pazzerellones to guarantee safety on the other side.

"Goddamn it, Elsa, just open the portal again for me," Vincenzo was arguing.

"Fine, if you insist." Elsa's muscles were jittery with adrenaline. "But we should test the other side, somehow; this is cutting it very close."

As the portal irised open, a blast of sulfurous air and ash particles came wafting through. Vincenzo lunged for it anyway, and Leo had to step in front of him and block his way, shoulder jammed against Vincenzo's chest and arm grabbing his waist.

"Let go of me!" Vincenzo shouted.

Elsa quickly shut down the portal. "It's over—the ashfall has hit the city."

Vincenzo slumped against Leo, the fight going out of him as defeat sank in. Then he shoved Leo away harshly and shouted a guttural, wordless cry, as if nothing from his plethora of multilingual curses was sufficient.

Elsa leaned closer to Faraz and quietly asked, "How bad is it, do you think?" Scribed worlds were typically too small to require active tectonics, so she had only passing knowledge of volcanoes.

"A mild ashfall would be mostly an inconvenience," said Faraz. "But with a heavy ashfall like this, we're looking at collapsed roofs, deaths by suffocation, and if there's ash flow, too . . ." His voice trailed off and he winced.

"You're saying . . . total destruction."

Faraz nodded.

Elsa struggled to fathom the enormity of what Aris had done. With the editbook her mother created. All those innocent lives—like burning the Veldana worldbook a thousand times over. "I can't . . . I can't believe anyone would do something like that. Decimate a city? It's too . . . big."

"Maybe Aris didn't know," Vincenzo muttered, more to himself than the others. "Maybe he didn't know I'd spent time stationed in Napoli."

"It wouldn't have mattered either way," Leo replied, his voice stripped raw with defeat. "Aris is Ricciotti's loyal soldier to the core; nothing matters more to him."

"No one had to die," Vincenzo snapped. "If pazzerellones

didn't hoard their inventions for themselves, we could have had emergency evacuation portals set up all over the city."

"If someone had built evacuation portals, then Aris would know about them," Leo said, "and he'd just plan a different attack that took the portals into account. It's called an arms race, Vico."

"An arms race that we're already in, whether the Order likes it or not, and guess what: *we're losing*."

Faraz rubbed his temples. "We don't have time for a political debate. We need to . . . we need to prepare."

Leo said, "Prepare for what? We don't know what my mad brother is going to do next."

Elsa exchanged a weighted glance with Faraz. She said, "The thing is . . . that's not completely true."

Faraz continued for her. "You remember when we explored the Jabir ibn Hayyan worldbook? Well, the Oracle spoke to Elsa and me—prophesied to us, really—and it saw this coming."

"Not the specifics," said Elsa. "Oracles don't exactly trade in specifics, but it said, 'A plume of ash ten thousand meters high blocks out the sun.' That was one of two predictions."

A muscle in Leo's jaw jumped, and he had to unclench his teeth to speak. "And the other prediction?"

Faraz recited, "'The waters writhe with eldritch horrors.' So, sea monsters. Presumably."

"Which," Elsa said, "as far as we know, hasn't happened yet. We don't know where they'll strike, but we know how."

Leo said, "The Italian peninsula has thousands of kilometers of coastline."

Vincenzo planted his hands on his hips, grappling to get control of his anger. "If the goal is to cripple the Kingdom of Two Sicilies, the next most strategically significant target after Napoli would be Palermo."

"You don't bury a city in ash because it's good strategy." Leo laughed bitterly. "What we saw back there was my father's rage. And rage could mean Marsala, or Nizza, or Venezia. Or hell, even Cagliari, if he blames the king for my grandfather's death."

Elsa scrubbed gritty ash off her face with her sleeve. "So we regroup and figure out where they'll hit next."

"Back to the ruins?" Faraz said. "Olivia knows to monitor for a fever, but I'd like to check on Sante anyway."

Elsa adjusted the settings on the portal device, but Vincenzo said, "I can't leave." His neutral expression seemed like a struggle. "Someone has to stay behind and figure out what to do with all these refugees. And I have to contact the Carbonari—we'll need to organize some kind of rescue effort to search the rubble for survivors."

Elsa had come to rely on Vincenzo's brash confidence, and it shook her to see the cracks in his facade where the grief showed through. She gave him a quick embrace. "Stay strong, my friend," she said, because it seemed like the sort of thing he'd want to hear.

He nodded. "You too, little pazzerellona. Now go."

When they arrived back at the Corniglia ruins, Leo checked in on his brother first. He found Pasca upstairs with the other children, though sitting off in the corner apart from them. Colette sat with him in companionable silence, a kitchen bowl in her lap, snapping the ends off snow peas.

Pasca clambered to his feet, eyes lighting up with questions. Leo couldn't bear to tell him what Aris had done, but the boy probably sensed something was wrong from the desperation in Leo's embrace.

Colette also sprang to her feet, hands clasped behind her back like she was expecting orders. Leo just said, "Thank you for all your help."

Colette shrugged, as if his attention made her uncomfortable. "I'm not much for swashbuckling, but I can keep a gaggle of children fed and out of trouble."

"Fed, certainly. Out of trouble . . . good luck with that one," Leo said, but he flashed her a grin to let her know he was joking.

He turned his focus back to his little brother. Part of him was tempted to ask Elsa for assistance, with that preternatural Veldanese talent for languages, but Leo had to figure out how to communicate with Pasca for himself. He should be the one to deliver this news.

Leo pointed to himself, to Pasca, and to the empty air beside them, and he held up a hand as if to measure Aris's height. Pasca understood and showed him the sign for *Aris*.

With his vocabulary of thirty-some-odd words he'd learned just yesterday, Leo began to fumble his way through an explanation— that Aris had done something terrible, that a lot of people were dead. That their brother had gone too far and was not coming back to them.

Pasca replied, but his hands moved too fast for Leo to understand; even when he repeated himself, slower this time, Leo caught only one word in four. Not enough to figure out his brother's meaning.

Pasca rolled his eyes. Then he placed his left hand on his throat and spoke aloud, using the vibrations as a guide. "Aris was only ever concerned with if we could—it was always you who thought, if we should."

Leo blinked at him, taken aback. Was that how little Pasca had seen him—the conscience balancing Aris's impulse? Young Leo had always felt his hesitation as a weakness holding him back from Aris-like greatness. How strange to discover that the smallest of the Garibaldi boys had a different understanding. A clearer one, perhaps.

Pasca said, "Do what is right. That is how I remember you."

Thank you, Leo signed. Then he added, *The clockwork creature, we will find her, bring her back. And I will learn.*

I know you will, Pasca replied.

Next, Leo went in search of Elsa. He found her tucked away in a dusty room down the hall; by the look of the supplies on the desk and the pages of notes arranged on the floor, Porzia had been working here. But now it was Elsa bent over a worldbook with a pen in her hand, scribing furiously. Her brow, already furrowed in concentration, deepened into a scowl as he walked in.

"What are you working on?" he asked.

"A stopgap I sincerely hope we won't have to use," she answered without looking up.

"How are you?" Leo tried. "What we saw in Napoli . . ."

"I'm busy."

"Can you please just stop for a second and take a breath and . . . *look* at me."

The pen stopped moving, but Elsa squeezed her eyes shut, as if the sight of anything else might pain her. "I have to keep working; it's the only thing that stops me from thinking."

Leo leaned against the windowsill beside the writing desk. "It doesn't have to be me, but please talk to *someone*. You're not alone in this."

For a moment he thought she would stay silent, but then she said, "I bargained their lives away. If only I had turned over the editbook to the Order, those people wouldn't be dead. But no—I wanted to rescue my mother, I wanted to get you back, and I wanted to save the world. I wanted to have it all my way, but instead I ended up buying Jumi's life by sacrificing an entire city."

"Elsa, listen to me: never in my worst nightmares did I suspect they would use the editbook to level entire cities. No one saw this coming. It is *not your fault*." He took a deep breath, steeling himself. "If the blame has to lie somewhere, it lies with me."

Elsa snorted. "What, you're going to fight me for it?"

"*Yes*," he insisted. "I am so sorry for not trusting you to make your own decisions. And I'm sorry I was jealous of Aris when it was my fault you were there to begin with, and I'm sorry for sometimes wishing you were a little less amazing—because I don't really want that, I don't want you to be less than what you are just so I can feel like more.

"But mostly I'm sorry that I put you in this situation, where you feel responsible for my father's war crimes. It's on me to stop him, not you."

Elsa shook her head. "The editbook is still a Veldanese invention. Let's just agree to handle this together, okay?"

"I can do that." He caught his hand fiddling with the chain of his father's pocket watch and made his fingers stop.

Elsa was running her thumb over the edges of the worldbook. "I should finish this."

"Yeah, I'll let you get back to it." Leo pushed off the windowsill and made to leave, but there was a feeling like a fishhook beneath his ribs holding him back—unsaid words refusing to release him. "Look, Elsa . . . the only part of my life that makes any sense is how I feel about you. So if it's all right, I'd like to keep loving you for a while, even though you don't feel the same."

He didn't dare look for her reaction; once the words were out he just wanted to flee. But then Elsa was out of her seat and she grabbed his hand, pulling him back like a rebounding spring. Her ink-damp fingertips found his cheek, and when he looked into those clear green eyes Leo felt as though he might happily drown in her gaze.

"It's not past tense," she breathed.

Their lips met, soft and tentative at first. He buried his hands in Elsa's soft black hair, and she pressed closer against him, as if she wanted to banish the molecules of air between them. The kiss deepened, and the small, terrible tightness in Leo's chest gradually relaxed. He wondered if this was what coming home felt like to everyone else—like he could step inside this moment and shut the door, and it would be strong enough to keep out the horrors of the world.

Porzia watched Sante breathe.

She watched him through the night as the candle burned low, and then watched him in the dark when it finally went out. When Faraz's sleeping potion wore off and he woke in pain, she fed him a small and exact dose of morphine. She watched Sante breathe as the sky paled and the birds sang outside the shattered window; she watched as Olivia checked his temperature and his pulse and changed his bandage.

When Faraz came back sweaty and defeated and flecked with gray ash to tell her the fate of Napoli, she stayed silent and simply watched. She didn't have room in her heart to grieve for a whole city right now—she doubted it was ever possible to truly have room for that, anyway.

When Revan visited she tried to ignore him as she had Faraz, but he came around her chair and perched on the edge of the bed, where there was no avoiding his gaze.

"You can't go on like this," Revan said.

Porzia held up a hand. "Don't. Please." Her voice felt drained of emotion, the usual edge gone from her words. "I think it's best if we don't see each other anymore."

"What?" His eyebrows drew together in confusion.

"My life is not my own. I have obligations, and I . . ." She struggled to spit out the words. "I can't afford a distraction, however pleasant it may be."

Revan rubbed his hand across his mouth. "Look, Porzia—there is nothing you could've done differently to prevent this. Sante's a daredevil of a kid who idolizes that Leo guy, and he was itching for some heroics of his own."

Porzia said nothing. Maybe he would leave her alone if she pressed her lips together tightly enough.

"I get it, I really do. Elsa and I were the firstborn of the Veldanese, and she was always occupied with her scriptology lessons, so I've done more than my share of looking after the younger children." He took her hand in his own. "If you allow the weight of your responsibility to crush you, you won't be any use to them. Or to yourself."

His fingers felt warm and calloused against her palm, and the fog she'd been mired in started to lift from her mind. "Huh. How did you get so smart?"

"Many years of inventing games with sticks and pebbles," he answered sagely. "So does that mean you'll stop trying to get rid of me?"

Her lips twisted as she tried not to smile. "We'll see."

"And the small matter of stopping Aris and saving the Earth . . . ?"

She squeezed his hand once and then let go, because the touch was starting to feel distracting. "Yes, I suppose we'd better see to *that*, too."

Porzia took a deep breath and stood from the chair that had been her private, self-imposed prison. Revan came with her.

"Elsa? Faraz?" she called, moving down the hall to look for them. "Where are you?"

She found Elsa in her makeshift writing room with Leo. They

were standing apart from each other in a manner that strongly indicated the space between them was only a few seconds old. Apparently they were holding up just fine—or perhaps holding *each other* up would be more accurate.

"We're ready to help," Revan announced. "Do you have a plan yet?"

The embarrassment seemed to vanish from Elsa. "You need to rest," she protested. "There could be side effects, after what Aris did to you."

"What I need to do is stop him from hurting anyone else," Revan argued.

"No," said Elsa. "I refuse to take you straight back into the path of danger."

"It's not up to you to decide!"

As Revan began to wear Elsa down toward a grudging agreement, Porzia was distracted by the blue-black smudge across Leo's cheek.

"What are you smirking about?" Leo muttered to her.

Porzia leaned closer. "You've got ink on your face, and I simply *can't imagine* how it got there, Casanova."

He flushed red and scrubbed at his cheek with his sleeve. And Porzia felt like it might just be possible to settle into her old self again.

Faraz arrived, having heard his name called, and they filled in the details for Porzia and Revan—how the eruption of Mount Vesuvius fulfilled half of a prophecy, so they knew what to prepare for next, just not where.

Porzia chewed the inside of her cheek. "That gives me an idea. If we can get to the Oracle worldbook, we might be able to squeeze some more details out of it with the right questions." She'd have to be very careful to avoid giving the Oracle any openings for self-fulfilling prophesies, but at this point they were desperate enough to risk it.

Revan asked, "Where's the book?"

"Therein lies the problem," Porzia answered. "For safekeeping, my mother locked it under glass in the library at Casa della Pazzia."

"About that . . . ," Faraz said, looking sheepish. "I *may* have borrowed it without permission to study it, and so it *may* have been in my room when Casa started misbehaving . . ."

Porzia glared.

Faraz finished quickly, "It's here, it's in my bag."

Leo laughed and clapped him on the shoulder. "My mission to corrupt you into a rule breaker is complete!"

Elsa smiled. "And just in time, too."

Faraz left to fetch the worldbook and returned with the old tome in his hands, and Porzia fell into the familiar role of delegating. "Elsa, you have a project to finish, right? Faraz, it looks like we'll need your disgusting tentacle monster after all, so it's time to pull Skandar out of hiding. Revan, would you tell Olivia to watch Sante?"

Leo grinned at her. "Someone's back in fine form, ordering us all about. And what shall I do, signorina, while you talk circles around an oracle?"

Porzia snorted. "Don't you have some knives to sharpen or something?"

There was a part of her that didn't want to admit it, but having Leo back . . . it felt *right*. Their circle was broken without him. She wouldn't know who she was without the people in her life, and Leo was one of those people.

Now they were all united again, and Porzia could do this. She opened a portal to the Oracle world.

Porzia stepped through into a cool, windowless chamber with a domed ceiling and four narrow alcoves arranged in the four directions. The atmosphere held some intangible, ancient quality; it felt like standing inside an undiscovered Egyptian tomb. There was light without any obvious light source, and standing in that diffused glow, Porzia cast no shadow. But these were hardly the strangest features she had ever experienced in a scribed world, and it would take more than a bit of ambiance to disquiet her.

As the alcoves appeared identical, Porzia selected one at random and walked inside. On the back wall of the alcove was a hamsa symbol, a carved stone hand with a blue glass eye in the center of the palm. The eye twitched and then focused on her with otherworldly intelligence.

"Here's the deal, Oracle," Porzia said. "I want you to refrain from speaking except to answer my direct questions. If you violate this rule, I will bury your worldbook beneath a poetic choice of ornamental—perhaps a fig tree—and you will degrade and slowly die in what I can only imagine would be a most unpleasant fashion. Do you understand?"

The resonant voice came from everywhere and nowhere. "I do, Heiress of the House of Madness."

Porzia narrowed her eyes, unsure whether the Oracle was being deliberately impertinent. "Very well, let's begin: a cloud of ash ten thousand meters high did indeed block out the sun in Napoli, and now I need to know where exactly the seas are going to be writhing. So—"

"With eldritch horrors," the Oracle corrected.

Porzia rolled her eyes. "Yes, yes—writhing with eldritch horrors. Don't interrupt me. *Buried in the damp earth forever*, remember?"

The Oracle harrumphed.

"Now, as I was saying, I want to know the precise current location of Ricciotti and Aristotele Garibaldi." In one of Leo's rare moments of openness, he'd once admitted to her that all his brothers were named after history's great polymaths: *Leonardo, Aristotele, Pasquale.*

Porzia waited. After a long pause, the Oracle said, "I await your query."

She took a measured breath to control her temper. "The query is, *where are they?*"

"At this moment they reside in the Floating City, but they will not stay long."

The Floating City: Venezia. They had a location.

"Thank you, that's very helpful."

Porzia turned to go, but before she was out of earshot the Oracle spoke again. "The balance cannot hold—you will have to choose whom to keep faith with and whom to fail."

The words burrowed deep into Porzia's heart, tapping into what she dreaded most—the choice she knew was coming, and wished desperately to avoid. But Porzia would be damned before she gave the Oracle the satisfaction of rattling her, so instead she glared at that implacable glass eye. "Don't push your luck, Oracle. Or I'll introduce you to my favorite fireplace."

"I have not prophesied my own demise, Heiress."

"Oh please, keep telling yourself that," Porzia said. "I'm a scriptologist. Fate doesn't apply to the writers of worlds."

23

I DID WHAT HE COMMANDED ME. I WAS A MERE TOOL
WHICH *HE* HAD THE TROUBLE OF SHARPENING.
—*Caroline Herschel*

Elsa and the others stepped through the portal into the central portico of the Rialto Bridge, perched above the wide green waters of Venezia's Grand Canal. The bridge was shaped like a shallow triangle, two ramps rising up to meet in the middle, with a row of little covered shops built into the structure.

Leo had described the bridge as a main thoroughfare bustling with commerce, but the walkway was empty and the shops stood abandoned. The sight gave Elsa a crawling sensation down her spine.

Porzia peered into the closest shop, poking at the wares left behind for anyone to steal. "Well this can't be a good sign," she observed.

"Look there," Leo said, pointing to the northeast.

They weren't quite high enough to have a clear view over the rooflines, but a flock of very large birds wheeled in the sky like vultures over a carcass. Leo passed his spyglass to Elsa; the birds' proportions looked all wrong, heads too large and tails too long. And there, just barely in sight above the red-tiled roofs—was that the curve of an airship's gasbag?

"Those . . . are not birds," Leo told the rest of the group. "Apparently my brother has edited flying monsters into existence."

Revan squinted at the sky. "Are they hunting or guarding? I can't tell."

Elsa said, "I think that's Aris's airship—docked on a roof, maybe?—so I'd hazard a guess they're guarding."

"Wait," Faraz began, "that's not exactly seas writhing, though . . ."

Porzia let out a shriek, and everyone spun around as she was knocked off her feet, a massive tentacle wrapped around one ankle. It was trying to drag her over the stone banister. Leo whipped out his rapier and stabbed the tentacle, and it let go and jerked away.

Elsa rushed to the banister and dared a glance at the water below. The beast's body breached the surface, longer than the narrow boats tied along the sides of the canal. Its tentacles slapped angrily at the water.

"Kraken," Leo reported. "Well, Faraz, ask and you shall receive."

Porzia got to her feet and dusted herself off. "High time for a scriptological solution, I'd say. Elsa?"

"Faraz, for this to work I'll have to borrow Skandar for a bit," Elsa said, "if that's all right."

Faraz put a hand up to his shoulder, where the beast perched. "Borrow for what, exactly?"

Skandar's one enormous eye blinked at her, and Elsa felt a twinge of guilt at the thought of endangering the darling creature. But they were all in danger here already. "I've scribed a world designed to transform him into Skandar, Lord of Sea and Sky, whose siren call no beast can ignore, et cetera."

Porzia raised an eyebrow. "You're going to turn that little thing into the king of the monsters. That's your plan."

Elsa ignored her skepticism and held the worldbook out to Revan. "Here. We'll return in a minute."

Revan accepted the book reluctantly, as if it might bite him. "What do I . . . do with it?"

"Well don't set fire to it or drop it in the canal if you ever want to see us again. Other than that, nothing—just keep ahold of it."

Elsa opened a portal and stepped through with Faraz and Porzia, and they emerged onto a flat-topped stone outcrop. On all sides, a dizzying drop led down to a black, churning sea, the froth-capped waves often broken by the rise of an enormous fin or tentacle. Other jagged brown peaks of rock projected out of the water, but they were all distant, accessible only by wing. The sky above was a mass of roiling clouds, lit from below with a sinister red light as if the sun were setting—except no sun was visible. The dark silhouettes of flying creatures circled over each of the rock islands; the three high above their own island glided like hawks riding an updraft.

Mere seconds after they stepped through, Skandar launched himself from Faraz's shoulder and arrowed off toward the largest island, his small profile disappearing against the constantly writhing backdrop of sea and sky.

"Where's Skandar going?" Faraz said, alarmed.

"Off to fulfill a destiny," said Elsa. "The monsters here have a myth that their true master will come to them from another world, and they will know him by his screech and rally to his call."

His brow drew together. "And that will help us?"

Porzia said, "Properties gained in a worldbook transfer to the real world, even if the mechanism of action is obscure. That's how Elsa and Revan can pick up new languages in a matter of hours."

"I was very careful," Elsa reassured him. "It's all subtext, so the script can't textualize Skandar. If anything, our failure mode will be that the monster-commanding property doesn't stick."

Faraz hugged his arms to his sides. "What do you think he's doing now?"

Elsa said, "He has to find the Throne of Aglarn-Shri and defeat the Tyrant in single combat."

This news did nothing to alleviate Faraz's alarm. "Single combat? You didn't say anything about *monster duels.*"

"I've dealt the cards in Skandar's favor, of course. The Tyrant's weaknesses are sensitive hearing and no resistance to electricity."

Faraz sat down on the rock. "I can't believe I agreed to this."

The wind howled. The waves crashed against the rocks below. They waited.

Elsa chewed at her lip, anxiety starting to soak in as the minutes ticked by. "This is taking longer than I thought. I hope Leo and Revan are okay."

"What's to worry about?" said Porzia with a dismissive wave of her hand. "They're resourceful boys—I'm sure they're doing just fine."

"Watch out!" Revan yelled, and Leo ducked an enormous tentacle, avoiding the blow so narrowly he felt a brush of air against his face. He rolled and twisted and came up from his crouch with rapier extended to pierce the kraken once again.

"Ugh, this is useless! I need a machete!" The beast's tentacles leaked green ichor from a dozen holes, but the stab wounds weren't slowing it down much.

Revan wound up and released another rock, which splashed into the water with little effect. "If I could just hit the head we might get somewhere, but it keeps submerging!"

There was a second kraken hanging out at the east end of the bridge, tentacles peeking through the stone banister rails, as if considering whether to join the fun. And when Leo looked up, he saw a third one swimming toward them, attracted by all the commotion.

"Seriously?" he muttered, dodging another swipe of a tentacle.

Revan saw it too. "You want to try running for cover again?"

They were exposed on the bridge, but to get away from the canal they would first have to descend from the bridge's apex and move closer to the water, which would make them easier for tentacles to reach. Leo said, "Our defensive position here is looking increasingly untenable. If we can just get an opening . . ."

Motion in the corner of his eye, but before Leo could react a tentacle hit him like a battering ram to the ribs and knocked him off his feet. He went down hard, the back of his head slamming into the stone with a blast of black-and-stars across his vision. The wind was knocked out of him, his lungs burning for oxygen, and the hand that should be holding his rapier was empty.

Leo rolled onto his elbows, trying to get his hands and feet under him, and gasped for air. Through his swimming vision he spotted Revan skidding to a stop at the west end of the bridge and turning to come back for Leo, his sling a blur at his side.

Leo pushed himself up to hands and knees, painfully aware of the precious seconds that the blow to the head had cost him. But as he tried to stand he felt the damp, terrible suction of a tentacle around his wrist and he was sprawling on the stone again, dragged along by an impossible strength.

"*Shreeeee!*" came a painfully high-pitched noise, and the tentacle grip vanished from his wrist.

Leo looked up to see the kraken retreating from the bridge in the face of the return of Elsa, Porzia, Faraz . . . and Skandar.

"Leo!" Elsa said, distress thick in her voice. "You're bleeding!"

Faraz crouched next to him, took a clean cloth from the small satchel of medical supplies he'd brought, and pressed it to the back of Leo's head.

"Remind me to buy a machete after this," Leo grumbled.

Porzia folded her arms, as if she suspected he'd injured himself just to inconvenience her. "How bad is it?"

"Look at me," said Faraz, examining his eyes. "Pupil response is normal. Any problems with your vision?"

Leo blinked. "No, it's clearing up."

"I think he's fine," Faraz said.

Leo took over bandage-holding duty and got to his feet with Faraz's help. At least his balance wasn't off. "Fine or not, we need to steal the editbook back before Aris can undo whatever you just did to send away the krakens."

Beside him, Faraz went still. "I hadn't thought of that. He could *erase* Skandar."

Porzia said, "Yes, so let's press the advantage while we have it."

"How do we get over there?" Elsa asked, shading her eyes with one hand. "The buildings are packed so tight together . . . does this city even have roads?"

"The canals *are* the roads," said Leo. "Come on."

One thing could be said for filling the lagoon with krakens: it certainly made it easier to steal a gondola. Not a soul was around to protest when Leo waved everyone into the nearest boat.

He stood at the rear and pushed off from the dock. He hadn't rowed a gondola since he was ten, but after a few awkward strokes, his muscles remembered how to handle the long oar. A kraken swam close, raising its tentacles curiously, but Skandar emitted a harsh *shree* and it backed off.

They rounded the bend in the Grand Canal, and Leo's breath caught in his throat as a too-familiar palazzo came into view. It was his childhood home, the one that burned in the riot; Aris must have scribed it back into existence for Ricciotti and himself to use as their headquarters.

The details looked a little off to Leo's eye—the arches on the second-floor arcade weren't pointed, and the windows were a smidge too narrow. How surreal to be here at all, and doubly so with their old home imperfectly revived from Aris's memory.

There was a guard posted by the canal entrance, standing on the small, private dock before the wrought-iron gate that would lead inside. Revan knocked him unconscious with a well-aimed pebble, and Leo maneuvered the gondola against the water-slick stone of the dock.

"Quietly now," Leo said, as everyone disembarked. He picked the lock on the gate and led them into an airy entrance hall with a marble staircase along one wall.

A sudden panic pressed on his chest. The exposed wood-beam ceiling, the checkered marble floor tiles, the intricate plasterwork over the arched doorways: it was here, it happened *here*. This was where he saw the dead bodies of his family as a child. Never mind that it had been a ruse, the bodies alchemical fakes, his father and Aris still living—the memory of the trauma felt as fresh as the day it happened.

Don't think about it, don't think about it.

"Intruders!" someone shouted.

Porzia muttered, "So much for stealth," as half a dozen guards flooded into the hall from the other end.

"Well, damn." Leo unsheathed his rapier.

Revan shifted to the front beside Leo, putting the unarmed members of their group behind him. "All this fighting other humans is just barbaric."

Leo laughed. "Thanks for stooping to our level."

But as the guards fell upon them, Skandar let out an ear-piercing "SHREEEEE!" and the hall was suddenly full of wings. The creatures from above the palazzo came streaming in through the open doorway, their toothy jaws wide and claws extended.

Everyone on both sides ducked, but Leo quickly realized the not-birds—flying lizards?—were only attacking his father's guards.

"Oh Lord I can't look," cried Porzia, and Leo had to agree it was horrifying to behold. The lizards latched on to the guards and rode them to the floor, a bloody mess of claws and teeth.

"What is going on down there?" Aris's voice at the top of the stairs. He stared over the banister for a moment, scowling down at the carnage, then rushed out of sight.

Leo shouted, "He's going for the editbook!"

Faraz grabbed Elsa's portal device, showed it to his tentacle beast, and said "Skandar, fetch!" then pointed in Aris's direction.

The creature shot up like a stone from Revan's sling and darted through the doorway at the top of the staircase. Leo heard an electric *bzzzt* and a surprised shout, and Skandar came gliding serenely back to deliver Aris's portal device to Faraz.

Aris emerged a second later, massaging the cramps from his singed hand, his expression furious. "Cute trick," he spat as he descended the stairs to them. "But if you think that's enough to stop me, you're sorely mistaken."

Leo held a hand up, signaling the others to hang back as he approached his brother, stepping carefully around the winged lizards feasting on guard corpses. "We have control of your monster army. It's over, Aris."

"It's over when I say it's over." Aris pulled his rapier from its sheath. "A few krakens in the canals is just the start of what's in store for Venezia. They rioted, and our home burned, and Pasca nearly died—don't you want vengeance for that?"

Leo threw his arms wide. "Vengeance against an entire city to repay the actions of a few? No! No, that's madness."

"We are Garibaldis: it is our kind of madness." Aris brandished his rapier, whipping it through the air in an intricate, showy pattern. "I see you still haven't learned your lessons, little brother."

Leo brought his own rapier to the ready position and let Aris step forward in a series of attacks. Deflect, deflect, deflect, but this was no practice session, and Leo had no reason to hold back anymore. His anger at the fate of Napoli gave him a sharp clarity of focus, and his movements flowed with an almost prescient precision, the rapier darting through the air like a living extension of his body. Leo saw his opening—slide, twist, and flick, and Aris's rapier went flying from his hand.

Aris stared at his empty palm as if it had betrayed him. "What . . . how . . ."

Leo shook his head. "Oh, Aris, how could you forget? This was always the one thing I could do better than you."

Elsa, portal device in hand, slid past the now-disarmed Aris and took the stairs at a run, going after the editbook.

"Revan," said Leo, "would you care to take charge of restraining my brother?"

"Nothing would give me greater pleasure," Revan replied.

After a minute, Elsa returned with the editbook open in her

arms. "Okay, this is bad. He built an earthquake machine into the foundations of the city. There's a trigger mechanism in the library room. You guys need to stop anyone from activating the machine until Porzia and I can figure out how to safely disable it."

Faraz nodded. "We're on it."

Elsa passed her lab worldbook to Faraz, and she and Porzia vanished through a portal into her laboratory with the editbook.

Leo said, "Come on, the library's this way."

"Father will never accept defeat," Aris declared, dragged along by Revan as they moved through the house.

Faraz gave an eye roll worthy of Porzia. "Oh, do shut up."

"Who do you think you are, street-rat? You can't talk to me that w—aaaah!" He yelped as Revan twisted his arm.

Leo rested his left hand on the library door handle, bracing for a confrontation, then pushed the door open and slipped inside.

Ricciotti stood at the old familiar library table, his back to the door, sorting through some papers. The tall bookshelves lining the walls seemed to lean in, turning the room oppressive, though Leo couldn't be sure if the effect was real or simply the weight of the moment pressing in on his mind. Rising from the floor in the center of the room was a narrow pedestal with one large red button on top; that definitely was new.

Without turning around, Garibaldi said, "Still no word from the city magistrate?"

"Father, quick! Activate the—" Aris tried to yell, but Revan clapped a hand over his mouth to silence him.

Ricciotti spun to face them, and Leo lifted his rapier in warning. "What's wrong, Father? The Venetian government not capitulating to your demands as fast as you'd like?"

Ricciotti stood still, folding his arms in a casual way that suggested he wasn't about to feel threatened by a boy with a pointy stick. "They will accept the terms of surrender I've given them, or they will suffer the consequences."

"Venezia is built on islands of sand," Leo said. "An earthquake would liquefy the ground and drop the entire city into the lagoon. The only thing your republic would gain is a giant underwater grave site."

"Exactly," Ricciotti agreed. "After Napoli and Venezia, who would dare oppose me? We will have a unified Italian Republic by the end of the month."

Leo's palm felt damp against the grip of his rapier. "If the idea of the Italian Republic is more important than the citizens who compose it, *it is not a republic*."

"Oh *now* you want to debate the philosophical ramifications? And here I thought the Order had successfully brainwashed you into eschewing politics altogether." Ricciotti narrowed his eyes. "You're stalling for time."

Desperate to keep his father's attention, Leo played his trump card. "Did you know Aris kept Pasca alive in secret all these years? Despite all your manipulations, even Aris can sense how toxic you are."

For the first time that Leo could recall, Ricciotti went pale. "That's a lie. Aris would never—"

"Am I lying, brother?"

"I'm not going to help you!" Aris spat when Revan allowed him to speak.

Leo kept his gaze locked on Ricciotti. "That didn't sound like a denial to me."

"You're just fishing for distractions," Ricciotti said with a sharp shake of his head. His usual confidence seemed to return. "What is Signorina Elsa up to, I wonder?"

A cold panic washed through Leo as his father moved closer to the machine.

"Don't," Leo growled, bringing the tip of his rapier near Ricciotti's throat. He stared into his father's eyes, searching for any sign of wavering resolve. "*Father.* Please. Don't make me do this."

Ricciotti gave him a funny look, as if Leo were behaving like a foolish child. "Don't be absurd. You're not going to kill me, Leo."

He reached for the button.

A hundred thousand citizens, Leo thought. Pasca had implored him to do what was right.

The movements flowed easy as breathing. Appel to catch his attention, followed fast by advance, extension, and the soft resistance as the tip pierced his father's throat.

Ricciotti's eyes flew wide, and he made a sound as if he were choking on the blade.

Leo swallowed, his own throat turning tight and raw in sympathy. Quietly, he said, "I tried to tell you, Father: you don't know me anymore." Then he pulled the rapier out.

"Noooo!" Aris shrieked. "Father! Father!"

Ricciotti stumbled, grabbing his wound with one hand, blood gargling in his throat as he tried ineffectually to breathe. But as he collapsed to the floor, Ricciotti Garibaldi spent the last of his strength to reach out and hit the button.

Elsa sat at the writing desk in her laboratory world, poring over the editbook, while Porzia scribbled physics calculations on a blackboard.

Elsa said, "So we're agreed we can't destroy the editbook now that it's been used, right?"

"Presuming that destruction would destabilize the reality of those regions most heavily affected by Aris's editorial changes . . . hold on . . ." Porzia's chalk flew across the board in mad strokes. "Yes, according to my calculations, it's likely the instabilities would propagate outward and cause massive collapse of core physical properties."

Elsa tapped her pen against the desk. "And if we tried to just eliminate the earthquake machine with the editbook, we'd be running the risk of an internal contradiction in the text, which could have the same effect."

Porzia held up her palms like a pair of scales balancing. "Maybe a twenty percent chance instead of a sixty percent chance, but I'm not fond of the gamble either way."

"Okay, so our only option is to add something to the editbook that can counteract the effects of the earthquake *without* the script contradicting itself."

"I don't love the idea of modifying reality even more than it already has been," said Porzia, "but yes."

Elsa read through Aris's edits again. His script was passable but a little clumsy—stealing the Veldanese spoken language hadn't given him a perfect understanding of how to scribe in Veldanese, and he was missing some of the syntactic subtleties. The thought of Aris messing around with the most dangerous weapon ever created sent a wave of hot nausea through Elsa. In his overconfidence, he easily could have made a small but catastrophic mistake.

"How would an earthquake dampener even work?" Porzia was saying. "Oscillate at a frequency that cancels out the seismic waves? I wish we could consult a mechanist."

"No . . . ," Elsa said, starting to grin. "The solution is simpler than that—we can add an off switch to the machine that already exists!"

"Are you sure?" Porzia abandoned the chalkboard to come look at the editbook, even though the script was unreadable to her.

Elsa pointed at the page. "Yes! In this line right here, Aris used the wrong verb tense, which leaves this whole section of script open to further modification. It'll definitely work!"

"So do it!" Porzia replied, gesturing excitedly for her to begin.

Elsa selected each word with precision and care, constantly aware that any mistake could have dire consequences. The finished lines of script were perfection. "There, it's done. Let's get back."

Porzia quickly opened a return portal to the palazzo. They came through into a disorienting assault on the senses, the whole library vibrating and the loud whine of the earthquake machine rising in frequency as it warmed up. Books rained down from the shelves, and beside her Faraz had his feet planted wide against the shaking floor. Elsa's heart kicked against her ribs; were they too late to stop it?

Only one way to find out. Elsa's focus locked on the emergency shut-off lever that her script had added to the control panel. She dove for it and yanked it down, the vibrations threatening to dislodge her grip, but she clung to the lever and held it in place. *Please, please work.*

Finally, the noise and the shaking faded. The machine was off; Elsa almost laughed with giddy relief.

Only then did she realize the carpet beneath her boots was squishy with soaked-in blood. Ricciotti lay on the floor, motionless, a hole in his throat.

Held fast in Revan's grip, Aris was shouting, "Listen to me, Leo! There's still time, I can fix him, it's not too late . . ."

Leo was not listening. He swept a dazed look over Elsa and the others as if they were invisible, or at least as if he did not see what he was looking for. His fingers relaxed and the bloody rapier dropped to the carpet with a muffled thump. He crouched suddenly and hid his face in his hands.

Elsa didn't quite believe this could have happened in her absence. "But . . . but I worked as fast as I could . . ."

"Leo, Leo!" Aris's eyes were wide and desperate. "We can make this right. We can put our family back together. Just let me go!"

Slowly, Leo stood and faced his brother. "I'm so sorry, Aris, but I don't want to fix him. Don't you see? Nothing could ever make our family right."

Aris let out a wordless scream of rage and grief. Faraz closed the distance and wrapped his arms around Leo, and Leo sagged into the embrace as if it wearied him to stand on his own.

A terrible guilt crept up on Elsa, and it felt as if it were pinching her heart. She had saved the city of Venezia, and potentially the rest of Earth, but she could not save Leo from this.

24

Elsa went with Porzia into the worldbook scribed with invisible ink. Once, that might have made her nervous, but the trust she and Porzia shared had grown deep roots.

They stood together in the square pavilion floating in a sea of Edgemist and shared a moment of silence. It was so quiet the absence of sound felt like cotton stuffed in Elsa's ears.

"Are you sure?" she said. "This isn't exactly going to please the Order."

Porzia smiled wistfully. "I used to be so sure about everything. Now I wonder if living with doubt is the price of growing up."

Elsa couldn't disagree. This editbook in her arms, with its eager pages and subtle Veldanese text—it felt like it belonged to her, like the book wanted her to use it. How could she not cling to her mother's greatest scriptological accomplishment?

How could she not shun the instrument of destruction that had killed thousands of people?

In the center of the pavilion stood a stone pedestal topped with a sphere of blue lightning. Porzia gestured to it. "This last part is entirely up to you—only Veldanese can reach through the sphere."

Elsa felt a swell of shame for hesitating. After everything they'd gone through to stop Garibaldi, how could she even consider keeping it? The editbook belonged here, under lock and key. She shoved it onto the pedestal, her hands tingling as they passed through the energy sphere.

Porzia sighed. "That's one problem sorted."

"On to the next," said Elsa.

They emerged from the worldbook back into the Venetian palazzo, which was more or less how they left it, except that Aris was now gagged and his wrists tied together—which Revan looked rather smug about. Leo stood at a window overlooking the Grand Canal, seemingly unaware of the rest of them, while Faraz wiped Garibaldi's blood off the rapier.

Pitching her voice low, Elsa asked, "How is he?"

"In shock, I think," said Faraz. "Must we really go to Firenze right away?"

Porzia said, "Turning Aris over immediately is the only way we'll convince the Order that Leo and Elsa aren't traitors."

Elsa glanced at Aris. Even considering the gag, he was too quiet, his eyes narrow and calculating. "It has to be now. We can't risk him getting away from us."

Unexpectedly, Leo announced, "The canals are still full of krakens."

Faraz passed him the cleaned rapier to sheathe. "A problem for another day, my friend."

Revan said, "So are we ready to get out of this nightmare of a city, or what?"

Faraz whistled for Skandar, Revan marched Aris over, and

they all took a doorbook portal to the headquarters of the Order of Archimedes in Firenze.

They stepped through into a cavernous lobby on the main level with a dark flagstone floor, leather armchairs arranged in a sitting area, and several tall sentry bots standing at attention, scattered around the space like decorative suits of armor. A bell chimed, announcing their arrival, and they were met by a small group of pazzerellones who looked them over with varying degrees of curiosity and suspicion. At the front of the group was a woman with steel-gray hair and an aquiline nose, whom Porzia seemed surprised to see.

"Signora Veratti, where is Signor Righi?" she asked.

"My, you have been out of touch, haven't you?" Veratti said. "Righi is dead—I hope you weren't close—and I've resumed my position as head of the Order until a more permanent replacement can be appointed."

Porzia took the news in stride, apparently refusing to let it shake her confidence, and launched into an explanation of all that had transpired. Elsa didn't know enough about the Order to guess what this shift in leadership meant for herself and Leo, but he was scowling as if it was cause for concern.

The revelation of Aris's identity elicited a wave of gasps and mutterings from the observers, and Veratti ordered a pair of bots to take him to be locked up. Leo voiced no protest, but Elsa could practically feel the tension vibrating off him as he watched his brother being led away.

She took his hand and whispered, "No day will ever be harder than this."

"I can only pray that's true," he muttered back.

Porzia embellished the truth somewhat, turning Leo into a kidnapping victim and Elsa into a rescuer. She made no mention of Vincenzo or the Carbonari at all—a carefully crafted omission, Elsa could only assume.

Veratti turned to Leo. "Can you swear off your father's political cause, and reaffirm your loyalty to the Order?"

Voice rough, Leo replied, "I killed him. So that's about as final a decision as one can make."

Veratti gave a solemn nod, accepting his answer. "And you, Signorina da Veldana?"

"Me?" Elsa echoed.

"You were reported for defection."

Porzia jumped in. "That was for Garibaldi's benefit. All part of the plan, you see."

Veratti's eyes darted to Porzia, and then back to Elsa, considering. "So then you swear off any association with the Carbonari?"

Elsa swallowed nervously. The Order's stance of political neutrality was a theoretical impossibility—avoidance was a choice that affected the world with as much significance as involvement would have. After a moment of indecision, she shook her head. "I regret to inform you that I do not."

Porzia muttered to her, "Shh, keep quiet and let me smooth this over."

"Thank you, Porzia, but no," Elsa said. "I will not pretend to agree with the Order's refusal to act." The Carbonari were not mad for power and vengeance like Garibaldi—they were simply people trying to build a better world for their fellow citizens. The same as what Elsa wished for the Veldanese.

Signora Veratti bristled. "You're saying you intend to keep actively assisting the Carbonari with their political agenda?"

"I can't in good conscience swear that I won't. I am not of this world, and I never agreed to behave in accordance with your rules."

"While you may not be of this world, what you do here has

consequences for those of us who are." She paused. "I am sorry, but Righi's arrest order still stands. Take her."

The security bots whirred to life from their quiet idling and began closing in. Revan and Leo reached for weapons to ward them off, and Skandar launched from Faraz's shoulder. The bots responded with guns unfolding from compartments in their forearms, and Elsa could all too easily envision how the situation would escalate.

She threw her hands out. "Wait! Stop! Nobody needs to get hurt, I'll surrender myself peacefully."

"Elsa—!" Leo protested.

She turned to him and rested a hand on his cheek. "There's been enough death today."

Something shifted in the amber depths of his eyes, and he leaned closer. Elsa pressed her lips to his, and they shared a kiss that felt like a sharing of strength, where paradoxically they both came away with more than they'd had before.

Then there were metal hands around Elsa's arms, pulling her back, their grip tight enough to make her wince. As the security bots dragged her away, she could hear Porzia yelling, "Elsa! I'll get you out, I swear it!"

The security bots brought her down into the basement, into a jail cell with thick iron bars, and they took from her all her tools and gadgets and books. But Elsa wasn't worried, because she still had something better than a portal device, better even than an editbook: she had her friends.

And together there was nothing they couldn't do.

EPILOGUE

Feeling incandescent with rage, Porzia burst through the doors into the council chamber in a neatly choreographed dramatic entrance, which had the desired effect of drawing all eyes to her.

The Order's council members—what remained of them—were gathered around the far end of the long table, poring over her worldbook.

"It's blank!" Porzia gasped mockingly. "How terribly inconvenient."

It was her own father who said, "Porzia, what is the meaning of this? Have you done something to the editbook?"

"Oh, that's not the editbook." She took off her gloves—gloves she'd donned specifically for the purpose of now removing them—and tossed herself down in the chair at the opposite end of the table, as if she'd purchased the room and were planning to move in. "That is the lockbox I put the editbook inside of."

At this pronouncement, everyone started talking at once. Porzia examined her nails while waiting for the din of protestation, disbelief, and outrage to calm down.

Signora Veratti called for quiet. "Explain yourself, Signorina Pisano."

"We designed safeguards to guarantee that no single person can gain control of the editbook, while still leaving it accessible in the event of an emergency," she said. "Well . . . accessible to *us*, anyway."

Veratti said, "When you say 'we,' who do you mean exactly?"

Porzia gave her a steady look. "I should think that obvious: myself and Elsa di Jumi da Veldana."

Elsa's name sent up another wave of protestations, like a gun-dog flushing a nest of pheasants. But Veratti put a hand in the air, demanding silence, and silence came. She was a highly respected alchemist and had been Righi's predecessor before she retired from the position. "Why have you done this?" she asked.

Porzia carefully avoided her father's gaze. She did not want to know if there was betrayal in his eyes. "It is our belief, now that the editbook has been used to alter the real world, that it cannot be destroyed without risking unpredictable consequences for Earth."

Filippo quietly added, "Unpredictable and potentially catastrophic." His voice drew her attention, almost against her will. Her father's gaze was not without respect, but still he looked at her as if she were a stranger, and that cut so deep her throat tightened. Filippo continued, "Which is why the Order must have control of the editbook."

Alek de Vries rose from his chair. "Now, now—while I'm sure the Order would prefer sole ownership of the book, there is arguable benefit to forging a permanent alliance with the Veldanese."

Porzia said, "Oh good, Signor de Vries is with us. Would you like to tell him the truth, Father, or shall I?" She paused just long enough to see a spark of panic light in Filippo's eyes. "Alek: Zio Massimo is alive, and you have been lied to. He was textualized, and rather than air our shame for all to see, my family hid him away in Corniglia and told everyone he'd died. Even you, the person most deserving of the truth."

"What?" Alek stared. He could not have looked more shocked if she'd pulled out a revolver and shot him in the chest.

A little flower of guilt bloomed in her heart at his reaction . . . though was there really a *good* way to break such news? Anyway, her anger held fast and carried her through—anger for Simo's exile, anger for Elsa's imprisonment, anger for the terrible choice Garibaldi forced upon Leo. And yes, anger for herself and the narrow road the older generation expected her to walk down.

She turned her focus back to Signora Veratti. "If you want to ever so much as see the editbook, you'll need one Pisano scriptologist and one Veldanese scriptologist—and the rest of the details I'll leave vague for now. I have to admit, I wasn't expecting to need this bargaining chip quite so soon, but here we are nonetheless.

Porzia allowed herself a moment to take in their indignant looks, and she saw the truth reflected in their eyes: the dutiful daughter was gone. This new Porzia Pisano was someone else, and for the first time in her life, it was entirely up to her to discover who that might be.

"So." Porzia gave them all a glittering smile. "Would you care to make a deal?"

AUTHOR'S NOTE

This novel presents an alternate history of the struggle for Italian unification; while I drew inspiration from historical conflicts and figures, the events described here diverge massively from reality.

First, I must offer apologies to the city of Naples for its total destruction (though it continues to strike me as a terrible idea to have three million people living in the shadow of one of the world's most dangerous volcanoes). In an odd twist of fate, my maternal grandmother was from Naples, so I have effectively erased myself from Elsa's timeline.

I have also taken liberties in my portrayal of the Carbonari. The real Carbonari were a secret network of independently operated cells without much in the way of a centralized command structure, and they were most active in the early 1800s. The café where Elsa meets them is based on Caffè Florian in Venice, which actually was used as the headquarters of an insurrection against the Austrian Empire in 1848.

The real Ricciotti Garibaldi was neither an alchemist nor a supervillain, but simply a son of the famous revolutionary general Giuseppe Garibaldi. However, the stories Aris tells of Anita Garibaldi are lifted straight from real life. Anita was the original badass woman—a pants-wearing, horse-riding, gun-toting freedom fighter—and she is indeed still a folk hero and symbol of liberty in her native country of Brazil.

Augusto Righi was a real professor from Bologna who made significant contributions to the study of electromagnetism, though as far as I know, he did not lead any secret societies, and he lived until 1920. His fictional successor, Signora Veratti, is perhaps a descendant of physicist Laura Bassi—the first female science professor in the world—and her partner Giuseppe Veratti. Even if none of Laura Bassi's granddaughters became scientists in real life, I prefer to think that her legacy is still alive.

The joy and the challenge of writing alternate history is envisioning how events could have turned out differently. In reality, the Risorgimento movement succeeded in liberating Italians from foreign rule, but fell short when it came to creating a popular republic. The invention of a unified national identity morphed over time into Italian Fascism, and Italy did not abolish their monarchy in favor of democracy until 1946. Perhaps in Elsa's timeline they can do better.